Praise for Mick Herron

'The new king of the spy thriller'

Mail on Sunday

'Herron proves himself to be a master of wit, satire and surprise'

Daily Telegraph

'Herron is spy fiction's great humourist, mixing absurd situations with sparklingly funny dialogue and elegant, witty prose'

The Times

'The new spy master'

Evening Standard

Also by Mick Herron

Jackson Lamb thrillers

Slow Horses
Dead Lions
Real Tigers
Spook Street
London Rules
Joe Country

Zoë Boehm thrillers

Down Cemetery Road
Why We Die
Smoke And Whispers

Reconstruction
Nobody Walks
The List
This Is What Happened
The Drop
The Catch

THE LAST VOICE YOU HEAR

MICK HERRON

JOHN MURRAY

First published in Great Britain in 2004 by Constable,
an imprint of Constable & Robinson Ltd

First published in 2016 by John Murray (Publishers)
An Hachette UK company

This paperback edition published in 2020

2

To Pat

'SHE'S THE ONE.'
    She wore black jeans, red top, a black leather jacket; she had dark curly hair and was old – forty, fifty, somewhere round that – with a shoulder bag that swung like an invitation: banging heavy on her hip, loaded with purses, credit cards and women's stuff; everything she'd need in the big bad city. Definite out-of-towner. She should have had *victim* tattooed on her forehead.

'Yessss . . .'

Andrew, who answered to Dig these days, let it out in one long breath. *Yessss.* She was the one. You waited long enough, your ticket to the party arrived. The party started tomorrow – all around, the old millennium drained away like dirty water from a sink – and here she was, just the ticket: a bag with a bag. Drifting down the arcade, her attention swallowed by a glittery window's expensive promises: they'd have the bag, that jacket off her back even, and all she'd ever know about it was Some You Lose. The credit cards, the money, were as good as in their pockets.

Beside him, Wez muttered something purple-sounding. He looked like he'd melt in your mouth, but had a vocabulary could stop a train.

And another spat of water hit Dig's neck. They were leaning on one of the concrete stanchions that supported the building overhead, and once every couple of minutes enough moisture

I

gathered up there to loosen and splash on Dig's neck. It would have been pussy to move because he was dripped on. So the thing was to pretend it wasn't happening, or if it was, that he liked it.

The way the woman walked – her bag slung over one shoulder; her left hand resting lightly on its clasp – she might never have been out of her village before.

Two hundred yards up the road, the Tube swallowed travellers. Here in the arcade, pedestrian traffic was slight: the shops were a low-rent jeweller's, a hardware store, a CostCutter, a chemist's, a dry-cleaner's, a newsagent's, a bagel shop. It was the jeweller's Black-and-Red faltered by. Dig had checked that window out himself: all crap, even he knew that. Naff engagement rings, and stuff, you hung it round your neck, you'd look like Miss Piggy on a bad hair day. The bigger the stone, the cheaper the lady, his bastard father used to say. This lady didn't look cheap, just old, and he wondered what she was doing here, where the shops were end-of-line, and all the expensive promises broken as soon as unwrapped. And then he thought: she must have been to the concert hall – there was a concert hall tucked inside the laby-rinth – a concert hall and a museum and some other shit. Black-and-Red must have spent the afternoon doing culture, and wandered past the Tube in the hope of finding more.

Wez said, 'Dumb bitch's about to have a shit-fit.'

Dig drew on his cigarette, and breathed out heavily – the cloud adding to the afternoon's mistiness; to the damp, the grime, the oil-patterned puddles at the kerbs.

Wez said, 'Fuckin twatlegs'll wish she'd stayed home,' and threw his own cigarette into the gutter.

The real clouds, what showed of them above the office blocks and skyline furniture, were an angry grey mess. The pavements shone weakly, stealing light from nearby windows. Dig tugged at his top's broken zipper. There was smoke in the air from some distant accident, and more in his lungs from a stolen

Marlboro, and water poured down his neck in a fine white wash of reality, and the woman was moving again – coming towards them, the bag slapping happily against her hip – and his insides clenched with the inevitability of everything, and he looked at Wez, voice hardly cracking at all when he said, 'Ready?'

And Wez looked pure scorn, because Wez was *born* ready, and this was his meat and drink. Was how he knew he was awake and breathing.

Dig freed himself from his pillar like, probably, some old statue coming to life, just as his cigarette scorched to the knuckle . . . He shook his hand and it jumped away, scattering sparks against the bagel joint's fogged window. This was *attention*, mad enough to get the stares coming, but the dumb bitch hadn't noticed; she'd turned to look at something – GET TWO SUITS CLEANED AND WE'LL CLEAN A THIRD ONE FREE! – so missed the fireworks; missed, too, Wez's split-second fury – *Cunt*, he mouthed, then turned and headed towards Black-and-Red, sidestepping to her right maybe twenty foot in front. Dig watched the stub tumble cartwheels in the draught, bloom one last time against a greengrocer's crate, then he set off to take his place in the dance.

. . . Once, the bitch mother had taken him to the ballet. That was what she'd called it: *the* ballet. He'd thought there was only one. And it was strange how some things you carried regardless: along with a couple of scribbled-over nursery memories, and a trace of her perfume he'd caught last night up west, he had the startling picture in his head sometimes of people producing impossible leaps and mid-air twirls; their limbs strangers to gravity, their hands gripping invisible ropes from which they swung like uncaged monkeys. *So beautifully choreographed, darling*, she'd said afterwards, practising for her friends while she lit a cigarette and stared into the crowds in the hope of somebody interesting. And so beautifully choreographed, he thought now, as Wez slipped the bag from the woman with a touch light as a ghost's, and turned and tossed it to Dig so sweetly it fell into his open arms even as he started to run – and this was what Dig did best. This was why Wez let him hang: it was Dig's run; nothing to flat-out whirlwind in point zero. Wez tarried long enough to do the rest – he pushed the woman sideways, with just enough footwork she hit the deck – then took off too. But Dig was away by then; darting like his feet were on fire the length of the arcade, and up the red-brick walkway, and into the concrete labyrinth.

It was heavy. That was the first and most important thing: this bag was heavy. Like the bitch collected bricks or something, except whatever it was, it wasn't bricks, and even while he was running, imagined contents took root in his head: what did she have in here, this bottomless black leather bag with its big clasp? Maybe she was stopping in town for tomorrow's blast, and this held her party gear: not just the money, the credit cards, the *stuff*, but strings of jewels, diamond tiaras, lengths of precisely numbered rubies. You never knew what you'd got till it was done. His feet had wings; they barely touched the walkway. At the top, he hit a hard left, then twisted right down a flight of steps: Dig was down them in one and a half clicks, and here came the danger – the big sprint across open space with bricked-in flower beds and litter bins, overlooked on all sides by office windows – here you could be spotted; your direction mapped; your destination guessed. He hugged the bag tighter. Today, he was winged. Today, the offices were deserted; everybody heading home, or filling the bars with their big-mouth suit-and-tie voices. He reached the shelter of the opposite side, the comfort of the next stairwell – up now, three steps a stride, which brought him to another walkway, this one bridging a traffic-choked road to end in a mini plaza with a wide-fronted entrance to a museum or something, closed already. He ducked a loop of builder's tape warning about overhead work which wasn't happening, and into another stairwell, and then there

4

were only two flights to go, and he was safe – there was a spot down here Wez had fixed on, and if Wez said it was safe, it was safe. Wez knew what was what. Dig was the legs but Wez was everything else, and both knew it.

The breath was hammering out of him in short hard bursts: his heart pounding, blood racing. Everything. He was alive, and it was all working.

The safe spot was a dark corner near the intersection of two walkways one flight from the car park; a strange nook the labyrinth's interlocking architecture had thrown up: accident or design, didn't matter. It smelt appallingly of piss. Waiting, Dig hefted the bag to shoulder height. Pretty weighty, yes. But he wouldn't open it till Wez arrived. That was the rule. Truth told he was scared of Wez, who had no boundaries.

The hand on his shoulder nearly killed him.

Wez said, 'All be dope?'

Dig swallowed the cry; re-anchored his heart. 'It's . . . cool.'

'Less check the stash.'

Wez reached and took the bag from Dig like cigarettes from a baby, but even he noted the weight – a sudden collapse at the wrist before he could correct it, correct *gravity*, and Dig felt a quick rush of pride: he had stolen this.

'She carryin fuckin stones.'

'It's not stones, Wez.'

'She carryin fuckin *lead weights*, dickweed.' But there was a gleam in his eye, and Dig knew Wez didn't think that; that there weren't no leadweights here, but pirates' treasure.

'It be dope,' he said, and felt the words come almost naturally; as if he were what they sounded like he were: king of the streets, big time.

Wez was unzipping the bag.

A splash grabbed Dig's neck – even here, buried out of reach of the weather, there was no escaping the damp.

What Wez pulled out was, indeed, a brick.

A couple of seconds they stood, looking at the brick in Wez's hand like it was the Ark of the Covenant. Another splash hit the stones. Wez opened his mouth. The sounds he'd been going to make disappeared.

And Dig jerked backwards, and whatever grabbed him this time was fiercer than raindrops. He made to squawk, but air vanished; it was half a second before he realised that an arm had scooped and clenched round his middle; an arm sleeved in black, with red at the cuff . . . He deflated instantly, and then his arms were wrenched back, and something snapped into place. He couldn't move. He couldn't breathe. Hands seized his collar and he was pulled backwards so abruptly he lost his footing; he was sprawling now, aching for breath. And the rain was coming down harder and he was flapping on the stones man, flapping on the fucking stones, and couldn't breathe, and it was the bitch with the bag, the bitch with the fucking bag, and all it held was bricks, and he couldn't breathe, and it was raining, and she was over him like fucking Wonder Woman or something, and if he didn't breathe soon he'd fucking die . . . They were handcuffs. The bitch had fucking cuffed him. And where was Wez: Wez was still in the fucking cubby. He breathed at last. The air felt like on fire.

Wez emerged, looking smaller, looking grey. 'Fuck you at, bitch?'

She held a palm out flat, like she was stopping traffic. Then bent and pulled at Dig's cuffs, so he was yanked to his feet like a puppet.

He still wasn't breathing properly. There were laws said you couldn't do this, couldn't just *squeeze* and *cuff* and *yank* people less you were a copper, and the horrible news hit him like that: she was a copper. What else was she? And his brain ran ragged, because a copper meant the beautiful game was over.

Wez was smiling. Dig had seen that smile before. It didn't signify happy. 'Muffcruncher,' he said.

'Back off.'

And this isn't her, thought Dig. This wasn't the slack-jawed woman they'd watched trawling the arcade, carrying her bag like a victim tourist – this voice was hard; it came from a place you didn't want to run into full tilt. It was a voice with rocks in it.

'Fuckin twat merchant,' said Wez bravely. It was as if he still didn't get it, but he got it. Beneath the words, Dig could hear something he'd never heard before from Wez; never imagined he'd hear from him. He was scared. But he was still giving it lip. 'Bitch.'

Then there was pain in Dig's wrists as he was pulled again: he was on his feet, and they were on the move. The woman took as much notice of Wez as if he were bruised fruit.

She had one hand on his collar and the other on the chain linking his wrists. He'd twist free any second; fling her away; give her some footwork . . .

He kept marching.

And two yards back Wez danced; never getting so close he was help or hindrance. 'Dishwashin scumsucker. Gunna give you fuckin *grief* lady, gunna give you fuckin *ballsache* . . .'

They were on the stairs now; he was being pushed down the stairs, her hand firm on the cuff chain, so he couldn't fall. The woman's hand felt like cable. Wez's voice wobbled after them, then his body followed.

'You juss fuckin *slice* bitch, you slice waitin to happen . . .'

Words tumbling out of him, and all Dig could feel, could think, was it's over. The game is over.

His hands ached, his chest ached, but at least he was breathing freely now as he was propelled in the direction of some piece-of-shit Nissan Sunny, anything less like an unmarked car he had *yet to fucking see* . . . Everything came to a halt when he was slammed against its bodywork.

'You're getting in,' her voice said. 'And no fuss.'

The door opened. Her hand squashing his head, he was poured into the back seat, which was what it felt like: poured. Outside, maintaining safe distance, Wez hovered.

'You lookin at *pain* bitch is what you lookin at . . .'

She could be anybody, thought Dig. Could be some serial pervert, and the next I'm known of, I'll be body parts in bags.

Wez came closer while Black-and-Red made an important suggestion to Dig. 'Mark my car, and I'm taking it out of your hide. Are we together on this?'

He said *muh* – or *wuh*. It wasn't clear which.

'That's good.'

The door slammed. For a fearsome moment he expected to find the insides smooth and handle-less: just sheer plastic-coated steel, soundproofed, against which he could slam and holler for days without drawing attention. By which time he'd have been taken wherever, and subjected to . . . whatever.

It wasn't soundproofed. There were handles. He didn't dare touch them.

Outside, Wez was making fists. Outside, Wez *looked* like a fist. There were new words streaming out of him now: biblical torrents of them. Black-and-Red straightened, checked the door was locked, and moved round to the driver's side. But she paused halfway and paid attention to Wez. 'You,' she said. She raised a hand to him, palm flat like a traffic cop again. 'Piss the fuck off.' Then she got into the car, and started the engine.

When Dig looked through the back window, crying now, at the last he'd ever see of Wez, what Wez was doing was some kind of war dance, there in the oil-patched damp of the car park – hopping from one leg to the other, waving his fists above his head as if summoning massive urban vengeance on the lady, and all the time the words cascaded out of him: damaged words, hurtful words he never seemed to get to the end of, as if this constant battery of noise were the only means he had of squeezing all the venom out of his poisoned nine-year-old heart.

ONE

KID B

I

W HEN SHE WAS BORED, which was often, she'd roll little paper balls (silver paper was best) and flick them one after the other, using thumb and second finger, at whatever target caught her attention: the clock on the wall, the door handle, the waste-paper bin. It was a strategy developed over years, one of the things she did instead of smoking, except sooner or later – mostly sooner – it became one of the things she did as well as smoking; another useless talent for her portfolio. Something to fall back on, when she was bored.

They didn't allow smoking on First Great Western. She didn't expect they'd take kindly to her flicking paper balls about, either.

The train bucked. 7:56. It picked up speed as it crossed the river. Zoë had bought her ticket with a full fifteen, nearly sixteen, seconds to spare; now she put out a hand to steady herself – she was on her feet; there were no free seats in sight – as a voice in her ear said *and with news of today's weather here's* and another, overhead, announced something about available seating at the rear of the train: carriage A. She was in D. Adjusting the tiny speaker in her ear – *a grey start with sunny intervals* – she followed the other seatless passengers trooping in that direction, as noise about buffet service began to compete with the headlines. Already, nobody was looking at her. Already, almost every passenger had settled into a morning ritual: newspaper, mobile phone, work-related papers.

. . . Zoë Boehm was at work. She was on her way to London to meet a man named Amory Grayling. Amory Grayling wanted to talk to her about Caroline Daniels. Caroline Daniels was dead.

on a housing estate in east London. The body has been identified as that of a twelve-year-old

The doors whooshed open automatically, or wished they whooshed – more of a clunk and slide.

This next carriage – she was in B now – was also full; its last free seat just being claimed by a grateful-looking thirty-something man in an aubergine top under a black jacket. For a second their eyes caught, and she wondered if he were going to offer her the seat – neither expected nor hoped; just wondered, with a detachment arising from pure science, whether he'd do that – and he broke contact, reaching to stow his briefcase on the overhead rack before settling down with a rueful grin directed more at himself than at her, Zoë thought. She moved on. If she'd been ten years younger, he'd have offered her the seat. But that too came with detachment, and she didn't look at him again as she reached the last of the carriage doors.

taken off the field last night after apparently being struck by a hurled coin. A spokesman for the club said

There were seats here, she saw immediately, and realised just how pissed off she'd have been to have to stand all the way. She took the first available – part of a four-seater round a table – making a small grateful noise as she did so. That was a thing about headphones: they made you over-ready to respond; compensating for the fact that you'd voluntarily cut yourself off from communication. This was merely an observation; not something that bothered Zoë. As she sat, though, communication happened anyway: the man by the window said something, pointing briefly at her headphones. She had to lean closer to hear.

say they have no leads at the present time. Charles Pars

'I said, this is the quiet carriage.'

He could have fooled Zoë. The train was bucketing along: she could barely hear her radio.

'I'm sorry?'

'No mobiles, no personal stereos.'

'Oh. Right.'

She turned it off. Not naturally an obeyer of orders, she nevertheless had a well-developed sense of when she was on somebody else's territory. The man had already forgotten her. He sat staring out of the window, or perhaps at the window itself: his eyes lacked that constantly changing focus of somebody watching a world flash by.

The *Today* programme presumably carried on broadcasting. Her mind, too, kept transmitting mixed messages: stuff she needed to remember; things she'd rather forget. Amory Grayling's address, for instance; she'd written this down, of course, but it would be pretty to think she could manage the trivia without depending on paperwork. Caroline Daniels had been his PA . . . And if the conversation had gone on longer, she thought, her journey now wouldn't be happening: Zoë didn't do death. What had happened to Caroline Daniels had taken her out of Zoë's league. Amory Grayling had finalised arrangements before she'd got round to telling him that . . .

We'll have to fix you up with an appointment.

She shook her head free of the unwelcome memory.

Anyway, she thought, she'd get paid. Look on it as a day out; a trip into the city. Her mornings were nothing special. Maybe life would be stranger on a train.

April was still new, still unsure of itself. The sky was grim, but a thick shaft of sunlight hammered down on some blessed event to the east. Through the window, in a field, by an electricity pylon, Zoë saw a tumble dryer. It was in her past a moment later, but that's what it had been – a tumble dryer.

13

How could anything get to be so out of place? And as soon as the question occurred, its answer arrived: somebody had dumped it; had loaded it into the back of a car or whatever, driven it out to that middle of nowhere, and left it for the weather to corrode. There was no real mystery why things ended up where they shouldn't. A better question would be: how come anything ever turned out to be in the right place? Which was as well for Zoë, probably. She found people – it was one of the things she did. She was a private detective. She found people who'd ended up where they shouldn't.

She caught the eye of the woman sitting opposite, who smiled briefly, then bent her head to her book, a history of the labour movement. She had arranged herself, it seemed to Zoë, for maximum comfort within the space allowed; a position in which she was not directly facing anyone – so probably wasn't too keen on repeated eye contact . . .

Walking to the station by the towpath, Zoë had encountered one of the city invisibles: a homeless man burdened with candy-striped laundry bags and a bashed-about holdall – a man of about forty, in a too big suit; intensely shy of human contact. When she'd rounded the corner on to the path, he'd been making the sign of the cross, his luggage forming a Calvary at his feet. But at Zoë's approach he'd stopped abruptly, gathered his stuff, moved on. He'd spent the night, probably, under an open sky, but couldn't carve a private zone out of all that space. And now Zoë Boehm sat in a crowded railway carriage, and all around her travellers had claimed territory for themselves and their morning tasks; areas the size of an unfolded newspaper, a laptop, a book, or a pad and pen. It was the unconscious reflex of the property owner, she decided; this unquestioning settlement of available space. Those with salaried functions took what they needed, while those without could barely cross themselves in the open air.

But she wouldn't get snotty about commuters. She owed her existence to one.

14

Zoë closed her eyes. The rhythm went on around her. Repetition was how you'd survive a daily journey like this; it was both what you endured and what got you through. It was there in the noise the wheels made; it was there in the landscape outside, patiently painting the calendar day by day. It was probably there in the thoughts running through the journeyers' heads.

She was on her way to London to meet a man named Amory Grayling. He wanted to talk to her about Caroline Daniels. Caroline Daniels was dead.

We'll have to fix you up with an appointment.

After a while the train slowed and stopped; people got off, people got on. When the man next to her departed he left his newspaper; snaffling it, she resettled by the window. A new woman claimed her old seat and produced from a briefcase an apple and a sheaf of email printouts larded with acronyms. As the train pulled away, Zoë unfolded the paper to a report of a football match in which a defender had been struck by a coin flung from the crowd: a tenpence piece had hit him above the left eye, and the resulting wound required stitching. What might have happened had he been hit an inch lower barely bore thinking about. She refolded the paper, and on the adjoining page found a photograph of Charles Parsley Sturrock, who remained as dead as he had been three days previously, when the same picture had been front-page news. A professional hit remained the popular scenario, though a police spokesman admitted no obvious leads. Which was likely, in Zoë's opinion. Policemen generally were too busy celebrating Sturrock's death to have done much in the way of investigating it.

A mobile phone went off, and harsh words ensued. The guilty party fled the carriage to enjoy his conversation in the vestibule. The woman opposite, Zoë noticed, had abandoned her history book for a paperback detective novel, and was looking happier.

And I wonder what she'd say, thought Zoë, if I told her what I did for a living.

There was a thought. The woman would probably not have believed her, but there were days when Zoë didn't believe it herself. She had recently read, in a novel review, that private detectives were unconvincing, and couldn't help feeling that the critic had a point. Not that she felt unreal, exactly; was, in fact, more aware of her physical self than she'd been in years – of her heart performing its extraordinary work. Of a tingling at her fingertips, here, now. But the job – the critic had a point. The job was part anachronism, part absurdity, and called to mind, when stated baldly, the usual suspect images: trench coat, bottle of rye, wisecracks out of the side of the mouth. Fact was, like everybody else, she spent most of her working life in front of a monitor.

Fact also was, she had once killed a man.

The fields outside gave way to industrial estates. The train passed a brick tower with a broken clock, its hands hanging at 6:30, or almost at 6:30; in fact at a dead version of 6:30, where the minute hand hid the hour at the parallax point; an inverted midnight. She wondered whether the mechanism had just snapped of a sudden, or whether this was the result of a slow surrender to gravity, observable only by those with the time and the inclination to watch. With most faulty clocks, you could tell when they'd stopped working. This one had ceased to function so completely, it had disguised the moment of failure.

The man she had killed (she had shot him dead) would have killed her, given the chance; a chance which would have arisen, if she hadn't shot him first. If it mattered, her job hadn't come into it. She'd been there, that was all; in his sights, and a gun in her hand. Him or her, the way it might have happened in a private detective novel. Nothing about her frequent rehearsing of the memory made any of it more convincing. There was no possibility of relating any of this to the woman opposite, and in any case, the information would only have frightened or depressed her.

It was time not to think about this any more. Zoë turned the page, an irritating business involving spreading paper everywhere, and when she was done, words anyway swam into nonsense; became a cacophony of newsprint containing too many adjectives. She had shot a man, and felt nothing about it, and this, in retrospect, was the problem. She felt nothing about it, but it had broken her heart. It was just that she had not known what a broken heart encompassed, imagining – or remembering previous occasions, when she'd thought she'd suffered one – that it involved hurt; an unfamiliar clenching of an overused muscle. But it meant, she'd learned, what it sounded like: a broken heart was one that no longer worked. It managed its daily labours all right – that extraordinary effort she was so aware of right now; the ceaseless pumping with its whoosh and splash of constantly propelled liquids – but the other stuff, the *heart* stuff, it just didn't do any more. She felt almost nothing. She was rarely happy. She was rarely sad. She got by, that was all. She felt almost nothing. And she had not noticed the moment at which this had started happening. Her feelings had ceased to function so completely, they had disguised the moment of failure.

She was staring at the woman opposite, she realised. It was as if everything had coalesced into one obvious point of blame, and this poor woman was it. Zoë closed her eyes. It wasn't entirely true that she felt almost nothing. There were times when she remembered how capable she'd once been of hatred.

The rhythm of the rails bore into her mind, singing *We'll have to fix you up with an appointment*. She rustled her paper. Tried to concentrate. The story blurred in front of her, then reassembled itself: letters, words, paras. A photograph. An echo of a headline from the radio news . . .

The body of a twelve-year-old had been found at the foot of a tower block on an estate in east London. The accompanying picture, a school photograph, showed a boy significantly younger than twelve, and it was not hard to draw the conclusion that this was the last available picture of him smiling – maybe the last time a lens had been aimed at him other than in anger. In the picture, the boy – Wensley Deepman, his name had been – was seven, maybe eight, and gap-toothed; and the teeth either side of the missing shone whitely out of a light-brown face in which glowed all the potential traditionally associated with children's beaming features; features in which a doting parent might discern a future doctor or lawyer, and the child himself in later years might rediscover the astronaut or engine driver he'd always meant to be. A broken twelve-year-old body was not generally included in such forecasts. And anyway, Zoë knew, most of whatever potential had existed in this seven- or eight-year-old had been squandered long before he'd taken flight from his grim tower: the last and only time Zoë had seen him, he'd been hurling abuse as she dragged his erstwhile sidekick back to his parents. *You*, she'd told him. *Piss the fuck off.* Three years later, it appeared, that's more or less what he'd done.

She laid the newspaper aside, her taste for knowing what was happening in the world quite undone. Beyond the window the North Pole appeared, where the jawbones of electric trains sat abandoned, like the remnants of a future civilisation, and just for a moment it appeared as if a dull grey rain were falling on everything, but that turned out to be dirt on the windows. Zoë closed her eyes. She didn't sleep. Everything stopped for a few minutes, nevertheless.

Paddington arrived: her 'station stop'. An intercommed voice reminded her to take her personal belongings when she left, and encouraged her to use the exit door, though there wasn't one specific to the purpose. From the platform, Zoë took the bridge to the Hammersmith line, and a little less than twenty minutes later caught a Tube in the City direction, which almost immediately reached an unexplained halt. She was standing – of course she was – in the middle of a strangely placid crush; its lack of angst born, presumably, of long practice. From the glass in the door her reflection stared back; and just behind that, another stared too, which could have been her older sister, if she'd had one. There were deeper lines in this one's face, and her eyes were more extravagantly bagged. This was Zoë as she'd be nearer the end of the line. And even as the thought occurred the train shunted, farted, and heaved into life, to carry her nearer to the end of the line.

2

A CROSS THE ROAD, AT an angle oblique to Zoë's vantage point, was the side of a building which had been sheared clean of its neighbour, leaving a four-storey windowless wall naked to the air; a blank, somehow painful expanse that put her in mind of a cauterised wound. Playing on it now – stacked one atop the other, about twelve foot apart – was a column of reflections that she realised, after a moment's thought, were of the windows of the building she now stood in. Four square, bright pictograms; light-prints beamed on to brick. They looked like they deserved a meaning beyond their accidental appearance; something suitably wise and epigrammatic. For the moment, though, they remained an unintended beauty, the way rows of TV aerials look like haiku.

'He'll only be a few moments.'

Zoë nodded. She had been on time for the appointment, and now was being asked to wait. It wasn't unprecedented, and it wasn't worth getting bothered about.

'Would you like a cup of coffee while you're waiting?'

'No. Thank you.'

Where she was now was an almost pathologically tidy receptionist's room. The paper-free office was an ideal, she supposed; this was photo free, art free, and quite possibly sterile, with the jacket on the back of the door its only concession to mortality. Its presumed owner, the Asian woman who'd just asked about coffee, was young to be so purged of frivolous gesture. Zoë turned back to the window.

She didn't know London well. It had never seemed necessary. But she knew that she wasn't far from where she'd found Andrew Kite, the day before Millennium Day; found him, squeezed the air out of him and dragged him home. And that it wasn't far again from where Wensley Deepman had fallen to his death. Some lives described tight circles. You could get born, grow up and die on the same two pages of your A–Z. Except growing up hadn't come into it with Wensley, and if he'd known his A and his Z, it was probably as much of the alphabet as he'd been familiar with.

Andrew Kite, on the other hand, had been educated, not that he was an advert for it. Even for a boy his age, he'd been deeply self-absorbed. In the car, heading back to Oxford, once he'd realised that's where she was taking him, he'd started talking. Some of it had been about his parents. Most, though, was about himself. Zoë had listened without responding. He'd been a startlingly beautiful boy, Andrew Kite, but it was his self-centred vacancy which had struck her; his rooted belief that everything impinged on his needs and wishes, as if he were still an infant in a pram, and the universe zeroed in on his well-being. The reasons he'd left were profound and important. The bastard-father. The bitch-mother. Zoë hadn't encountered the father, and what Andrew said about the mother might have been true, but the woman she remembered had been sad and nearly broken; whatever middle-class outrages she'd inflicted on her only child – raising, feeding, clothing him, and spoiling him like a bastard – hadn't been intended to drive him away. Maybe he'd know that by now. Keeping in touch hadn't made it on to Zoë's to-do list. But one more thing she did recall: that whole drive home, he hadn't mentioned Wensley once. Already, Kid B had been out of the picture.

'If you'd like to go through now.'

We'll have to fix you up with—

'Ms Boehm?'

'Yes. Fine.'

Through meant a walk along the corridor; a knock on a door; a responding invitation. The young woman went in briefly and said something inaudible. Then she was leaving, and the job beginning. Zoë was meeting Amory Grayling; was shaking his hand.

If she'd passed him on the street or a market square, she'd have clocked him as a farmer, she decided later; or as someone who worked with brick and mud – this not just because of the weather-beaten cast to his face (he had large, chipped features, like a totem pole's) but for something that seemed to nestle behind them; an intelligence of the kind Zoë associated with people who favoured dogs and fresh air, and long walks planned with big-scale maps. Not people she'd care to spend a whole lot of time with, necessarily, but nobody she'd instinctively dislike. But here he was on the seventh floor, which supposed a different nature of intelligence, and his handshake was a city one: its calluses moulded wielding pens and mobiles, not shovels. His suit looked the price of a season ticket. His office was large, square, neat, and its view, beyond the usual rooftops, boasted a fingernail paring of St Paul's.

'I'm sorry to keep you waiting.' He made a gesture she was never meant to interpret, beyond the vague things-to-do-ness of it.

'That's fine.'

'It's good of you to come.'

'I hope I haven't wasted both our times.' The time of both of us, she almost added. These times of ours. Whatever. She wished she'd had a cigarette out on the street.

He showed her a chair, asking, 'What makes you say so?'

It took her half a moment to remember what she'd said.

'This is about your PA. Your former PA.'

'Caroline Daniels.'

'You said that she was dead.'

A pained look crossed his eyes.

Zoë said, 'I run a private business, Mr Grayling. I don't investigate deaths, not any kind. Not even for insurance purposes. If Ms Daniels's death, if you think it's suspicious in any way, it's the police you need to talk to.'

'Caroline's death was an accident.'

'. . . I see.'

'She fell from a crowded platform. In the underground, I mean. It happens, Ms Boehm. They tell you to mind the gap and hold the handrail, but every so often the system comes unstuck. Most systems do. Especially those involving crowds.'

She wasn't sure what response that expected, and merely nodded, so he'd know she was paying attention.

There was a knock and the young woman returned carrying a tray with coffee, milk, biscuits. Amory Grayling thanked her in a tone suggesting he usually remembered this courtesy. Meanwhile Zoë, for no reason, felt her mind leave the building. She was standing by her car, loading one cuffed boy into the back, while Kid B hawked and swore in infant venom at her wheels. *Piss the fuck off*, she'd told him. He must have been all of nine years old: a pre-adolescent wreck trying to make his voice heard over the feedback of his own short life. *Piss the fuck off.*

She came back to the kind of space in a conversation which indicates something's been missed. 'Just milk. Thanks.' It was a good guess. Then she said, 'Tell me about her.'

'Caroline Daniels worked for me for twenty years. Twenty-two years.' The woman had gone, either on silent runners or Zoë's mental absences were disturbingly thorough. 'Not always here, I can tell you.'

'This building, you mean.'

'Nothing like. When I started, that is, when Caroline started

23

working for me, I was with another firm. It was a good, steady job – hers, I mean. She was my secretary, but she wasn't employed by me, she was the firm's. When I left, she came with me. That's the sort of person she was. She was loyal, Ms Boehm. She was a very loyal woman.'

Zoë thought: maybe the original firm would have had a different slant on that. But she said nothing.

And now this newer business – Pullman Grayling Kirk – was a going concern, and had been for eighteen years. Zoë had checked them out; their website was one of those just barely informative areas, keener on graphics and mission statements than fact, but she'd found enough references to be satisfied of the important details: Pullman's existed, made money, and was successful enough that Grayling was unlikely to stiff her on the bill. *Providing management services* was what their scrolling text promised: essentially they troubleshot ailing businesses, special-ising in the light industrial end of the spectrum, and happy to boast they could turn a £10 million deficit round inside half a year and save jobs while they were about it, though Zoë guessed this was probably at the expense of other jobs, which would turn out expendable. But maybe she was wrong about that. Maybe Pullman's people wore white hats, and circled their wagons round small businesses, defending them from evil asset-strippers. It didn't seem to especially matter right at the moment, though went on long enough for her to finish her coffee.

What mattered more was what she learned about Caroline Daniels, who had been with Pullman's all those eighteen years; who had been forty-three when she died – a shade younger than Zoë – and had lived in Oxford.

'She commuted, then.'

'Uncomplainingly. She liked Oxford. Always said she'd rather live there and have the journey.'

'That must have been tough on her family.'

'She never married.'

As epitaphs go, this bordered on obituary.

Zoë became conscious of her empty coffee cup, and leaned across to place it on the desk. 'Did she have a partner? Boyfriend, girlfriend?'

He might have flinched a little at 'girlfriend'. 'That's what I want to talk to you about.'

There had been a boyfriend. It had been a recent development. Amory Grayling held on to his cup, though it too was empty, while he told her. There had been a boyfriend since about the previous November, and maybe a little earlier. He had certainly been on the scene by Christmas. Prior to that was speculation, but it was difficult for a man not to notice such things: an increased lightness about her; a new softness. Something in the way she moved, Grayling turned out not to be too embarrassed to say. Caroline developed a tendency to hum under her breath, and to move her lips slightly, but in a happy way, when she thought herself unobserved, as if rehearsing lines for later. Zoë, listening to this, wondered if Amory Grayling had been in love with Caroline Daniels himself, or was simply, as seemed more likely, a touch miffed that she'd found someone.

'Did you ask about him?'

'Not at first. I didn't think it was my business.'

'But she offered the information.'

'After Christmas, yes, I suppose so. I asked her how her break had been, and she kept saying "we" – we did this, we did that. It would have been churlish not to ask.'

'What was his name?'

'Alan. Alan Talmadge.'

He was assuming the spelling, but Zoë made a note of it anyway. No obvious variation occurred.

'But you never met him.'

'No.'

She wasn't sure where this was going. It seemed he wasn't

either, for he veered away suddenly; began talking about the day of Caroline Daniels's death – her unusual lateness: it was true the trains delayed her at times, but she always called in when that happened. It seemed to him now that he'd had the sensation there had been phones ringing, unanswered, all that morning. Two police officers had turned up shortly before lunch. Grayling had arranged cover by then: there was another woman in Caroline Daniels's office, pulling away at the loose threads of Caroline Daniels's job. Of the officers, the male had been sympathetic. The female, he recalled, had found it worthwhile to emphasise the disarrangements caused on the City line.

'Disarrangements,' he said. 'I remember thinking at the time what an ugly word to use.'

'This was at Paddington?'

'That's right. She must have used that platform hundreds of times. Quite possibly thousands. And one day there's a crush, and . . .' He didn't finish the thought. Didn't have to. After a moment, he said, 'Every so often it happens, and you read about it, and nobody ever thinks it'll happen to them. But that's who all the people are it's ever happened to. They're people who read about it happening to somebody else once, and never thought it would happen to them.' He became silent. Zoë said nothing. She was remembering reading in a newspaper about a couple whose tiny child had drowned in their ornamental pond. And even at the time of reading, she'd been remembering another report, maybe two weeks previously, of exactly the same thing happening somewhere else, to somebody else. And she'd wondered if that second couple had read the report of the first drowning, and thanked God it hadn't happened to them.

At length he said, 'There's a sister, and I'd met her occasionally. I offered to help with . . . arrangements, and she let me do so. It was the least I could do.'

Zoë said nothing.

26

'There was a cremation, in Oxford. She wasn't religious, and those were the instructions she'd left. She was . . . organised, I suppose you could say.'

She said, 'And Talmadge wasn't there.'

He looked at her sharply. 'How did you know that?'

'You said you'd never met him.'

'Oh. So I did.'

'Had they broken up?'

'No. Not that I know of. And I think I'd have known. I think Caroline would have . . . I think I'd have been able to tell.'

'She'd have been upset.'

He sighed. 'Ms Boehm. In all the years I'd known her, in all the years she'd worked for me, I was never aware of Caroline having a boyfriend. And while she was never an unhappy person, I don't remember her humming around the office before. So yes, she'd have been upset. And I'd have noticed.'

Zoë was thinking of all the ways upset people might find of making their feelings known, and coming up with few more extreme than landing in front of a Tube train.

'And I can tell what you're thinking. And no, she wouldn't have done that either. She wasn't religious. But she had firm principles, and suicide would have offended them. She thought it was . . . She thought it an insult, somehow. I know what she meant by that. But please don't ask me to explain.'

She didn't need him to. Which did not mean she was in agreement, quite.

She said, 'Did the sister know about Talmadge?'

'Terry? Yes. Caroline had mentioned him. But they hadn't met.'

'Were they living together?'

'I don't think so. But they were lovers, there's no doubt about that. Caroline told Terry as much.' He paused. 'He was younger than her. That's something else she told Terry.'

27

'Did she say how old he was?'

'No. She was forty-three. He could have been younger than her and still been forty himself.' Grayling noticed he was holding his cup, and put it down as suddenly as if it had grown hot. 'I can't . . . I don't really think he could have been terribly younger than her. Late thirties at most, probably.'

'Why do you say that?' asked Zoë, though she suspected she probably knew.

Amory Grayling said, 'She was a fine woman and I both liked and respected her very much indeed. I trusted her absolutely. We might have begun as employer–employee, but we became friends years ago.'

'But,' said Zoë.

'She was not what you'd call the world's most . . . She was not physically an attractive woman, Ms Boehm. Not by the standards we're encouraged to adopt.'

'I see.'

'I've long thought physical beauty overrated.'

'So have I.'

This apparent accord, which both knew for a lie, silenced them a moment.

Then Zoë said, 'So. They met, they were lovers. Caroline dies in an accident. And Talmadge doesn't show up at the funeral.'

'That's right.'

'Was he notified?'

'I had no means of doing so. No number, no address. But he couldn't not have known what happened. I mean, thinking about it, there is no way he could have remained unaware of her death.'

This was true. He would have had to have really not wanted to know to successfully maintain such ignorance.

She said, 'What is it you want me to do, Mr Grayling?'

'I want you to find him.'

'All right.'

'It's a matter of . . . I suppose it's a matter of unfinished business. You could even call it a debt, of sorts.'

She didn't reply.

He said, 'Caroline never left an untidy desk. Not in twenty-two years.'

And Zoë, who'd messed a few in her time, nodded, as if she'd just had a glimpse of what truly pained him.

3

O N THE PAVEMENT, SHE lit a cigarette. A group of shirt-
sleeved men and jacketed women were doing likewise
on the steps of the building opposite: there was probably a new
word, or a recent one at any rate, to describe this group behaviour. 'Smoking' would do for now. And this was something she
was now starting to think about promising herself she was
going to stop soon: or so, at any rate, she reminded herself.

When she glanced up, she saw that the pictograms lately
reflected there had risen; the column was only two reflections
tall now, as the upper pair had escaped into the sky: a trick of
light and angles, she supposed; to do with the way the earth
moves, but buildings mostly don't. And she wondered where a
reflection went when there was nothing for it to project upon,
and whether the air was full of the ghosts of things that had
almost happened, but lacked foundation. But this was whimsy,
and she had no time for that. One of the smokers opposite
sketched her half a wave as she tucked the lighter into her
pocket, but she pretended not to notice, and moved on round
the corner.

There was now a job to do. It wouldn't necessarily prove
difficult.

What potentially made the difference was whether Talmadge
had meant to vanish.

It was Zoë's experience that finding people was harder when they didn't know they were missing. There was a whole category of people liable to fall off the edge of the world; whose grip on contemporary reality, never marvellous to begin with, was weakened further by what, to others, might appear no more than the average slights – and then they were gone. They didn't know where they were going, so wouldn't recognise it when they got there, and left no clues as to where it was. Often, theirs wasn't a journey so much as an act of divestment; a shedding of all that had anchored them in the first place: mortgages and bank accounts, mobile phones and credit cards, enmities and friendships – something snapped, or something else got stronger. It was hard to know whether it was pull or repulsion acting on them, because these were the ones who were never found, so never answered the questions. And she thought again of the man by the canal whose prayers she'd interrupted; who carried his history in a collection of laundry bags. Impossible to tell if he was lost on purpose, or missing by accident; or whether, after enough time had passed, it made the slightest difference.

. . . Because things happened, she told herself. Volition, intention, desire, regret – sometimes these took a back seat, and events just got on with it. Not everything had somebody responsible.

It was important to remember this, as she crossed the road at the traffic lights. That there was no conceivable pattern of belief, for example, under which anything that had happened to Wensley Deepman in the years since she'd encountered him – all the missing parts of the story which it hardly took genius to fill in – could be laid at Zoë's feet. She had had a job to do and had done it. Wensley, either way, was background colour; an extra in a story about how Zoë had gone to London to bring back Andrew Kite; or perhaps one in which Andrew Kite had gone to London and somebody had brought him back.

Wherever you stood, nobody was giving Kid B top billing. *Piss the fuck off* she'd told him, but she hadn't meant him to die.

This wasn't guilt she was feeling. It was an awareness of an absence of guilt that she might once have felt, when things were different.

She needed coffee. From an obscure need to punish herself, Zoë walked past the branded outlets to an extreme-looking dive on a corner with road spatter scaling its outside walls, whose misted windows made it clear what lay within: stained formica tables, plastic chairs and scuffed lino. It also contained the biggest spider plant she'd ever seen. She sat in what was nearly its shade, while her coffee, which was too hot and too weak, cooled. Against the wall opposite an old man with indescribable eyebrows and a throat raggy as a tortoise's chewed on a roll-up. In front of her eyes, its mouse turd of ash dropped into his mug of tea, and her hands, which had automatically gone seeking her cigarettes already, quit their hunt.

It ought, she thought, to have been raining outside, but it wasn't.

Caroline Daniels, though, was the job in hand. She tried to clear her mind of the unwanted image of a nine-year-old kid making his pass for her valuables – that brilliant pair of bricks she'd secreted – leaning into her so clumsily she'd had to drop her shoulder to let the bag fall into his hand, then push against his foot to achieve her stumble . . . This wasn't what she was supposed to be thinking about. When starting on a job, Joe had always said, first evaluate the client. He'd been clueless, Joe, most of the time; stealing what he thought he knew from that black-and-white fiction that gave detection a bad name. But it was a mental exercise, if nothing else; something to keep her from that picture of Kid B lifting her bag, then stepping off the edge of a gap three years wide and a lifetime deep . . .

Amory Grayling . . .

Yes, Joe.

When she'd been younger, she'd have had less trouble with Amory Grayling; would have pegged as good or bad his reasons for wanting to find Talmadge, and filed him accordingly. Life had become more complicated. Now, she couldn't even be sure that Grayling himself knew what he was about. Amory Grayling had been Caroline Daniels's employer and her friend, had viewed her with respect and affection, and had taken her for granted for twenty-two years. She'd doubtless been a paragon as a secretary, and doubtless too been a little in love with her boss. And maybe he'd never taken advantage of that, but it was a racing certainty the knowledge had given him ego comfort over the years . . . And suddenly, she'd found a man. This wasn't, perhaps, the most astounding development, but Zoë pictured Grayling's puzzlement anyway . . . Maybe she was being unfair. But over and above the personal – no matter whom these women yearned for from afar – men liked, she suspected, the idea of single women; of single women no longer in first youth. It was less to do with there being an available pool than with simple market economy. To women who lacked, but wanted, men, men were blue-chip stock, valued for their wit, their charm, their opinions. Women no longer in those straits were less likely to overlook their nasal hair, their corpulence, their lack of tact.

She thought: but maybe I'm wrong; maybe Grayling simply cared, and still cares, and worries that Caroline's lover is distraught, and in need of attention. Nobody should grieve alone, some thought. For Zoë, solitude and grief were necessary partners, but she was aware that some well-meaning people felt otherwise. It would be nice to believe there were good motives for doing things, things like paying Zoë to do her job. But she didn't need to dwell on that long before deciding that the main thing, after all, was that she was paid to do her job, and since Grayling had written a cheque, perhaps she ought get on with it.

So she left the café, with this idea taking root: that she should trace Caroline Daniels's steps home, as she'd traced them so far to her office. The woman's working day had finished at 5:45: it wasn't difficult to work out which train she'd have caught. Zoë might find someone who'd known her. *We were all shocked by the news. And tell me, how's Alan?* This wasn't likely. But it was the nature of the trade to play the odds, and besides, it gave her the rest of the day in London. She'd passed a sign a minute down the road, pointing the way to the local library. Before second thoughts set in, or better judgement, she was headed that way, thinking: ten minutes. It was ten minutes out of her life. *Lay your ghosts while you have the chance.* That wasn't something she remembered Joe ever saying, but it was his voice that formed the thought in her head, or so she decided, and while it wasn't true that it was always a joy to remember him, or that she could ever pretend he was anything like a constant presence, it was nice to reflect she'd have him to blame when this turned out a mistake. Which chain of thought occupied her all the way to the library.

Her first impression, reaching Rivers Estate, was: it reminded her of film of anonymous Soviet cities, those postwar dystopias created in the middle of vast emptinesses, whose architecture seemed all featureless concrete and light pollution so fierce it blinded the stars. It was always the light that disturbed her, seeing such footage; the way it seemed less intended to keep the enormous darkness at bay than to remind the marooned citizens they could be clearly seen. The cities were like literal-minded reconstructions of those shopping centre maps with YOU ARE HERE printed in big red type. Wherever you came across one, it always knew exactly where you were.

But then, there were always ways you could be tracked down, model citizen or not. There were databases, electoral rolls; there were credit listings and people-tracer sites. Zoë subscribed to all major available finding services, and not a few that were neither major nor well known, nor even especially legal. All, though, could be reached at a public library, if it had internet access, and they all had that. She'd found the Deepmans within minutes: fewer than the ten she'd promised herself. It occurred to her, as long as she was online, she might as well have gone ahead and put out tracers for Alan Talmadge, but by the time she'd thought that, she was already outside, and soon after that, on the streets of Rivers Estate.

Which, from what Zoë could make out, were arranged like the spokes of a wheel, at the hub of which stood a pair of high-rises, probably twenty-odd storeys' worth: she didn't count. These streets were named after rivers. Zoë wondered if local councils had naming committees, or whether each hired a Womble to do this for them. The Deepmans lived on Severn Street. And there was no need to check the numbering: as she turned the corner and saw the mid-level chaos there, she knew which house it focused on, and what it was about.

There were cars and vans parked both sides of the street; some with people inside, talking on phones; one with a man standing next to it, working a laptop resting on its roof. And there was a crowd milling about a house, more or less kept at bay by two uniformed policemen. This would be number 39: the Deepmans'. The crowd broke down neatly into crews as Zoë studied it: teams of two and three bound together by umbilical cabling. One of each bore a camera on one shoulder in pseudo-military manner, and each of these cameras was aimed at a tall black man who was standing outside 39, saying: '—in the next twenty minutes. So if you'll all just be patient until then. Thank you.' He went in. The door that closed behind him had a bouquet taped to it. The house's curtains were drawn. She didn't really know what she was doing here, and the crowd offered no clue as it turned inwards and burbled to itself. At what seemed the exact same moment, every member of it not

35

holding a camera produced a phone and punched a number. Zoë imagined phones in different offices all starting to ring at once; a finely orchestrated moment far too scattered to have any impact. Another car pulled up beside her, with three men inside, each of them smoking. When they clambered out, it was like watching heroes emerging from a catastrophe: the smoke that clung to them, that blew away on their exit, was a souvenir of the danger they'd brushed. One glanced at Zoë in passing, but in a way that rendered her unimportance absolute. He was saying something about the PC to his companions: PC, press conference.

Zoë had made the papers, when she'd shot a man. This had happened not long after her husband had died, been killed, though at the time – and didn't the press just let it be known? – he was thought to have killed himself in remorse after supplying drugs to a dead teenager. It had not been a good time for Zoë. She received a lot of letters, most of them from men. And it had taught her this much, her brief and uncoop- erative encounter with the press: that when it came to the red tops, there was no such place as the right side. The tabloid press was like the pub drunk. You didn't want it picking on you, and you didn't want it telling the world you were its best fucking mate. You wanted it to not notice you, and that was all; its eye to pass over you, registering your absolute unimportance. It could leave in the air behind it a trace of stale tobacco and brimstone, and that was okay, just so long as it wasn't there any more. She felt a shudder as the men passed, but managed to keep it internal. As soon as they'd gone, she was on her way.

. . . There's a feeling that's almost but not quite déjà vu: the sensation you're creating a memory even as you're doing some- thing for the first time. Zoë had that now, leaving Severn Street. It was unsettling, like finding that somebody else had packed her bags for her. She didn't want to remember this scene; neither the gathering crews of journalists, nor the way the dead boy's house had become part of a set: Act I, Scene iii. It was part of the commercial wrapping that packages premature death, and you couldn't read a paper, watch TV or turn on a radio without being part of it, but that didn't mean you had to wallow. So she turned her back before the instant memory could dig itself deeper. When somebody else packed your bags, you never knew what was going to turn up in them. That was why the question was always asked at airports.

Around a couple of corners, from a kebab van at the side of the road a young Turkish man was selling tea, coffee, sandwiches; probably kebabs, if the demand arose. Three men and one woman stood in the shelter of the van's raised panel, drinking from polystyrene cups. Passing, Zoë caught the word 'Deepman', and slowed as if hit by the sudden need for a cuppa.

One of the men nudged a companion. 'Another victim, Abdul.'

'I make the best tea in London,' said Abdul, unless that wasn't his real name.

Zoë smiled at him – it seemed an unfamiliar exercise; maybe her first of the day – and guessed tea was the thing to order. The average age of the four customers was, say, eighty. This was a second estimate. Her first was a hundred and three. By the time her tea was poured, they'd established she wasn't a journo, wasn't local, that she had 'known' Wensley Deepman, though she kept the details to herself. Perhaps, by the time she was a hundred and three, or even eighty, her own interrogation skills would have been honed like theirs: the unembarrassable direct questioner was a formidable opponent.

'His folks shown their faces yet?' the woman asked. She had a face like an apple, but a very old apple; one you could probably poke your finger through without trying.

Zoë told them about the man on the doorstep; about the conference happening soon.

'Vin'll have sorted that.'

Admitting she didn't know who Vin was might have damaged her credentials. She said, 'Does anybody know how it happened?'

'He'll have been on the drugs, that's right.'

'Or drunk.'

'He was twelve, but.'

'It's a crying shame,' said the woman. And her eyes agreed, but there was something else there too; something that said yes, but it had happened, and it was getting the TV crews in. Or maybe that was Zoë reading stuff that wasn't there. She'd long ago accepted she could be wrong about things. She still needed telling twice sometimes, though.

'Know what I heard?' Abdul said.

'Tell us what you heard, son.'

'I heard he threw himself off.'

The group on the pavement shared looks. A new ingredient had been chucked into the mix.

'He was twelve, but,' one of the men said again. 'Why'd he want to do a thing like that for?'

Abdul shrugged. 'It's what I heard.'

Zoë was wondering about the speed of information. This had happened yesterday. Time enough for the truth to have got lost; at the same time, what made this so unlikely? Of the six of them there, Abdul was the youngest, and he hadn't been twelve for a while. Everything was more extreme than it used to be. Everybody knew that. The older four here, they knew the kids drank and drugged. It wasn't much of a reach that they also despaired.

'Where'd you hear this?' she asked.

But the young man didn't know. It was word, that was all. There was never any telling how it got on to the streets.

She was going to go now. That was the plan. This was emotional tourism, without even the excuse of an accompanying buzz. Because Zoë didn't care; not exactly. At least these others had known the drama's participants. At least they shared the same postal code. For Zoë there was just the splinter of unfinished business; the same insistent irritation she used to get whenever Joe got a bee in his bonnet and demanded it be followed. Those were the times she'd slam doors, exit premises; find out about it later. It never amounted to anything. That always made it worse when it happened again. Nothing Joe ever thought important amounted to anything, so now he was dead.

One of the four said, 'Wonder how Joe's taking it?'

It was one of those blips when you have to call reality into question. She had a custard-pie moment: face blank, mouth open, all signs of intelligent life fled.

'His own bloody grandson,' one of the others reckoned. 'How'd you think?'

. . . Joseph Deepman. She'd come across the name in the library; guessed he'd be a relative – how could he not be? Same area, though the address escaped her.

'There's some'd be glad to see the back of the bastard.'

It was the woman who said that.

'There, now. Ill of the dead.'

'He eyed my handbag a time or two.'

'Well, he'll not be round to do that again.'

'Where does Joe live?' Zoë asked.

One of the men pointed. It took her a moment to understand what he meant by this, because he seemed to be aiming at heaven, and her first response was the obvious; a fleeting sense of the luck that befell some people. But he meant, if anything, the opposite, because what he was pointing at was the fourteenth floor of one of the tower blocks in whose shadow they were standing, though she hadn't realised it until that moment. She'd taken it for ordinary shade; the gloom you stood in, obviously, in areas like this. But it was a concrete object casting it upon them, and just for a moment they stood looking, the six of them, as if it had never been visible before; one of a pair of obelisks wished upon the landscape by planners who'd set them there, and moved on. A flat-faced solid structure, not so much characterless as character negating, and definitely lacking in humour. But the hub of a wheel; a building of unignorable weight, if nothing else. And very like one you might throw yourself from, if you ever intended to die.

Zoë had long given up constructing theories as to what made people what they were. It was fatuous to imagine you understood a stranger's motivation when your own felt massively involved, like a complicated piece of legislation. But there was no denying that there were places would dwarf potential, and when every horizon was hidden behind the New Brutal, and uncloseted smells hit you every breath you took, you'd probably reached one. This was what she decided in the stairwell, on landing six. Everything stank, here. Her heart was hammering; her breathing was a mess. Around her, names tagged on walls laid claim to territory nobody sensible would set foot in. Many of these names were ugly, and threatened violence. If you gave a zoo-born gorilla a sketch pad, it would draw the bars of its cage.

. . . Her own motivation was something she'd lost track of. There were hours to kill before her train; that was part of it. But she didn't allow herself to fool herself often, and then only when it wasn't important. She was here because of something she'd said and everything else she hadn't done. *Piss the fuck off*, she'd told Wensley. It all came back to that. He'd been nine years old. Probably past saving already, which anyway wasn't her job. But while it was possible, and in most cases desirable, to wipe your hands of involvement, if you were an honest woman, you saw that through. Which meant turning up afterwards, to make sure everyone knew you weren't to blame; to let them know you hadn't been involved, and hadn't altered any outcomes. To give them a chance, in fact, to hate you.

Landings eight, nine, ten, were deeply purgatorial. She hit a second wind then; as if her body had accepted this as part of the punishment, and would keep climbing until she told it to stop.

At fourteen Zoë stepped out on to the walkway running round the outside of the block. She had met nobody coming up the stairs, and there was nobody here either, on this concrete balcony. When the lifts didn't run, she supposed, you boarded yourself inside until things got better. One of those circumstances you filed away with the weather, as being beyond control. She had been given the flat number by the crew down at the kebab van, and hoped now they'd not misled her, because then she'd have to go back and kill them all. At the first corner she stopped one moment, registering the height. A slight problem with heights, Zoë had, but only a slight one. The door she was after was the next one along; a blue door, like all the others.

She knocked, and turned her back as she waited, and looked down on London. It appeared more complicated from this perspective. She could trace the way the streets collided, and the odd, ill-fitting shapes of the mismatched buildings. Many flat roofs had extra, small buildings atop them, as if there were a parasite city feeding on the ceiling of the main one. This was not, she supposed, terribly high, but it was unnaturally high all the same. This would foster isolation. Penthouse suites were well known to be desirable, but generally came equipped with working lifts. Towers were where the condemned were banged up, and usually had steep stairs and broken lighting.

After a while she turned and knocked again.

The people down there, she thought. They look like ants. Or about the size of ants, she amended, and engaged in what might be ant activity, inasmuch as, from this distance, it could be mistaken for purposeful, pre-planned industry. And she felt the sudden rush of vertigo: an anxious high that threatened to sweep her off her feet, the way they say love does, leaving you nothing to cling to, and only the certainty of flat-out closure ahead. 'Deceleration trauma,' Bob Poland called it once. He had not been talking about love. He'd claimed emergency crews used plastic bags, which were rinsed out after, for reuse. And Wensley Deepman had gone this route. For the splittest of seconds, she caught a glimpse of his last view: a freewheeling vision of some miserable backstreets and unkind architecture, and then nothing – then just the only possible end of such misadventure, and with the stark and violent blankness of it came the vertigo pang again, and Zoë felt cut off at the knees. She took a deep breath, steadied herself on the railing. Way down yonder ants milled strategically, scurrying picnic-wards. Behind her, the door opened.

She had almost forgotten where she was, or why. It was so long since she'd knocked, the buzzing at her knuckles had faded away.

'Who are you?'

'Mr Deepman?'

'Who are you?'

'My name's Zoë Boehm, Mr Deepman. I wondered if I could have a word.'

'Who are you?'

It occurred to her, brief as a passing moth, that his repetition had purpose; that this old man – and he looked pretty old, pretty decrepit, with sagging skin and rheumy eyes, and nico-tined wisps tufting randomly from his scalp; he was white, but only in the broadly used sense of the term, actually being a cross between grey and yellow, as if he'd been finely mulched, then left out in the rain – that this old man, it occurred to her, had seen through her pretence that she was who she thought she was, and intended now to get to the bottom of Zoë Boehm. But this was a wild thought; one of those off-message moments like a pop-up for the brain, offering a second's irritated distraction before you close them down. She took a breath. 'My name's Zoë Boehm. I wondered if I could talk to you, Mr Deepman.'

'What about?'

'About your grandson.'

'Wensley.'

'Yes.'

'Wensley's dead.'

'I know, Mr Deepman. I'm very sorry.'

He was looking beyond her now, down at the messy city, at its excess of angles and sharp corners. Probably, all he was seeing was blur.

'You press?'

'No. I'm not press.'

'What you want to talk about Wensley for?'

Frankly, she didn't know. 'I met him once, Mr Deepman.' I was a link in his chain, she thought of saying. 'It was . . . I met him, that's all. I wanted to pay my condolences.'

'Tried to rob you, did he?'

She blinked.

'Not much way Wez was running into your likes. Less he was trying to rob you.'

She found herself nodding, though he wasn't looking at her. 'Something like that happened,' she said.

'He was a devil from hell,' the old man said.

There was a moment, maybe half of one, during which Zoë felt an impulse to contradict him. But what was the point of that? This was the grandfather: he'd known the boy. The indications were, he was right.

'A devil from hell,' he said again. Then: 'Do you do bulbs?'

'Do I what?'

'*Bulbs*. Light bulbs.' He stepped back inside, leaving the door hanging open. Zoë breathed deep, and followed.

The door opened on a hallway which seemed narrower than it ought – narrower than the door, almost – and it struck her, entering, that if all the flats matched this, each of them of dimensions just slightly more disappointing than expected, there could be a hidden chamber somewhere in the block, made up of all the left-over spaces. It was dark, too, and she assumed this was where the bulb was needed. But Deepman was already elsewhere: she tracked him through the sitting room – an area focused on an absence, somehow – and into the kitchen, where the guiding principle seemed to be that nothing should be washed up until everything needed to be. That point might easily be reached inside the next two minutes. He indicated the bulb, a foot above his head. It was intact but scorched, as if its burning-out had been wilfully exaggerated. 'It's been like that for days,' he said.

'And it's not likely to get better by itself.'

'I know that. I know that.' Deepman held his arm out, so she could admire its tremble. 'I can't lift this above my head.'

'Where's the bulb?'

'Drawer.'

He gave her a little more help than that, though; showed her the particular drawer. In addition to a single bulb it held a neatly folded, though long discoloured, tea towel.

Zoë checked the switch was off, changed the bulb, and turned the light on. Its unshaded glare pointed out that it wasn't only the dishes needed doing: what could be seen of the surfaces was grimed and streaked with grease.

'What about the hallway?' she said. 'Do you need a bulb there?'

'I've only the one. You've used that.'

'You want to get some more. You could fall, break something. There must be someone would change it for you. A neighbour.'

'Wensley used to come round.'

She said, 'To help?' Not keeping the doubt out of her voice.

'He'd kip on the sofa. Whenever Vin kicked him out.

'Vin?'

'Our Jet's boyfriend. It was her mother's idea. It means a stone, not an aeroplane.'

The light seemed to have activated him.

Zoë said, 'Did Vin kick him out often?'

''Bout as often as he deserved. He was a devil from hell.'

'But you let him sleep here.'

'Couldn't keep him out. He had a key.' He sniffed, but there was no sentiment in it. He just lacked a handkerchief. 'I was forty-eight when his mum was born. How'm I suppose to cope?'

There was no answer Zoë could usefully supply.

'Vin an' him were like cat and dog. Funny, really, 'cause Vin's the spit of Wensley's dad. Another what-you-call-'em.' Zoë braced herself for a racist term. 'St Lucian.'

'Right.'

'Used to curl up on the sofa, prowl round when he thought I was asleep. I get up one morning, the TV's gone. He's back later like butter wouldn't melt. "Wasn't me," he says. "Honest." Honest! That's a word in the dictionary, that is.'

'I'm sorry.'

'And how'm I suppose to watch the cricket with no telly?'

She followed him into the sitting room, whose sofa and upright chair were aimed at the vacancy in the corner. It would have been cruel but neat if there'd been a dust-free area the shape of a TV set on the table there. Instead there was a plastic spray of wild flowers in a small vase. It was dim in here too, but Zoë didn't want the light bulb discussion again.

'What will happen now?' he asked suddenly.

'What will happen?'

'To Wensley. To his . . . remains.'

'I expect,' said Zoë, 'there'll be an inquest. I mean, I know there will be. There'll have to be.'

'To find out why he did it?'

She looked at him and saw now, clearly despite the grey-stained light, that what she'd taken as a surface slackening, a loosening of the skin that was all that was holding a beaten spirit together, was more immediate than that; was the product, not only of years gone by, but of grief and puzzlement now. And she'd taken at face value his *devil from hell*s, his *often as he deserved*s . . . It wasn't that he'd hidden his sorrow well, it was that she'd lacked the emotional talent to read it; a talent she'd once had, but had boarded away in some internal chamber made up of the unused spaces the rest of her life had produced. And he was still looking at her, Joseph Deepman. It was more than just his flat he'd wanted light cast on. 'Why he did it?' she repeated, and it came out a whisper.

'It's what they're saying.'

She cleared her throat. 'Who?'

'Everyone.'

That was too many people to argue with. She'd already met some of them.

'A policeman,' he said.

'A policeman told you that?'

'He wasn't talking to me. But . . . you hear stuff. What gets said.'

'Is that what you think happened?'

'How'm I suppose to know?'

'I'm sure,' she began, and stopped. She wasn't sure of anything. 'Mr Deepman. I'm sorry about what happened. Wensley . . . when we met, it wasn't great. You weren't wrong. But nobody wanted this. I'm sorry.'

'I stopped touching him,' said Deepman. 'Not since he was a mite. Never touched him after that.'

Zoë looked at him.

'Cuddling an' that,' said Deepman. 'You don't, do you? Not when it's a boy. You don't hug them or pet them. Don't want them turning out soft, do you?'

'You shouldn't blame yourself.'

He looked at her, then through her, briefly, as if she'd opened

46

into a window. He didn't seem to enjoy the view. 'Not like it comes with a choice, is it? Who you blame.'

'Mr Deepman—'

'I need a lie down, now.'

She could have done with one herself. He left without further word, stepping back into the hall and through a door the other side of it. She waited a while, but he made no noise. So there she was standing in his dark living room, fourteen levels up, all the furniture concentrated on something that wasn't there any more. But then, her whole day had been like that: Wensley Deepman, Caroline Daniels . . . There was nothing Zoë could do for the old man, and nothing she was obliged to try. She picked a figurine from a shelf, and studied it for no special reason: a small shepherdess; a reminder of a world that used to exist somewhere else, though never as cleanly or as prettily frocked as this. She put it back. Wensley might have lifted it once himself, she thought; maybe sized up its value, then evidently put it back. And this filled her with disgust, not Wensley's action but her own baseless imagining of it. She left the flat, careful to pull the door to behind her. What could be seen of London still stretched like an electric mat way down below. Zoë had no plans until 6:30 . . . But she'd had days with larger empty spaces in them, and those had passed too.

4

PADDINGTON WAS GREY, DAMP and tense, with crowds knotted beneath departure monitors, waiting for their platforms to be signalled. Zoë foresaw a serious trample when that happened – she didn't want to be standing between any part of this horde and the last available seat. Somebody brushed past, and it took half a second to place him as a face from the morning train: a balding, upright man, with a clockwork twitchiness to his movements. On the ground that a regular might have the inside track, Zoë followed him rather than hang round with the masses, and he led her to the far end of a platform, coming to a halt just as a train ploughed into view.

She had a moment's horror as it passed. Even slowing down, it was weight, brute force and metal: an exercise in practical physics, juddering with the effort of coming to a halt. This, or something like it, had done for Caroline Daniels: a Tube train was smaller, of course, but that was like weighing the difference between a bus and an articulated lorry when you were underneath one. And she wondered what it would be like, to step out in front of this juggernaut – no, not step, be *pushed*, even if that push was the involuntary swelling of the crowd behind. There must have been a moment during which Caroline Daniels had known everything. And then it met her: her travelling death. The way it happened for Wensley Deepman, except in his case, he'd been doing the travelling . . . But it did not matter, in the end, whether what you collided with was irresistible force or immovable object. Something had to give, and – in the end – that would be you.

Hard landings teach us we are flightless things.

The train halted. Passengers disembarked. Trusting she hadn't been led astray, she boarded once it was empty: the quiet carriage again, she saw from the sign by the door, so turned her mobile off. Taking a table seat, she leaned back. Days in the city wore you out. She'd have known that anyway, from the people arriving now: nodding at each other, saying good evening, but mostly sitting separately. Tired again, like this morning. But there were different kinds of tired; the kind you haven't shaken off yet, and the kind you earned in the course of a day. She'd earned tired, she supposed – killing time was as wearying as most other things you did with it – but she'd been waiting for the job to start, not doing it. She closed her eyes. *We never sleep.* That had been a detective agency slogan, Joe had told her. She forgot which one. It could almost have been her own, though; she slept, of course, but never well, never soundly.

And now it was time to think about Caroline Daniels.

Before leaving Pullman's, she'd spoken to a woman who'd known Caroline: one of the partners' PAs. 'I didn't know her well. But we shared a room, we have this restroom? For breaks?'

Her name had been Corinne, and she was twenty-four; a natural blonde, with that brittle prettiness you never find in the country-born. While they spoke, she barely left off fingering her engagement ring.

Zoë had said, 'Did she ever talk to you about Alan?'

'About who?'

'Alan Talmadge. Her boyfriend.'

'She had a *boyfriend*?'

Which answered that.

Corinne said, 'She never told me she had a boyfriend. I always thought she was, you know. Single?'

It was a word on a sliding scale, or so it fell on Zoë's ears. There was 'single' and there were other words, and you could grade the gravity of your situation by the level of pity in Corinne's voice; the amount of sympathy withheld calibrating the precise degree to which the condition was self-inflicted. From 'single' right the way up to 'cancer'.

'He must have been quite old.'

'What makes you think so?'

'Well, she was in her forties, wasn't she?'

Zoë said, 'I believe he was some years younger.'

Corinne stroked her engagement ring. 'Well,' she said at last. 'That makes it even sadder, doesn't it?'

'That she's dead?'

'Yes,' said Corinne. 'Just as she was starting to have a life.'

A man took the seat opposite Zoë; in his fifties, by the look of him, and wearing a nice dark overcoat, which he removed, folded carefully, and laid on the rack overhead. He was narrow-faced and seemed frayed – well turned out, but with stress levels visible. He carried a copy of the *Evening Standard*, which had found something new to say about Charles Parsley Sturrock, whose dead features Zoë glimpsed below the fold.

He was looking at her – the man opposite, not Sturrock – and she realised she'd been staring. 'Was somebody sitting here?'

'No.'

'Well, then.'

Well indeed. Somebody cycled past the window, an odd thing to do on a railway platform, but he turned out to be loading his bike into the guard's van. People bustled – all over, people bustled. It wasn't everywhere you saw the verb in action.

She turned back to her fellow passenger. 'I take it you do this journey daily.'

He nodded, then raised an eyebrow, as if granting her permission to continue.

'I was wondering,' she said, 'did you know Caroline Daniels?'

'I'm sorry?'

'Caroline Daniels. She used to catch this train.'

'A great many people catch this train.'

He used the tone the English middle classes use when they want you to know you're an imbecile without their having to say it.

'She caught it for twenty-two years. Every day.'

'Ah.'

'Oxford to Paddington.'

'I go on to Charlbury, myself.'

'Still . . .'

'Still. Yes. I must have known her, if only by sight. Most people pick up habits, of course. Same carriage, same seat, where possible. I always sit here myself. But twenty-two years, I must have seen her.' His eyes narrowed. 'I'm not sure, though, why we're discussing her.'

'She had an accident.'

'I see. On the train?'

'Not this train, no.'

'And you're, what? Some kind of insurance person?'

'Something like that,' said Zoë.

'Well, then. I hope you do your best for her.'

'So do I,' said Zoë.

He nodded to himself. Caroline Daniels: total stranger. But a stranger who'd fought in the same war, sort of. He looked like he wanted to say more, but wasn't sure what it might be. Instead he nodded again, as if in response to some significant intelligence, and returned to his newspaper.

The train emitted a high-pitched beeping Zoë assumed announced the locking of the doors, and began to move. Most seats were taken now, but not all. Paddington began sliding away behind them, and a no-man's sprawl of workers' huts, prefabs and cars parked at awkward angles on cratered bombsites shunted past. All available wall space was cartooned over in primary spray paint. Above everything hovered the Westway, its concrete ugliness a match for the sky above. Zoë stood, prepared to make her way the length of the train if necessary. She had no photograph, which was a pain, but then, how many bosses kept pictures of their PAs? Married bosses, of their unmarried PAs.

'Eighteen years,' said the man suddenly.

She looked him full in the eye.

'I've been doing this eighteen years,' he said. 'Seems quite long enough to me.'

She nodded, and moved a few seats further down.

None of the others she asked in that carriage knew the name Caroline Daniels. One woman thought she remembered a familiar face not being round any more, but that happened. Sometimes, they came back.

'They take a sabbatical, if they're academics or medical. Or the job sends them abroad for a bit.'

'Or they have a nervous breakdown,' a man put in.

But Caroline Daniels: no.

To the south, in the sky, planes were leaving Heathrow, at the rate of what must have been one a minute. So many people, getting out of this place. She'd seen them in the morning too, when relative directions of travel had made them appear stationary in the sky. Like everything else, it fell to points of view. One person's speed of flight was another's standing still.

Zoë moved on. In the next carriage down, she stopped a woman on her way back from the buffet car holding a bottle of water and a plastic cup; asked her if she'd known Caroline Daniels, and received a confused, slightly frightened negative in reply . . . It was pointless, this random interrogation. She knew that already. She might as well have stood in Paddington throwing sticks, hoping to hit Alan Talmadge . . . But it had caught hold of her, the urge to ask questions of strangers. There were connections to be made. Caroline Daniels couldn't have made this journey daily, with the same collection of people, without forming bonds, even invisible, silent bonds. If Zoë had kept routines – which she didn't. But if Zoë had kept routines, she'd have noticed when elements went missing; she liked to think she'd have questioned the difference, if only for her peace of mind.

Outside, dusk was falling, though it wasn't so dark yet she couldn't see. They were into fields now; in one, a bunch of rabbits – 'bunch' was not the proper term, she knew – sat by the track eating something; all except the chief rabbit, which was fixed bolt upright, ears tuned for maximum reception, attention focused on the carriages walloping past. There's a trainspotter in every crowd. Maybe she should be questioning him instead. She spoke to three more people, two of whom had never been on this train before in their lives. This was how they put it: 'in their lives', as if an alternative opportunity existed. Such random thoughts were born of tiredness, but the suggestion was enough to stir the possibility that Caroline Daniels was here yet, using the train again not in her life but after it, like that Dutchman doomed to be eternally on the move. His sin, if Zoë remembered, was selling his soul to the devil. Caroline's problem had been falling in love. The cynical might find a parallel, she supposed.

In the next carriage, by an empty window seat, sat a youngish blond man in an aubergine top, who recognised her, she could tell, from the morning's journey. He had not, then, offered her his seat. He stood now as she approached, looking like he intended to block her way, though in fact he was gesturing towards the space next to him.

'I saved you this,' he said.

'That was kind.'

'Least I could do. I was rude this morning. I hope you were okay. Didn't have to stand, I mean.'

'You couldn't let me past, could you?'

His face fell; an exaggerated collapse. 'You're sitting somewhere else?'

'It wasn't difficult. It's not a full train.'

She could have asked him about Caroline Daniels, she supposed, but he would have taken it as invitation. It was better to wait while he delivered a rueful smile, made a boyish pass at a lock of hair that had dropped across his forehead, and stepped aside. 'Nice almost meeting you,' he said.

She reached the buffet car; began questioning the woman working there, but gave up when told she'd only been doing the job three days. Then Zoë sat with a cup of coffee, having brilliantly resisted the temptation of a miniature vodka; sat opposite half a face looking back at her from behind a newspaper; an attractive man, or so he seemed until he lowered the paper, but whatever it was that seemed handsome in isolation was rendered null by symmetry. She looked away.

. . . The train pounded on. It stopped once, somewhere it shouldn't, and pulled into Oxford as a light scatter of rain was departing. Zoë stood on the platform while the crowd, a good third of the train's passengers, dispersed; most of it over the bridge across the line, thence to cars, buses, taxis, bikes. A dozen or so took the exit west. This was the exit Caroline Daniels would have used; it was the one Zoë used once she'd lit a cigarette; once the train had pulled out of the station, abandoning her along with a few stragglers waiting for another train . . . An air of fatigue hung over the evening, as if everybody involved in it had had enough; as if nobody, the weather included, could be bothered to finish what they'd started.

Smoke caught the back of her throat in a way that didn't often happen; she had to lean against a wall as the fit passed. Bloody damn, she thought, when she could think, instead of cough. She must look like a derelict; as if she'd been sucking on a roll-up made from other people's throwaways. She tossed it while she could still breathe, and it bounced, scattering sparks into the path of a cyclist, who gave her a look . . . She was past caring; visions of sterile white rooms were swimming into view again: *We'll have to fix you up with an appointment* . . . She put one hand to her heart, but it felt normal.

Whatever that is.

. . . Panics came in different colours, but Zoë's were always white. This white panic began with a lump in the breast. If anyone else had access to it, she thought she'd have to kill them . . . Because this was a vulnerability beyond sex, beyond her deepest, private thoughts; it made gynaecology look like amateur fumbling. She was not frightened of death, nor even of the different forms death took. She was frightened, though, of the pity of strangers; disgusted, too, at the weakness of a body that threw up unexpected lumps; that held for years, getting its owner from place to place, doing everything expected of it; producing pleasure and pain in more or less equal doses, attracting the admiration of lovers and strangers, and then coming up with a life-fucker like this . . . They talk about nursing a traitor to your bosom, but when your bosom itself turned traitor, language ran dry. Zoë wasn't the first woman this had happened to, and wouldn't be the last. But it was the first time it had happened to her.

All of this rushing out of her, as if the day's mantra, *We'll have to fix you up with an appointment*, had rattled it loose at last; the storm generated by a doctor's words, or not even by the words so much as the knowledge the words were coming – the knowledge that had fastened deep the morning three mornings ago she'd found the lump. *We'll have to fix you up with an appointment*. Like one of those magic formulae, like 'open sesame', it took you into a world of wonder, except the wonder wasn't what you wanted it to be; was more like everything you didn't. She felt almost nothing, she remembered. She was rarely happy. She was rarely sad. She felt almost nothing. But that seemed to be coming to an end, and what she felt that moment was a massive, yawning nostalgia for the emptiness she'd been numbed by these few years; that, and a blinding horror of the intrusions ahead. Unless it was a false alarm, she told herself. This was always the standby of fools and cowards – it could easily be a false alarm.

She waited, then, until it passed, which it did. This was what she relied on: the permanence of what lay beneath; the rock-solid knowledge of who she was, had always been. This was what would carry her through. Meanwhile, there was work to do. She took a deep breath – didn't light a cigarette – and set off for Caroline Daniels's house.

TWO

OTHER PEOPLE'S
ACCIDENTS

5

THIS WAS NEITHER FAR nor hard to locate. She was still in earshot of the railway when she found herself beneath a streetlight that didn't work, looking at a narrow two-storey house on a quiet road leading to a park; a house with a minimal patch of front yard, which contained nothing. This was where Caroline Daniels's workday ended and her private life began, and having arrived, Zoë felt dead-ended. There was little more she could do tonight, bar head for home and hit the Web. She closed her eyes, and opened them when someone said, 'She doesn't live here any more.'

It took a moment to place the voice: where it came from; where it was. It came from Lancashire, and was currently in the shadows of the passage between Caroline's house and the neighbour's. This would be the neighbour.

'Did you know Ms Daniels?' she asked.

'Who's interested?'

Zoë stepped forward, and as she did the streetlight popped into life. It should have been a moment to burst into song. Instead, she rested her palms flat upon the neighbour's gate. 'My name's Zoë Boehm,' she said. It was like talking into a void; sending words down a wishing well. The light above was a faint moth glow which hadn't yet blunted the shadows. Whoever was there, threat or promise, remained invisible. 'I'm looking for somebody. I wonder if you can help.'

'I'm somebody. Would I do?'

'I can't see you. You're in the dark.'

The woman – Zoë had got that far – moved forward. She wasn't tall, and was maybe in her fifties, with a head shaved smooth as a nut. This lent her a pixie finish her clothing did nothing to counter: it looked like a dark green sack, tucked at the waist. Which must have had pockets, because she produced a lighter from one now, and used it on the tightly made roll-up fixed between her lips. In the lighter's flare, her face was a vision of Emerald City.

Smoke drifted Zoë's way, delivering an instant nicotine stitch. She reached for her cigarettes. 'So you knew Caroline Daniels.'

'I lived next door to her for eight years.'

'Is that a yes?'

The woman laughed – a raw noise, like a tropical bird's. 'She kept to her own half of the drainpipe, Caroline did.'

First name terms, though. Zoë said, 'It must have been a shock.'

The woman shrugged, or maybe a goose crossed her grave. 'It happens. Shows us not to take it for granted. Life.'

'It's a fragile circumstance,' Zoë agreed.

'Well, you don't want to go putting it in front of a moving train.'

Somewhere down the road a real bird – not an owl – hooted.

The woman took another step closer. Zoë hadn't realised that the passage in which she'd been standing was raised. Now she'd stepped down, Zoë saw she was about four foot six. Your physical borders, Zoë thought: you got used to them pretty quick, but they were the first thing every stranger noticed. Unless you shaved your head.

'Is it her man you're after?'

'What makes you say that?'

'Who else would it be?'

Zoë, unlit cigarette in hand, wondered if this was the day

she took a job, and the first person she asked said 'Oh, yeah, him', and gave her a working address.

She said, 'I don't suppose you'd know where I might find him.'

'Alan . . . something.'

'Alan Talmadge. Do you know where I'd find him?'

'I have no idea.'

'Okay.' She lit the cigarette. If work turned that easy, they wouldn't call it work; they'd need another word.

Lights in windows up and down the street had come on now; curtains were drawn, and various shadow plays were happening against their patterned backdrops. Only Caroline Daniels's house looked forgotten.

'He's not been round for a while. But then, he wouldn't be, would he?'

'What was he like?' asked Zoë.

The woman tilted her head. 'Never met him. Saw him in the garden, once. I assume it was him.' A shrug. 'He looked okay.'

'Do you know how they met?'

'I never asked.' The woman bent, and squashed the end of her cigarette against a brick. 'I suppose she'd have told me if I had. We do, don't we? We like to boast about our little conquests.'

'Is that what he was?'

'She could hear wedding bells.'

'She told you that?'

'I just knew, that's all.'

Zoë thought: when you say 'I just know' about something you can't possibly have a clue about – like what somebody else is feeling – it doesn't mean you know, it means you've stopped thinking about it. You've reached the limits of your under-standing, and that is all. But what she said was, 'I don't follow.'

'She was forty-three, dear,' the woman said, and that 'dear' was a harsh addition.

Zoë tossed her cigarette so it bounced neatly down a drain.

Forty-four, herself. She didn't pretend not to take the woman's meaning, but knew it didn't apply to her.

'You want to come in, don't you?' said the woman.

'I was looking for a way to ask,' Zoë admitted.

'What do you want with him when you find him?'

'I just . . . Somebody wants to know that he's all right,' she said. 'Somebody cares,' she added.

The woman gave this some consideration. 'I suppose that's not so common I can ignore it.'

'I knew you'd see it that way,' Zoë said, opening the gate.

The woman's name was Alma Chapman, and in the light of her kitchen, she was fiftyish for certain. This kitchen was small and cluttered; emphatically lived in. On its table sat a half-full ashtray and a half-empty bottle of gin, and neatly sandwiched between them was a paperback called *DeTox In 28 Days*. Zoë, largely held together by toxins, knew a lost cause when she saw one. Magneted to the fridge were two wedding photos; both featuring Alma, though with different grooms. Alma saw her notice. 'Have you been married, dear?'

'Once,' she said.

'Divorced?'

'He died.'

'They're not terribly reliable, are they?' She began rolling another cigarette. 'He must have died young.'

(He had died at his desk, when a vile man, now deceased, had cut his throat.)

'Pressure of work, was it?'

'Something like that.'

Alma looked to her photos. 'I'm glad I married,' she said. 'And I'm glad I did it twice. One bad experience, I might have been unlucky. Two's a policy basis.'

'Right.'

'Don't get me wrong. I'm not a man-hater. Marriage, though,

that's taking it a little far.' She turned back to Zoë. 'You ever think of marrying again?'

'No.'

'You should. You're still young enough. You don't think all men are bastards, do you?'

'No, I think most people are bastards,' said Zoë. 'It leaves less room for error. You say you saw him in the garden?'

'If it was him. Maybe Caroline snagged another towards the end. Like buses, sometimes, aren't they?'

'I've heard it said.'

'Maybe it's a conspiracy. Men show up occasionally, throw the odd fuck about, it keeps us from getting over them, and planning a revolution.'

Zoë shrugged.

'You're not a believer.'

'I think most conspiracy theories are invented by the government,' said Zoë. 'To spread paranoia and uncertainty among the masses. What did he look like?'

'If it was him.' She thought about it. 'I didn't get much of a look. He seemed ordinary. Hair a little long. He was standing by the pond, Caroline has a pond. Just standing staring at it. He was twirling his hair round his fingers, that's why I remember it being long. Fair hair.'

'Age?'

'I'm not good on ages. He was a grown-up. Who's looking for him?'

'Caroline's boss.'

'This is the one who cares?'

'Seems to. I don't suppose . . .'

'You want to get in, don't you?'

'You have a key?'

Alma Chapman said, 'This could be one big wind-up, couldn't it? You could be the coolest burglar ever. I'd look a right idiot then.'

'Can't argue with that,' said Zoë.

Alma gave a short laugh: a surprisingly tinkly one, like a dying coal fire. 'I've got a key, yes. I suppose, legally, it's her sister's now, isn't it?'

'If that's who she left it to.'

'Next of kin. I expect so. Caroline was a stickler for doing things right.'

Like leaving the spare with the neighbour, thought Zoë. 'I think her boss is much the same.'

Alma said, 'You think something bad's happened to him?'

'Talmadge? No, not really. I think he's just done a bunk.'

'But there might be a clue next door.'

'A clue would be good. Yes, I hope there'll be a clue.'

The woman gave it more thought, then opened a drawer in the dresser behind her, and produced a key, tagged clearly NEXT DOOR'S FRONT. She said, 'I'm sorry she died.'

Zoë nodded, and Alma passed her the key.

'Still,' she said, as Zoë stood. 'All that business towards the end there. Finding her man. It must have done her poor heart good.'

Zoë Boehm wasn't big on the supernatural. Once, years ago, she had holidayed with friends in a borrowed apartment in Rome, and late each night they'd been woken by skitterings that came from all around them – underfoot, overhead: it was hard to tell. A ghost, her friends had agreed. A former occupant, haunted by nameless horrors. A dog, Zoë had countered. A well-trained pet in the apartment upstairs. The friends had preferred their theory. If you asked Zoë, the dog was the only thing round there not barking. But the main reason she didn't believe in ghosts was that Joe wasn't one, and he'd never been a man for a clean exit. If there'd been an obvious route back he'd have found it, if only to double-check he'd turned the heating off, and cancelled the milk.

So as she turned the key and entered Caroline Daniels's house, she wasn't expecting ghosts, but all the same, uninvited notions crowded in . . . There were urban legends you couldn't help hearing, even if you tried never to listen. The surgeon's patient turning out to be her own child. The fireman cracking open the concertinaed car, to find the severed head of his twin. Sometimes what you thought was somebody else's accident was your own. This was what the legends meant, and Zoë couldn't argue. Here, now, entering the house, it was as if Caroline's death had been a pretext allowing Zoë this experience: the cataloguing of a stranger's effects; sifting through the detritus of unexpected foreclosure. It was a reminder that you couldn't be sure of any of your tomorrows. *We'll have to fix you up with an—* Enough. But endings happened suddenly, and you couldn't be blamed if they caught you on the hop. Death was never more than a heartbeat away.

For someone who had not expected to die, Caroline Daniels had left little mess.

A Klimt print hung in the hall; the one that looked like a particularly tragic woman seen through a broken stained-glass window. Other than that there was a small table, and, on the mat, some unopened pieces of mail. This was part of the life process that carries on regardless, the way hair appears to grow in the coffin. You sicken, you die, and the junk mail continues. Zoë piled it on the table, and moved into the house.

A good part of her day had been Caroline Daniels's – Zoë had caught her train, traced her steps; stood in her office while Chinese patterns climbed the building opposite. And now she'd walked the same route through the gathering dusk; had used the same key, or a reasonable copy thereof, to let herself into the same house, and she wondered whether the feelings that assaulted her now had ever touched Caroline Daniels at day's end: that for all the journeying, nowhere had been reached – that it was all just killing time. You got through one day so you could get through the next. Though Caroline Daniels, of course, had found love at the end. Or a reasonable copy thereof.

Alan Talmadge. He too would have left traces here, from the minutely intimate (flakes of skin and shed hair; fingerprints; the oils from his body's corners) to the everyday portable: clothing, bathroom kit; the odd book or CD – the stuff you owned which was useful or necessary, and could easily wind up at your girlfriend's. He had been in the picture six months. To a forensic scientist, he might as well have chiselled his initials on to every available surface. But Zoë was no forensic scientist; she was looking for those larger, more obvious signs of man.

This is how she searched:

First, the kitchen. Some men cook. The kitchen is compact, designed for single living, and puts Zoë in mind of a room you might find on a ship. Even the electric kettle is half-sized. There is a fridge-freezer, a cooker, a washing machine. On the window ledge a potted plant is dying. A further door, its top half ruffled glass, leads to a back garden invisible for the moment. Zoë takes the cupboards first, and finds cups, glasses, plates and bowls in one and various tinned goods in another: soups, pulses, fruit in syrup, all with labels facing outwards. The lower cupboards hold pans and electrical appliances; bags of flour and cereals; cleaning materials – bleaches, scourers; a plastic washing-up bowl. In the drawers are cutlery and cooking utensils; also bin liners, clothes pegs and vacuum cleaner bags. In the herb and spice rack on the wall, none of the small glass jars is less than half full. The pans she finds are dark blue; a matching set.

A tea towel hangs from the handle of a drawer. In drying, it has creased into cardboard folds, which retain their shape when Zoë lifts it.

Nothing about the kitchen reads Alan Talmadge rather than Caroline Daniels.

★

And the same with the rest of the house. Zoë moved through it with the growing feeling that there was nothing to find, though without picking up any sense that this was deliberate. There were no dust-free absences in bathroom cabinets, or empty halves of bedroom drawers. It was simply that the house was Caroline's alone. Presumably Talmadge had grazed its surfaces as he visited, but he'd left no substantial luggage in his wake. Perhaps he too had an obsessively neat apartment somewhere, where no trace of Caroline Daniels survived. And all she had to do was find it.

It was a bit odd, though. No toothbrush, no spare shirt, no unfinished paperback by the bed. Except, just six months in, reading in bed wouldn't have been a priority.

In a mirrored cupboard in the bathroom, she found a healthy collection of face creams and ointments in tubes and jars and bottles. Most related to complexion and anti-ageing; most, too, were designer branded – Christian Dior, L'Oréal – but there were also supermarket labels, as if Caroline Daniels had been prepared to try anything. All were less than half used, like the spice jars in the kitchen. But whereas there, Zoë had had the impression that Caroline had not been a woman to run out of anything, here, it felt more as if she'd still been searching for something that would work. It was impossible not to draw a connection between Alan Talmadge's arrival in her life and this interest in reversing time's damages. Zoë closed the cupboard door.

From its mirror, she stared back at herself. This both was and was not the face she'd always had. Presumably, below its surface, other, older faces were waiting to make their appearance, and no amount of magic lotion would hold them at bay for ever. Most days, she felt quite strongly that this did not matter at all.

The bedroom showed no outward sign of shared occupancy, but in the drawer of a bedside table, she found an open box of condoms: a packet of twelve, with ten remaining. The discovery gave her pause: she already knew that Alan Talmadge existed – why did she feel as if she'd come across proof of a yeti? The bed was made, and this must have been one of Caroline Daniels's last domestic actions. The sheets seemed clean, or not noticeably soiled. Forensics again. She did not spend long in the bedroom; being there made her feel exactly what she was: a snoop.

In the hallway she paused, listening for she didn't know what. She supposed, on some level, noises continued to pulse through the house (electricity coursed through it; water shifted tidally in its pipes; its battery-powered clocks ticked on), but she felt, nevertheless, dead centre of a large numbing silence. A person's passing was best measured by the grief they left behind them. But their physical absence – their no longer being in the place they belonged to – was another means of weighing loss. This house waited like a bomb for Caroline Daniels. Without her it lacked point, like a photograph without a subject.

The spare room held a sturdy, old-fashioned desk, its drawers full of neatly filed accounts, bills and letters. These, Zoë scanned quickly. Most were from the sister, Terry. None were from Talmadge. The bills were marked *paid* and arranged chronologically, going back twelve months. The desk's surface was a hymn to neatness and order, the only items disturbing it a pot containing two pens and three pencils – the pencils freshly sharpened, identically lengthed – a tablet of bright yellow Post-its and a Tippex mouse. This last, in the context, an almost crazed outburst of frivolity. Zoë, about to leave, looked under the bed instead. Pushed against the wall was a box, the size of a shoebox. She brought it into the light.

. . . Horrible, the things you do. The dead must weep. She opened it anyway.

Inside, swaddled in tissue paper, lay a pale pink vibrator of a size Zoë would class realistic. A trade name on its handle identified it as a LadiesMate. Also in the box was a cellophane packet containing spare batteries. After a moment, she wrapped everything the way she'd found it, and pushed the box out of sight beneath the bed.

All the retraced steps, she thought; all the opening of cupboards and the looking into drawers. All forgivable – Caroline would understand – but this was trespass, pure and plain.

Zoë went downstairs. She had already searched the living room, and found nothing especially male. The books were androgynous, Penguin classics leavened with middle-brow blockbusters, and nothing about the alphabetically shelved CDs suggested a merged collection. It was varied and contradictory, but music collections were. Caroline Daniels had liked classical, specifically piano recitals, but had had a weakness for seventies soft rock and some of the spunkier bands of the early eighties. The music she'd listened to in college, Zoë surmised. Record collections were as effective as carbon dating. The player itself was a CD/radio/tape deck, and a glowing red light showed it was still plugged in. When she pressed a button, Radio 3 came softly to life. Zoë turned it off, and after a moment's thought unplugged it.

It was time to go. There was nothing to be found.

It was time to go, but first she passed through the kitchen, and tried the back door. A brief search located the key on the ledge above. Outside it was full-on dark, but light spilling through the window showed that the garden was paved, with a water feature at its centre. Terracotta pots lined the wall. The air was cool, and city-fresh: Zoë tasted traffic and standing water. She breathed it in, then lit a cigarette, of course. Something needle-like spasmed in her heart. She stepped into the dark, and reached the pond.

Which was four foot square, and easily skirted. By the back fence, a garden bench sheltered in the overhang of next door's tree. Touching it she felt damp wood, so stood instead, smoking and studying the night sky, a tiny fraction of whose available stars could be seen. Paradise, some thought, was five miles high. Zoë, who believed in heaven no more than she believed in ghosts, didn't expect Caroline Daniels was looking down.

She dropped her cigarette and ground it underfoot. Facing the house, she noted how the window's light fell on the pond, and in that same moment made out, floating on the water's surface, a pair of bloated rubbery tumours . . . For one disgusting moment, she thought she'd found the two missing condoms. And then realised she was looking at a pair of frogs, limbless, and entirely dead. There was a disease did this to frogs . . . Well, it killed them. But in doing so it caused their legs to drop off, which seemed so venomous and direct – so *frog specific* – as to suggest that nature had a psychopathic streak.

Revolted, she shuddered. The frogs bobbed on the water, dead as yesterday. Zoë went inside.

Where she locked up, and took a last look round. She was past the stage of expecting discovery; there was nothing of Alan Talmadge to find here – he had been and gone; had left such a perfect absence, he must have been the ideal guest. The only thing keeping him from being a ghost was Zoë's belief in him.

So she'd go. But first she stooped and replugged the CD player. It would have niggled her otherwise: leaving an unnecessary difference in her wake. If Alan Talmadge hadn't, neither would she. The player's red light blinked into life, and on impulse Zoë turned it on. Before the radio could clear its throat, she changed mode, pressing *play*, and the CD display lit, counting upwards from minus three. Whatever Caroline Daniels had last listened to was still loaded, though whatever it had been at the time, it was requiem now. Zoë held her breath. There was a fine change in the quality of the surrounding silence.

Whatever she'd expected wasn't this.

A drum roll, then a swooping bass. And hard after both, a

brass section, punching a hole through everything in its way: a riff so deeply familiar it hadn't been written but discovered – it hurled Zoë back twenty years or more:

This old heart of mine been broke a thousand times
Each time you break away I feel you're gone to stay

The Isley Brothers. Strange how the mind retained stuff that barely mattered, though listening now, it was hard to pretend this didn't matter.

So Zoë stayed while the song played; stood in Caroline Daniels's home, listening to words and music Caroline Daniels had listened to, and wondered, at first, what the dead woman's feelings had been, hearing this – whether it had been the soundtrack to her mood, or just the first thing to catch her attention – and then stopped wondering anything, to do, in fact, what Caroline Daniels had done – which was close her eyes and sway to the music, moving her lips to words she hadn't known she still knew, after all these years, after all these years.

When the song had faded, her eyes were dry. She turned off the player before the next song broke in, then locked up and pushed the key through Alma Chapman's letterbox. As she did so, a familiar noise disturbed her and she turned, to hear its echo – it had been a car door opening, then closing, that was all: no ghost, no urban nightmare awakening. There was something wrong with this picture, but whatever it was wouldn't come to her yet. She waited but nothing happened, and at last she shrugged it away like an unwanted attention, and walked home in the dark.

It was after three when she woke, and pitch black.

Lately, Zoë had been dreaming about childhood – its physical specifics, its smallness. The being at both centre and periphery at once. But unlike the dreams of youth remembered from her thirties, from which she'd woken wet-eyed, confused by loss, these were funny. In what way, she could never quite recall, but coming awake she carried the sense of having just left a comedy, the best comedy ever, though exactly what made it so escaped her. It was possibly to do with childhood's potential. Everything was funnier then, because no one was wholly fucked up yet.

Except that wasn't so any more, was it? Being fucked up was no longer the prerogative of age. It wasn't only Wensley Deepman who'd found childhood foul and complex; open any newspaper and once a month there'd be a pre-adolescent suicide staring back. There were few prisons, thought Zoë, without an available exit: you just had to not mind about the exit not leading anywhere. Sometimes escape mattered more than anything; it was easy to forget that, in all the tales, when you found your deepest desire it brought you grief. When the Tin Man's wish was granted, the first thing his new heart did was break. And now Zoë wasn't thinking about Wensley Deepman, but about Caroline Daniels, and possibly about herself. And she put a hand to her breast and closed her eyes, and wished – one heart's wish that couldn't turn sour – for one good night's sleep; eight hours' dreamless sleep. That was all she asked.

It wouldn't come. She rose and padded to the kitchen bare-foot, where she poured a glass of water and thought about the young woman, Corinne, who had twisted her engagement ring while delivering crass opinion. *Just as she was starting to have a life*, she'd said, as if everything Caroline Daniels had done, public or intangible, counted for nothing against the absence of a man – not a good man or a worthy man; just a *man*, an absent man. Nor was this an age thing. Zoë knew women in their forties who felt the same; maybe without that degree of blind certainty, maybe with an awareness they'd be trading an absence for subtraction, but still, it persisted, this sense of incompletion. Zoë didn't feel it herself, but felt it in the attitudes of others towards her, which sometimes came coupled with resentment that she didn't appreciate what she was lacking.

But this was what she'd chosen. There was only one heartbeat under her roof. And who was anyone to say whether a life had 'started' or not? How could you weigh what was still trapped inside you, scampering through your body like a thing apart? Zoë stood by the window and tried to listen to the sounds life was making deep inside her, and wondered if this happened everywhere, to everyone; that there came a day when you woke to find something had altered, had broken, and there was no telling what it was. So you ended up alone at night and sleepless, drinking tap water and staring out of windows, trying to ignore the evidence that suggested you hadn't made much of life. Remembering that you weren't measured, anyway, by the possessions you'd leave behind, so maybe you needed another you could have an effect upon . . .

And maybe that was when you went looking for Alan Talmadge.

Because everybody needed a friendly ear; a voice that would say only yes. Candidates in Zoë's life were few and far right now, but there was always the telephone. She could just about see herself picking it up, and calling the only person she wouldn't freak out by doing so this time of night. *Sarah?* she'd say. *It's me. It's Zoë.*

It was three o'clock in the morning, but all Sarah would say would be *Talk to me.*

And Zoë would say, *There's a lump* . . .

But she could do without this right now. There'd be no calls. If she needed a friendly voice, she had Radio 4. Tomorrow, she'd go looking for Alan Talmadge herself. She put the glass down and returned to bed, and as she killed the bedside light, it occurred to her what had seemed odd leaving Caroline's house – the moment she'd heard the car door open, then close. There had been no courtesy light showing, that's what was strange.

When a car door opened, the courtesy light went on: this was the usual arrangement. Whoever had been out there had disconnected his – or hers – perhaps so as not to be seen. And this was just another incident in a crowded day, but coming on top of everything else, it proved enough to foil her heart's desire until grey light smudged the corners of her bedroom window.

6

EVEN SO, SHE ROSE early. She'd heard the thump of the
letterbox, but there was no brown envelope on the doormat;
no neatly sealed time bomb with her examination date enclosed.
We'll have to fix you up with an appointment, the doctor had said.
It's quite likely nothing to worry about. But when you were
outnumbered, it was always something to worry about. When
there was only one of him and he still outnumbered you, panic
wasn't out of the question.

That, though, was an ordeal for another day. Coffee mug in
hand, she went online and began searching for Alan Talmadge.
It didn't surprise her when she got no hits on any of the
obvious sites. She'd have been pressed to explain why. She just
felt she'd started on something big.

Radio 4 burbled in the background. *Today*, these past weeks,
had been delivering regular bulletins from a professor of
psychology who was investigating love. A partner had been
chosen for him, at something very like random. Now various
encounters were being engineered; sessions edging towards
romance, though focused for the moment on communication
– you listened, you spoke. The *coup de foudre* across a dance
floor remained the teenage daydream, but love was program-
mable, apparently. In the end, the professor said, an enduring
relationship – a caring, loving bond, indistinguishable from the
real thing – would be built. It was difficult not to picture him

Baron Frankenstein. And it was all very interesting, but Zoë wasn't sure what they'd do with the knowledge once they'd acquired it. Though possibly they hoped to find a cure.

She thought: Caroline Daniels, now – would someone who'd kept a tidy desk for twenty-two years really have welcomed love's turbulence in her forties? Wouldn't she have been better off without it? Because there was this possibility tugging at Zoë: if Caroline hadn't fallen in love, would she have fallen off that platform? They say the ground drops away beneath your feet: yes. But they say it like that was a good thing, and they never tell you what comes after.

It was gone eight. She spent an hour signing into sites she generally used one at a time, feeding *Alan Talmadge* over and over into hungry boxes. Deep down, she already knew this wasn't the way to find him. It was just the quickest way of proving that.

Once she'd run out of sites, she showered and dressed. She'd check for answers later. Meanwhile an itch needed scratching; clean and caffeined – wired like hell – she went off to scratch it.

An alley ran from what had been the old market square and was now the new one – and remained the same, only with cappuccino bars – and a college lived on it, though not a real one; one of the city's crammers, offering force-fed GCSEs to the offspring of the middle classes, and jobs to otherwise unemployable graduates. This was where Andrew Kite studied; Andrew Kite, once and briefly 'Dig', whom she'd hauled kicking and swearing from London, when his parents paid her to bring him back.

For reasons a profound mystery to Zoë.

Except there was no mystery really; it had been the same old same old story. Andrew had been a troubled, confused, *conflicted* kid – a spoilt little bastard. The first Zoë had heard of him had been from his anguished mother, a tall ash-blonde strung like a pro-tennis racket. 'He's fourteen,' she'd said. 'He could be anywhere.'

Her focus kept shifting, as if there were events flitting about that needed keeping an eye on. Her distress seemed both real and faked to Zoë, but there was nothing unusual about that. Charlotte Kite was too intelligent not to know that if her son was screwed up, it was partly her fault. But Zoë wasn't in the business of judging others. Not until she'd invoiced them. 'I'll find him,' she said.

And she would, because he couldn't be 'anywhere', not really. He wasn't at his expensive day school, from which he'd disappeared before, and he wasn't upstairs in his bedroom-cum-video-arcade; a Santa's grotto of the dying millennium, where the only things not plugged in were the still-wrapped Christmas presents. Which left London or Ibiza. It was sad, the narrow horizons of the adolescent male.

So she found him; followed the trail of plastic he'd slung like a clew through a labyrinth, and even when it dead-ended in an off-licence, where a tired intelligent woman had retained his mother's credit card, he wasn't hard to find. He'd been tall even then, and privileged-looking, and would have been meat if he'd not hooked up with Kid B. Since when he'd been on the rob, a detail he shared on the trip back to Oxford. 'On the rob.' This, too, was depressingly ordinary; not the downward spiral into crime, but the laboured appropriation of street lingo that went with it.

Zoë hadn't asked him about Kid B. Kid B had ceased to matter.

And now she waited by an estate agent's, resisting the impulse to smoke. Colleges like this ran on hourly timetables; he'd be there or wouldn't; she'd find him or not; either way, this would happen by ten. It barely mattered. It was as if the absence of that envelope had left her in limbo; somehow, this was where she'd always been: waiting for a brown envelope that never came. She realised she had one hand pressed to her breast. She must look like a heartbreak just recently happened . . .

Shortly after ten, Andrew Kite came through the glass door of the college with a Quiksilver backpack over one shoulder and two pretty females in his wake. A moment later a fourth student followed: a boy with either a shaving wound or more likely a running boil on his neck. Zoë stepped forward just as Andrew noticed her.

'Hello, Andrew.'

He blinked. He was no taller than three and a half years ago, but he'd filled out; looked like a CK poster boy. His hair flopped in a passable Hugh Grant. Acne happened to other people. 'Do I know you?'

'We ran into each other once.' He didn't react. 'In London.'

'Do you know this woman, Andy?'

The girl thinking: it was so just barely likely *that* could happen.

Andrew looked directly at Zoë. 'I think you've got the wrong person,' he said politely. 'I'm not in London much.'

She showed him the palms of her hands. 'You sure about that?'

He nodded, then strode down the alley, girls and boy behind him. The boy cast a puzzled glance back at Zoë – unsure what she thought she'd been doing, trying to bridge this chasm of age and beauty – then did a catch-up lollop after Andrew, who was being audibly badgered by the females. Zoë couldn't make out words, but had no trouble imagining them. 'Really' and 'awful' and 'woman'. Whatever did she *want*, Andy? She let them turn into the square before following.

The square was milling: students and shoppers and others with no obvious excuse. Andrew and Co. breezed through to colonise a table outside a coffee bar on the far side. Zoë lit a cigarette. After a while a waitress came and took their order. After another while she came back with drinks.

Watching, it seemed to Zoë that Andrew Kite sat in a shaft of sunlight, as if weather had singled him out for treatment: he was young, strong, healthy; worth caressing. He had fucked up once, but everybody got a second chance, except Kid B. He was drinking coffee-coloured froth from a tall glass. As she watched, he ran a slow hand through his rich hair. Zoë dumped her cigarette, and went to join them.

Andrew was saying something about a monster DJ, or a DJ monster. He broke off at her approach. 'You're back.'

'I'm back,' she agreed.

The others stared as if she were an unexpected natural disaster: a typhoon in the English countryside, or a broken TV anywhere at all.

'I've already explained, you've got the wrong person.'

Zoë shook her head as she pulled out a vacant chair. 'The wrong person was the other boy, Andrew. You going by Dig still? Didn't think so.' She sat.

'We don't want you here,' one of the female children said. Zoë ignored her.

'The wrong boy was Wensley, Andrew. Wensley Deepman, remember? The wrong boy in the wrong place leading the wrong fucking life. I just thought you should know, Andrew. He's dead.'

It took an expert, but something shimmered beneath Andrew Kite's surface.

'They found him under a tower block. He'd just taken a shortcut nowhere. He was twelve years old. Am I ringing bells?'

He licked his lips. Then said, 'I just think you should piss off, that's all. I think you should just leave us alone.'

'I will. But you should know this first, Andrew. Call it a lesson in responsibility.' She turned to the others. 'Your friend here, he's got a bit of a past.'

'We don't need you telling us anything.'

'Maybe I need to tell it.' Zoë felt a tremor trap her right

hand, as if a nerve had spasmed. 'Last time, well, he ran away to London. Did a little thieving, a little smash-and-grab. Real Jack the Lad, weren't you, Andrew?'

He said, 'These people are my friends. We're not interested in your opinions.'

'And you found a friend there too, didn't you? Wensley Deepman. A little thug. Took you under his wing. He was nine years old.'

The boy looked from Zoë back to Andrew. The girls didn't waver.

Zoë said, 'So I found you and brought you home. Mummy and Daddy paid for that. And now you've grown up a bit, and you're studying, and you've got nice-looking friends, and here you all are drinking latte in the sunshine. But Wensley had nobody to take him home. He was already home. And now he's dead.'

'That's not my fault,' Andrew said.

'No. But he's still dead.' She stood. 'I wish you luck, Andrew. You look like you've sorted some stuff out. But these things cost. You should be aware of that.'

She stuffed her hand in her pocket before it could spasm again. The kids would think her drunk. There was probably something else she should say, but she couldn't for her life think what; and nor did she look back as she walked away.

The encounter left her feeling stupid minutes later – *What was the point of that, Zoë?* Joe's voice, she thought, then: no, not Joe's, Sarah's. Which was a laugh, because if there was anybody you didn't need as the voice of your conscience, it was Sarah Tucker. You'd enjoyed your last moment's peace if you had Sarah Tucker telling you right from wrong. Which didn't mean Zoë didn't love her, she supposed, but there was tricky history involved. Since getting Joe killed, which was part of the tricky history, Sarah had gone to live up north, where she'd met someone she said was a nice man. Zoë hadn't seen her in some years, nor ever laid eyes on her 'boy and two girls'.

'I worry about you,' she'd said, last time she'd called.

'You don't need to. I'm fine.'

'You'd say that tied to a railway track,' Sarah diagnosed. 'You'd say, "Go away. I'm perfectly all right."'

It was good to have friends, but it was also good when they lived miles away, and you never saw them.

Home again, she checked her emails. Nothing had come through on Alan Talmadge, or nothing that wasn't negative. He did not hold a driver's licence; was not registered to vote. He had no credit card, no mortgage, no – slightly off the wall, but it had borne fruit before – season ticket to any Premiership club. He did not belong to a major political party, subscribe to a national newspaper, or shop at Amazon – he'd never bought anything online at all. Which might have had something to do with his not having a credit card, of course. After a while, you were searching in the same places twice; if he'd not been there the first time, he was unlikely to turn up the second.

. . . Alan Talmadge had no telephone, no mobile, no email address.

Zoë rose abruptly; paced the small room. Aside from her computer and a fold-away bed, it held a lot of books: she'd been a reader once, though that was a habit she'd shucked without noticing. Also the music she'd once needed: the usual rock and roll; the odd piece of soft classical or easy jazz. Mostly on vinyl, of course.

. . . Alan Talmadge had posted on no music fan-sites. Alan Talmadge had not possessed a TV licence.

The TV was also in here. Occasionally she'd wheel it out, usually when it was late and she needed numbing, but that happened less and less . . . Either she was developing a puritanical streak, or very slowly she was ceasing to exist.

'Fuck this,' she said, under her breath. She had no idea who she was addressing, or where her sudden anger came from.

. . . Alan Talmadge existed: that was a given. But he was either a throwback, or he wasn't called Alan Talmadge . . . It was possible Grayling had got the name wrong, of course. Larger matters had foundered on smaller details. But if he had, fuck him too: Zoë had better things to waste time on than clients' misinformation. Given a moment, she'd come up with some.

She had never noticed before how dumbly vacant a TV set looked, like a mistreated puppy. If she had any sense, she'd junk the damn thing.

. . . And there was Sarah's voice again, telling her right from wrong. It wasn't just the TV needed junking, Zoë told herself twenty minutes later, loading the bastard into her car. It was her whole damn history, beginning with everybody she'd ever met. Maybe that way she'd get some rest eventually. She glanced in her mirror; pulled out. She wasn't so paranoid as to check whether anyone was following, but it wouldn't have made a difference if she had.

On the way, she rang Bob Poland. It was his day off, but if she was disturbing him, she was disturbing him. Theirs wasn't a relationship based on kind regard.

'So what are you doing anyway?'

'Oh, you know. Sitting down. Drinking a beer.'

'And they say men can't multitask.'

'Funny woman. You ring just to piss me off, or what?'

Because that's the only time she ever called him: when she had a problem.

The first time she saw Bob Poland, she thought: here's a man who's been given the wrong head. It was a moonish addendum to a frame otherwise angles, straight planes, edges. She didn't know how he kept lean – every time she saw him he had a drink in one hand and another behind the bar – but it worked, except there wasn't much he could do about the head. 'Like a stick of rock with a tomato on,' Joe had said. Then added: 'Never tell him I said so.'

No, Joe.

Bob Poland, anyway – a six-foot jawless stringbean – was a cop. Joe had known him first, of course; Joe had bought him, to start with, drinks and smokes, and finally just bought him, or that was how Joe told it. In his mind, Joe had always walked tightropes. In the real world, Zoë suspected, he'd had the same experience she'd enjoyed: shovelled a bundle of money Poland's way to keep him on-message, and in return got whatever he felt like giving, which was mostly nothing. Though she didn't expect he'd wasted so much effort trying to get Joe into bed.

He'd contacted her a couple of months after Joe was in the ground.

'If you're thinking of carrying on, you'll need someone like me. Maybe you'd like to buy me a drink.'

And after all, whatever else he might have been, he was verifiably a cop. There was bound to be a time when one of those would come in handy.

. . . None of this was what she'd intended. The day Joe died Zoë had been in Paris, armed with a man and a plan. The man hadn't lasted – had never been meant to last – but the plan was built and sorted: she would cut her last ties with Joe (their marriage, by now, was one of those linguistic anomalies anyway: a word that covered its own opposite meaning, like 'cleave') and go back to college, convert her law degree. It was a getaway stratagem; a running from, not a moving towards. But at least it would work.

It was not entirely Joe's fault. (This was a revision of her earlier stance, which had been that it was entirely Joe's fault.) For as long as she'd known him, he'd harboured a dream of being a private eye, and there had been in him this quality that over the years she'd defined in turn as steadfastness, whimsy, pig-headedness and bullshit that had kept the dream alive even when the reality demonstrably sucked. Process serving. Credit checks. It was work, if you didn't know it was glamorous, you could mistake for the daily drudge: work done over the phone or in front of a monitor; work done murdering countless hours outside strangers' houses, hoping they'd not turn violent when you served them. Work that called for patience and shorthand, neither of which Joe had in great supply. So he'd kept his dream alive by hiding it where reality couldn't touch it; Zoë, meanwhile, kept the office alive with credit checks and process serving, and kept her sanity by blowing off to Paris once in a while. They were still man and wife when she made that last trip, but were no longer cleaving to each other – were doing, in fact, the exact opposite. She would cut her last ties with Joe; go back to college, convert her law degree. But before she could do that, somebody cut Joe's throat instead.

A couple of months later she was meeting Poland, and law college was a bunch of prospectuses gathering dust on a shelf.

What he'd said first, after taking the top off his lager, was: 'Joe talked about you. A lot.'

'Did he really.'

'He reckoned you were ace. He reckoned there was nobody you couldn't find or turn inside out without leaving your desk.'

'Did you know Joe well?'

'Yeah.'

'Then you know he was full of shit.'

'My point is, Mrs Silvermann—'

'Boehm. *Ms* Boehm.'

'My point is, Zoë, if you plan to carry on without him . . .' He put his glass down and repeated himself. 'You're going to need someone like me.'

She still remembered that moment. They were sitting in a pub garden; the sun was shining; a loose piece of guttering hung from the roof – details. Somewhere nearby a TV showcased a

Mexican soap. It was 3:45 p.m. Joe was dead, as was the man who'd killed him. And Zoë had encountered a borderline case who'd announced his intention of shooting her, mistakenly confident she wouldn't shoot first. After that, somehow, law school was out of the question. But it was only listening to Bob Poland that she knew she was stuck in Joe's dream.

'And why's that?' she said.

'You're wondering what use a friendly policeman could be?'

'I'm wondering how expensive he gets.'

'Joe always got his money's worth.'

'Joe bought batteries from street traders. He wasn't the best judge of value.'

'He ever get a speeding ticket while he knew me?'

'You know what I heard? I heard the system's so up-stuffed they let eighty per cent of the fines go hang, because they can't process them before the deadline.'

'You're a cynical woman.'

'Thank you.'

He laughed. 'You're one of those people, you've got like a tortoise mentality, don't you? I don't mean slow. I mean like totally armoured. You're one of those people carries your defences wherever you go.'

And he was one of those people who said 'one of those people' a lot, as if he'd already sorted everybody into neat categories.

'I do a lot of liaison work,' he told her. 'I've contacts in every force south of the border. See how handy that might be?'

'And what does it cost?'

'Whatever works.'

'I think we're finished here.'

He put his hands up. 'Can't blame me for trying.'

She could if she wanted. They batted sums of money about, then Zoë made the mistake of asking what happened, she paid him up front and he didn't deliver? He grinned a tooth-heavy grin, and separated a coin from the change in front of him. When he tossed it her way she snapped it from the air like a lizard catching lunch, but the grin didn't waver, and the line came out pat: 'Call your lawyer.'

Zoë remembered Joe saying Poland did this. She didn't suppose Joe caught many coins.

Flipping it back, she promised: 'You'll do that once too often.'

'You're saying we've got a future?'

'We'll see how it goes.'

And as things go, so had this. Occasionally, Poland had been of use; often, he'd taken her money. And frequently she'd wondered if he weren't a mistake, because there was an underlying ugliness to their exchanges. It came down to sex, like most things were supposed to – he was pissed off she'd never responded to his advances. That was something else about men (the list headed *Men* was very long): rejection wasn't a thing they forgave easily. And definitely something practice made them worse at.

But now they were miles distant, and getting further apart by the second. She told him: 'I've a couple of names for you,' and gave him Caroline Daniels's details, including that she was dead. Then Alan Talmadge, though with no accompanying colour.

'Some kind of spook, huh?'

'Some kind.' Then she realised he meant *spook* – a spy. 'That hadn't occurred to me.'

'Sounds pretty fucking likely though, don't it? James Bond porking some old lady from the typing pool.'

'This particular old lady was younger than me.'

'Yeah, well, that was bound to happen, wasn't it? Sooner or later.'

Instead of replying she swung abruptly into the fast lane to overtake something redder and sportier than her.

'I'll do what I can,' said Poland. 'But if he's a spook, you're screwed. And it's the same rates for failure.'

'If we didn't have those, you'd starve to death.'

'And I didn't have a sore head, I'd laugh.'

'That's nature's way of saying too much beer.'

'You kidding? Charles Parsley Sturrock's underground.' He belched loudly. 'Every blue in the country's tied one on on the strength of that.'

'Real nice, Bob. I can tell you're in touch with your feminine side.'

'I tried that once. My phone bill went through the roof.'

'Boom boom.'

'You know what your problem is, Zoë?'

'Mostly it's hating being told what my problem is.'

'Also, you smoke too much. But your real problem, you're one of those people with a case of the not-to-be-fucked-withs. Makes you kind of bitter, know what I mean?'

'Tell me when you've run those names.'

'Business, business. Maybe I'm not the one needs to get in touch with his feminine side.' He broke the connection.

Zoë realised her foot was approaching horizontal, and eased up.

The red sporty number cruised past. There was a kind of insulted arrogance in this – like it was pointing out, she wanted to race with the grown-ups, she'd have to concentrate every step of the way.

And she remembered something else Bob had once charmingly told her, picking up on what he'd called her tortoise mentality:

The big thing about a tortoise isn't that it carries its armour round with it. The big thing about a tortoise is, it winds up on its back, it's fucked.

7

S HE HIT AN EASY run into the city. Even getting lost didn't take as long as it usually did. When the two high-rises broached the skyline, she steered by them as if they were hills seen from the sea.

And the lift worked, which showed that the universe was sometimes benevolent.

Remembering her moment of near vertigo, Zoë did not look down from the fourteenth balcony; she was anyway struggling to keep her grip on the television, which was gaining weight by the minute. When Joseph Deepman opened the door, he seemed not to recognise her; the look on his face suggesting that one or the other of them was seriously out of place.

But when he spoke, he said, 'You're back.'

'I'm back,' she agreed. 'Can I put this down?'

He stood aside, and she carted the TV into the sitting room; set it carefully in the space where the lost one had sat. Deepman gazed on this as if the whole process were something he had arranged and paid for, and was already bored by. Zoë had to remind herself this wasn't the biggest thing happening in his life right now.

She stepped back, as if admiring a complicated piece of handiwork. 'You'll be able to watch the cricket, anyway.'

'It's April.'

'I know.'

'Cricket's not for ages.'

There was this to be said for kindness to strangers: it didn't take long for the strangers to put you off. You could be cured immediately, and never have to bother again.

She plugged it in. Deepman pointed out the cable for the aerial: she connected that too. When she turned it on, an American chat show brawled into life; one of those horrors featuring overweight crackers who'd slept with their siblings, or eaten their neighbours' dog. Like other acts of global terrorism, this had an hypnotic quality; she switched it off before it sucked the life force from her.

'Did you speak to them, then?' he asked her.

'Speak to who?'

'The police. You said you'd speak to them.'

Zoë tried racking her brain for a memory of saying that, then realised there was no point. It didn't matter that she hadn't, or even that he didn't really think she had. What mattered was, he was telling her now that's what she'd said. It had become established fact, and denying it wouldn't get her anywhere.

Not for the first time, she reflected there were advantages to age.

'What did I say I'd speak to them about?'

'Why they reckon he did it.'

'You mean, why they think that? Or why he did it?'

Deepman looked at her with scorn. 'You speak English? Why they reckon he did it.'

He turned his back on her and disappeared into the bathroom. A moment later, Zoë was on her way, reflexively flipping the light switch as she passed, which made nothing happen. He had yet to resolve the light bulb problem. The front door was hanging open; she closed it as she left.

Behind the wheel of her car, she sat resolutely ignoring the fact that she'd just wasted two hours dispossessing herself of a working television set; concentrated, instead, on the idea that she might be hungry. It was a little off the track for salad bars and soup parlours, so she started the car and cruised. Telling herself as she did that she definitely had no memory of promising Deepman she'd speak to the police. Inasmuch as she owed him anything, which she didn't, she'd paid in full.

There was a small parade of shops not far distant; among them a café, where she chose a sandwich from a list on a blackboard. An alarming – if approximate – twenty per cent of everybody Zoë had ever heard say 'espresso' said 'expresso' instead, and here it was, up on this blackboard: EXPRESSO COFFEE. But now she discovered that maybe she'd been wrong all this time, because whatever they gave her, it wasn't espresso. When she'd finished, she wandered the length of the mini-drag, whose shops were a clutter of grocers, video outlets, betting shops. And a hardware store. She went into the hardware store.

Back at the high-rise, the lift still worked. This time Zoë paused on the balcony, reminding herself of height and danger. It occurred to her that she did not know from which building Wensley had pitched to his death. For no reason she could pin down, she was sure this was not the one.

The door to Joseph Deepman's flat was ajar. She knew she'd closed it on leaving.

Her grip tightening on the paper bag she held, Zoë called his name. There was no reply. She stepped into the flat, wondering if she was imagining the icy touch on the back of her neck. In the hallway, she heard nothing, not even the ticking of a clock: time's heartbeat. She called his name again. Putting the bag down, she moved into the sitting room. Nobody there. In the kitchen, she found a bottle on the table. Whisky, not a great brand, an inch or two from full.

Somewhere in the larger world of the high-rise, something slammed.

'Mr Deepman?'

The bathroom door swung open at her finger touch. His body lay piled in the bath: a complicated mess lacking arms, legs, a head; in the fraction of a second before she recognised this for what it was – his dirty laundry, dumped here for convenience – it struck her what a hell of a job it must have been, to accomplish this in the space of a lunch hour. To remove his extremities, and rinse away his blood. Then she was turning away, moving towards his bedroom, because that was where the body must be: the only room in the flat unaccounted for.

It lay on the bed, so stiff it might have been its own sarcophagus.

Then it farted, loudly.

Zoë, backing out, backed smack into the man behind her:

'*Fuck*ing hell—'

He moved aside just quickly enough to avoid her kick, and was covering his face, visibly frightened, by the time she was ready to hit him. So she waited, instead, until he'd lowered his hands, and his fear turned to outrage; she shifted from attacked to attacker in the time it took him to say 'What the *hell*—'

'It's okay. I'm a friend.'

'What's that mean? I've never seen you in my *life*.'

He was younger than Zoë; somewhere in that vague arena of the late thirties: medium height, hair buzz-cut to suede; light, but it might have been mouse-brown, given the chance. He had pale eyes, pale skin; eyebrows so much an afterthought, they looked plucked. His top was light blue, with rolled-up sleeves. And his mood was finely balanced; things could get ugly, or he might be laughing about this soon.

'Of him, I mean. Of Deepman.' She lowered her hands. 'The door was open. I thought – I thought something had happened.'

'Like what?'

Like somebody had chopped him into sections and decorated

the bathroom with him didn't seem a good answer. 'Who can tell?'

'You services?'

'No.'

'So what, then? You're not really a friend.'

She said, 'I'm doing an old man a favour, that's all.'

'Right.'

'That's hard to believe?'

'You're not from round here, are you?'

She didn't like being interrogated, but he had a point. Not for the first time she regretted getting involved; wished she could wind back the days, and do it differently. *Mr Deepman? I scammed your grandson once; gave him a really foul instruction. Probably not the only adult to do that, but every little helps, right?* She could have walked away if she'd said that. He could have sorted out his own bloody TV, his sodding light bulbs.

'What's your name?' she asked.

'Why?'

'Because it saves me making one up.'

'It's Chris.'

'I'm Zoë. Were you here all this time?'

'I'd just popped next door. I didn't mean to startle you. Not if you're what you say you are. Doing him a good turn, I mean.'

'He was short a TV.'

'There's a lot of it about. Theft. Burglary.'

'Has he been drinking?'

Chris said, 'He's had a couple, he's lying down. Asleep is the only place he'll fall,' and Zoë wondered if she were that transparent, or if he was just good at between-the-lines.

She said, 'Have you known him long?'

'Not really.'

'And you're, what? Are *you* services?'

He said, 'I'm not religious, if that's worrying you.'

'It crossed my mind.'

92

'There's people round here, they've enough problems. They don't need someone trying to buy their soul in return for a little grocery shopping.'

'Speaking of which,' she said. She retrieved the bag of light bulbs, and emptied it on to the table.

'That's good,' he said, 'I'd been meaning to get some myself,' and for the first time he smiled, and Zoë saw that his ordinariness – the pancake mask his features seemed ready to settle into – could vanish as smoothly as if a switch had been thrown.

They roamed the flat, replacing bulbs that didn't work. It didn't feel like kindness once the lights were on; more an act of exposure, training light on to corners best hidden. Zoë remembered the scrum of reporters on Severn Street, their cameras aimed like torches. Meanwhile, here in the flat, surprising amounts of dust swam upwards, as if magnetism were involved. And in the old man's room, he lay fully clothed on the bed; the smell of used alcohol tainted the air, along with others she didn't want to dwell on. When she closed the door, he didn't stir.

In the kitchen, Chris was washing up. 'It doesn't matter how long they've been on their own,' he said. 'The ones who had wives. They still expect a woman to turn up any time, to clear away.'

'Do you do a lot of this?'

'No. The bare minimum, to keep my conscience quiet.'

It seemed like he'd accepted her; he was easier now.

'I didn't realise he was a drinker.'

'He's not, much. Couple of glasses, he's away with the pixies.'

'Did you bring it?'

'Bring what?'

'The bottle.'

He flushed. 'You think I'd do that? Go round supplying booze to frail old men?'

'Possibly. I don't know you.'

'Well . . . Well then stuff you, all right?'

'I didn't say I thought it was a bad idea.'

He was shaking his head. 'You're kind of weird, you know that?'

'I think of myself as normal. I suppose most people do.'

She took her cigarettes out, and he said, 'I don't think you should smoke in here.'

'What do you do for a living, Chris?'

'Is that your business?'

'No.' She put the cigarettes away. 'Do you think he's all right?'

'You were just there.'

'Still . . .'

'He doesn't need strapping in.'

'I'll take your word for it. If he rolls off the bed and breaks his neck, though, I don't want to be the one tells his daughter.'

Chris said, 'If it makes you any happier, I'll go and check, all right?'

As soon as he'd gone, she unmagneted the note stuck to the fridge she'd not noticed earlier and pocketed it. He was back immediately: 'Sleeping like a baby.'

'Did you know Wensley?'

'. . . No.'

'He used to call here.'

'I'm sure he did. I don't visit to a regular schedule, is that all right with you?'

'I think we got off on the wrong foot, Chris.'

'You tried to break my face.'

'No. I almost tried.'

He said, 'You're probably a nice lady underneath. I mean, you brought him a TV and all. If you didn't think you were Roy Keane, we might get along.'

Chris might not be the pushover he appeared, she decided.

She left him to it, and on the drive back home half managed to convince herself that that was a line drawn, a chapter closed;

that the Deepman story was separate and different, and her own job clearly defined. But she couldn't quite banish the old man's words – *You speak English? Why they reckon he did it* – and the second set of lights she stopped at, she fished the swiped note from her pocket, and transferred it to her wallet.

A name – just 'Chris' – and a mobile number. Just in case.

8

THAT EVENING SHE FELT restless; animated, but not in a good way. Animated like one of those East European cartoons, where the figures jerk and the background never changes. She ate standing up, brushed her teeth and headed for town. The bars on George Street had big glass frontages, and from outside might have been broadcasting widescreen footage of a good time happening elsewhere. She drank a large glass of white wine in one, then moved next door and ordered another, and lit a cigarette while waiting. When it came, it was already paid for.

'Gentleman down the far end,' said the bartender.

Something about 'gentleman' in a Geordie accent made it a slur.

It took a second to place the gentleman in question – she'd not noticed him on arrival. He'd been on yesterday's trains, wearing an aubergine top and a rueful grin; had offered her his seat on the journey back. He was dressier now: jacket and tie; the jacket urban khaki, as if he were a hunter of some sort. Well, that figured. Zoë nodded, then he disappeared from view behind a crowd of young excitables.

She was glad she'd ordered a large glass.

There were only so many directions once you'd ruled one out. She could study the Cunard posters on the walls, or just stare into the mirror behind the bar – one of those mirrors that didn't tell a true story. It made Zoë younger, somehow. This would be the effect of distance: the mirror you can't get close to is the mirror that likes you best. This one had erased some living, and it was a curiously smoother Zoë looking back at her. The kind of Zoë this Zoë should probably take under her wing; drop a few hints about situations best avoided. What struck her, though, was what they had in common: the dark tight crop of curls; the darker eyes giving nothing away.

'You managed to find a seat this time, I see.'

(He'd worked his line out, then.)

'Only there are tables back there, if you'd prefer.'

'I'm good.' She hesitated. 'Thanks for the drink.'

'You're welcome. You weren't on the train today.'

'It was a one-off,' said Zoë.

He was a little old for the bar, which made Zoë beyond redemption. But the difference was – Zoë Boehm thought this – he was hoping no one would notice, while she didn't give a damn. Even in the mirror, he was late twenties. Allow him the light and some high maintenance, he'd be mid-thirties, still ten years too young.

'Do you mind if I join you?'

She shrugged.

The crowd had dissipated or moved elsewhere. Jay Harper took the stool next to her, explaining that he'd been Jamie until that TV chef took off, and then rebranded because he 'wasn't what people expected a Jamie to be any more'. Zoë nodded, wondering how many times he'd said that; wondering, also, what people expected a 'Jamie' to be, and what kind of grown man worried about such things, and changed his name so easily, as if slipping from one identity to the next. He helped her out on this by filling in background detail; polished enough that he could have released it as a single. She took in the outline – PPE, job in the City, long-term relationship foundering on the twin issues of children and marriage – while fleshing it out with observations of her own: he wasn't a real drinker; he had a good dentist; and his tousled hair was tousled the way a cobweb was an accident. There were bald spaces there; not huge, but to a used-to-be-Jamie, they probably shone pillar-box red.

'And what about you, Zoë? Was it business took you to London?'

'That's right.' But she didn't want him pursuing that topic: some people got antsy when her line of work was revealed. Joe, glibly, had used to say this was because everyone had something to hide. Zoë felt it had more to do with justifiable distrust of the secret-hunters.

She bought another round. Not a real drinker, he had something with Coke in it. The last sticky half-inch of his previous stood abandoned on the counter.

'This is probably not a sentence that should pass my lips,' he said, 'but do you come here often?'

'It's my first time.'

'Bit superficial, isn't it?'

'I don't know. I'm not sure what a genuine ocean liner's wet bar looks like.'

'Good one.' He touched the knot of his tie briefly. His fingers were surprisingly worn. She wondered if he gardened, or dug an allotment, and with a sudden wave of weariness wished he did, and would talk about it. Instead of this tired ritual. She should get up and leave, but didn't. 'Gets busy later, so I'm told. All the thirty-something lonely hearts, looking for love in all the wrong places.'

She said, 'So where would the right place be?'

'Wish they knew.' He placed his glass on the counter, and Zoë heard the ice ring. 'Do you know what the collective noun is? A "desperation".'

'That's kind of cold.'

'I don't mean to be. But something's going on, more than

98

just the biological time bomb. Something almost . . . feral. It's like the last-chance saloon, you know? A man could announce he was clean and single and get damaged in the rush.'

'Nice for you.'

'I'm just saying that's what it's like. It's a sad indictment of our society, if you ask me, and I'm sure there are plenty men taking advantage. Me, I'm just making an observation.'

Zoë said, 'I've often thought, the downside of those Bridget Jones books is men read them and think they've learned something about women.'

'You're not a man-hater, are you?'

'I pick my hatreds carefully, Jay. I wouldn't waste one on a whole gender.'

'Well, I'm not talking about all women either. I'm talking about the ones, they're single, they're looking at forty, they come to places like this, they might as well be carrying neon signs.'

'What did you have in mind when you bought me that drink, Jay?'

'You don't think I'm classing you with them, do you?'

She didn't reply.

'You're an interesting-looking woman.'

Zoë nodded thoughtfully; swirled her glass. There was a hint of debris in her wine, settling at the bottom.

'That was a compliment.'

'I could tell.'

'You're not strung too high, are you, Zoë? I like that in a woman.'

She said, 'When I hear a phrase like that . . .'

'Sorry.'

'. . . I start wondering which decade I wandered into.' She finished her drink. 'You're probably a nice guy, Jay, but somehow I don't think our future's written in the stars.'

Outside a chill had set in, and underdressed people leaving

bars and restaurants clouded the air with their breath, and shivered. Zoë fastened the top popper on her leather jacket, and thought about smoking, but didn't. She also thought about Caroline Daniels, and wondered if her romance had started like that – if Caroline had come to a bar, *looking for love in all the wrong places*, which was probably a song. But then, it was only the wrong place if you didn't find what you were looking for. Zoë was unaware of any rule that said love couldn't begin with a pick-up.

Or a lonely hearts column. Or a stranger on a train. Or a conversation in a lost property office.

There were, in truth, a lot of avenues unexplored.

Tonight, though, she thought – lighting a cigarette; a reward for not having lit one a minute earlier – tonight was not a night for discovering them. She felt a slight tenderness after her encounter, as if she'd bumped an old bruise, and wasn't sure if the ache was on her own account, or Caroline Daniels's, or just for every woman who'd ever sat in a bar, hoping a man would talk to her. Was any of that true, what Jay had said? Or was it just what men thought true, or hoped true, because it made their roles easier; bestowed upon them a sense of superiority and confidence? And did that mean they viewed women with contempt, or just that they didn't understand them? Or worse, did it mean that they understood them too well: that a single woman, about forty, wasn't much more than a target. One who'd drawn the concentric circles on herself of her own accord: come and get me. And what about me? she thought. Am I like that? But if she was, she'd have stayed there and let Jay keep talking. He'd been clean, good-looking, articulate, well dressed. In a seller's market, he was a prize. But that was the problem; that that's where he'd put himself. In the seller's market.

He'd not been repulsive, and if something about him had left her with this quiet unease, it was to do with her own private demons. With her own damn heart that didn't work the way it used to. And also, perhaps, because she knew that every encounter left a trace – that half an hour with Jay Harper, and she knew enough about him to find him any time she wanted. And yet Alan Talmadge had shared Caroline Daniels's life for six months, and now that that life was finished, he hadn't left enough of himself behind for Zoë to truly believe he existed.

And there was no way that was an accident. We don't allow accidents round here, she thought, and carefully made her way home, smoking.

9

*I*MAGINE, THEN (HE THINKS), *a life. A life without the trappings we're encouraged to expect — it's the emotional trappings he's thinking about. The happy ever after with the One True Love. The handsome prince who chopped through evil shrubbery, or the beautiful princess so pure and good she was force-fed poisoned apples. Take all that away. Now: imagine a life, one no longer young. Not old, exactly, but enough of it gone that mornings aren't the rosy-red adventures they once were, and New Years come tinged with regret. There are no children underfoot. No queue for the bathroom after breakfast. It's a temptation to check the horoscope listings, to see if there's company coming.*

Imagine a woman, he thinks.

Because for a woman, all this is harder. It's not just a matter of reality; it has to do with perception. For a lone man, even one drifting through his forties, single life is freighted with the envy of friends and colleagues; not a deep-seated, trade-places-in-an-instant envy, but an undertone that whispers to them during their boring, domestic weekends. The single man, to the coupled man's thinking, is Out There, Doing It. It doesn't matter if the reality's Cup a Soup and Film on Five. The perception remains Doing It. The single man's a Lad, and lads know how to have fun.

But imagine a woman, and remember, too, the importance of perception. A single woman, marooned in her fifth decade, is not having fun. Accomplishments don't matter — we could be talking world-class businesswoman or international eventer; novelist, racing driver, brain surgeon — a single woman in her forties is the object of pity and derision. She has failed at the one thing society expects of her, which is to be half of a pair. It's not even necessary that children happen. Children are a lifestyle choice, but coupledom's a must. A single woman in her forties declaring herself happy is many things – brave, a treasure, inspiring, impressive – but she's not happy. That's the perception.

The trouble with this scenario is that the perception is always true.

He wishes it were not so. If he could believe in a world that allowed women to be happy, content with their lot, he'd have few problems with that world. The other stuff – the Big Stuff: famine, floods, geno-cide – is always going to happen, and there's not a lot anyone can do about it, but the Women-Being-Happy thing – that's always struck him as within our reach. But what do you do about heartbreak?

What you mostly did was, you watched it happen every day. Here was something else about women: they were all beautiful, young or old; the ones who'd had heartbreak happen, and the ones with it yet to come. It didn't take significant technology to tell them apart. Heartbreak was inevitable, even for those who thought they'd found their happy ending. Because a happy ending demands an ending. The key to happy-ever-after is keeping eternity short.

And now, meanwhile, here's a new beginning . . .

She has black hair, which makes her pale face paler, or maybe it's the other way around, and her eyes are also dark, and look like they've seen secrets, and kept them. The creases at their corners used to be laughter lines, but it seems they no longer recognise humour in the situation. And this is one of the things he means by heartbreak: it's not just dancing partnerless, it's no longer hearing the music . . . She dresses well: she knows what suits her. Forty-four, he thinks. That's something he's always been good at: knowing the age, the range of ages; both the one they hope they're passing for, and the one they've really earned.

And he already knows what he's decided, but says it aloud anyway, as he has done twice before, just to hear the words break into the air around him and stain it with their promise.

He says: She's the one.

THREE

KAMIKAZE HEARTS

IO

THE AISLES WERE FULL of music – boom box beats, long-hair rock; the migraine thump of techno – and up and down them Zoë wandered, recognising the odd band she'd assumed long dead and gone to nirvana (Heart; Love): were they really still around, or was this CD repackaging; old whines in new bottles? There was no chance she'd summon up the interest to find out. But meanwhile here she was, trawling the local record fair, belaboured on every side by noise; all of it with roots, she supposed, in the rag-and-bone shop of the heart.

Never underestimate the power of cheap music, somebody once said.

Never underestimate its volume either, she appended.

Earlier, she had spoken to Terry Hill, Caroline's sister, who was married, lived in Darlington, and had three children, who were audibly staging an extinction-level event in the vicinity.

'I'm sorry, who did you— Will you *stop* that!'

'Zoë Boehm. I'm working for Amory Grayling.'

'I'm not telling you again! I'm sorry about this. Who— Enough!'

(This was perhaps a recognised syndrome: maternal Tourette's.)

'Grayling,' she repeated. 'Caroline's boss.'

There were clearing-away sounds; the noise of the end of a rope being reached. Zoë wondered how she'd have coped, and doubted she'd have found the resources. There were many –

Zoë sometimes among them – who acted as if the mothers of young children had had their IQs shaved in the process, but that was the idiot view. When it came to patience, strategy and multitasking intelligence, child rearing was like running a small country single-handed.

She was back. 'I'm sorry. You want to know about Alan?'

'Whatever you can tell me.'

'Not a great deal. She mentioned him, of course, but – well, she thought the phone was a business instrument. She wasn't one for long chats.'

'Did she tell you how they met?'

'If she did, I don't remember.' She was quiet a moment. Zoë realised Terry Hill was weeping. 'She was older than me, you know. This man, he might have been the best thing ever happened to her. I should have taken more notice.'

Because it was probably the right thing to do, and because short of hanging up, there was little to prevent it, Zoë let Caroline's sister grieve. Barring the odd lunch, the occasional letter, there had not been enough contact: there had not been enough *time*. It was a grim perspective, the one found over your shoulder. Terry knew that: everyone did. And Caroline had left her her house and its contents; everything, in fact. Which counted for something.

'When did you last speak?'

'A week before she died.'

Zoë asked if Caroline had sounded different.

'She sounded happy. I don't mean that was especially different. She'd sounded happy a lot lately.'

'Because of Alan.'

'Nobody likes being alone, do they? Oh *do* stop that!'

Chaos was flexing its muscle again, up in Darlington. Zoë, glad she was alone, was ready to ring off when Terry said: 'I'll tell you one unusual thing. She was talking about going to a record fair.'

'Where?'

'Oxford, I think. Some place they sell CDs. Rock and pop and whatever. That must have been Alan's influence. Caro grew out of pop years ago, she only listened to classical.'

And 'This Old Heart Of Mine', thought Zoë . . .

It was difficult to live in Oxford and not know about the record fair. First Saturday of the month, Town Hall: there were posters on most available spaces. Zoë had never been. This being a Saturday, though, and the first of the month, it seemed, from a distance, like a lead – maybe she could stand in the lobby, and pick Alan Talmadge from the queue. The number of times his name had echoed through her brain, she'd know him by his shape in a crowd . . .

And besides. She was remembering leaving Caroline Daniels's house, and the car door that clunk-clicked without the courtesy light showing. There was a simple explanation: lights, like everything else, could be broken. But the question still insisted: had he been watching the house? This was where Caroline Daniels had lived, where Alan Talmadge had loved her. The reason for loitering lay deep in their story's bones – lovers, like murderers, return to the scenes of their crimes.

Zoë had walked home tired that night; tired and buried in thoughts. She'd not have noticed if she'd been followed.

It was possible that Alan Talmadge had found her before she'd found him.

On a stall playing Smokey Robinson were two men in their twenties, looking more like weekending City types than Motown fans. There probably wasn't a law said you couldn't be both. They were at opposite ends of their operation, both in chinos and collarless shirts. The one she addressed wore rimless spectacles.

She said, 'I wonder if you could help. I'm looking for somebody.'

'We're more a record store than a dating agency,' he said. 'But I'll have a bash.'

'Do you know an Alan?'

'An Alan?'

'An Alan Talmadge?'

He called to his companion. 'Do we know an Alan Talmadge?'

'I don't believe we do.'

'Sorry.'

'He might not be going by that name,' said Zoë. 'Which complicates it a bit.'

'Not really.' He called out again: 'Do we know anyone not called Alan Talmadge?'

'Loads.'

'There you go.'

'You've been a help.'

But he said, 'What makes you think we'd know him, this Alan? Or not-Alan?'

'He likes music,' said Zoë. 'Your kind of music. And he was planning a trip to the fair.'

'Are you Bill?'

'No. And he's not in trouble, or not with me. I'm just trying to find him.'

'What's he look like?'

Good question. She said, 'He has this thing he does with his hair. He plays with his hair. Runs his fingers through it.'

'That's it?'

She shrugged.

He laughed. 'Well, I see that happen, I'll send up a flare.'

She moved on.

It was busy, mostly a young crowd, but there were plenty of fortyish men around, any one of whom could have been Talmadge: how would she tell? There were marks life laid on you when things went wrong, and she knew about these, but wouldn't recognise them on a stranger's face. Would Talmadge have collected himself enough to come here anyway? Death wasn't a twenty-four-hour thing. You didn't shake grief overnight. Or did you?

There were no other golden oldie stalls, and the stuff assaulting her ears wasn't likely to achieve the status. She did another circuit anyway, studying people with the glazed stare of the collector pasted on to their faces; a visible junkie craving for rare material. There were some who'd waited all month for this – it was in her to wonder what sad lives they led. But she found herself wondering about her own instead, absent passion of any kind for longer than she could tell. So which was worse: a misdirected energy or an energy that wasn't there – energy she'd spilled somewhere and hadn't found since? She'd come to a halt; had picked up a CD; was examining it minutely as if it held the key to survival . . . This was what her body did: it covered for her mind. Made her look ordinary, rational, just another collector, while her thoughts peeped over the abyss. She put the CD down without registering what it was, and moved on.

This was what her body did for her, when it wasn't plotting her destruction.

But there had been no envelope that morning; there was no possibility of an envelope before Monday, now. *What can't be cured must be endured* was the stupidity that floated into her head. *What can't be cured is likely inoperable* . . . Shut up, she told herself. She shut up.

Back at the corner, she was hailed from the Smokey stall: 'Three Rodneys and a Derek. No Alans yet.'

'Right.' Her voice crashed like static in her ears, as if she'd been gargling electricity. 'This stall of yours. Do you run a shop?'

'God, no. We do a couple markets a month, weekends. Some internet selling. Rest of the time, we write software.'

This was not as big a surprise to Zoë as he thought it might be. 'Do you know of any shops?' she asked.

'Record shops? You kidding?'

'Specialising,' she amended, 'in Motown. Soul.'

'Oh.' He glanced at his companion, who was schmoozing a customer: Al Green in one hand, Marvin the other. 'London, of course. And there's one in Reading.'

'Anywhere nearer?'

'Not desperately.' He stroked his shirt cuff. 'You're keen on finding this bloke, aren't you? Does he owe you money?'

'Something like that. This market, it moves round, right? Is it always the same stalls?'

'Mostly. There is a shop, you know. Soul Driver, I think it's called.' An abstract look occupied his face while he thought about it. He was used to gazing into a screen for solutions, Zoë surmised. Part of a generation for which large slabs of everything crumbled into digital format. He looked to his friend again, who was tucking folded notes into a tin box. 'Soul Driver? There's a Soul Driver Records, isn't there?'

'Soul Rider. Wallingford.'

'Wallingford. There you go.'

'Thanks,' she said. Her voice sounded normal; her volume fine. 'Thanks' was what you said when somebody did you a favour.

He was looking her in the eye: a little amused, maybe a touch concerned too. 'And you're heading there on the off chance, right? In case he shops there? This guy you've never met?'

Zoë said, 'It's what I do.'

It was what she did, but she wouldn't have given it serious consideration if he'd not said that. *The off chance.* You played the odds, but waited until they were halfway sane, generally. She went, though, because it was what she did.

And driving, found herself thinking – it was an image hard to relinquish – of the pale vibrator under Caroline Daniels's bed. A trespass – being dead must be like having the world go through your handbag. And what had it cost Caroline to procure it? She couldn't have gone mail order, risking her name on God knew what ugly list. It would have been a cash deal: a face-to-face in one of Soho's female-friendly sex outlets. Zoë could just about picture this: Caroline's two (or four, or eight) feints, until the shop was empty . . . It was another world to the one she'd inhabited of alphabetically arranged CDs, of matching sets of pans, but one she'd had a right to experience. And how many men had there been? Not many, was Zoë's guess. This wasn't relying on Amory Grayling's estimate. Men based such appraisals on what they hoped the answer to be. But Zoë felt she understood Caroline Daniels. There had not been many men. There had been dreams and desires, fantasies and fictions, even something like desperation, and then Talmadge had come along, and maybe all the dreams had come true. The vibrator had been tucked away, its spare batteries carefully preserved. You hoped for the best but prepared for the worst. Yes: Zoë Boehm understood Caroline Daniels.

So maybe the worst had happened.

Maybe there was no sign of Man in Caroline's house because Man had left: packed razor and toothbrush, the clothes and paperbacks Zoë hadn't found, and carried them back to his life. Maybe, even – Zoë hated to think this. Maybe, even, the vibrator had been his parting gift, wrapped in pity and contempt. And this version left no room for accidents: if this were halfway true, Caroline Daniels had fallen from no platform. If it were halfway true, she'd jumped.

But it was speculation, and there were missing facts. How had they met? Not at work, or Grayling would have known; not in a pub or club – Caroline Daniels was the wrong age, the wrong sex, the wrong *person* to fall in love in a crowded room. But they might have met on the train. Dozens of relationships kicked off that way; more than a few of them irregular. It had to do with the everyday, she guessed; the establishing of patterns inside a sealed environment, apart from home or work. Domestic routine calcifies. Picture hefty deposits of plaque encrusting a tooth. But friendly habits tenderise: when the first kind word of the day comes from a companion on a railway platform, it would be an easy thing to grow to rely upon. Caroline had no domestic partner, of course, but it would explain a lot about 'Alan Talmadge' if he had a wife back home. Explain, for a start, why it wasn't his name.

. . . Once you had the frame, you could arrange the details inside it. That was the thing about speculation into other lives: other lives were always simpler – moved in cleaner directions, with more obvious motivation – than your own. Everybody was a mess, it was true. Everybody else was doing okay, though.

So what had it been like for Caroline, falling in love in her forties, maybe for the first time? It would have been full of the same sensations first love ever was; the same lies, the same mining for significance in every passing comment – even Zoë remembered the thrill of the phone ringing. Even a phone she didn't pick up in time. Love was kidding yourself, mostly. And first love came with built-in obsolescence: one minute you were a couple enflamed; the next, you were a spent match.

A shiver crawled up her spine. But it was history, that was all; history trying to nudge part of her back into life. It wasn't going to happen. Zoë bit down hard on nothing at all, and wiped her mind clear of everything but the road.

Soul Rider Records was tucked into an upstairs nook in a barn of a building whose interior had been hived into individual shops the size of kiosks: selling antiques mostly, or stuff that could kindly be called antique. Old junk. Framed prints of dead pheasants were stacked twelve deep in the corridors, between dangerously tilting bookshelves crammed with dusty paperbacks. Zoë wove past trays of mint condition coins and piles of stamp albums and found it on the second floor: SOUL RIDER painted on a bit of driftwood nailed above a doorway. This gave on to twenty square foot of floor space, into which the history of popular music had been condensed, with enough room over for a man with fifteen inches of grey beard and bright green eyes behind thick black glasses. He wore a painter's smock and sat on a stool, talking into a mobile phone. This was incongruous. He looked like he ought to be wielding a peace pipe or crystal ball. Everywhere Zoë looked, stacks of CDs wobbled: music was filed in alphabetical rows in plastic troughs, but was also thrown higgledy-piggledy wherever space allowed, and a few places it didn't. It was the sort of arrangement, you could sneeze and have a week's work putting everything back together. She'd bet he knew where it all went, though: it was that sort of outfit. He was that sort of bearded man.

On walls hung posters of the great and good: Aretha, Otis, Sam. Framed behind glass was a concert ticket montage, complete with ink scrawls suggesting autographs.

'Help you at all?'

Zoë didn't do this often: she gave him her card. She managed this without spilling music. 'I'm looking for a missing person.'

'Enquiry agent? Is that like Spenser or someone?'

'There's less shooting involved, but basically, yes.'

'Cool.'

His surprisingly soft voice was surprisingly free, too, of irony. Like he really thought that's what she was doing: cool things. This made enlisting his help easier, of course.

So she described Alan Talmadge – described him? Said that such a man existed. Late thirties, forty. A Motown fan. With slightly shaggy fairish hair he had a habit of running his fingers through.

'That's all?'

She wasn't positive about the habit.

'It's not a description, is it? More like a template.'

'He might be a regular.'

'I can think of a couple blond guys. But younger than yours, most likely.' He swiped at one of his lenses with a forefinger. 'One's a Pete. Probably not him, then. Don't know the other.'

'It's a young crowd you get, is it?'

'Crowd'd be nice. But young, yeah. On the whole. Though we get a few second-time-rounders, soundtracking their mid-life crises.'

This with the air of one who'd been there, done that.

'Mostly men?'

'I'd have to say ninety per cent.'

She nodded. She could have written these answers herself. 'This man might have been here with a woman. A woman about my age, does that ring bells?'

'What did he do?'

'He's missing, that's all.'

'I wonder, if I went missing, would anybody come looking?'

Zoë didn't answer.

After a while, he said, 'We don't get many women. Your age, I mean. No offence.'

'So she'd have looked out of place.'

'That's why I remember her,' he said.

She'd been glancing back at that montage – did he really have Wilson Pickett's autograph? – and for a moment didn't register what he said; that he remembered someone: remembered who? The possibility that this was Caroline Daniels sent something like pleasure pulsing through her, though it was gone too quickly to be sure. And was dashed for good a second later:

'She works in the shoe shop down the road.'

'Oh.'

'Name's Engalls, or Ingalls. Victoria. I don't know her. But she had one of those name badges they wear in shops, you know?'

Zoë knew.

'She'd not been in before. Or since.'

Because she was a detective, and because you always kept the witness talking, she said, 'So was she on her own?'

'She was talking to a guy. I don't know if she was with him or not, they might have just met on the stairs. Hey.'

Zoë waited.

'He was, you know, fortyish. Late thirties.'

'Was he blond?'

'Kind of mouse brown, I think.' He squinted back inside his memory. 'I can't say for sure. I might think blond just because that's what you said. You reckon he's who you're after?'

She didn't rightly see how he could be. 'The woman I had in mind,' she said slowly, 'was somebody else.'

'Oh. Still, no pain, no gain, right?' He paused. 'I don't know why I said that, actually.'

'When was this?'

'Ages ago. Six months?' He waited a beat, then added apologetically, 'There's not a lot of traffic. Lady from the shoe shop comes in, it's hold the front page.'

'But you didn't recognise him?'

'No. I wouldn't now, to be honest. I mean, he walked in this minute, I wouldn't know him from Elvis. Some guys fade, you know?'

She thanked him, and made to go. He called to her as she was leaving.

'Hey. You ever get to shoot anyone?'

'Only once.'

'A bad guy, huh?' he said, not believing her.

'Real bad,' Zoë said. 'But mostly, he just pissed me off.'

11

S OME DAYS, PEOPLE COULDN'T get more helpful.

'Do you need assistance?'

'I was looking for somebody,' Zoë said.

This woman was in her teens, and her name tag claimed her another Zoe, but without the diaeresis. She tilted her head now, processing Zoë's reply, and her mode shifted from professional – or possibly vocational: this *was* a shoe shop – to the personal: 'Someone who works here?'

'Her name's Victoria, or Vicky. Ingalls, I think. I might have that bit wrong.'

'Oh.'

And some days it only takes a syllable; just that brief release of air – some punctures you know about, soon as they happen. Zoë watched the other Zoe struggle for the right face, the right tone, and should have saved her the effort: *I know*, she could have said. *I don't need to hear you say it. Just tell me the where, when and how . . .* Victoria Ingalls was dead, and this was the story of Zoë's life. There were living women everywhere, and she never got to know any of them.

'I'm sorry—'

'But she died,' said Zoë, and it came out harsher than she'd intended. 'How did it happen?' she added, more gently. Thinking: cancer.

'She fell. It was one of those . . . Last year, last August, you remember we had that rain? She fell, out walking. She fell and broke her leg. I'm sorry. Was she a friend?'

'No. No, I didn't know her. How did she come to die of a broken leg?'

'She lay all night in a drainage ditch. And it was one of those rainy nights, so she just lay in the cold and wet . . .'

Zoë asked, 'How old was she?'

'About fifty.' This other Zoe paused; made a quick scan for customers. 'I didn't know her either. I'd only been here a couple of weeks.'

'Who were her friends?'

No one really.

But her name had been Victoria Ingalls, and she'd been single, and lived nearby. Never in great demand while alive, she'd achieved popularity by the manner of her death, which had been stark and Learlike. She'd been on her evening walk (and everybody knew this about Victoria Ingalls: she liked her evening walk), and from nowhere it had come on raining; one of those sudden semi-tropical downpours last summer had made famous. She'd started to run, but the ground was slick and treacherous, and next thing she'd been in the drainage ditch, her leg broken, and the rain coming down like God never promised a thing. And that was it. Exposure. It was hard to credit, but you could die the most natural death within five minutes of the nearest street lamp. Somebody had found her the following afternoon, when Victoria was beyond all help.

It seemed to Zoë that the girl's eye held an unshed tear, finishing this.

'Where was her flat?' Zoë asked.

'I don't know. I could find out.'

'Would you?'

So she did, by the simplest means available: she looked in the phone book, which still listed Victoria Ingalls among the living. Zoë watched while the girl traced a finger down the relevant page. She was thinking of recording angels; of a girl like this with a thick black pen, picking names at random and scoring them through. She was so lost in it, just for a second, that this other Zoe had to read the address out twice.

Victoria Ingalls had lived in a large and shabby town house that had been converted some decades earlier into flats. Its facade formed an arch giving on to a yard that once sheltered carriages but now seemed barely big enough for two cars and a dustbin. The building didn't look like it was going to fall down soon. It looked like it was going to crumble slowly. Zoë wrote a quick mental history of tenants hard to dislodge; of a filthy landlord resorting to lack of maintenance. Victoria's flat sat empty, of course. Of the remaining three, the first was inhabited by a young couple; the others by single men: one in his thirties, the second older. Saturday afternoon, and all were home. She showed each her business card. And these were some of the impressions she gathered, in the course of sixty minutes:

'She wasn't friendly. Not *un*friendly, exactly, but she didn't go out of her way.'

'I always thought Victoria was unhappy. She had that look, as if life had done her down. That it wasn't what she meant it to be.'

'She loved the opera. There was always opera coming out of her flat. I'm not saying she was loud.'

'Didn't go out much. Fridays, Saturday evenings, nothing like that. She was usually in.'

'She had a man friend, though.'

And this was said suddenly, by the female half of the young couple; a blonde girl, pretty in the way that comes with admiration – like a flower that only blooms when looked at. Her husband, who was tall and bony, and wore glasses the wrong shape for his face, said, 'We don't know that for a fact.'

'I saw him leaving her flat. It was early one morning.'

'He could have been . . .'

His wife, and Zoë, waited.

'. . . reading the meter.'

Zoë said, 'Do you remember when this was?'

'Last summer, sometime. During one of the good patches. The weather, I mean.'

'What did he look like? Was that the only time you saw him?'

But she'd seen him from the back, and yes, it had been.

The husband said, thoughtfully, 'You know, she seemed happier last summer. Less . . . uptight.'

And the young woman hugged herself, as if she were storing a secret he really should have known about.

But when Zoë brought it up with the other tenants, neither could remember seeing a man about, or having heard noises a man might be expected to make.

'I'd like to think she'd found somebody,' the younger said. 'But I never saw signs of it.'

And the older man said, 'I'd have less trouble believing she'd snared a unicorn.'

Every evening, Victoria Ingalls had taken a walk after supper. She would make a circuit of a footpath beside the river, which the path followed a short distance before cutting through a patch of woodland. Then it skirted three fields to reach a drainage ditch, which it ran alongside until joining the road again. All of which Zoë gleaned from these fellow tenants – knowledge they'd absorbed without being sure how they'd done so. Certainly, none had ever accompanied her. But all agreed she'd had a routine, and stuck to it religiously. In this, and in much else:

'Saturday mornings, supermarket. Sunday afternoons, she'd do the front windows.'

'On the first of October, she'd switch to her winter coat. Didn't matter what the weather was.'

'You could set your calendar by her.'

Though her calendar had now stopped.

Routine was bigger than habit. Routine was a bulwark; a dike against messiness. Its obvious enemy was paranoia. Zoë wasn't paranoid – she'd told herself so many times – but avoided routine, just the same; she spent too much time finding people to want to make it easy for anybody to find her. But she understood the need for routines. Some locked rooms were for keeping people out, not keeping them in.

'She liked opera?' Zoë had asked.

'Yes. It was a big part of her life.'

'How about pop music? Soul, rock? Motown?'

'. . . Hardly.'

So what had she been doing in Soul Rider? Not exactly part of her routine.

'What about family? Friends?'

But Victoria Ingalls had no family her fellow tenants were aware of. Her closest friend had worked in a surgery in town until cuts had done for that; she'd moved to Oxford, and their friendship's regularity – its comforting weekly rituals – had given way to occasional outings: holiday efforts. Some short while after Victoria died, there'd been a flat clearance, and all her belongings – clothes, art, books, kitchenware – had been roughly tea-boxed and delivered to the local animal sanctuary shop.

'She was fond of animals?'

'I don't know she was, especially.' It was the young woman who'd known all this: and why, thought Zoë, was that no surprise? 'Maybe it was just simplest.'

Or maybe she wasn't over-fond of people.

There was no chance of entering the vacant flat; no point, anyway. The woman's possessions had gone, and there'd be no clues in empty walls. If clues were available, or mattered: Zoë had to remind herself she wasn't here to investigate Victoria

Ingalls's death – there was nothing here that withstood examination. She'd followed a trail that might have been Caroline Daniels's, and found instead another dead woman, linked to the first by the frailest of threads: a man who might not have been there, and a sudden, unverified interest in soul music. The only common point was the women themselves, and what kind of story was that? Two unconnected women dying in accidents meant nothing. The same women falling in love – if they had – meant little more.

Unless it was with the same man.

There was a kind of maze whose starting point was a room with many doors, each leading to other rooms with many doors . . . However lost you got, you remained connected to your starting point.

But however tenuous this link, Zoë had at least traced it. And once you allowed the connection, the story took shape: there was no love; there were no accidents. When you'd passed through enough doors, you were back where you started, but seeing it from a new angle . . .

She'd watched a bird once, frozen to a lawn, a cat hooked round it like a tarpaulin – one forepaw blocking its flight; the other stroking it gently, head to tail. If she hadn't known what she was seeing, she might have taken it for tenderness.

If both men existed – if both were Alan Talmadge – he had murdered them.

She said, 'Which shop was this?'

It was tucked on to a side street, and was closing when Zoë arrived; she got just enough foot in the door to discuss opening hours with a frosted, brittle woman in a green cardigan and a string of pearls that was surely a joke.

'Monday morning. Ten o'clock.'

'It was a particular donation I wanted to talk about. Victoria Ingalls?'

'I just do the till,' she said, ushering Zoë out with a force-fulness that suggested pro-wrestling was a missed opportunity. After barely enough time to take in the floor plan Zoë was on the pavement, watching a cardiganed shape organise the takings through the window. Something about animal charities brought out the worst in humans. She made her way back to the car, and sat and thought.

. . . 'Murder' was a huge word, probably bigger than 'love', and just as hard to let go of, once spoken. Not that it was spoken yet. There'd been no reason to suppose Caroline Daniels's death other than accidental, nor Victoria Ingalls's either. They only became suspicious if connected. They only became connected if the same man was involved with both. And so far, the only sighting of a man in Victoria's life was a shadow leaving her flat one breakfast time; a shadow spotted by a young woman who'd have been glad to think Victoria happy too, and whose definition of happiness was no doubt self-generated. The dead woman had had nothing to say on the subject.

We do, don't we? We like to boast about our little conquests.

Alma Chapman's words: she'd been sure of herself, too. But people were generally sure when basing observations on their own behaviour, and didn't necessarily take account of human difference. The little Zoë'd gathered about Victoria Ingalls, she wasn't from the same planet as Alma. 'Boasting about her little conquests' would have been anathema to her . . . Zoë tried to recall the last time she'd imagined herself in love: eight or nine years ago, with a married man. (Zoë, then, had been guilty of optimism, and this had been part of her cure.) It was like trying to remember a language she'd once been fluent in but had lost, as if she'd been refugeed at an early age. All she'd retained was the memory of being one half of a conversation that was constantly happening, even in the other's absence. And the last thing conversation needs is remorseless background chatter.

It was no stretch to imagine Victoria Ingalls feeling the same.

I always thought Victoria was unhappy . . . She had that look, as if life had done her down. She was a disappointed woman: that was the nub of it. Once, Zoë had overheard a man say there was no domestic hell like living with a disappointed woman, and had found herself agreeing: none at all, save being the disappointed woman yourself. Victoria Ingalls had been an opera lover who worked in a shoe shop, and it was hard not to see the gulf dividing reality and desire. Opera was thunderstorms and grand device, with passions that rattled the scenery. Shoe shops were shoe shops. No wonder she'd hemmed her life with routine and private matters. So what did a woman like this do, finding herself with a lover? – she subsumed him into her life; made him part of those routines. Steered clear of public demonstration. Because opera would have taught her this much: that love was not safe harbour, whatever the paperbacks said. It was a condition that left you subject to the ministrations of others, your safety and survival depending on their talents, their concern for your well-being. They had to be gentle or very very sharp, with a touch like a feather or a scalpel. You had to trust them completely, or failing that, hope they made it quick.

She was holding a hand to her breast, she realised, and let it drop.

Down the road, the green cardigan was locking the animal sanctuary place. The shop kept charity hours – everywhere else would remain open another hour.

After sitting ten minutes, Zoë went for a walk.

It was dark blue afternoon when she joined the footpath, and breezy enough that she was glad of her leather jacket. There were others around, dog walkers mostly, and a young couple strolling arm in arm; an older pair who looked happy together. It wasn't difficult to trace Victoria's route, because her route followed the path.

By the time she reached the drainage ditch, Zoë was alone.

She stood at the lip, gazing into it at the point where the footpath right-angled. There was no telling exactly where Victoria Ingalls had slipped and fallen: they'd have slung accident tape at the time, no doubt, and scraps of it might still linger, bright yellow edges snagged on knots of bark. But to the woman who'd died, the precise geography would have been an irrelevance: neither here nor there. What would have mattered was that this was the last place she'd ever notice; whose banks, slick with mud, must have oozed to liquid at the touch. This with a broken leg. So after a while she'd have retreated inside her body, trying to coax resilience from it as the rain came down and everything grew darker. The walk was part of her routine, but this was not. It happened anyway.

Alone and in the dark; in pain, with water falling. If you were lucky, Zoë thought, the last voice you'd hear would be your child's or a friend's or a sensible stranger's, telling you you were loved. Otherwise it would be your own, asking 'Why me?'

She stood in the near dark herself now, wondering what there'd been of evidence – what the police might have found after a night of rain. Or how hard they'd have looked. Because why would they look? Victoria Ingalls took her walk alone each evening. This was her routine. There'd have been no reason to ask hard questions, because Victoria's life was one easy answer after another: her flat, her job, her opera. On Saturday mornings, the supermarket; Sunday afternoons, the front windows. On the first of October, she'd switch to her winter coat. It didn't matter what the weather was. Did she have a lover? Why would they ask, with the answer staring them in the face? Lovers didn't die in ditches. Not in the usual stories.

Lost in this, she forgot herself so much, she didn't even smoke. What she did remember, at last, was that she had nothing – no evidence, no clue, no firm ground at all. *Firm ground*, standing here by an unfirm edge. If she wanted that, she needed to act. Zoë turned, and walked back the way she'd come.

★

Back at the car, she still had time to kill. There were people around, though the shops were now shut: people heading out to eat and drink; to remind themselves why they spent the rest of their week at work. As long as she was sitting, she might as well be useful. She called Bob Poland again, who wasn't happy about it – Saturday evening, what was she expecting: miracles? She told him that would do for a start, and hung up before he could whinge further.

Waiting again, she found a scrunched-up note in the glovebox – *Chris*. She hadn't got round to his surname. She considered calling him, for no better reason than not liking loose ends, but in the end didn't, in case Poland tried to get through.

When he got back, he said, 'Tom Connor.'

'Got a number?'

He read it – quickly, but she was good with numbers – and finished by reminding her it was Saturday evening.

'I'd not forgotten yet. Anyway, don't you guardians of the peace work twenty-four seven?'

'You fucking wish.'

Then she was on her own, dabbing out the number he'd given her while it was fresh.

Miracles: here's one. Connor was on duty. The switchboard connected her.

'I got your name,' she told him, 'from Bob Poland.'

'Bob who?'

'Poland.'

She waited while somewhere on his side, another phone rang. Tom Connor said, 'Bob Poland, okay. You a journo?'

'No.'

'Name?'

When she'd given it, he said, 'Call back in five.'

She gave him six, but had to wait a couple more before getting through again. First thing he said was, 'So what's your interest in Wensley Deepman?'

She said, 'I know his grandfather, that's all. And he's been left out of the loop.'

'Not much of a loop to be in, Miss Boehm. Kid threw himself off a high-rise. Sad thing to happen, but what can you do? Teen suicides, it's like there's a rash.'

'And you're sure he jumped.'

'He was on the roof alone.'

'Drunk? Drugged?'

'Traces of cannabis in his bloodstream, but he wasn't high at the time. I didn't mean that the way it sounded. Miss Boehm, what can I tell you? The inquest will likely call it an auto. The death isn't actively under investigation.'

'Wensley Deepman,' Zoë said, 'wasn't exactly a model child.'

'Not news. His nick had a calendar posted, ticking off the days until he passed juvenile. Maybe he took a hard look at his future. Was there anything else?'

'The papers said there was a witness.'

'There was. Ground level, but he saw it happen. Kid stood on the edge, launched himself off.'

'The witness wasn't named.'

'Not everybody wants to be a celebrity.'

'I don't suppose you'd tell me—'

'Poland's a contact, not a friend. He got you this conversation, but that's all.'

'It would mean a lot to Mr Deepman.'

'You give Mr Deepman my condolences. Nice talking to you.'

Out on the street, there was still activity; mostly boy–girl stuff. Zoë attracted all the attention of an empty crisp packet. She slipped her mobile into her pocket, and recovered last Tuesday's *Independent* from the back seat. Front-page news then had been Charles Parsley Sturrock.

. . . Sturrock had been one of those soaps the world transmits on occasion: avidly watched by a sizeable minority;

intermittently glimpsed by all. In the end, as with all soap operas, his career highlights boiled down to a few scenes etched on the national consciousness: the equivalent of a fire in a farmhouse, or a shooting by a canal. In 1987, he had stood trial for his part in a bullion robbery netting £8.4 million: the robbery had happened three years earlier, and the trial was an act of desperation, held in the absence of concrete evidence, or any of the proceeds. Charles Parsley Sturrock was acquitted, of course, along with his alleged confederates. His next move had been to publish a book – not the My Trial Hell, which might have been forgivable, but a novel entitled *The Haul*, which described in painful detail a successful bullion robbery masterminded by a charming rogue tailor-made for the young Michael Caine. Zoë had read it, and her memories were of gritty, unconvincing dialogue and a lot of night scenes involving trucks. But she'd smiled more than once. The joke was in bad taste, but that didn't stop it being a joke. Caine would have had a field day.

The force spat nails.

Over the following years, Sturrock was arrested many times – driving offences; VAT irregularities: he owned a road haulage firm – but rarely reached court. He claimed harassment, and obviously had a point. Zoë knew policemen who used his name as an obscenity, though the nation at large still viewed him on Michael Caine lines. Then, one hot August night in the early nineties, Charles Parsley Sturrock stabbed a policeman to death, and the nation changed its mind.

The policeman, Daniel Boyd, had been twenty-five years old: black-clad, balaclavaed, armed; part of a Serious Crimes raid on Sturrock's Surrey manor house – a 'controlled and appropriate' response to information received, a force spokesman claimed. The exact nature of this information remained vague. Sturrock, on the other hand, argued terrorist outrage: he had been attacked in his home by a man dressed in black with a gun, and reacted accordingly. The outcome was tragic, but hardly his doing. He didn't go so far as to say he was holding a knife and Boyd jumped on to it, but his lawyer inked the dots and handed out pencils. The jury joined them. When Sturrock walked, one of its members was snapped giving him the thumbs up; rumour had him cruising the Med two weeks later. As for Sturrock, he returned to Surrey and redecorated. 'Tragic,' he was quoted as saying. 'But life goes on.' In his case for ten years, which was when his body turned up in an underground car park.

'Slowest fucking bullet in the world,' Bob Poland reckoned. 'But at least it had his name on it.'

Thus, she passed twenty minutes.

Along the lane stood a row of wheelie bins. The properties here had backyards: a pyramid of wooden crates crested the wall of one, while NO PARKING AT ANY TIME peeled from its padlocked gate – ACCESS IN CONSTANT USE. If she'd counted right, the door she wanted was midway along.

Zoë never went anywhere, except aeroplanes of course, without her multipurpose penknife.

If she wanted evidence she had to act, even if the act was pointless: what would she find of Victoria Ingalls in a charity shop, eight months after the event? It was more to do with being sick of inertia. The back lane was empty. She stooped to jam a bin's wheels with a chunk of brick, then hoisted herself on to it and over the wall, landing on tiptoe, instinctively dropping into a crouch. The air smelled damp here. Mildew thrived round an overflow pipe. But no dogs barked.

The back door looked only mildly locked. Zoë saw no alarm box; no obvious wiring. What were the chances that an animal charity shop was hi-tech secure? A pile of broken-up cardboard boxes and deconstructed packaging was stacked to one side; she rearranged it against the back wall, in case she needed a quick boost on her way out, then turned to the door, whose upper half was chopped into panes of frosted glass. No light shone. Its lock was tarnished and familiar. Zoë fished her penknife from a pocket.

. . . Years ago, Joe had decided he should learn to finesse locks, and had been genuinely surprised to find few available texts on the subject. So he'd taught himself, up to a point, that point occurring fairly soon: a large and mostly gentle man, he'd had a tendency to become cross with fiddly objects. Some doors, you just kicked down. Zoë, it proved, had more patience with inanimate objects than with people, and patience, in this field, was the key. But here was a fifteen-year-old lock and a handle that rattled. The door didn't meet the jamb properly. Even Joe could have schlepped it without resorting to violence.

Inside, she paused. There was a qualitative difference to air you weren't authorised to breathe – it had a tart, forbidden edge, like fruit on the turn. And dust; the rough leathery dust of old books, and of clothes left hanging too long in one place. She was in a passageway leading directly to the front of the shop. To one side was a toilet; to the other, a cabin-sized kitchen, where an upside-down mug dried quietly next to a kettle. The kettle ticked softly, recalling its last boiling.

Every noise, now, was a warning. Zoë had stepped through more than a poorly locked door; she'd jumped the invisible ditch that bordered the straight and narrow. And for what? – the outside chance of a clue to she wasn't sure what. She had more chance of finding a jacket that fitted her, or a nice hat.

Things being what they were – her job being what it was – she'd met burglars, some of whom were charming. Zoë remembered an evening in a wine bar, a progressively drunken raunch with a well-dressed, immaculately presented burglar whose cut-glass vowels matched a filthy sense of humour. Her name was Alison, and at thirty-seven, she'd been twenty-five years into a criminal career without ever enjoying an inside view of a prison.

'Rules, darling,' she'd told Zoë – drawling, two bottles in. 'There are rules for everything – dating, fucking, breaking up. These are the rules for burglary.'

One. Ensure the premises are empty.

Once, Alison had been doing a flat on a winter's evening: the place in darkness, quiet as night, and in the bedroom she'd found a middle-aged man, trussed like a Christmas parcel. PVC had featured largely. Seeing her, his eyes grew round as planets. 'I think he'd been expecting Cruella de Ville.' She'd left before his playmate returned.

Zoë didn't expect, an animal sanctuary shop, there'd be bondage in train on the premises, but still. She held her breath and waited. The only sounds were external: traffic minding its business; the average evening hum.

Two. Turn a light on. 'Nothing more suspicious than a torch-beam in an unlit house.' Not that Zoë had a torch.

The light took a moment to respond – one of those low-wattage power-savers that burn dimly for a long long time. The passage grew narrower; smells crowded in: a tang of bleach through the toilet's open door, instant coffee from the kitchen. She could see into the front of the shop: a trove of knick-knackery on shelving. Eighties fashions dangled from a coat rail. Somebody passed outside. The newly lit light drew no attention.

Know what to ignore. Too much choice is like wearing divers' boots.

She stepped into the shop and found the stairs behind the cash register. Ignoring a sign reading PRIVATE STAFF ONLY she took the stairs swiftly, ears piercingly alert. When something clicked or sighed, a vacant house noise, her heart's tempo quickened. She was embroiled in illegality here; had broken into a shop which sold nothing worth stealing. She wasn't sure if it was criminality or stupidity speeding her heart. Punishment for either would boil down to the same.

Zoë left the upstairs light off. *Ensure the premises are empty* was still tattooed on her mind. There were two rooms up here, and a bathroom; she checked for humans first, and found none. In the bathroom a tap dripped steadily, painting a green oval on the porcelain. She closed the door behind her, dampening its beat.

. . . Downstairs would be the usual cast-offs: clothes hats toys jewellery. No telling where anything came from. But a flat clearance needed administration. In one of the rooms, a space had been cleared for a desk and an ancient computer – any older, it would have been an abacus. Quickly as she dared (*Four. Move deliberately. Your body bloats with tension; you're bigger than you were. You knock things over.*) she turned it on and rummaged for a program disk: it really was that old. The screen groaned into green life. The necessary disk sat on the monitor, USE THIS stickered to its case. Probably the closest Zoë'd ever come to a useful clue.

She'd owned one of these herself once. Inserting the disk, she recalled wasted hours – hell, months – spent watching it boot, so made quick inventory of the room while she waited. People who liked animals no longer liked, it seemed: the novels of Wilbur Smith, lampshades decorated with stars, wooden figurines, PlasterMaster kits, wax fruit, and much else Zoë sincerely hoped she'd not have found room for in the first place. Everybody thought that in charity shops, though. Nothing had PROPERTY OF VICTORIA INGALLS stencilled on it, and it wasn't clear how helpful it would have been if it had.

When the computer was ready, it took her a moment to remember what to do next. There were more disks neatly stored in a plastic box, and she studied their labels now: CONTACTS. ACCOUNTS. MERCHANDISE. ROTA. MERCHANDISE contained thirty files, and the machine took an actual two minutes to open the first, which was a pricing guide. Scrolling through – Zoë had learned to drive in less time than it took this program to run a search – she found no names. The computer's electric hiccuping reminded her of the damn *Star Wars* robot: the pedal bin. Her famous patience with objects was wearing thin.

A car pulled up outside, and she froze.

There came voices, laughter, a car door slamming. Then a novelty horn blast, which hung in her ears while the car drove away. She had stopped breathing meanwhile, and again her heart pounded. The consequences of being found here, her inner Zoë remarked, far outweighed any possible benefit she might derive from it. Remind me of the purpose of this?

Five. Keep your eye on the ball, darling.

It was easy to drift under pressure; to forget, while burgling, what burglary meant. Alison had once tried a dress on mid-job. 'I could have just put it in my bag. What was I going to do if it didn't fit, take it back?' But she had forgotten, momentarily, that she was a burglar, not a real person. Zoë pulled open drawers; found a pack of unused disks. They were of a size and shape no longer familiar, and she had to close her eyes and let her fingers remember the copying procedure. One instruction to store the information to memory; another to write it to the clean disk. The process could take ten minutes.

She began anyway, picking MERCHANDISE, as it was handiest. While the machine growled she foraged the room, but found nothing significant among the tat. The window looked down on the back lane; the cardboard boxes she'd stacked for an emergency exit were just visible. And so was she – she'd broken rule whatever: she had no torch, but the monitor's glow would be framing her in the window . . . She moved aside quickly. There'd been nobody visible outside. This didn't mean there was nobody outside.

But Zoë felt alive. Felt more vital than in months, performing this illegal – this stupid – invasion.

The machine fell silent, half its job done. She inserted the clean disk, started it copying, then took herself to the other room; beginning to get used to this; beginning to move like a professional – on the balls of her feet, making next to no noise.

And so busy congratulating herself she hit the light switch without thinking, and the sudden harsh brilliance of a naked bulb split her vision in two.

It sounded like sirens going off in her head.

She froze, making sure they really were in her head, not out in the world. On the street below, life continued: people going about their evening; none of them remotely bothered by a light above a closed charity shop. Get a fucking grip, Zoë instructed herself, very nearly aloud. There was a painful dragging sound somewhere close; it took her a moment to register it as her own breathing. She let it calm before turning to the room's contents.

Like next door, there were boxes here; unlike next door, most had labels attached – DOG/CAT FOOD, JIGSAWS, PAPER-BACKS, MISC. ITEMS. Sometimes, you had to trust the paperwork. Ignoring food, games and ornaments, she opened the first book box and checked the topmost paperback's flyleaf for a signature: somebody called Debbie Squiggle had owned it, once upon a time. The box held maybe forty similar; there were three boxes labelled BOOKS, and Zoë asked herself how useful examining each and every one would be, and found an answer quite quickly.

Clothes on the floor in a corner managed to be both neatly folded and piled in a heap at the same time. No knowing if any had been Victoria's. An unmarked box held nothing but blank sheets of paper. Wild geese suggested themselves, but alongside other qualities, Zoë could be seriously pig-headed. There were other boxes; there were more corners. If she found nothing, she was at least going to know there'd been nothing to find. But *Six. Set a time limit*. Five minutes more, tops. Enough to copy a second disk; to check the rest of this room. But she forgot about the second disk immediately she found the auction boxes.

This was how they were labelled: FOR AUCTION. The same

careful hand that had printed the rest. They sat below the window; neither hidden nor prominent – they were, after all, just four more boxes; whose contents, the records (heavy boxed sets of thick black vinyl), were all of operas; their names at once familiar and incomprehensible to Zoë, to whom the form was a locked room. The boxed sets made an impressive, heavy-looking mass comprising God knew how many hours' music. If she started at one end and listened right through to the other, she might emerge significantly less ignorant, she supposed. But perhaps significantly less inclined to carry on living, also. It occurred to her that you could cram all this on to few enough CDs to snugly fit a shoebox, but the expense had presumably been beyond Victoria Ingalls – or perhaps she'd preferred the old-fashioned way. The CD boom gave everyone a chance to purge their musical history, though most went on to make the same mistakes again. But Victoria must have been happy with her choices.

There was never doubt in Zoë's mind that these were Victoria's records.

It made every kind of sense: how often did a shop like this – not the high end of the charity market – wind up with a treasure trove? A collection this size must be worth thousands. Too valuable to sell piecemeal downstairs. So it had been kept for auction; meanwhile, here it rested, arranged according to principles Zoë didn't have the first clue about: Puccini next to Janáček next to Mozart. Chronology or theme or taste: light and heavy: whatever. Now that she'd found them, what did they tell her? The answer remained an obstinate zero.

There was shouting out on the street, briefly – pub-bound youth – but it neither startled nor worried her; she was entirely inside her own space. The maze she'd thought about earlier came to mind, the one where you passed through door after door, moving ever further from your starting point, with no idea where you were going. She was hearing from her inner

Zoë again, and the tone was unimpressed. *So what, exactly, were you expecting?* That *exactly* irritated. Zoë knelt, and ran a hand across the top edge of the ranked sets of records in the first box; automatically began to count, but stopped when she noticed. There was something here, but it meant nothing to her – one more language she was unversed in. Victoria Ingalls was dead as ever, and all Zoë'd found was something of the life she'd left behind. *So what were you expecting? Exactly?* She felt she'd won an argument she didn't even believe in herself.

She ran the same hand across the second box, feeling mute music in cardboard packaging.

Next door, the disk had finished copying. She should take it, for what it was worth, and run; she should remember the final rule – the same as it ever was: for dating, fucking, breaking up. For burglary. *Don't get caught.* Ultimately, Alison hadn't taught her anything Zoë didn't know already, and this, too, was the same as it ever was.

She ran a hand across the third box; felt the same rank of unknown pleasures beneath her fingertips, and tried to imagine owning them – their being part of her life's furnishings; the physical objects the backdrop to her daily events, and the music they held the soundtrack. To collect them – not just the expense, but the actual time involved in choosing them, in learning them, in keeping on collecting – must have been immense; must have demanded commitment and tenacity. Which was what she was thinking when she became aware of an oddity she couldn't put her finger on.

Putting a finger on, though, was the answer . . . She ran her hand across the tightly jammed boxes once more, and registered what had snagged her attention: something tucked between two records, pushing them apart so a slight gap intervened that her fingers had noticed, but into which they wouldn't fit. A chime struck in her brain, and she knew her five minutes were up, that she should be out of here – risk increased exponentially, and her chances of walking away were shrinking by the moment – but shrugged these mental warnings off, and eased a record from the box instead, to give her fingers room. *The Cunning Little Vixen* caught her eye; words unattached to any tune her mind remembered. Laying it aside she pulled another out, then another, until she had enough space to pull the foreign object free. When she'd done so, she barely glanced at it; its existence, right that moment, was enough for her purposes.

Zoë replaced the records in the order she'd removed them, then stood and scanned the room, to check what difference her presence had made. None, as far as she could tell. Another of Alison's rules swam into mind, but swam out again too quickly for the words to form. It didn't matter. She was done. She switched off the light and went next door, where the old computer had managed its trick, and was waiting, churning asthmatically, for somebody to make it perform another. Zoë retrieved the copied disk, put the others back where she'd found them, then shut the computer down. Downstairs, she killed the light in the hallway, and stepped into the yard. Way up yonder was a full moon, or a moon so very nearly full it made no difference. By the time she was over the wall and in the lane she wasn't a burglar at all, but a woman out on her own, mid evening: pretty respectable-looking on the whole, though her jacket had seen better days.

12

I T HAD NOT ESCAPED Zoë's attention that she was growing older. A dozen reminders nipped her daily, which in time would double then double again . . . But it was only lately, sifting dead women's relics, that it had struck her how much everything else was ageing too. Her possessions, like theirs, were well embarked on the bleak trajectory from newly desirable to shabby familiar: one day, everything she owned would be packed in boxes, and junked or sold for charity. Even gifts once cried over. And there wasn't a lot could be done about this. The physical form – the body you tenanted – could be shored up: there was no shame now in going under the knife; it was an available alternative you'd be a fool to dismiss out of hand. And there were other measures, varyingly drastic – Botox injection, HRT, laser correction, toy boy: whatever worked. But it was all throwing money on top of a weary infrastructure: things looked brighter, gleamier, as if they'd probably work, but irreversible corrosion ate the foundations below. The high-speed trains all stopped when the signals failed. And the things you owned grew worn and faded, and were destined for boxes in the end.

Do I need a drink or what? she asked herself.

Zoë was in the car, heading back to Oxford; smoking, driving too fast; still agitated from her break-in, and alarmed at how alive it had made her feel. Was this what she'd been missing?

And was it illegality or triumph boosting her? A triumph that tasted oddly like ash, because what it signified was somebody's murder. It was the reason Victoria's possessions had ended in boxes.

It lay barely examined on the seat beside her. She didn't need to examine it: the fact that it existed was enough. It wasn't proof of anything, not to anybody else; to Zoë, it was all the proof she needed.

As I walk this land of broken dreams
I have visions of many things

She didn't know she knew the words. But there was this about pop music: it crept into you like mist under an ill-fitting door, until words you didn't know you knew had taken up residence – words like 'love', heartbreak', 'forever'. People her age spent years having poetry hammered into them at school, and emerged without a couplet intact. But each and every one knew what followed 'I'll never dance with another'.

What becomes of the broken-hearted
Who had love that's now departed

Jimmy Ruffin. Motown Records. 1966. She couldn't begin to remember last time she'd seen a seven-inch single in a paper sleeve; it was like something recovered from a time capsule, meant to remind you what you'd been doing while Armstrong walked the moon. And it had been tucked into Victoria Ingalls's record collection, as out of place as a cat in a kennel. Zoë, looking for Caroline Daniels, had found this instead: two jigsaw pieces that didn't lock together. Now, instead of stubbing it in the ashtray, she tossed her cigarette through the open window and saw in her rear-view sparks scatter the dark road behind her. *I know I've got to find some kind of peace of mind.* It was always a mistake to look for solutions in a lyric, but there was a point here, that was true. Peace of mind. Easier sung than found.

And now that I know this, she was asking herself, what am I going to do?

Her flat was in darkness. There was no wine in her fridge. Zoë couldn't remember finishing a bottle, but then, couldn't remember starting one either. She put the record on her desk, then in afterthought in a drawer instead, which she locked. It wasn't terribly late yet; it felt terribly late, but wasn't. Not too late to drink coffee, but coffee wasn't what she needed. Alan Talmadge, she thought. She spoke the words aloud, to hear a killer's name in the open air. 'Alan Talmadge'. Which wasn't his name. She felt absurd, as if she'd essayed a satanic rite; uttered a fiendish name to conjure evil. What did she do with what she knew? Which wasn't quite suspicion – felt like certainty – but boiled down to less than conjecture (this song, that song; two tunes in two wrong places).

She had a man friend, though . . . I saw him leaving her flat.

We do, don't we? We like to boast about our little conquests . . .

. . . It was still coursing through her veins; that life force she'd generated performing the break-in. She said his not-name aloud again. 'Alan Talmadge'. I'm going to find you. Proof or no proof: I know you're out there, whoever you are. Sitting at her desk, in the pool of light her anglepoise cast, her index finger made a pile of the scatter of paperclips it found; a slow methodical gathering she was barely aware of. I know what you do. I'll find you. Trust me.

The phone rang.

So on edge, so alive she was, it might have killed her.

She picked up, spoke her name, and in the moment before the silence broke wondered if she'd conjured Talmadge out of the ether, by discovering what he did. A cigarette called to her, but it was trapped in her jacket pocket, on the far side of the room.

'Zoë? It's Jay, Zoë. Jay Harper? We met—'

'I remember.'

I'm talking about women, they're single, they're looking at forty, they might as well be carrying neon signs.

'Zoë?'

'But I don't remember giving you my number.'

'You're in the book. I don't remember you saying you were a private eye.'

'You didn't ask.'

'It goes to show, we have unfinished business.'

Her finger disrupted the tidy pile it had made of the paper-clips. 'You can't be finding things that difficult.'

'Difficult?'

'You know what I mean.'

'I'm not ringing you because I like a *challenge*, Zoë. What would that make me?' He didn't leave a pause. It wasn't really a question. 'I enjoyed your company. I'd like to see you again. That's all.'

At the heart of the paperclip pile she found a tightly rolled ball of silver foil. Hardly aiming – choosing a target, but not looking at it – Zoë flicked, hard. It missed the door handle by barely an inch.

'You keep going silent.'

She sighed. 'Jay. I must have ten years on you, and that's adding five to what you think you're getting away with. You seriously imagine I need that kind of grief?'

'So how old do I think I'm getting away with? Twenty-two?'

'Nice try.'

'All I'm asking is, a drink? Seriously, Zoë, you strike me as more used to giving grief than getting it. You've nothing to worry about where I'm concerned.'

That had the air of famous last words, she thought: the kind that get said by somebody else. Like *This isn't going to hurt, much*, or *It's all right, I'll catch you.*

'I'll make it easy. I'll tell you where I am right now.' He told her: a pub, one she knew well. This was because it was five minutes' walk away. 'And unless you save me from myself, I'll be here until kicking out. Which, given my regrettably unmacho capacity for alcohol, means I'll get hopelessly drunk, sleep in tomorrow, miss my train, miss a *very* serious meeting, and lose my job. Which will be your fault.'

'So no pressure, then—'

'Later.'

—and he was gone, like that. She was listening to a dial tone.

It's Sunday tomorrow, she thought.

And: not a chance, she also thought . . . She spread her hand, and swiped the paperclips across the desk, on to the floor, into the bin. There was a tingling at her fingertips, at her toes, the roots of her hair – none of the obvious sexual playgrounds, but if her body thought it was fooling her, it had another think coming. Not a chance, she thought again, but she wasn't even kidding herself.

There were various reasons Zoë liked this pub, among them its blackboard listing available cocktails: Guinness and bitter, bitter shandy, lager top. In the back room, where there was a sofa and an armchair, she found Jay Harper, who'd bagged the sofa. A pint glass, almost full, sat in front of him. He was reading the *Independent*.

'I was beginning to think you weren't coming.'

There was a piano, and, on the walls, photos of obscure jazz performers, along with ancient revue bills and vinyl recordings from best forgotten eras, such as the polka craze of the fifties. A young man on the piano stool was studying sheet music, while two women talked quietly in a nook. A drift of crushed monkey-nut shells littered the floor. 'Well, you don't look dangerously intoxicated.'

'Don't underestimate this stuff. It's called Monks' Brain Mortilyser, or something. More than a pint, and you're technically dead.'

'Sounds tempting. But I'll stick to wine.'

While he fetched it, she claimed the armchair, trying not to wonder what had brought her here. Wine, but not only wine. The body, after all, was a traitor. But wasn't this research, of a sort? – it brought her closer to Caroline, to Victoria, and might bring insight into their story. Though largely, they'd always remain mysterious to her. Sometimes, it was as if other people had minds of their own. And the most unlikely among them ran on kamikaze hearts.

. . . And the body, anyway, was a traitor . . . The thought hollowed her out, dried her mouth; she had forgotten for whole hours thoughts of envelopes and examinations and *We'll have to fix you up with an appointment* . . . Murder and love had edged out cancer, but only for a while, only for a while. There was probably an equation awaiting calculation; some very precise formula which would balance these extremes. For the moment, cancer was winning; it had swamped Alan Talmadge and his murderous loves, and everything around her grew larger of a sudden, while noises boomed as if the room had become a sound tunnel. She very badly needed a drink. Because the body was a traitor. And then Jay was back, handing her a glass, which she took without a word. She had her first large swallow before he'd even sat down.

He looked at her. 'Bad day, or just thrilled to see me?'

'You have no idea.'

'How thrilled—'

'The day I've had.'

He sat, and resumed his pint. In this light Jay seemed older than he had in the bright bar; it should have been the other way round, but somehow the softer context was hard on him, and didn't let him get away with much. She decided she preferred this. Pubs were realer than bars. Here, Jay looked like he worked for a living. He was relaxing, but obviously had a life to relax from. 'Want to tell me about it?' he asked.

'Not really.'

'It's going to be a long evening.'

'I didn't mean to come,' she told him. 'I'm not sure why I did.'

'So long as you're here.'

Reaching for a cigarette was easier than replying.

He said, 'I think you got the wrong idea about me last night.'

'Why would you think that?'

'You seemed mistrustful. I might have said some rubbish.'

'Is that why we're here? So you can correct my first impression?'

'Do you fence?

'Why do you ask?'

'You seem keen on duelling.'

'I've never fenced,' said Zoë. 'I've done a bit of shooting.'

This seemed to amuse him.

She said, 'So what's the real Jay Harper like? Sensitive, concerned, mildly feminist?'

'I'm just me. I'm not pretending to be anybody else.' He drank some of his beer. 'What's it like, being a private detective?'

'It's a job.'

'You don't give much away, do you?'

'That kind of goes with the job.'

'What are you working on at the moment?'

'I'm looking for somebody.'

'Have you found him yet?'

'What makes you think it's a man?'

'Fifty-fifty shot.' He had tucked the *Independent* down the side of the sofa, from where half of Charles Parsley Sturrock's face grinned out at her; one of those sardonic, hand-it-to-the-jury expressions he was specialising in circa 1993. Jay noticed her noticing. 'That happened near where I work,' he said. 'Sturrock's execution.'

'You think that's what it was?'

He shrugged. 'Thieves falling out. The money never turned up, did it?'

'I was kept out of the loop on that one.'

'Have you ever been married, Zoë?'

'Seamless switch.'

'I'm just trying to get to know you.'

And since when did that work, Zoë wondered. When you had to try. 'Yes,' she said. 'I've been married.'

It was like that moment in any siege, she thought later, when you yield the first stone to the marauders. Give up one tiny part of the city, even if it's hurled in anger, and next thing you know, the towers are tumbling down. Was that how it happened with Victoria and Caroline? Had they thought they were succumbing to love? And did it mean it wasn't love, just because Talmadge killed them? There was a big 'just' in that sentence. Jay Harper was looking at her as if she were missing her train, and Zoë bent to her wine again, already regretting the admission, the trivial surrender. But *let it go* a voice inside suggested. She had no idea if this were her inner Zoë, or Joe, or Sarah, or what. It was a long time since anyone had been interested, and that was the truth. Maybe she was just ready: ready to let go.

'Talk to me,' he said.

And now she found herself deep in a dream of a white room equipped with sleek medical machinery. *We'll have to fix you up with an appointment* something a bit like a tannoy said. A fixture rang like a telephone, and woke her. She was drenched, everywhere; her cotton tee limp as a dishcloth. Still it rang.

The luminous hands by her bedside quietly informed her it was five past two. Nothing good happened suddenly in the single-figure hours. The late-night phone call was the weapon of stalkers and other perverts. Her feet almost lost balance on the firm, level floor, as if she were still on dream legs, which couldn't handle reality.

When she lifted the receiver the sudden silence was like something breaking. 'Hello?'

She could hear breathing, but not aggressive breathing. A ragged swallowing of air, as if whoever had been crying.

'Hello?'

But there was only breathing, and beyond that, a freighted emptiness which sounded like the world outside.

Zoë hung up and returned to bed. There was probably a reason the phone was on the far side of the room. Closing her eyes she saw the white space again; heard its equipment begin to tick. Something small and lost, not quite pain, shifted in her breast. She'd drunk two glasses of wine: fewer than she'd wanted, but more than was sensible. Talk to me, Jay had said, and she almost had. Almost talked as if she knew him well; as if he were more than a stranger in a bar. You might call it charm. The phone rang.

'Hello?'

This time, she heard rain – not a downpour, but a gentle pattering of water on glass. But when she peeled the curtain with her free hand, there it was: rain brushing the window here and now.

'I'm hanging up.' *You son of a bitch.*

'I didn't know.'

'. . . Didn't know what?'

'I didn't know he was dead.'

She'd been right; there was rain down the line, too. Wherever he was, it wasn't far, and he was out in the rain, talking to her.

She pulled the phone as far as the cord allowed, and sat. Her own abandoned warmth rose from her bed. Drenched in sweat, she was cooling fast. 'Where are you, Andrew?'

'It doesn't matter.'

This was what Zoë wanted: teenage drama. 'Look, I meant what I said. It wasn't your fault. And I could have handled it more sensitively.'

'I don't deserve sensitive.'

'Oh—' She'd been about to tell him to fuck off. Decided that was not a good direction. 'Have you been drinking?'

'Bit.'

Great.

'He was my friend.'

'Right.'

'He was my only real friend.'

'No, Andrew. Those people you were with the other day, they're your real friends. They're where you belong. Understand?'

'If I'd stayed with him, he wouldn't be dead.'

'No. If you'd stayed with him, you'd both be dead. You'd not have lasted six months. Sooner or later, he'd have turned on you himself. That's the way it is.'

'He was my *friend*.'

'He was a street punk, and he was using you. He didn't get a fair crack at life, true. But lots of people don't, and they're not all thieves and muggers.'

'You don't understand.'

'I don't pretend to. Understanding's overrated. Most of us settle for surviving. You had a tough lesson in that. Take it to heart.'

'Who killed him?'

She sighed. Teenagers were impossible to avoid, and she'd heard this about them: they had their own agenda. Don't bother telling them anything they're not listening to. They wait for a gap and plough right on. Sometimes without waiting for the gap.

'Nobody killed him.'

'He can't have just *died*. He was twelve.'

'There was an accident. He fell.'

The wind kicked up. More rain hit the window. Zoë was trying to remember where the nearest cigarettes were, and worrying they'd turn out to be under lock and key in the local newsagent's.

'Fell where?'

A great height, she almost said.

'What, was it off some building or something?'

'A tower block.'

'He didn't like heights.'

'No. Well.' Sensible aversion, in the circumstances. It wasn't like falling from one had done him any good.

'He wouldn't go somewhere he'd be so high, that's all.'

'That kind of depends on his plans,' she said.

She had remembered there were cigarettes on the kitchen sill; a mostly used packet that had gone through the wash some days ago. They were likely to be dry by now. Or likely to become so, once she set fire to them.

'What do you mean?'

'I lied. It wasn't an accident.' She amended that. 'Nobody thinks it was an accident.'

She heard, or thought she heard, that same sudden squall on his side of the line. With a map and the wind speed and a weathervane, she could pinpoint exactly where he was, if she'd timed the interval. An interesting exercise in futility.

'He killed himself.' Andrew's voice was flat, morbid; he wasn't asking a question.

She answered him anyway: 'That's what they're saying. Yes.'

'Why would he do that?'

Zoë thought: why wouldn't he?

'He had his whole life in front of him.'

149

'There are those who'd call that reason enough,' said Zoë. 'He'd used up a lot of options.'

'I spoke to him.'

'Spoke to him when?'

'He used to call me. Not often. Every six months or so?'

'And say what?'

'He wanted money.'

Of course he wanted money. 'Did you send him any?'

'He said he'd come looking if I didn't. Said he could fuck me up no trouble.'

'And this was your friend?'

'You were right. I'd not have lasted ten minutes without him. Not on the streets of the city.'

'Go home, Andrew. Go to bed. Maybe you're right to feel guilty, I don't know. But get over it, okay? Go home, go to bed. Get on with your life.'

'Last time, he wasn't asking for money.'

I really don't care any more, she thought.

'He said he was quids in. If I'd stuck with him, I'd really have it made.'

'Andrew? He was a con artist. No. He was a street thug. He was *hoping* to be a con artist.'

Andrew, formerly Dig, said nothing.

'Andrew?'

There was more rain, but it was hitting her bedroom window, that was all: in her ear was the dial tone. Just for one moment – something to do with the rain, with the dark; with the day she'd had and what she'd learned – it was the sound of every sundered relationship she'd ever known.

After a while, she got back into bed.

13

*T*HESE ARE THE THINGS *he knows he knows: what she drinks, what she wears, how she moves. And these are the things he thinks he knows: that she grieves after dark, and carries sorrow whose weight sometimes catches her by surprise – when no one's looking, her mask slips, to reveal the effort, the frank outrage, of a woman who's learning that she's not equal to everything life can throw. Though what she's yet to learn too is that there's never no one looking.*

He has fixed a tracking device to the underside of her car.

And naturally, he has chased her down the Web. She doesn't enter chat rooms or post mad diatribes, but she's a user (unlike Victoria) so there are footprints to be found. Besides, she's a feature. Once, she killed a man. The details are fuzzy – the man was a neo-Nazi, an undercover policeman or a rogue government agent, depending on your source – but the fact is cold and blunt as paving slab: she took a life. What was once warm muscle and cardiac machinery, she turned to meat and bone. This was almost something they had in common, though the circumstances were different.

(He had wooed and won Victoria because her whole life cried out for it. It was that simple, and started by accident. Overcome by the need for shoes while far from home, he had been struck by the woman serving; by her air of . . . disappointment. It was no big thing to strike up conversation. What many people don't understand is that lives are not locked boxes, but open easily to the right touch. He

wooed and won her because that was what she wanted. And it made him happy and proud that for the last few months of her life, Victoria had known what it was to love and be loved. He had opened her ears to the music. Though when push came to shove, it ended, of course.)

. . . And these are the things he knows she knows: that he exists; that he is out here in the world. She doesn't know his name. It was Alan Talmadge she was looking for in Caroline's house, and Alan Talmadge no longer existed, just as Bryan Carter – whom Victoria loved – was no more either; both vanishing like a quick fade once their work was done. (He knows she knows about Bryan Carter, because he knows she went to Wallingford. He has fixed a tracking device to the underside of her car.) This makes life interesting. He would shy from the word 'challenge'. This is not about conquest. It's about love; about bringing love where it's needed, to the lives of those who lack it.

(Once, walking by the river – on a cold evening, towards the end of their time together – Caroline had turned on him suddenly. You talk about love, *she said.* You say you love me. But what does that mean? What does love mean?

Nothing, *he told her.*

And even in the dark he saw her eyes come over weepy, as if, for all the harshness of her tone, she'd been looking for reaffirmation; for him to insist again that it was true, that he was true, that love could flourish. Even here. Even now. His blunt rejection robbed her of what she'd started to believe, and seeing that belief made him glad, although it meant their time was coming to an end.

In tennis, *he said.*

Tennis?

In tennis. Love. It means nothing.

But here and now, *he added,* it means us.

And he felt, in their linked fingers, a sigh pass through her like the ghost of sex.)

. . . These are the things he thinks she knows: that what she is

lacking, he can give her. That that's why she's looking for him. And though she doesn't know it yet, she's found him now, or he's found her. When push comes to shove, the difference barely matters.

In love, he's found, push always comes to shove.

FOUR

NEVER NO ONE
LOOKING

14

WHEN THE FIRST THING you noticed in the morning was the weather, it set the tone for the day ahead. Monday morning was blue skies, but Zoë traced a stiff wind in the limbs of next door's trees, and knew clouds might turn up out of nowhere. Spring days could turn to autumn. The lift your heart got might be the kind that dropped you at the next exit.

Sunday, she'd written to Amory Grayling, a report which didn't mention Victoria Ingalls. It did, though, outline Zoë's reasons for thinking 'Alan Talmadge' an assumed name. He was married, Zoë concluded, leaving Grayling to draw what he wanted from this – that people are not framed for good behaviour; that where men love they also lie, and that some men lie and call it love. These mild conclusions would be based on incomplete knowledge, but Grayling didn't want to learn that Caroline had been pushed under that train. By this stage, he might no longer even want to find Talmadge – a guilty adulterer now; not a bereaved lover – but that was barely relevant. Zoë had made her own connections, to Caroline, to Victoria, and would keep pushing doors, regardless of what lay behind them.

When Bob Poland called, Monday morning, she'd been about to use the phone herself.

'What did you say to Connor the other night?'

For a moment, she couldn't remember who Connor was, let alone what she'd said to him when. 'Why?'

'He called me. He wants to know about you.'

'Wants to know what?'

'Where are you?'

Which was Poland asking, not Connor.

She was halfway into town – she had things to do – but she was curious as to what Tom Connor wanted. It was probably knee-jerk – when you asked a policeman questions, you were by definition wasting police time. But it was better, too, to know what Poland's answers had been.

He was drinking an Americano in a café in the covered market.

'Why were you interested in this kid?'

'Hi, Bob.'

'What was his name? Deepling?'

'I'll have the same. Thanks.'

He gave her a stare, but went to fetch it. Zoë watched him join the short queue, which was not quite short enough to forestall his impatience: she read this in the tightening of his shoulder muscles; in the thrumming of his fingers on his thigh. There was a violence in Bob Poland she'd never seen in action, and doubted she would. This would be all it amounted to: an annoyance with people in his way; an epithet spat at those unlikely to spit back. All the boring qualities of cowardice. Not that she underestimated this. When cowardice came to the boil, it could burn those who strayed too close. Poland liked to hear about it too: violence. He'd asked her more than once about shooting that man. Most people tiptoed round it: it was the elephant in the kitchen, the one nobody mentioned. But Poland wanted to know. He wanted to imagine the trigger, and what was happening at the other end. For this, among countless other reasons, she never answered.

And besides, some experiences rendered you ineligible to discuss them. Your point of view became irrelevant: it was like trying to find magnetic north while standing at the pole. Evel

Knievel was once asked what it was like, being in a coma. 'How would I know?' he'd replied. 'I was in a fucking coma.'

When Poland returned she said, 'His name was Wensley Deepman.'

'Whatever. Kid took a header off the fortieth floor, right? Connor was wondering what made him important, on account of he was this half-caste punk looking at life indoors. What could I say? I don't know what you're up to.'

'Because it's not your business.'

'That's what I'm getting at. You want me onside, Zoë, you've got to keep me informed.'

'What did you tell him?'

He said, 'I'm a liaison officer, or did you forget? What's it gunna look like I start telling him lies? You think I'd be trusted tomorrow?'

'You think you're trusted today?'

'Your mouth'll get you in trouble, Zoë. Sooner or later.'

'I'd hate to think you were threatening me, Bob.'

Instead of answering, he drank his coffee. It occurred to her, she'd not seen him without alcohol to hand before.

Then he said, 'Where's this happening, anyway, somewhere in the Smoke? How come you're involved?'

'Nobody calls it the Smoke, Bob. Not in about fifty years.'

He used the fuck-off button on that. 'So where's the money?'

'There is none.

'How's that work?'

'I'm not being paid, Bob. It was just . . .' It was what? She could barely name it. 'It was something happened a long time ago. I owe it to him.'

'How can you owe a kid?'

'I'd explain that, but I only talk human.'

'Jesus.' He picked up his cup, but it was empty. He put it down. 'He wasn't yours, was he?'

'Wensley?'

'He was half black,' Connor said. 'Black your type?'

She looked at him. He smiled without it touching his eyes. 'That would cover some ground, wouldn't it? Zoë Boehm with a little lost boy. Explain why life's so tragic.'

Part of the energy that had washed through her on Saturday came flooding back, now coloured as hate. Some experiences rendered you ineligible to discuss them, sure. But the practice helped, on the days you felt like murder.

The non-smile was still plastered to his face. He had stalker's eyes, Bob Poland: how come she'd not registered this before?

He said, 'You're one of those people think you're invulnerable. You always have done. But you want to be careful about screwing with me, Zoë.'

'Trust me, Bob. Screwing, you and me are things that are never going to occur.'

It was the best she could manage off the cuff.

'Bitch.'

She left, hatred pulsing through her veins. This was what it was like to be coming back to life: old emotions stirring, catching like barbed wire. The alleys of the covered market throstled with shoppers and would-be looters; a creep with a car salesman's coat and a face that belonged on Gollum oozed past. Bob Poland had been part of her scenery so long, she'd forgotten he was venomous. Sometimes a good memory was more important than anything else. Remember to hate him.

There'd been something she'd planned to do, but it slipped her mind right now.

On Market Street the wind's edge cut through leather. She turned towards Cornmarket, zipping her jacket, and felt in her pocket the familiar lump of her phone: talk to Andrew Kite. That's what she'd been planning to do when Poland interrupted. Standing on the corner, her neck pricking as if she were being watched, she rang first his house, and got no reply, then the ersatz college he studied at. She had to pretend to be his aunt, but ascertained he was there. By now the pricking was worse, but when she turned, she saw only the usual crowds, the usual butchers' vans; the usual homeless man with his newspapers clutched to his chest. Poland, she decided. That was his speed: to follow, to watch, but to shrink to the fucking shadows when she felt him. She lit a cigarette, and moved on.

And found herself in that alleyway again, waiting for Andrew to appear; smoking, and thinking about Alan Talmadge – where had he met Victoria and Caroline? Wherever he wanted, was the answer. Talmadge didn't choose at random, he stalked. Talmadge was looking for women of a certain age, of a certain lifestyle, who had room in their lives for a man bringing little baggage – no books, no photographs; maybe soul music. Everything else was theirs. But then, most relationships involve one half providing the detail (the friends, the location) while the other slots in. It was conflict avoidance, as much as anything else. And when the woman has little background, and the man no being, what's left is vacuum.

How easy would it have been for them to fall so hard? Very easy indeed.

Zoë ground her cigarette underfoot. They had been, she thought, walking invitations to a man with no morality, which would have been bad enough if all he'd wanted was sex. But he'd insisted, she supposed, on love. And what they'd have thought was what everybody thought: that they were the only people this had ever happened to, when they weren't even the only people it had happened to with him. Love was recyclable, unfortunately.

. . . It didn't matter, anyway. It didn't matter how he'd met them. What mattered was what came after: we are in the realm of results, not causes. He preys on women. I know this, but can't prove it. If she could, she'd take it to the police. But all she could point to was two women dead in accidents, and her reputation was not such that anyone would care.

The doors to the college opened and a pack of students emerged; somehow uniform, despite their individual striping. A clamorous number headed towards her; distracted, she almost missed Kite, who was heading the other way: jeans, blue-black fleece, Quiksilver backpack. She caught him before he reached the market square. 'Andrew.'

His face was that same polite blank of Friday morning.

She said, 'I'm not having a good day. You wanted to talk the other night. You want to talk more, talk now. Otherwise, next time you ring, I'll hunt you down and feed you your mobile.'

And here he was: Dig, not Andrew Kite. The sly but frightened boy who could steal and run but was wholly out of his depth.

Less savagely, Zoë said, 'Okay. I'm told I'm not that likeable. You want a coffee?'

He nodded, then cleared his throat. 'Yeah.'

They walked to one of the less crowded cafés, and sat at a table in the bright cold sun. Zoë lit a cigarette, and absently offered him one, then caught herself; shrugged an apology. Before their orders came, he was talking about Wensley Deepman.

. . . She'd drunk so much coffee already she was zigzagging, or that was what it felt like, while Andrew Kite spilled all he'd ever known about Kid B: how they'd met, what Wez had said; all the ins and outs of being rough in the city. Their drinks came, and he kept talking. Kid B knew all the rules: that's what Dig reckoned. Between the lines, Wez had been another punk wannabe, but to hear Dig they'd been Butch and Sundance, carving a hole in the wall. In his mind he was reliving grainy walls and neon puddles. Only when he'd wound down – when the words gave way to a middle-distance stare that might have been aimed at the gaggle of girls across the way, or possibly three years further – did Zoë say: 'When did he call?'

'Late at night, mostly.'

'To your home?'

'Once. 'Fore I gave him my moby number.'

(So his parents didn't need to know.)

'And he asked you for money.'

Fifty quid a go; the odd hundred, Andrew told her. Told her as if such sums were the usual ones; sums you couldn't expect to be smaller; sums most teenagers could lay their hands on no problem.

'Were there threats?'

Andrew said, 'If I hadn't sent it, he'd have come for it.'

Zoë wondered what that would have been like; a door opening on one world from another. From this safe present, Andrew looked back on his wild-side walk as if it allowed him a broader perspective than the children he moved among daily, cushioned by their parents' love and money. He might even have been right. But he knew – it was obvious – that he was back where he belonged, and that when Zoë had brought him home, she'd been rescuing not relocating him.

'Did he?'

'No. I never saw him again.'

'On Saturday,' she said, 'you told me he'd come into money.'

'He said he knew where he could get some.'

'Did he say where from?'

Andrew shook his head. 'But it was a scam of some sort. Something dangerous.'

'How do you know?'

He looked at her as if she were forty-four, and he only seventeen. 'Because he was Wez.'

Right.

'Did he ever talk about his grandfather?'

'He mentioned him.'

'What did he say?'

But Andrew couldn't remember. It was too removed from anything that could matter: an old man, somebody else's grandparent . . . As for Wensley, Wensley was an image, when he'd not been a voice on the phone; an emblem of something exciting Andrew had done once. The fact that he was dead was exciting too, Zoë suspected, though Andrew would never admit it.

'He ever take you there?'

'Wez only went when he needed to hide.'

Right, she thought again.

He said, 'You know something funny? The day he died? It was my birthday.'

Zoë tried, but couldn't think of what to say.

'Ain't life a bitch?' Andrew asked, as if he'd rehearsed it often.

She watched him make his way across the square. A grown woman, easily in her thirties, looked back at him as they crossed. Then turned to notice Zoë noticing this, and smiled at being caught.

Zoë sat on a bench by the tourist office, watching buses dispense the morning's travellers. There'd been a reason she'd come into town – groceries – but it was fading fast. Her other concerns divided neatly in two. She needed to know more about Alan Talmadge; enough that she could convince the world of what he was. But had to find him first. And then there was Wensley Deepman, who wouldn't take much finding because he wasn't going anywhere ever again. Who didn't like heights, but had been on that roof by himself. Who'd found a way of making money, and boasted about it to Andrew Kite. She wondered if he'd boasted to anybody else.

It was about now she'd normally be lighting another cigarette. She'd had a vague resolve on waking, though, and while giving up wasn't going to happen here and now, cutting back was worth thinking about. So was whatever it was she was doing.

Nobody reached Zoë's age without formulating rules for life. Some were obvious – never trust a man with a sunlamp tan, or anyone who smiled while delivering bad news. Others were more to do with the way things were: that it was a hard world, with a sentimental streak a mile wide. That traffic slowed for nuns and ducklings. That everyone else took their chances.

That it was best not to get involved.

But this was a rule she'd broken before. Once, she'd done a brave thing, putting herself in danger to help a woman she barely knew. And afterwards, wondering why she'd taken that decision – to stand with Sarah Tucker rather than walk to safety – she'd known that beneath whatever rationalisation she'd cite, whether of valour or morality, lay her sense of self. Whichever course she'd chosen, that was who she'd be for the rest of her life. The woman who'd stayed or the one who'd walked away. What she hadn't realised was that being the one who'd stayed wouldn't necessarily make her feel better afterwards. But either way, that Zoë had at least cared: cared about what people thought of her, and cared too about Sarah Tucker. She wouldn't be pondering her choices on a bench outside the tourist office. She'd have felt no more for Wensley Deepman than this Zoë, but she'd have known what was right. In the long run, she was already involved – this Zoë/that Zoë. Both of them.

The bright sun caught the windscreen of a London coach pulling in, and its reflection smashed into supernova, dazzling her the way tears might. For a moment she could see nothing for the bright ghosts seared on to each retina: sunbursts and lava spray. But slowly vision returned, and with it a little clarity of thought; a little insight. She was frightened of having cancer. That wasn't outrageous: a lot of people were. But she was nearer than many, at this point in her life, to the reality. So much of the woman she'd continue to be, or grow into being, depended on the envelope that hadn't arrived; the appointment she'd yet to keep. And what was she doing to hold that at bay? – she was dazzling herself with her own private sunburst; a distraction from the cold possibility of her near future. What, after all, did she know about Alan Talmadge? One CD on a dead woman's player; one vinyl forty-five among another's lost possessions. All she knew was nothing. She was kidding herself. She had cancer.

And maybe it's this that brings back the pricking at her neck. Maybe it's nothing external at all, but a fear of what lies within. And as she stands, acting on a decision she hardly knows she's made yet, the old words come back to her, cast in a different form: that she has nothing to fear but fear itself; that she has nothing to fear but herself.

15

*S*HE DOESN'T SEE ME, *he decides, because she's not ready to see me yet.*

This is a satisfying explanation, as it covers many ponderables. He has been watching her for days, and if what he's read is true – and he has no reason to disbelieve it; her appearance, somehow, verifies her reputation – she should have noticed him: this is her domain, her duty; she sees things others don't, finds things they have lost. That's the story in those internetted abstracts he's uncovered; the mini-histories culled from tabloids and the occasional official report, pasted on to the ether by men with an interest in women who've taken life. So if she hasn't seen him, it's because she's not ready to. That explains her lack of observation. Though it's also a testament to the subtlety of his approaches.

And he's not immune to alternative possibilities. Perhaps she's distracted by an as yet unrevealed heartbreak. That can take the edge off a woman (he knows this), and there are men who'd regard it as weakness, but he recognises it for what it is: a courage most men aren't aware exists. Men hurt themselves because they blunder into havoc unaware, but women walk wide-eyed into the danger. That's the difference. If she has a heartbreak, he'll find out what it is. He's just getting started.

As for her, she's moving; rising from her bench as if released by a starting gun. And watching her, he's aware of her body; not just that she's in good shape – note that he doesn't add the poisonous for her age – *but that she houses various tensions that exercise, always supposing she takes any, can't reconcile. She has set herself at an angle to the world, and this is part of her allure; her willingness to go to battle to defend her right to suffer. He finds this incredibly moving. And all the while she too is moving, of course, and she moves right on to that London coach.*

He watches while she produces money, buys a ticket, chooses a seat; becomes semi-anonymous behind metalwork and glass, and for a moment he imagines boarding, sitting next to her, enjoying her reaction. What are you doing here? *she'd ask.* Shouldn't you be at work? *And he'd laugh it off, discover a plausible reason, and they'd smile and joke all the way to the city . . .*

The bus is away, out of the station; a foul exhaust storm in its wake, despite its company's claims to the contrary. And then only the cloud shows it was ever there; that and (he'd like to pretend) a similar ghostly energy on the bench where she'd been sitting; in the air she passed through, heading for the bus. This was a spur of the moment decision. When she left her flat, she had no plans beyond shopping. Don't ask him why he's sure of this. It's to do with the connection between them; the perfect understanding she's not yet aware of.

(This is one of his truths: that love is clairvoyance. Love means knowing what happens next. Or at the very least, love is the ability to improvise, so that when the unexpected happens next, love is quick to catch up, and make as if it never faltered. Like love knows what it's doing all the time.)

The night he followed her from Caroline's, he immersed himself in researches into the small hours – her address gave him her name, gave him her job, her car, her history. Her whole life unfolded in a pixel stream. And as knowledge gathered in his head like bees, he kept recalling the way she'd looked, walking home in the dark: a woman carrying a burden she had no intention of dropping; no intention of anyone knowing about. Nothing catches the heart like vulnerability unwittingly revealed. This was the chorus of his thoughts, later, as he attached the tracking device to her car's undercarriage.

And now he is moving too, before his vigil attracts notice, though he appreciates that that's not likely, on this crowded corner. And if it does, what of it? – he's in love with a departing passenger: that's all the explanation necessary. Which is why the songs last for ever, the ones that tell you that love satisfies everybody; that love is the answer.

He checks his pocket for his mobile. There it is. He checks around for unwarranted attention. There isn't any. And he knows that if he were a woman there wouldn't have been this same indifference; if he were a woman there'd have been sizings up and markings down; there'd have been that almost but not quite inaudible muttering that follows a woman everywhere, until she's of an age to lay male interest to rest. But not for him; for him, only the white noise of human traffic and motorised locomotion. It's not difficult, being invisible. It's only exactly as difficult as being charming, but in reverse. He leaves the bus station. In the air all around him, in the sky above, in the expressions of passing strangers, nothing happens.

16

'IT'S NOW.'

'What is?'

'The inquest.'

'Aren't you going?'

He regarded her with a mournful face that put Zoë in mind of wet newspaper. Since Friday Joseph Deepman had lost an inch of height, as if he were one of those complicated buildings in the City that adjust their dimensions to fit the burdens they accommodate. And what he was accommodating was death. This hit her like a blow to the breast. Why had she just now noticed this? He was sheltering death, and not only his grandson's; he was carrying his own as if it were a load of shopping that needed fetching up to the fourteenth floor, on a day the lifts were down. One word of permission, and he'd let that shopping fall. And she pictured the contents of a long life spilling from torn carrier bags down flight after flight of stairs: youth work marriage daughter grandson food drink lies. All tumbling into chaos at the bottom, while many landings above an empty husk relaxed at last.

He was waiting for a response, but the last question she'd heard was her own.

To cover her lapse she said, 'Have you been eating?'

The words, in the hallway of his dismal flat, sounded like accusation. What are you chewing? Spit it out.

He shuffled into his kitchen. After a moment, Zoë followed.

More debris had accumulated since Chris's attempt to clean up on Friday, which at least answered her query. Two empty tins sat by the sink; one had held sausage and beans, the other beans. Sauce trimmed their rims like savoury lipstick. Her stomach threatened revolt, whether in hunger or disgust she wasn't sure.

He said, 'Why would anybody want me there?'

'You're his grandfather.'

He sighed, wetly. She'd have liked to grip his shoulders and shake life into him.

For something to do, she set the kettle boiling. It shook and rattled, like old-time rock and roll. 'When did you last see him?' This earned a blank look. 'Wensley, Mr Deepman. When was the last time you saw him?'

'The day before.'

'The day before he died?'

He nodded.

Zoë found cups, and rinsed them. 'What was he doing for money?'

It was an unfamiliar sound, his next. She had to check to make sure. But it was true: he was laughing, if mirthlessly. 'Same as always,' he said, when the tremors ceased. 'On the rob. Is that tea you're making?'

'It can be. He told somebody he was coming into money. How was that?'

'Not likely to tell me, was he?'

'I don't know, Mr Deepman,' she said with studied patience. 'That's why I'm asking.'

And it was his turn to regard her, as if he'd just noticed she had no great call to be here; that her questions were her own; that she might leave at any moment.

'He told me nothing,' he said at length. 'Wensley . . . didn't tell me nothing.'

Then, in a bewildering display of hostly control, he opened a cupboard and found teabags.

She put them in the cups, added hot water, and stared at the wall while they brewed. There was no window. Only the front room had windows, which gave out on the walkway: you could see sky, and the companion block across the way, but from inside you couldn't see down. You could be scared of heights, and stay unbothered.

As if reading her mind, he said, 'You get used to it. You could be underground, really. 'Stead of halfway up the sky.'

'He didn't like heights, did he?'

'He never admitted being scared.'

She fished the bag from his mug, and added milk. He said, 'But he didn't like heights. No.'

Zoë said, 'So . . .'

His blank stare told her she'd have to spell it out.

'Mr Deepman. If he didn't like heights, what was he doing on the roof of a tower block?'

'I don't know.'

Nobody knew anything. That's why her job kept on going.

She had made herself tea, and she didn't want tea. A small problem in the scale of things. 'I spoke to a friend of his,' she said after a moment. 'He told me Wensley only came here when he needed somewhere to hide.'

Joseph Deepman gave this some thought. Whatever conclusion he reached expressed itself as a shrug.

'So you've no idea who he might have been hiding from?' she persisted. 'The day before he died?'

'You think somebody killed him?'

'I don't know what I think.' She thought he was quicker than she'd given him credit for. 'I'm just asking questions.'

'You ask more than the police bothered.'

'I don't think the local cops were too fond of your grandson.'

'Not only them.' He looked down at his cup, then at the

floor, as if he'd just become aware that he was standing up and drinking. 'I want to sit.'

He carried his tea to the other room. Leaving hers by the sink, Zoë followed. When you acted on impulse, this was what you suffered: consequences. She'd boarded the bus in Oxford because it seemed the right thing to do at the time; because Alan Talmadge was less real than her own problems; because she wasn't sure she wasn't kidding herself in what she thought she knew about him. Wensley Deepman, though, had been indisputably alive; was indubitably dead. This was less a mystery to Zoë than a foregone conclusion, but it bothered her that Tom Connor had checked up on her. He'd established who she was on Saturday. Why had he talked to Bob Poland?

Deepman's cup was balanced on the arm of his chair, and he was staring at the TV set, Zoë's old set, though it was off. 'He had no friends round here. There're people glad he's dead.'

Some kind of response seemed called for. Zoë, unable to think of one, stayed silent.

'One of the neighbours, he had his pension from him once. Never spoken to me since.'

Between the tortured pronouns, Zoë saw frosty meetings on stairwells and in lifts; looks cast like daggers at retreating backs.

He lapsed into quiet again. Zoë was thinking: maybe the little bastard deserved it. On any ranking of the not much missed, Kid B scored about the same as Charles Parsley Sturrock. She shook away these probably vile thoughts, and noticed the empty bottle in the bin. Friday's alcohol.

Association prompted, 'Have you seen Chris?'

He looked at her blankly.

'Chris? Who was here Friday?'

'Oh. He said he'd come back. And he did.'

'Since Friday?'

'On Friday.'

173

Some conversations it was best to escape from as quickly as possible.

'I have to go,' she said. She was tired again. Last night's sleep had been the usual aggravated nuisance, like hunting somebody through a viciously thorned maze.

'You're going to the inquest?'

'That was not my intention.'

Strange how sentences came out formal when they least needed to be. No fucking way, she'd meant.

'Somebody should be there.'

'Somebody no doubt will be.'

On the walkway the chill wind slapped her sideways like a cardiac incident. It brought tears to her eyes, the way things used to do. She paused to catch breath, to get steady – to feel, perhaps, the icicle stab of the weather; to *punish* herself: what for? – and heard Joseph Deepman's telephone ring inside his flat. So she wasn't the only one spared him the odd thought. This ought to have eased whatever it was she carried, flight by flight, down fourteen floors, because the lifts were broken again.

On the street she looked round for her car, feeling a brief flare of fear-cum-outrage at its absence, before remembering she was on foot. There was barely a soul in sight – an elderly woman doing the corner shop shuffle; a man watching his unleashed dog crap on the pavement. The wind kicked hell out of an empty lunch bag. No way was she going to the bloody inquest, damn it. There was no obligation laid on her. She'd left no debts unpaid. Zoë felt the first heavy drops of rain begin to batter as she reached the junction, as she stood there for a full half-minute, with no idea where she was headed next.

At the library, the computer area was decorated with a mural made by pupils from a local primary school: it pictured a green field grazed by fat and stupid sheep; an image of the countryside designed by city children who didn't know much about it but suspected it was rubbish. Ignoring it, she went looking for Wensley Deepman, who was dead. This was the first thing you noticed about him, trawling the Web: all the hits were recent, and all concerned his death. That was as much footprint as he'd leave: this ghostly electric newsprint, describing his end on an unforgiving pavement.

But last time she'd hunted Wensley, all she'd wanted was his address; now, she devoured the details of his passing. The *Guardian* had covered it in depth; most of the others had let it drown in the wash from the week's big story: the death of Charles Parsley Sturrock. The tower block he'd fallen from hadn't been anything like the forty storeys Bob Poland had quoted, but anything over ground level was high when you hit the road head first. She had a sudden dizzying moment, living it – the acceleration beyond anything achievable by non-fatal means, and then the dead stop, sudden as a diagnosis. A bead of sweat trickled down her back: what is this? she thought. This isn't about me. Some kid I never knew; some kid I swore at, long ago. One of the tabloids had run with it a little, once its angle was established. *Death plunge boy was tear-away.* Another way of saying that everything worked out for the best in the long run.

It was the *Guardian* that confirmed the half-remembered detail she'd taxed Tom Connor with: that there had been a witness; a man who, from the ground, had seen Wensley leave the roof. His name wasn't given. (*Not everybody wants to be a celebrity*, Connor had said, his voice tightening with the words, as if Zoë were a rubbernecker at a traffic accident.) The boy jumped, said the witness. Stood on the ledge and spread his arms like the Angel of the North. The block had been just west of the City, not far from where Zoë had grabbed Andrew Kite, and transported him home to his parents. A life's small circle, though this circle had a finishing point.

. . . *record of street crime* . . .

. . . *involvement with drugs* . . .

The witness would be at the inquest; the story would roll on the same. Wensley Deepman had killed himself.

Other stories, meanwhile, unfolded, only a mouse click away. The internet was another version of that maze of connecting doors, through which you could wander secure in the knowledge that there was no way you'd truly lose yourself, except you always did. On the newspaper's opening page she found Charles Parsley Sturrock: the familiar photo, with that fuck-you grin that was his default expression. Until they took him into the car park, probably. Which, she saw, was just this side of the City: a long way from Sturrock's own patch, but not that far from Wensley's. Calling up a map, she pinned the distance to less than a mile, which was neither too small nor too big to be anything other than what it was: a fact. Playing with it further would be like rearranging sheep in a field. Sooner or later you'd find a pattern, but only because you wanted one.

That was always the danger. That you'd end up designing your own maze, just to be sure you'd know your way out again.

The inquest had taken place in the magistrates' court not far from where Wensley Deepman had died, as if in this, too, he'd been keen to demonstrate how circumscribed a life could be when its poles were street crime and thuggery. By the time Zoë arrived, it was over. From one of the news crews on the pavement she learned the verdict: misadventure. It was the one preferred to suicide when there was family extant, or a child involved. She lit a cigarette and held back, keen not to step into camera view. The red-brick building was tall and flat-faced. Its barred windows put Zoë in mind of orphanages.

When people began emerging it was clear who the focus was on. There was nothing like a grieving mother to shift copy. Jet – the name came back like magic; Joseph Deepman saying *It was her mother's idea. It means a stone, not an aeroplane* – Jet Deepman leaned on her man's arm, her bright blonde hair belying her name. If that was natural, Zoë didn't smoke. Zoë smoked. Jet wore a black dress, which showed she'd read some of the etiquette books, but even from here Zoë could see the scarlet tips to her fingers. It was easy to judge, so Zoë judged. The man she leaned on was broad and solid: black, bald, wearing a rather fine knee-length coat. His expression in the face of press attention was utterly inscrutable.

Jet Deepman, though, wept as if she'd had lessons.

Zoë watched for a while, thinking about motherhood. Some instincts, you couldn't fake. Love was inimitable, evidently. There were times she imagined she'd felt that tug – had wondered what it would be like, being woken by a crying child – and expected, in all honesty, she'd have fallen short. She'd always been too much Zoë to happily submit to another's demands. But a small steady part of her was sure she'd not have touched up her nail polish to attend her child's inquest. She dropped her cigarette, ground it underfoot, kicked it into the gutter.

'You're Zoë Boehm.'

She looked round. The speaker was mid-forties, tall and lean, with thinning sandy hair, and that seen-it-all edge Bob Poland affected sometimes: enough of a clue for Zoë. Cop. He must be Tom Connor; Tom Connor in tan chinos and dark jacket, an expertly knotted black tie. Tom Connor wore thin-framed spectacles; behind them, had brown eyes with lines creeping away from their corners, like fine fractures. Tom Connor wasn't smiling. Tom Connor looked like the kind of cop you didn't want to meet when you were guilty, and possibly the kind of cop you didn't want to meet, full stop. Bob Poland must have described her to him.

'DI Connor,' she said.

A blink was as much surprise as he showed. 'You're still ferreting, then.'

'Interested party.'

'Who lives in Oxford. Who isn't getting paid.'

Zoë said, 'You know a lot about my business.'

'None of which you're denying. Thanks. I will.'

She was holding her cigarettes, so extended the pack. He slipped one free and held it between finger and thumb, as if it were a whole new experience.

He said, 'Public spirit, that's good. Nothing like seeing a member of the GBP taking an interest in the workings of justice.'

'You're about to say "but".'

He leaned close for a light. As soon as he had one he dropped the cigarette, and trod it out. 'Filthy habit.'

This was meant to annoy her. She said, 'That's pretty clever.'

'Biggest favour anyone'll do you all day. You're right, Ms Boehm, there's a but. There's a big difference between taking an interest and interfering. There's nothing to find out.' His voice was surprisingly gentle: that was probably an asset. Cops, you expected to be brusque and loud. When they weren't, it took you aback. You might end up believing their every word. 'A boy's dead. Very sad, but nobody's fault. All you're doing is upsetting people.'

'Like you?'

'Ms Boehm, I don't want to come across like some pillock from the TV. But you're way off home ground. If I say you're upsetting people, you're upsetting people.'

'Go go go,' said Zoë.

'What?'

She shrugged. 'That's what they say on *The Bill*, isn't it? I don't have a telly.'

He said, 'The coroner's verdict's in. Misadventure. We both know she was being kind. The kid killed himself.'

'If you say so.'

'I just did. So it's over. You can leave now.'

'Last I checked, I still had freedom of movement.'

'Okay. That was inappropriate. But there's nothing to find out. We know what happened. We've drawn a line.'

Her next cigarette was still unlit. She remedied this, while wondering how to respond. He was a clean-looking cop – not just the tie, the jacket, the close shave, but what he didn't have: the weasel glint to the eye that told you he was in it for himself. You couldn't spend more than ten minutes with Bob Poland without knowing he was after a bite. Of course, it was always possible Tom Connor was better at undercover.

'Zoë.'

Both turned as if operated by the same string. It was Chris, whom Zoë had met last Friday at Joseph Deepman's. Slightly dressier (black jacket, black jeans, white shirt), but otherwise still pale and plucked. In daylight, his buzz-cut looked like a fight he'd lost.

'I didn't mean to interrupt,' he said, and she realised they'd been staring at him, wordlessly.

'Chris,' she said. 'This is Detective Inspector Connor.'

Zoë thought it wise to make clear who was the policeman. 'Chris Langley.'

Connor nodded, without offering his hand.

Chris said to Zoë, 'I just thought somebody ought to be here. For the old man. The daughter tells him nothing.'

'I was late, myself.'

He said, 'It was the usual thing.' He looked round. Cameras were still running; Jet still crying. She looked capable of continuing for as long as the situation demanded.

'You'd be a friend of the family?' asked Connor.

'Of the grandfather.'

'Give him my condolences.' He looked at Zoë. 'I don't mean to come on the hard guy. But all this, it's done with. People get aggravated, people get upset. When it's the death of a black kid, well. We don't want anybody making more of it than it is. I'm sure you appreciate that.'

Chris Langley was watching this conversation more than listening to it; watching, too, the way she raised her cigarette to her lips. Zoë was having one of those slightly hyperreal moments: time slows down, and every action seems invested with a significance beyond reason. She inhaled, then dropped the cigarette. How many was that today? It was a good job she'd cut down, else she'd probably be dead by now.

. . . She was tired and pissed off, and really needed to get a grip. 'Was he carrying cash?'

'Was who carrying cash?'

'Wensley. He was coming into money. So he said.'

'As far as I'm aware,' Connor said carefully, 'his pockets were empty.'

'As far as you're aware.'

'They were empty.'

'Did you know he was scared of heights?'

'No. I'd say it was a moot point now, though.'

'He was running a scam, Inspector. Something he'd seen, something he'd heard.'

'He was always running a scam. Mostly the smash and grab kind.'

'But maybe he got ambitious. Maybe he was putting the squeeze on somebody. That's the sort can easily go wrong.'

Connor looked at Chris, newly aware they had an audience. He turned back to Zoë. 'I don't recall that being mentioned inside.'

'Little bits. Details. They add up.'

'Ms Boehm? Do you have anything you want to make official?'

'She's only saying,' Chris said.

They both stared. He flushed.

'She's only saying, maybe not enough attention's been paid. He was a kid. He's dead. He might have been a handful. That doesn't make it right.'

There was an edge to Connor's voice when he said, 'I don't think any of us are saying it's right.'

'Well . . .'

Zoë said again, 'Details add up.'

'Coincidence.'

'Is that the best you can do?'

Tom Connor nearly smiled. 'If they didn't happen, we wouldn't have a word for them.'

'Are you working the Sturrock case?'

If the switch fazed him, it didn't show. 'Not my patch.'

'Not far, though.'

'Borders have to happen somewhere.' He looked at Chris as if about to say more, but unsure what it should be. Chris had that earnest, left-leaning, actions-speak-louder air that worked on policemen the way salt works on wounds. Except Connor had used 'inappropriate', so maybe he'd had sensitivity training. He turned back to Zoë. 'You have a point?'

'He was a street kid. Maybe he heard something.'

'I thought you said you didn't have a telly?'

'Who was the witness?'

He said, 'Ms Boehm, I don't want to appear rude, but you've had your fifteen minutes of fame. Was that not enough?'

Zoë said, 'You've looked me up.'

He glanced at Chris, then back at her. 'You shot a man. Killed him. He wasn't armed.'

'He was armed.'

'Reports vary.'

'I don't give a fuck what reports do. He was armed.'

Along the pavement, the news crews were packing up. Maybe Jet Deepman had stopped crying. Chris was watching Zoë, his expression unreadable. This might have been the most shocking thing ever. It might have been an update on the weather.

She noticed, as if it were happening to somebody else, that she was trembling. *Zoë is trembling.*

And said, 'My history has nothing to do with this.'

'Not everything you're involved in has to be newsworthy.'

'That's not what this is about.'

'No?'

Her mouth dried. Behind his glasses, Connor's eyes narrowed. She'd lost the ability to read: maybe there was sympathy there; maybe contempt.

He said, 'Either way, perhaps he was asking to be shot. That happens sometimes.'

Her voice returned. 'You're saying Wensley—'

'I'm saying, don't make something out of nothing. People can get the wrong impression. Reports vary. The truth doesn't.'

Chris said, as if it remained the important thing, 'He was just a kid.'

'Nobody's forgotten that. It's a sad event. But don't—' He turned from Chris to Zoë to continue. 'Don't go taking minor details and building fantasies on them. Coincidences happen. They mean nothing.'

'Like dates.'

'Like what?'

She said, 'I was thinking about birthdays. It wasn't important.'

Everyone leaks history. Stray remarks draw blood, sometimes. Tom Connor stared and she saw she'd hit a chord, the way it can happen with strangers.

He said, 'It would have been nice to have met differently. After what Bob Poland said about you.'

This alarmed her. 'He spoke highly?'

'No. But he's always struck me as a prick. Goodbye, Ms Boehm.' He nodded at Chris, and left.

So then there were two, standing on the pavement, watching the policeman walking away.

After a while, Chris said, 'That was like arriving right in the middle of the show. I have no idea what's going on.'

'Welcome to my world.'

'You're some kind of detective, aren't you?'

'Some kind.'

182

'What did he mean, about you shooting somebody?'

'It was a long time ago,' said Zoë. 'I don't make a habit of it.'

The last of the journalists was looking their way, wondering whether they'd amount to a paragraph. Evidently not. He held up his hand and a black cab appeared and pulled a U-turn to reach him. Zoë had never seen this done before. Everyone else – Jet Deepman, her man; the kind and the curious – had left.

'So,' said Chris. 'Well . . .'

'Tell the old man I'm sorry,' she said.

'You won't be seeing him again?'

'No.' What would be the point? But because she was, after all, some kind of detective, she asked, 'Did you ring him, Chris? A short while ago?'

He paused before answering, as if assessing her right to know. 'I did, actually. Why?'

'No reason.' It was a mystery solved, that was all, and it was good to clear up even the small ones.

He *was* armed, she wanted to tell him. But why did she need him to believe that?

She told him goodbye instead. He seemed an all-right man, but there was no serious need to prolong their conversation. She didn't look back as she headed up the road, and reasoned that, even if she had done, he'd be gone anyway.

Zoë needed to get west, to pick up her bus. The rain had subsided, but would return before long; the skies were scribbled over grey, and the pavements had a dirty, half-washed look, as if the shower had simply smeared their grime, releasing sealed-in odours. It was the smell of rained-on overcoats. Something to look forward to on the Tube.

The best she could figure, walking to King's Cross was simplest. The walk would do her good. Orienting herself by a street map on a corner – trusting that its stylised angles, its shading away of complicated junctions, wouldn't leave her lost in minutes – she cut through a park to a thriving little street with a delicatessen, where she bought everything she hadn't bought that morning. It was late before she moved on; offices were closing, and the streets becoming crowded. Beyond the pedestrian area lay a main road, which she crossed at a set of lights. Halfway over, she knew she was being followed . . .

It was nothing solid. It wasn't as if she'd looked back to see the same stranger twice. It was just a pricking between her shoulder blades, like this morning back home – but how likely was it she'd been followed from Oxford without noticing? And you couldn't second guess a journey that hadn't been planned.

When she turned, the crowd was the usual fluid monster, weaving in and out of itself like a box of snakes; never quite knotting, never falling still. There should have been a snarl-up; the follower should have tried to fall back, or veer aside, but whatever happened happened so smoothly, it might not have happened at all. People wove on, breaking round her, reforming; the obstacle she presented no more than half a moment's interruption, and less thought.

Either he was very good, or he wasn't there.

She stood a little longer, oblivious to the picture she presented. There were instincts she trusted, and the sense of being watched ranked high among them, but what if that too was falling apart? – after all, she had trusted her body; relied on it to carry her through life, and here it was: attacking her from the inside, eating itself, until what was left would mulch at the touch like forgotten fruit. *Stop it, Zoë.* She was bumped, quite fiercely, probably deliberately, from behind, and for a moment lost her direction; she moved, stopped, corrected herself; made sure she was heading for the station . . .

From the corner of her eye, she caught a hesitation in the crowd.

It was that tiny. It might have been a man wondering which

pocket his keys were in, or a woman hearing her mobile chirp. A fractional hiccup almost smothered by the Brownian movement of the homeward-bound. Any other time she'd have shrugged it off, but now it registered loud and clear, and she knew that all the day's tiny misgivings were proven; that somewhere within this anonymity, a watcher had her in his sights. The knowledge shifted something heavy within her, and for a moment she felt redefined; felt downgraded from Zoë to victim, as if that were all it took: a brief anonymous hostility from deep within a crowd. She had to take an almost physical grip on herself to know where she stood; who she was; why she mattered. It was . . . *pug-ugly* that this could happen; one creep of a man (it had to be a man), reducing her to a cipher. It was fucking outrageous. It wasn't going to happen.

. . . A week ago, days ago, feelings like this were alien. She'd been numb. Closed down. It was the waiting, she knew; the waiting for the envelope . . . The possibility of a lethal diagnosis – or a mutilating one – had rebuilt her connection to the everyday. Had reminded her what vulnerability felt like.

As if to underline the matter, the skies opened.

King's Cross lay ahead, a busy throng cramming its concourse. As she watched, the crowd bloomed sudden mushrooms; dozens of umbrellas opening at once like something in a musical. And the rain heaved down; thick unbroken lines of it, or unbroken until it met umbrellas, car tops, gutters, heads, whereupon it spattered in all directions at once. Zoë had slipped into professional mode; trying to watch everything, without giving the impression of doing so. This crowd was a practised one. People moved quickly, to minimise the rain's impact, but obeyed an urban choreography that allowed for few outright collisions . . . Reaching the junction, Zoë stepped into the road a second late, and the blast of a horn drove her back. Kerb water kissed her legs. Turning, she saw nothing she didn't know about. Buildings, roads and rain; a hustling mass of nameless humanity.

Lights changed. She crossed the road without looking back again.

And then she was in the station, which was dry overhead and wet underfoot, and she almost missed her footing. Somebody shoved her in passing, but this wasn't hostile; just how things were. The shover disappeared into the underground. Zoë followed to find tropical warmth; people visibly steaming all around her. A man paused to wipe his glasses on his tie. She fell in step with him and they headed for the turnstiles together; anyone would have thought them a couple. But he peeled off suddenly, as if worried he was being collected, and she was on her own, without a ticket. But if she altered course now – for the machines or the queue at the booth – she'd be losing minutes, and all she had going for her was that her watcher didn't know she knew he was there . . . She had to make him hurry. She couldn't hang about.

Alongside the turnstiles people pressed through a gate, showing tickets to a uniformed man. Zoë squeezed behind a fat guy with a briefcase the size of an ironing board; he thrust a pass at Ticket Man, who glanced, nodded, turned to Zoë just as that briefcase caught her knee; she'd have hit the floor if not for Ticket Man's reflexes . . .

'A'right, there?'

He'd caught her by the elbow. She gave him her most grateful smile. It had been a slick fall. It had looked real. 'Thanks. I'm . . . thanks.'

'Got your ticket, lady?'

'Yes, it's in my . . .'

Behind her people surged. It was like the zoo at feeding time: everybody trying to get to the lions' cage. Somebody stepped on Zoë's ankle, and this hurt. Somebody else, or possibly the same somebody, pushed past, and Ticket Man released her to remonstrate – 'I didn't see your ticket!'

Or Zoë's. She was through; swept like a cork on a current

down the escalator. There was a train leaving, and for a moment she wasn't sure if she wanted to catch it or not . . . She'd be leaving him behind, but didn't she want to see who he was, what he looked like? She wasn't scared, was she? Didn't matter: the doors' pips sounded; she had a hand to the glass as it pulled away. When she turned her face was fixed into a snarl; a look, if she'd seen it on anyone else, she'd have crossed the road to avoid.

Somebody said, 'Jesus. Two minutes, bitch.'

Which was what the electric overhead said: two minutes. People were flooding the platform: all with homes to go to, and anxious to get there. Every face was a stranger's, and none was pointed her way.

Two minutes, her inner Zoë stated flatly. One thirty. No sweat.

Move down the platform, a tannoyed voice suggested. She felt calmer; there was nothing like having an option removed to force focus on the here and now. She moved down the platform. The voice said *Owing to an event on the District line,* but detail deconstructed into static. 'An event' was code for 'death'. Along with 'incident,' 'passenger action,' and, sometimes, 'death'. *Owing to an event on the District line* something was either about to happen or not about to happen. She stepped back against the platform wall; tried to capture the gathering crowd; its constituent elements of faces, hands, gestures. Somewhere in this sinuous mass was a man who was following her. Realistically, it could only be one man. For all her earlier doubts, he existed. Alan Talmadge had tracked her to London.

You couldn't argue, in the end, with your instincts. So maybe she was paranoid, a little. The right amount. It wasn't a bad thing. Paranoia was akin to love: it heightened your senses, peeled a layer away, left you tender to the lightest touch. With this difference: it was intended to protect. You could imagine it deserting you, your ability to recognise danger, but it came back when it mattered.

And then he stepped clear of the crowd, and she saw him.

He was looking her way, and he was good, but not good enough: the moment he glimpsed her a little of his tension dissolved, as if he'd been worried he'd lost her. But here she was. And there he was: older than she'd have expected; about six foot, with hair (the hair he liked to drag a hand through) that began way back on his forehead, growing in tight greasy curls like a farmyard pelt. This, too, was not as advertised. But the predatory element was present and correct. The moment he saw her, he knew she'd seen him too, and pegged him for what he was. And he smiled, a smile stripped to the bone of kindness and humour. There was conversation here, over ten yards' distance; conversation so loud, she was amazed nobody could hear it.

You can't run.

I can run.

You can't hide.

And you can't touch me. Her eyes left his for half a second, taking in the crowd around them. *You think you can touch me here?*

You think they'll help?

And she couldn't answer, because you could never tell. Did she think they'd help?

Something was coming. She could hear it in the track, and feel it in the draught shifting litter along the rails. And in that moment, she knew exactly how it had been for Caroline Daniels; standing on a platform, with a crowd pressing close. Like a train, Alan Talmadge had been approaching, and causing things to happen before he got there. Causing Caroline's surroundings to be the last she'd know: this press of people, with their smells and noises; those raucous adverts; that chocolate machine somebody was thumping, because it didn't work. Unseen, Caroline's lover had stepped behind her, and ended her life with a well-timed push . . . How would anybody know? A crowd couldn't tell what was happening in its heart.

He had pushed her unseen, and walked away. And he was walking towards her now.

The train thundered into the station. There was a surge, as people jockeyed for position. Most of Zoë's recent life had involved trains and buses. She stood unmoving for a moment, trying to relocate Talmadge, who'd disappeared in the mass. This was his talent: not being there any more . . . People were boarding and Talmadge was still lost, unless that was his arm hanging out of the door, next carriage down – a dark sleeve, an overcoat: did this match what he'd been wearing? She could stay where she was; he'd jump right off. Then they'd still be here, but with fewer people around. She stepped in, forcing room, while those already on board squeezed back, making a Zoë-shaped space for her, or possibly one a little smaller. Facing downtrain, she tried to see into the next carriage. X-ray vision might have helped. Short of that, she was dreaming.

And her heart was pounding. She was crammed between two males: a young black man in pinstripes and an older white guy wearing bin-lid earphones – huge, with no sound leaking out, though his head nodded in synch with their noiseless rhythms. It kept brushing Zoë's hair, but she was too anxious about Talmadge, about where precisely he was now, to dwell on it.

. . . Unless it wasn't Talmadge. Did this look like a man sensible women might love? Like a man with music in him? And how, anyway, had he followed her? It was an unpleasant thought, akin to finding spiders in bed. He might have been tracking her since that evening at Caroline's. All the while she'd been mapping the house, looking for his traces, he'd been outside spinning webs. She shuddered. The young black man opened his eyes . . . For a second they stared at each other, inches apart. Then, embarrassed, he looked away as the train slowed, and a new station rolled past the windows.

Few people disembarked. A slightly larger number got on.

Zoë would have stepped on to the platform, if only to see if Talmadge did the same from the next carriage along, but trapped in the crush, she was subject to its intentions. It didn't intend that she do any such thing. There was no room for frivolous movement here. She let out an involuntary sigh, which bothered no one. Then closed her eyes, in case that helped. The doors beeped; the train shuddered, and pulled into deeper darkness. When she opened her eyes, she was looking straight at him.

. . . It might have been worse. She might have gasped or shrieked. As it was, there was a kind of inevitability to the moment, one her body seemed aware of before the rest of her caught up. Of course he'd changed carriages; that's just what he'd do. And what else had the past days been working towards? You could not hunt somebody without ending up this close: not if you were Zoë Boehm. Even if you'd wondered whether they truly existed. So her body, which had much to atone for, did right; she neither gasped nor shrieked, but stayed as calm as if she were studying an aquarium, and this man were an entirely expected shark.

He smiled from a two-foot distance. The only barrier between them was a young Asian woman with a tiny jewel stud through her nose.

What were her options? She could point and scream. But madwomen melted down in the Tube all the time. People pretended something else was happening, or watched to kill the time until their stop. What they didn't do was anything about it. Never wedge yourself between a screamer and her psychosis.

Besides, she was Zoë Boehm. Never a screamer.

His teeth were small but sharp in his orcish smile, and was she imagining them flecked with white scum? In his eyes she recognised a look she associated with her own worst mornings. She couldn't believe these people were indifferent to this; couldn't sense a soul gone bad in their midst.

There was a change in the rhythms around them as the train slowed without reaching anywhere. The crowd swore silently. Knowledge hardwired within it recognised which slowings-down meant stations, and which a ten-minute wait in the dark. The Asian woman sneezed loudly into her open hand. The train heaved to a halt, and lighting flickered.

It was as if he caused this too: trains to stop, lights to dim. And finding herself imagining so she squeezed the fist that held the carrier bag from the deli. *This man will not do this to me.* He had the look of a late-night caller, a lurker on corners, and again she half doubted he could be Talmadge, because this was not a man to win a woman's heart. Not a woman with history; one who knew her mind.

But who else could he be?

The sudden pull of motion would have had her on the floor, if there'd been room. Relief rippled the carriage like wind through leaves. The train shunted. Talmadge licked his lips, and she had the immediate disgusting thought that he'd like to lick hers. Her natural response – *In your fucking dreams* – she swallowed. The train picked up speed. The young woman pressed closely against her as another man edged for the door. It helped, if this was your life, to know which side the platforms fell.

Light burst all around as the train smashed into the station.

It slowed, it stopped, doors opened. There was more traffic; more people alighting. It was easier to go with the flow, so she stepped out while passengers disembarked, her eyes never leaving might-be-Talmadge, who hovered by the open doors. She was boiling up inside, and the Zoë who'd stopped feeling anything slipped further from view. When those waiting climbed on board she climbed with them, pushing past Talmadge as if he were just another traveller, then swivelling to face the back of his head. She let her bag drop to the floor.

He turned as the beeps announced the closing of the doors. 'Mind the gap,' she said, and shoved him, hard. His face as he fell ran the cartoon gamut from fear to indignation to rage: he caught his balance by windmilling wildly on the platform – she thought the doors would open again, but they didn't – then imagined him hopping on one foot then the other, shaking his fist at the vanishing train. Hieroglyphics sprouting in a bubble above his head . . .

'You do realise,' said a measured male voice in her ear, 'that you could have killed that man?'

'Then he shouldn't have felt me up.'

'Reclaim the Tube,' said the Asian woman.

For a moment Zoë stepped into a sunlit meadow, its atmosphere rich with mown grass and lightly falling rain. And then she was back in captivity, crushed against these fellow subterraneans, the stink of stale tobacco on her clothes and theirs. And the train walloped back into darkness, and she picked up her carrier bag.

Adrenalin, when it went, took everything with it. Zoë slept on the bus back to Oxford. Dreams in a moving vehicle are shambolic, greasy affairs: in this one, Zoë pokes through a huge pile of junk with a sharp stick – garden rubbish, broken radios; the refuse from a thousand kitchen bins. She has to stop and rest every so often. Whatever she's doing, it's too much for her. And then the tip shifts, and he's breaking out of the mess beneath her feet. She steps back while he emerges into light. You're Alan Talmadge, is all she can think to say. No I'm not, he replies, and bares once more his weird unsuitable teeth. There's music playing, and she recognises the tune, but can't for her life recall the words. She's still trying when the bus reaches home; when its cessation of motion jolts her back into the real.

She almost left her shopping on board. She almost couldn't remember what it was. Stepping out on the High, she was glad of her leather jacket for the hundredth time that day; the world was in between showers again – the rain tracking her from London. Yawning, she walked. Taxis were decadent. Zoë had never quite freed herself of the habit of thinking so.

As for everything else, it was easier not to think, because every thought had the stale, wasted air of the underground. Had it really been Talmadge she'd pushed? How had he followed her, without her noticing? Creepier still was the ease with which she'd done it: pushed him from the train, the way he'd pushed Caroline, pushed Victoria . . . Push came to shove, and that was the way of it. But you know, she decided, as she headed into Jericho, I don't care. A man had stalked her, which only cowards and vermin did. She'd pushed him off a train. That seemed fair.

Turning off the main road, passing the fenced and empty children's playground and a row of parked cars, she felt rain again: if the day had a theme, it was that Zoë was going to get wet. But she wasn't far from her flat. She unzipped her jacket, and with her free hand probed her inside pocket for her keys. The streetlight up ahead was out. Civic souls made phone calls when this happened; Zoë, like most others, let them get on with it. Her carrier bag – which held pasta, olives, pimientos, oil, stuffed peppers, bread and anchovies – had grown heavier, but that was okay. She found her keys. Bob Poland stepped out of the shadows in front of her. 'You're not popular, are you, Zoë?' he asked. 'You dumb bitch. I told you your mouth would get you in trouble.'

She dropped her bag. Behind Bob, another shape appeared; the man from the Tube. There was someone behind her, too. It began raining in earnest.

FIVE

DIRECTION OF TRAVEL

17

H ANDS FELL ON HER shoulders and forced her down; she twisted aside, kicked Poland in the leg, and would have run but the hands grabbed her again. And then she was squirming, and her jacket slipped from her shoulders as the man from the Tube reached for her with a meaty, thick-fingered paw which held her breast in the least sexual way Zoë had ever been touched. It pushed her against a car, one without an alarm, though she made up for this with a full-throated scream that drew everything to a halt for half a second – there were three of them; three of them and Poland. This she took in while screaming.

A door opened over the way.

'What the *blue hell's* going on?'

Poland, limping over, was already pulling out his warrant card; holding up one calming hand.

Zoë seized breath.

The man from the Tube – no *way* was this Alan Talmadge – leaned and put his finger to her mouth. 'Shut. Your fucking. Face.'

She bit him.

He swore and bunched his hand into a fist. It would have been so final, if he'd done what he intended – even in that moment, scared and furious, Zoë knew this. It would have ended her normal life, if she'd been hit as hard as he wanted to hit her.

The second man stepped between them. 'Ross, are you out of your mind?'

He was talking to Tube Man.

Squashed hard against the car, Zoë blinked. A door handle clawed at her back.

A front door shut. Poland returned. The third man grabbed her left hand and cuffed her wrist before she knew what he was about. Oh Jesus, she thought, they're all cops. Then Poland was in front of her, the others shifting aside as if he mattered. 'I warned you about screwing with me,' he said. He'd prepared this beforehand. No way was he not going to say it. 'This didn't have to happen.'

It surprised her but her voice was still there: it even sounded steady. 'You're a bastard, Bob. This comes round. I promise.'

And he was doing it, the sad fuck, like he was taking part in his own private movie; tossing her a coin, which caught light from over his shoulder as he said his magic words: 'Yeah, right. Call your lawyer.'

With her free hand she snatched the coin out of the air.

You'll do that once too often . . .

He said, 'Whatever you think she did, she did it. Don't turn your back on her.' Then he turned and walked away, leaving Zoë with the three of them.

Man Two, the one who'd stopped her being punched, said, 'No more rough stuff. Let's be calm. But we have to cuff you. Put your hand out.'

'Fuck,' said Ross. 'You're asking?' Pushing him aside as he spoke; stretching for Zoë's left hand, which she snatched from the third man, one bangle of the cuffs hanging free.

It was a tableau moment. Four frozen figures; none of them touching, though all of them reaching, and about to connect.

With her free hand, finger and thumb, Zoë flicked the coin as hard as she could into Ross's eye, then ducked beneath his outstretched hand and ran.

Leaving pain. She had heard terrible sounds before – the worst was the silence after she'd shot a man; the way he died without making a noise, though the expression on his face, for the short time she'd left him with either of those things worth mentioning, had indicated his grave disappointment with the turn events were taking – but Ross's cry was really bad, and bounced off the architecture all around as she hit the corner running. This would have the neighbourhood opening doors. Running without ever stopping was a good idea. There was no way she wanted to encounter Ross again in this life.

. . . Or any of them. They were policemen, but this was no arrest. This was . . . *blue hell*.

But running without stopping was for champions. Zoë was a smoker. Boy, was she a smoker.

This wasn't only about distance, though; it was about direction. As in a maze, you made choices everywhere, leaving behind you a puzzle of possibilities. Each available corner, she took. It was dark, and the rain had emptied the streets. She ran past a pub, its windows throwing rainbows on the pavement, and imagined laughter, beer, safety; then realised with something like pain that this was where she'd come with Jay, what, two nights ago? She could step inside and claim help. But they were policemen. Whatever else they were, they were policemen. So she kept running, stomping puddles, while air raged in and out and burnt her up – lungs were bags of air. Hers were punchbags. She'd been beating hell out of them so long, it was a wonder the idiot things still knew how to breathe.

Round the next corner she reached the bridge across the canal. It was accessed via a concrete stairwell, in which she rested a second and retched, while lightning flashed in her mind. This is how it is, then, when someone is trying to kill you . . . Like a lot in life, it was instantly comparable to everything else. That moment you step out of your depth, and feel the undertow's tug, and something deep in your stomach respond. Or stand cliff-edge and understand the height you're at, the depth you might fall. Or notice you're not loved any more. Zoë felt white panic loom, and clamped down hard; tried to lock it in a box.

Breathing was murder; all the same, crouched in this nook, she almost felt safe — it was close and dark and she couldn't be seen from the street. But the moment anyone arrived, it was a trap. Staying put wasn't an option. The loose handcuff flapped from her left hand. She caught its loop in her fist, and gripped it like a knuckleduster. Learned how to breathe again: in–out. Then took the stairs at as much of a jump as she could manage, and raced over the bridge.

It almost felt like a game. That would be the inner Zoë; the one to whom things were funny, until they pissed her off. The stairs on the far side led down to darkness, and this was where the game came in: that notion of reaching a den; a place of safety. She sheltered a moment in the lee of the bridge. Canal boats were moored along the towpath. Bars of light escaped their windows to splash on the muddy, pitted path, almost seeming an extra obstacle, as treacherous as the upjutting edges of brick. Inside the boats was food, heat, television. Outside, rain fell cold and steady. She could bang on doors and summon help — they weren't all tie-dyed and helpless, these water-folk; there was the odd ex-foundry worker among them: tradition-ally muscled; genetically wired to assist damsels. But it wasn't help Zoë needed. It was a clean getaway.

She paused to look back at the bridge. No one was crossing. But there were only so many directions she could have taken. Sooner or later, they'd be coming her way.

And from here, there was only one direction left: down the canal. On the move again, she inventoried herself. She wore flat shoes, in which she could run; she wore jeans and a cotton top over a tee. Her leather jacket was history. A pair of hand-cuffs hung from her left wrist. She had no money; no plastic;

no mobile. She probably had her usual penknife. She checked: she did.

But she didn't have her car keys. Inasmuch as she had a plan, it was to loop through town, and reach her car. But Zoë didn't have her car keys.

Rain was pasting her top to her body, and without shelter – soon – she'd be a helpless wet rag when they found her.

Beyond the boats, she picked up speed. Lights from across the canal reflected on the water, where they broke in the rain and rippled into jigsaw shapes. A bramble snagged her, and she ripped free. Her breathing sounded louder than a train. She hadn't had a cigarette in ten minutes. She wondered if that counted as giving up.

Then she heard something louder: the weight of a man hitting the towpath behind her, one big foot at a time.

Zoë turned. He was emerging from the dark, the rain, and she couldn't tell which one he was, if it mattered. Twenty yards away, but easier to read every moment: wide chest, clenched fists . . .

There were some small things Zoë had learned about self-defence. The first was, a big angry man will kick the crap out of you every time.

She ran. There was no choice involved: you did *not* stand and fight when all that could happen was pain and broken teeth. But she was drowning on dry land, with the ground dragging at her every step she took, so she dropped to the ground instead, to make as small a target as possible; squeezed into a ball which the first thing he did was kick.

Her arm went instantly numb. But she barely had time to register this, as his attack sent her sprawling to the water's edge. If she'd had trouble breathing before, this was new territory: an airlock. Nothing was reaching her lungs. He piled at her on all fours like a woolly beast. For a moment, she thought it was okay. Not that things were going to end happily, but that they were at least going to end: that this was better than alternatives lately dwelt on – the scalpels; the drawn-out treatments. But only for a moment. As soon as he grasped her leg, she knew she'd fight. She kicked, and the sudden spasm jerked everything back into motion; she swallowed air again, and her vision cleared. She was on her back, her head over the edge of the path, inches above the water; her left arm was frozen, but her right was operational, and her legs worked. What she'd kicked was his head, and he pulled back with an animal grunt of rage. Then his weight hit like a chimney collapsing, and she was on her back again, the force of collision ringing loud and clear in every numbered bone. This couldn't last long. It was already almost over . . . She was further over the edge now. Her hair dipped into water, and there was time for panic to squeeze her heart before his hands were on her shoulder, on her chin, and her head went under . . .

So this is how it is, then, when someone is trying to kill you.

She'd clamped her mouth shut. You did this swimming; you did this in the *bath*; but against your will, it was different . . . A small detached part of Zoë kept on whirring like a black box. *This, too, will pass.* Lights whizzed and popped: her own New Year, exploding in the privacy of her brain. Then something melted in her head as he pulled her clear of the water; pulled her face so close to his own, they were near enough to kiss.

The black box told her this. Zoë's eyes stayed firmly shut.

'Calmer, bitch?'

He didn't wait for an answer. She was back underwater immediately; those same lights flashing and bursting in her head.

And isolation and numbing cold and raw black nothingness.

His body locked her legs down. Nothing they did mattered. And her left arm was worse than useless; as limp as if she'd slept on it awkwardly . . . Odd that your last sensation might be one of vague pain, vague irritation, way out there in your second-best limb. That the last voice you'd hear would be calling you *bitch*. She batted at his head with her right hand, but it was like swatting a wall with a handkerchief.

. . . And again he pulled her free of the water, and the air she swallowed was almost too much; she felt like she might burst. He was speaking but her ears were full; she was too busy breathing; she had no fucking interest in his opinion. Besides, her right hand was being interesting: reaching into her jeans pocket; fishing out her penknife . . . He was pulling her to her feet; one fist on her collar; the other twisting her right breast, which was a whole new kind of pain. 'You're gunna behave, right?' he seemed to think. Zoë sank the knife as deep as she could into his thigh, and he let go.

She wrenched it free. The blade wasn't huge, but it had caught gristle and caused damage. She was light-headed, streaming water; must have looked like a vengeful mermaid. Lights became brighter up the path as his scream brought people out of boats. Where'd they been when she'd needed them, cowards? He dropped to a crouch, hands wrapping his thigh, his mouth open wide – the scream was all finished, and he made a hoarse whisper as he tried to inhale. Not good, is it? Zoë wanted to ask, but she had no words. She turned and ran.

Or lolloped, anyway. A battered, breathless lunge from the lights. A voice rang after her, a woman's voice, but women were far too sensible to chase violent strangers in the dark. Adrenalin pumped through Zoë, and her movements became fluid; began to resemble human activity. There was a humpback bridge ahead. She sped up on the downslope. Night vision kicked in; her breathing came easier. The penknife felt welded into her grip. She passed another canal boat. The light flickering through its curtains was the blue-grey ghost of television; some cop drama about riverside damage, knife fights, fugitives.

The energy violence had generated was wearing thin already.

She needed warmth; she needed to get dry. Most of all, she needed to be far away. Her car would be a start, but she still didn't have the keys. Life was a series of problems, of variable difficulty. She had stabbed a man in the leg. The memory was tucked into the muscles of her right arm, was throbbing in her wrist: the resistance his flesh had put up for a second; the scraping of cartilage.

And then she'd reached the road, and traffic, and people, but she was way past asking for help. She'd just committed mayhem on a policeman. Dog-legging right, she sprinted over – all her movements felt faster than they were – then leaped down the steps to the path beside a pub. She was Bede's sparrow: seconds of light and noise all she knew between two stretches of darkness. Then pain hit her side, and forced her to stop.

It was a stitch, bad enough that she leaned on her knees, short of breath, hurting all over. Her hair was plastered to her skull. She was wet and freezing and about to throw up; she was unsure if it was the cold, the wet or the violence sickening her, or simply the fact that you could now do this: run across a busy road wielding a knife, and have no one stop you.

But she didn't throw up. When her vision cleared she had to reorient. She was between two roads. To her left ran the river; to her right was a bush-lined patch of green, with benches for the weary; beyond that, a high wall. Her option was to go forward. Meanwhile she was a target in a lamplit pool, outside which somebody now coughed. Zoë's heart leaped in its cage; might have jumped free if not for her fierce intake of breath. It was a man, two yards away, watching her. How had she not seen him? Because he was one of the invisibles; he was one of the invisibles, and she recognised him now. He was the homeless man she'd interrupted at prayer the other day. The one who carried his life in a collection of laundry bags.

Those bags lay at his feet, and the expression he wore was one of blank absence: she might have been a door, a shoe, a missing sock. He wore a wide-brimmed hat from which water fell in a steady stream, and a thick black overcoat which reached his knees. The bushes behind him looked about as alive.

Zoë stood upright and faced the road ahead. The rain was heavier than ever, and without a coat she'd stick out like a leprechaun. She turned back to her new companion and saw that his gaze had shifted to the knife in her hand, and his face altered at last, as if whatever signal he was receiving had been blocked. He stepped back. That's great, she thought. That's just great. This is where I am now. This is what I'm about to do.

'I'm not going to hurt you,' she said.

He didn't answer. This did not necessarily indicate agreement.

'I'm really really sorry,' she said. Her voice had a metallic quality, as if it were being processed through something useful but soulless: an electric tin opener, perhaps. If she could pretend that's all she was – a single-purpose tool, empty of volition – it would be easier to forgive herself afterwards. 'And I promise I'm not going to hurt you. But I need your coat. I need your hat.'

He was shaking his head, she thought at first, but no: he was only shaking. And still she was holding the damn knife, and it was hard to see in this light, but it might have blood on it, it was highly possible he could see blood on it, and no wonder the poor fuck was shaking: it's hard enough finding shelter in this life without some knife-wielding bitch stealing the only things keeping you dry—

Enough!

'I'm sorry. But I need them now.'

And God help her she waved the knife.

She must have closed her eyes for a second, to stop seeing what she was doing, and when she opened them he was taking his coat off – not unbuttoning; it wasn't buttoned; probably didn't *have* buttons – but slipping his arms free, bundling it up, handing it to her; his blank face with an extra wrinkle now; another little mark left by the world. Just when you think things can't get worse: meet Zoë. It's always possible I deserve to have cancer. And now he was removing his hat, and shaking water from it. She took the coat and pulled it on. It stank. (And didn't have buttons.) The hat stank worse.

What she was thinking was, this is so easy . . .

He stepped back, looking wetter already. Without somewhere to go he'd be drenched in minutes, and if he had somewhere to go to, why was he here? Thoughts Zoë pushed away, like she tried to push the next one away, but couldn't: it had wormed into her, and wasn't going anywhere. I'm sorry, she said again, then realised she hadn't spoken. 'I'm sorry.'

He might have nodded.

'But, look . . .'

Feet clattered on the road behind them, but when she turned it was a couple flashing past en route to pub or restaurant or taxi . . . Somewhere dry, where they always let you in, unless you were desperate.

'But look, I need money.'

He might have tilted his head to one side. Maybe she did. A matter of perspective. And maybe the whole damn world shifted on its axis: little fucking point in making an opera out of it. 'I need money,' she repeated, her voice harder. 'A tenner. Five, even. Whatever, I'll find you and pay you back. Ten times over. But I need it now.'

If there'd been something to hide behind or crawl under instead of doing this – a blade of grass; a stone – she'd have hidden, she'd have crawled. But his gaze had dropped to the knife again, and her grip on it tightened without apparent intention on her part. He reached into the pocket of what had once been somebody else's jeans. If he'd speak, she thought, if he'd say *anything*, if he'd tell me to fuck off, tell me he'd die tonight without his coat and hat, I'd give them back and take my chances. I would rather face three men with guns than live through this again.

She didn't look at the coins he handed her; just stuffed them into the pocket that used to be his.

'I will find you,' she said.

He said nothing.

'I will.'

He said nothing.

She turned, pocketing the knife. There were steps up to the road. At the top she looked back, as if to underline her promise, but he'd gone, of course, with his laundry bags; had melted into the shadows of a bad world that had just got worse.

A left turn took her towards the city centre. Beyond the junction she hopped a bus heading north: coins from her new hoard paid the fare. The driver wrinkled his nose as she boarded, but that was mild compared to drowning her. At the back, Zoë sat staring out. This rain wasn't giving up any time soon. Nothing you wanted to be out in without coat and hat. Survival, though, meant prioritising. Survival meant forgetting what was done and concentrating on what came next. She had no plan. She had little idea of what was going on, except that the possibility that it concerned Alan Talmadge had receded, unless there was a conspiracy; unless there was a whole raft of Talmadges out there, enraged she'd cottoned on to them . . .

. . . The shakes were setting in. The warning was deep in her bones. Her arm, where he'd kicked her, was still buzzing: she didn't think it was broken, but he hadn't done her any good . . . This, though, was dwelling on the past. What she needed was a plan.

The bus pulled up outside Borders. She counted her money: a little over nine pounds. For some while, she'd kept a thousand pounds' fuck-you cash taped in a recess behind her kitchen sink, but this would have been as handy if she'd mailed it to the moon. One of those three would be watching her flat. She'd have to be an idiot to return there, but they didn't know she wasn't an idiot. It was possible they held conclusive proof that she was. So nine pounds, which would barely get her out of the county. She needed food; she needed shelter. There were only so many places you could go to demand such treatment.

And all of them, she needed soon. These shakes, her bruises, all the rough treatment: they'd knock her off her feet. This, too, was what survival meant: knowing when to lick your wounds. She needed her car, was what it came down to. She didn't have her car keys, but that was the smaller problem: if she had her car, everything else she could cope with.

She stepped off at the top of St Giles and cut through the churchyard, where the ghost sheltering under a tree was another poor soul with nowhere to go. Hallucinating was one thing; entertaining sentimental versions of winos another: get a grip. Desperate to stop and rest, to buy cigarettes, she forced herself on: down Little Clarendon, into Jericho. Her brand new hat, she wore over her eyes. Her bruised old eyes, she kept fixed on the pavement. If the bastards found her now, there wasn't a lot she could do. She was used up. All she had left was her inner Zoë, who was good at the voices, could be pretty fucking caustic, but wasn't much use when it came to bonework. *You're a mess,* she encouraged now. *If you have to run, you'll get five yards.* Brilliant. Thanks. *Remember where you parked the car?* She remembered.

At the corner, she waited. If it had been her, she'd be watching the car. She'd know the car was useless without keys, and she'd know the keys were in the leather jacket she didn't have any more, but still: if it had been her, she'd have been watching the car. Because there might be spare keys. And while there weren't, in fact, spare keys, there were other ways of starting cars, and Zoë knew one.

I think we should learn to hot-wire, Joe had said once.

(He'd been watching a TV account of life in Blackbird Leys.)

Yes, Joe. Why?

But 'why' wasn't Joe's favourite question. Either you thought something or you didn't. What he thought was, they should learn to hot-wire.

To give him credit, he'd learned; or had found someone to teach him, which was close enough for jazz. The kid had spent most of a Saturday with Joe; equally bemused, Zoë reckoned, by the fact that somebody was paying him for this, and that the same somebody had the exact grasp on essentials as a goldfish. At last, she'd joined them.

'Show me,' she'd said. 'I'll show him later.'

Ten minutes, and the kid was on his way.

Okay. You can show me later, Joe had said.

She never had.

. . . The longer she stood, the colder she got. It was now or never. She made her move.

With a piece of brick plucked from a skip, she smashed her car's window. Sliding into the seat, feeling glass crunch beneath her, she had to trust her hands to do her remembering. Closing her eyes did not make this easier. When she closed her eyes, she was flicking a coin at a big man's eye . . . She opened them. Sometimes, ordinary days turned into shortcuts through hell. Her hands were frozen to the bone, and rain on the windscreen blurred the world to a celluloid cliché. It was her inner Zoë came to her aid; who let go the rain, the dirty streets, the chances of anyone watching, and grasped the task in hand. *It doesn't matter who you've hurt,* she said, joining the wires as a long-ago boy had directed. The engine sputtered to life. *You didn't ask for this. All you need do is live through it.* When Zoë put her hands to the wheel, they were her own again. For a moment, she wanted to rest her head, let the car's motion fibrillate through her like a giant life support system, but no. Rain heaved at her neck, and she turned to close the window she'd broken. How stupid was that? she wondered, redirecting her attention to escape, as an arm snaked through the same broken window and slammed her head back against the seat.

'You are so. Fucking. Mine.'

But she wasn't. She was already pushing the door with all the strength she had left; it struck her assailant hard enough to break his grip. As he stepped back swearing she slammed him with it again. This time he slipped and hit the pavement. Before he could get to his feet the door was closed and the car moving. The first thing she hit was the car in front; the second, the one behind. It was possible she was shouting. The man was on his feet now, and had his hand to the window as she pulled into the road; with luck, the ridge of broken glass lacerated his palm. He yelled, but she was gone. The third thing she hit leaped out from between parked cars at the corner. The Sunny shuddered as it sideswiped him, but kept the road nicely. She forgot to indicate before turning. There was no approaching traffic, so this was not important.

It was nice to know the old skills hadn't deserted her.

Before she reached the roundabout on the main road leaving the city, she pulled into a lay-by to lose the broken glass. She had a nearly full tank of petrol; she had nine pounds in her pocket. In the glove compartment was a three-quarter pack of low tar cigarettes she'd bought by accident. None of this was brilliant, but it was a vast improvement. Smoking held the shivers off was the theory, though when she coughed, it racked through her like she was a wardrobe full of empty coat hangers. Once the glass was mostly at the side of the road – that familiar urban sight: the jewelled carriageway – she drove on. She knew where she was going, even if she had only the vaguest idea of how to get there. Whichever way you looked at it, that was more of a plan than she'd managed in weeks.

When she looked back on that drive, it was like seeing through a broken mirror: everything fragmented, refracted; the only constant, a bright swift procession of cars zipping by on urgent business. She had the dim idea the radio was on, but all it broadcast was broken bits of news from another time: *on a housing estate in east London. The body has been identified as that of a twelve-year-old . . . taken off the field last night after apparently being struck by a hurled coin. A spokesman for the club said . . . no leads at the present time. Charles Pars . . .* Light had abandoned the sky, and the world had no limits. It was an endless stretch of darkness she was condemned to drive through for ever, or until her mind and body gave out, and surrendered to the deep.

This is a very good road map of the British Isles. We keep this under the passenger seat.

That was her inner Zoë, unless it was Joe. Or maybe it was Sarah Tucker, still telling her what was what. Whoever, it got her where she needed to go, or might have done, if it hadn't failed her eventually: either new routes had been built, or she was too exhausted to fathom the arrangement of the old ones. Off the main roads, everything became complicated. Hills appeared where they had no business. Zoë was good at map reading. Joe had mentioned this often. *You are good at map reading,* he'd say. *Cartographers are frequently rubbish, though. They make mistakes, you end up lost.* When she reached her fourth last cigarette, she got out to smoke: very near her destination, or possibly nowhere near it at all. Before lighting up she climbed a five-bar gate to pee behind a hedge, and startled a dozy sheep. Every bone in her body ached. This road disappeared at the top of the next hill. It was a small, disappointing road, too narrow for comfort, and far removed from the brash, confident motorways she preferred. When she'd finished smoking she sat for a moment on an uninformative stone post by the roadside, and dozed. Silence jerked her awake. It was past five. The sky was grey, but in a hurry. The car wouldn't start.

Any other morning she'd have sworn to raise the dead. Here and now, it was just the next thing happening. She hugged herself, then ran a hand through ratty, filthy hair. Shutting the driver's door, she reached through its broken window to depress the lock: this struck her as a funny thing to do, though not enough to make her laugh. She should take the map with her. Yeah, right. Before cresting the hill, she reached a right-hand turn sheltered from view by a very old tree. On the principle that, when navigating a maze, you kept your right hand to the wall, she turned.

This lane dipped further. It was lined by ditches either side, and by trees the other side of the ditches, and heading down it she picked up speed. Slowing down was not an option. Events created their own momentum. She would reach the end of this lane, and when she did, she would decide what to do next. This might be anything, though smoking her third last cigarette was the clever-money favourite. The lane levelled at a cattle grid, one bar of which was pitched wrong, and tripped her. Zoë broke her fall with outstretched palms.

It would have been nice to lie there, but that too was not an option. She heaved herself up and brushed grit from her hands while her vision slipped out of focus; she had to shake her head before the picture returned to normal. Even then, there was something wrong with reception. Either that or a bird from another planet was eyeing her from behind a wire mesh fence.

'Oh,' she said, and she was speaking out loud.

It strutted closer, then halted. Bent its neck low, and made a threatening noise.

'You are so . . . fucking . . . not normal,' she said.

At which it pulled itself up to its full height, like a ladder unfolding. There were two more birds behind it, and both seemed to be studying her, though you could never tell with birds. When she blinked everything swam: filmy ripples washed the landscape, and for a moment the big fuzzy birds were cartoon monsters, or TV puppets, lacking only primary colours and huge letters branded on their chests. Soon they'd be dancing and reciting the alphabet backwards. Zoë could barely wait.

'Hello?'

And now a man approached from wherever this lane led: striding between trees as if he owned the place. The possibility existed, of course, that he did. He was dark-haired; wore a donkey jacket and a pair of wellies he'd tucked his jeans into. Beyond that, he blurred.

'Hello?'

She was suddenly too tired to reply. I've done my best, she wanted to say. You think that was a picnic? Dealing with those men? Getting here? Wherever here was. It was unclear what this man would do with the information, but the list of things Zoë considered her problem was shrinking by the moment.

'You,' he said, as he reached her. 'You're Zoë Boehm . . .'

He was quick, then, though not quick enough to catch her as she fell. But this, too, seemed somebody else's problem, and while she undoubtedly hit the ground, the lights went out long before impact.

18

*T*HERE WAS A FILM *once, he remembers – and everyone knows the film – and it had a line, and everyone knows the line.* Love means never having to say you're sorry. *Of which he hates every syllable. Because some idiot got it the wrong way round – love means always saying sorry, and that's the truth. It means always being aware of how far you're falling short of the grand ideal. But at the same time, love means never having to forgive, never needing to forgive, because there's never anything wrong with what the loved one does. Case in point:*

He's standing on a corner in the rain, near where she parks her car, and there's broken glass on the road and painful strangers on the pavement; one with a handkerchief to his eye; another who's clutching his leg. The handkerchief blooms red. As for Man Three, he holds himself gingerly, like a marionette with suspect strings; he looks like he's recently had a concrete interlude. And watching this – the men, their obvious pain; the anger steaming off them in the wet – all he can think is: That's my girl.

Nothing to forgive.

So maybe she's done wrong. Maybe these men represent whatever justice looks like on a wet night, out of uniform, but he Just. Doesn't. Care. *Which is not a matter of refusing to accept the possibility of her wrongdoing. It's that the need to forgive's been obviated. Whatever she's done, he'll applaud: she could blunt her knife on these men's bones, and he'd champion her right to inflict damage. That's the pact and that's the promise. Even if she's not aware of it yet.*

You and I must make a pact
We must bring salvation back . . .

But that's not to say there's no responsibility involved.

As he watches, the men move to a nearby car. Two of them are limping, and the one with the handkerchief to his eye makes a noise halfway between wounded animal and broken machinery: it's not especially loud, but carries on the wet air to the corner where he watches. And he trembles, as if there's a bass being played right here beside his elbow. Nothing outrageously funky. A ballad, perhaps; dripping regret and pain and loss, but making a promise. Exactly what you might feel if you'd encountered Zoë, and appreciated her worth, and experienced rebuff. Judging by the blood, this one had experienced rebuff.

. . . And she's some kind of woman. Turn your back on her five minutes and she starts her own casualty franchise. The men are in their car now. Choosing the designated driver has to be some kind of uphill struggle, but that's their problem, and now they're gone. And what's left is the blank space after the jigsaw puzzle's been tidied away unfinished: the splash of broken glass by the kerb; the echo of a one-eyed man's pain . . . A black leather jacket on the pavement. Whatever happened here was serious, and possibly Zoë's hurting. Though it's clear she got away.

He could go to her flat. Ring the bell. She won't answer. But it would be a gesture of solidarity; the keeping of a promise, even if she remains unaware of the pact they've made. Because this is where responsibility lies. You do not turn away when things become difficult. Such never happened with Caroline or Victoria. They had been needy not needful, hungry for love in their lives, and the simple fact of his presence had supplied what they'd lacked. Nothing more had been asked or given. And perhaps – painful as it is to admit, even to himself, even in the dark – perhaps that helped, when it grew time to let them go. Perhaps the knowledge that their love had reached its natural conclusion triggered a kind of . . . He hates to call it boredom. Boredom has nothing to do with love. But completion was achieved, sooner than might have been expected. And push came to shove. But that's behind him now.

He waits a while longer, enjoying the moment's melancholy: the lover in the rain. It might look like he's planning his next move, but that was settled back when he first cast eyes on her, and knew she was the one. Because what kind of man would let her drift now, with these strangers on her case? Finding her might be a problem – the tracking device on her car has a limited range – but not a grave one; not knowing her like he does. Superficially, theirs is a passing acquaintance, but they connect on a deeper level, and he knows what makes her tick . . .

A sudden draught sprays water from a gutter overhead, and he shivers at the contact. It will be another long night. But in the end you do what you do, and if your motives are pure, you reap the reward. Love is the storybook ending, but it has to be earned. He already knows this.

One last look at a scene that is over, then he turns and walks away. But first, he retrieves her leather jacket. Near the main road, he passes a homeless man, a wanderer whose life packs into three stuffed laundry bags, but he barely notices; doesn't give him a thought. He's too busy listening to words that spin and tango round his head. Words to live by. The old songs are the best.

Just look over your shoulder
I'll be there

19

LIGHT HUNG SOLID IN the air where it sabred through chinks and flaws in the shed, which held the usual shed paraphernalia – a reasonably well-organised display of tools and feed bags; of gardening stuff (rakes, hoes, shears) hung on walls; of cans of white spirit and paint ranged on shelves – and also a metal-framed camp bed on which Zoë lay, the pain in her elbow pulsing with every heartbeat, while those light sabres pierced her mind with brittle stabs. To recover control, she focused on her surroundings. There was shelving above her head, but she couldn't see what it held. Beside the bed was an old and child-sized wooden chair, which had been painted white at some stage of its existence, and had some of this paint removed at another. The patches that remained had the stained and yellow unpleasantness of old snow.

The man on the chair said, 'They're flightless, but that doesn't mean they're slow. They can hit forty miles an hour, where they've space to reach full throttle. Ratites, that's the family they belong to. Ratites are running birds. Ostriches are not defined by their inability to fly. They're defined by their ability to run.'

Zoë closed her eyes, and decided to keep them this way for some time.

He said, 'Mr O, he's the male, is a shade under nine foot. That sounds pretty big, but when you get right next to him, you realise it's actually bloody huge. And he weighs God knows how much, because trust me, I've never tried to lift him. Your adult male ostrich is like a large smelly piece of furniture. It's not surprising they can't fly. I mean, gorillas can't fly either, and they don't get a lot of bad press on the issue.'

The more he talked, the more Zoë's head throbbed. Every third word, she grew nearer busting. She'd already learned more about ratites than she needed. But stopping him meant speaking, and she wasn't ready for that.

'He's about thirty, best guess. They can live to seventy-five, did you know? It's surprising how little people know about ostriches, it's as if they're not entirely on the agenda. Anyway, we reckon he's about thirty, and the girls – Nicole and Gwyneth, by the way – they're probably younger.'

Some of this, Zoë already knew.

He paused, as if he'd heard something outside, and for a moment Zoë stopped breathing, and they were just two bodies in the cramped air, straining for what might have been a distant car changing gear. Even her heart stopped, it felt like. A momentary suspension of service. And then their silence was broken, and there was no car anywhere, and nothing to be worried about.

He said, 'Personally, I think of them as a potentially major barbecue, but that can stay our secret.'

Zoë's bearings were beginning to slide; when she opened her eyes the shed's walls were swelling out then sucking back in, as if she were trapped inside her own lung. Her power of speech was quite gone.

'Maybe you should get some sleep.'

That was the first sensible thing in a while. A while which roared suddenly, becoming much much longer and much much darker, and so large, it swallowed her whole.

*

Next time she reached consciousness, she felt drugged or flu-struck. The air was unpleasantly warm, as if she'd been her own heater, and left herself on too long: par-broiled, her clothing stuck to her damply. The chair was empty. The door shut. Light filtered through those chinks and flaws in the woodwork. Something specific had woken her, but she couldn't tell what. And despite her strong desire to know whether the door was locked, the effort of finding out was beyond her . . . In this grey nowhere, she was sure of nothing but exhaustion and thirst. Next time she woke she'd find a jug of water by the bed, but for now she lay aching a few minutes longer, her throat beginning to rasp and catch, before mist took hold of her once more, and wrapped her in forgetting.

When he came back he approached so quietly, he was in the shed before Zoë heard him. She'd been awake fifteen minutes, and had found the water along with a couple of serious-looking painkillers. After some hesitation, she'd taken these. Maybe they'd slowed her reactions. Either way, he was in the shed before she heard him.

'You're awake.'

'Yes.'

Her voice sounded as if it belonged to someone older.

'I looked in a while ago. You were still on planet nowhere.'

His looking in undetected while she slept would have worried her in most moods, but right now she was more concerned about his burden: a tray holding a pot of coffee, and possibly food, but most importantly a pot of coffee. He poured for her as soon as he'd settled on the ridiculously small chair.

'Thanks.'

'Feeling better?'

Well, not a hundred per cent, but she wasn't going to die soon . . . The thought brought a twinge, a reminder of mortality in her left breast. But she nodded, and sipped her coffee. 'What is this place?'

He looked around, as if just noticing it. 'It's a shed. We pretend it's a barn, but it's not very big.'

'So why put me in here?'

'Seemed like a good idea.' When she raised her eyebrows, he added, 'Sarah's always reckoned, if you ever needed to run, she's who you'd run to. And anything bad enough to get you running would call for a hiding place. Do you want more coffee yet?'

His name was Russell, and he and Sarah Tucker had lived here a little over two years: Sarah freelance editing, while Russell was 'mostly retired' at forty. 'Wondering what to do next,' was as much as he'd elaborate. Sarah's 'boy and two girls' – Mr O, Nicole and Gwyneth – they'd rescued, expensively, when a nearby farm found that ostrich rearing wasn't the gold mine expected. And Sarah would be back that afternoon. 'She's in London, seeing a client. She's doing well. Turning work away.'

'Did she tell you how we met?'

'Yes. But I don't scare easy.'

Zoë didn't reply.

'Sorry, that was macho. But Sarahs don't happen often. I'd be an idiot to be frightened off by a little history.'

'Multiple deaths and chemical warfare.'

He said, 'We were visited after we moved in together. A couple of men with polite smiles and minimalist ID. I had to sign an official secrets form. Sorry, was *asked* to sign. I think they'd have insisted, but Sarah made them ask.'

'She was a pushover when we met. But she had a steep learning curve. You haven't asked why I'm here yet.'

He shrugged. 'Like I said, Sarah's told me her story. I don't care who you're hiding from.'

'It's not a debt I ever meant to call in.'

This made him laugh. 'Sarah won't help you because she owes you, Zoë. She'll help you because she loves you. Do you want to eat yet?'

She thought she'd better. She couldn't remember last time she'd eaten.

In her letters, in her phone calls these past few years (which had always been Sarah ringing Zoë), Sarah had talked about Russell. In the flesh he was much as she'd painted: five eleven, dark, thinning a little on top, with brown eyes Sarah called kind. He didn't swagger, didn't roll. He wasn't especially broad, but wasn't weedy either. Thickening around the middle, possibly, but that was life: it plumped you up, ready for market. He wore jeans and a dark blue V-neck, and was softly spoken. For what it was worth – Zoë had been wrong about men before – Sarah probably had a point: this Russell was maybe a good one. But Sarah had been wrong about men before, too.

And he'd made a lot of money, though Sarah hadn't said how. Advertising, Zoë expected. Architecture, at a pinch.

Outside, in the proper world, the sun struggled behind grey swaddling.

The ostrich pen was to the left, and on its far side stood another shed, much like the one she'd emerged from. The ostriches were nearby, looking deeply weird – a trio of giant feathered anomalies: not the first thing you'd expect in an English farm scene. It wasn't a working farm; the land around belonged to the neighbours. Still, it made an Oxford flat look cramped.

The biggest, Mr O, stared at Zoë as they passed. Zoë had been scrutinised by bastards lately, but this chilled her nevertheless.

The farmhouse – if you could still call it that – looked like a bungalow from the rear, but getting nearer Zoë saw that its lower storey, from this approach, was below the level of the land. A kind of dry moat had been dug round it, so the lower windows at the back looked out on a stone wall holding the earth at bay. But the land dipped sharply, and from the front the house was a plain two-storey of old grey stone: broad and squat, with a mildewed patch below a leaking overflow pipe, and windows either a little too wide or a shade not deep enough. Squared-off chimneys at either end looked vaguely military, for no obvious reason.

It wasn't an attractive building, and lacked ivy or window-boxes to soften its façade. Zoë liked it. Houses built for people who looked after pigs and tilled earth deserved this no-nonsense style. No prizes for guessing Sarah felt the same way.

There were lights pegged just below the guttering at each corner. Russell saw her notice them. 'Motion sensitive,' he said. 'We're a bit vulnerable to burglars out here.'

He pushed open the hefty, weather-beaten front door. 'Kitchen's straight ahead,' he said. She walked through a hallway littered with shoes and upturned wellies, into a kitchen stretching half the length of the house. Not enough daylight spilled through the windows – the moat blocked it – but the internal lighting was recessed, subtle, and the moat wall had been whitewashed, which counteracted the gloom. Below the windows was a double sink with a huge draining board, and in the middle of the room a table so large and scarred it left no doubt that this used to be a farmhouse kitchen where serious business happened: the plucking of poultry and skinning of lambs. A double-fronted oven dominated one wall, with a large and heavy pan on its back ring. More pans hung on hooks and from an overhead metal rod spanning the room. The chairs around the table were wooden, but didn't match. There was even space for a bookcase, heavy with cookery tomes all different sizes and shelved at problematic angles, interspersed with paper-back novels, phone directories, and, unless Zoë was misreading the spine, a sex manual. There was no sign of dog or cat life.

'I'll assume you're not a vegetarian.'

'That's very civil.'

He began assembling ingredients from the fridge. 'You're Jewish, right?'

'Is this the bacon question?'

'Uh-huh.'

She shrugged. 'Whatever.'

Which was the right answer, the smell assured her.

He made more coffee in between making everything else. Zoë could feel life coming back, and everything that had happened in the last twenty-four hours started to assume the haunted fuzziness of a late-night movie watched while drunk. It was Tuesday morning. That seemed a strange time for it to be; an odd fact worth repeating. It was Tuesday morning. When he placed a plate in front of her, she cleared it without talking. The loudest noise in the room – crowding out her chewing, their breathing, the ticking of the clock – was the way the handcuffs jangled on her left wrist, like a musical illustration of a promise breached.

At last he said, 'You're wearing handcuffs.'

'I know.' She finished eating; reached for cigarettes, but evidently wasn't wearing her smoking clothes, because all her pockets were empty. 'It wasn't my idea.'

'Does that indicate police involvement?'

She said, 'So it would seem.'

'They didn't finish arresting you, though.'

'I'm not sure they were real policemen.' Then she said, 'No. They were real policemen. But they weren't doing their job.'

Something about the way he was looking at her – something, she amended, about his face, those *kind* eyes – invited her to continue.

This was not how it worked, though. This was not how Zoë worked. You broke down with the first man prepared to listen, you might as well jack in the game at the start: there were men who understood this trick. Which was why women like

Caroline died. So instead of going on she said, 'You don't smoke, by any chance?'

'I wish I did,' he replied with feeling.

Oh. One of those.

She made to cover a yawn and almost took her eye out with the cuff.

He said, 'Perhaps we should do something about that.'

While he went to find tools she took in her new surroundings. There was something unreal about visiting for the first time a place you'd been told about. Like seeing the film of a novel you'd enjoyed, it was usually either disappointing or not quite as bad as you'd expected. But this felt like Zoë had been reading a different book altogether. She wondered how much attention she'd been paying while Sarah talked or wrote to her, and decided not enough.

When Russell returned he was carrying a very man-at-work toolbox, which accordioned open to show compartments full of shiny implements and different-sized nails. From among them he chose a vicious pair of cutters, their seriousness only partly mitigated by their kiddy-orange handles. 'I don't think I can get through the cuff itself,' he said. 'Not without endangering your hand. Do you want me to endanger your hand?'

'Guess.'

'So what I'll do is take the chain off. That way you won't be clinking like the bride of Frankenstein.' He had her lay her arm on the tabletop, and didn't mess about once she'd done so: using both hands to force the cutters, he sheared the links as close to her wrist as he could, and the second cuff, its silver worm attached, shivered to the table. Zoë felt no freer; actually, it made her realise how much she hated having this thing hooked on her. But she was quieter, at least, and she thanked him.

'I don't mean to get personal. But could you use a bath?'

'I was going to ask.'

He showed her the bathroom, laid out some clothes of Sarah's, and left her to it. Then she ran the bath high as it would go and still leave room for her: it was a deep tub that sat on iron claws, and held a lot of water. While it filled she unclothed and stared into the mirror. You hurt some people, she told herself. You stole a coat and hat from a man who has nothing. The face looking back might have been somebody else's, for all the grief and guilt it held. The mirror misted, and Zoë was glad. There was something about that face's determination not to give anything away that made her tired.

But water was good. Water was hot. She slipped into it with a sense of release; it made her both more conscious of her body – soothing its outline; stroking its bruises – and detached from it at the same time. She looked at herself, basking like a porpoise. This is what was happening: her body either was, or was not, harbouring an unwelcome guest, which right now either was, or was not, eating her healthy cells. There were other possibilities, and while none were pleasant, all were preferable. None would kill her. None would maim. None would harm her *body*, not for ever, and it was with this thought that something confused until now became clear: that it was not her body doing this to her. It was something happening to her body, something separate and unwelcome. This was worth hanging on to, and it followed her into a cloudy warm nothing where she closed her eyes and forgot, for a while, men who'd forced her to hurt them, who would have hurt her too. And a man who'd allowed her to wrong him, instead of making her work a little harder for what she'd robbed him of.

It was the cuff prevented her falling asleep. Its unrelenting presence, the way it grated against the bath and scratched her flesh, dragged her back before she could slip away altogether.

When the water grew cold she washed herself, then let it drain away; then, wrapped in a towel, she sat on the edge of the bath and wondered what was going on. The men who'd come for her had nothing to do with Alan Talmadge, that was for certain. It could only be Wensley. Wensley was the only other thing she'd done lately, and judging by the outrage, one thing was clear: he hadn't fallen off his tower block. Like Caroline, like Victoria, he had been pushed. Because it seemed Zoë lived in a world devoid of accidents; one where every rotten thing that happened could be traced to a rotten cause. No great leap was involved in reaching this conclusion. Though it kind of figured – would have made Joe's ghost laugh if he'd had one – that it was the job she wasn't being paid for that was causing the havoc.

It had to be Sturrock. She bent and dried between her toes, always an aid to concentration. There'd only been a mile between his and Wensley's deaths, halfway along which sat Zoë. Why anybody thought she knew anything was a mystery, but she knew about kicking over stones: sooner or later, something crawled out. She opened the window and steam billowed for a few frantic seconds; just another of those moments where casual action provokes visible tumult. Then the air cleared, and all was fresh and cool and positive. She needed thinking time. Zoë was a strong believer that there was nothing she couldn't get to grips with, given time and cigarettes. Which was another reason for alarm; she was perilously low on cigarettes.

She dressed in Sarah's clothes; a small and not terribly important surrender of identity. She couldn't help wondering what had become of her beloved leather jacket, and whether she'd see it again. Downstairs, she found Russell in the kitchen making coffee again, as if he were engaged in a not terribly subtle campaign to become her favourite human being. He said, 'I'll show you around, if you like. Around the fortifications. It's not the usual guest situation, is it?'

'I guess not.'

'Are they likely to come after you?'

She looked at him a long while, then said, 'They don't know I'm here.'

'Maybe not. But Sarah's always said you'd come to her if you needed help. And, well . . . here you are.'

Yes. This had occurred to her. She said, 'I don't want to bring trouble on you. I won't stay long.'

'That's not an issue. All I'm wondering is, do I make up the spare room, or will you be in the shed?'

'I think the shed.'

He fussed with the coffee machine, as if it were a gadget unfamiliar to him. 'Does this happen often?'

'No.'

'Me neither. Well, never. In case you'd not guessed.'

She said, 'You're doing fine, Russell. I'll go tomorrow. I just need a breathing space.'

'Zoë. You can stay as long as you need. That's a given.' He poured the coffee at last. 'I just don't want to let anybody down, that's all.'

'You've already been a saviour.'

When they'd finished, he led her outside. It was a bright chill day, and the surrounding hills were sculpted clean against the sky. Zoë breathed deep, and remembered cigarettes.

'It's always different,' he said. 'Not just the seasons. Every day.'

She nodded. None of the obvious comments seemed worth saying.

'Plays buggery with a mobile, though. You can't get a signal for miles.'

They walked past the ostrich pen, where the birds were strutting aimlessly. Mr O, the biggest by far, pinned them with a beady gaze and stayed put, but one of the females trotted over. Watching her, Zoë remembered that birds were the closest living relations to dinosaurs. 'Which one's this?' she asked.

'Ah,' said Russell. He looked embarrassed. 'This would be Gwyneth.'

'Gwyneth,' repeated Zoë.

When Gwyneth arrived, Zoë was glad of the high mesh between them. Not as tall as the male, she was still sizeable, and her feet were deadly weapons – couldn't they open you up with those feet? She was about to ask the fount of ostrich lore, but was distracted by the bird, who was sinking to her knees, fluffing her wings. She was making a plaintive noise – part croon, part groan – and her attention was focused on Russell.

After a moment Zoë said, 'Why is she doing that?'

'Um,' said Russell, 'she's being friendly.'

'How friendly?'

'Very friendly, actually.'

'You mean—'

'Yes. I do. It's quite common, apparently.'

They watched the lovelorn ostrich a few moments more before walking on.

Behind the second shed sat a small blue tractor.

Zoë said, 'I thought this was a no-farming zone.'

'It belongs to next door.' He nodded in the direction she'd been heading in before turning down the lane. 'They keep it here, and its fuel and gear in the shed. We've space to spare.'

'Code of the country?'

'Just neighbourliness. They're away at the moment.'

There was a drainage ditch bordering the road on which Zoë's car had quit. She mentioned the car to Russell, who said he'd collect it, if she'd give him the keys.

'I don't have keys,' she said.

He gave her a look. 'I'll think of something.'

The trees along the lane were hard, knotty and old; hawthorn, she thought, though her knowledge was not great. Was mostly made up, actually. She could identify all major brands of cigarette blind, though. 'What do you do for shops?'

'We get in the car and drive two miles that way.'

'What about pubs and post offices?'

'We get in the car and drive two miles that way.'

'It would drive me crazy.' This did not sound especially complimentary, she realised. 'I'm sure it's lovely most of the time.'

'I suppose it depends what you're used to.'

'How did you make your money, Russell?'

'Did Sarah not tell you?'

'If she had, I wouldn't need to ask.'

'Well, then. I'll leave it to her, I guess.'

Together, they walked a stretch of the perimeter, until Zoë noticed, shockingly, she was tired. Her arm still hurt; her whole body, in fact, felt racked, as if her bath had drawn new bruises to her surface. Russell must have gathered this – maybe she was walking stiffly – because their route took them back to the shed. He didn't once ask for anything like detail. Nor did he make a big deal out of not doing so. He left her, telling her he'd wake her to eat in a few hours, and she stretched out on her bed once more. Then got up and rifled the pockets of the stinking overcoat she'd stolen and recovered her cigarettes. The box still held three, and after thinking about it for a second – two *miles* – she lit one. There was doubtless a whole range of directives and nanny-type instructions about not smoking in confined wooden areas, but if she listened to good advice, she'd not be smoking in the first place.

Then, she slept.

When she opened her eyes again, she was not alone.

20

STANDING AMONG THE TREES, he feels different – but then, he usually feels different. A city block; a small town house; a leather jacket – he slips into one as easily as another. What matters is that his core being remains undiluted; burns brightly as it ever did. He's gone by different names; worn different outfits; different hair. But his heart beats same as ever; even here, under weirdly stunted trees.

Zoë's car sits up the road. Speaking her name has that gorgeous, tantric effect he can't get enough of: Zoë. It tastes on his tongue. And this is love: standing under trees alone, saying her name out loud just to hear it get lost among the branches . . . The moment he knew he'd found her – the moment the transmitter on her car responded – was like the silent yes of tongues first meeting; it was validation. Having traced her history in the ether, he has written it on to the world. Though if he can do this, so might others.

But before he can follow this thought to its conclusion, and reach an estimate as to when those men might show up, he sees movement through the trees, in the field near the shed. It is curious how little it surprises him that this is an ostrich. But then, at a certain stage in any affair – the anxious hours before words are spoken – everything appears equally normal, equally abnormal. Something to do with heightened awareness. It's as if he's wearing a new, very effective, pair of spectacles; spectacles which affect all the senses, not just vision. Colours are brighter. Edges sharper. Ostriches happen. And the trees around him murmur in the wind; he can nearly make out their meaning.

. . . Female ostriches, he's read, can fall in love with their human keepers; so much so that they fail to mate with other ostriches. One of the reasons ostrich farming was a failure. An ostrich in love drops to her knees, spreads her wings, and groans. Apart from the wings, that wasn't so different, was it? Love is non-species specific, amusingly. And ostriches thwarted in love can pine.

He has driven through the night to where Zoë's friend Sarah Tucker lives; here on the edge of the Peak District, where the air breathes clean and the sky looks fresh. It didn't take genius to know that this was where she'd come. It didn't take love. *And that's where worry raises its head again: if it had taken love – if only the truly connected could join these dots – he'd know she was safe. As it is, anything could happen.*

More movement: human this time. But nothing desperate yet. When push comes to shove, he'll know about it. He's reached that point before.

He remembers his mother after his father left; how her life shrank until all it contained was the record player. She'd play her songs over and over: the old songs. Except they were the new songs at the time, of course.

'Dance with me,' she'd say.

And: 'You're my white knight, that's what you are. My knight in shining armour.'

She'd been forty-three. He'd sworn that would never happen again; he'd never watch a woman fade away before his eyes. He would take measures to prevent it. Even measures that seemed harsh at the time.

And he remembers how Zoë looks when thinking hard; how she grows disconnected from the world, as if plotting an escape route from it.

Danger might come from any direction, but most likely, he knows, from the road up above.

As for Zoë, he knows where she is.

She's in the shed.

He tugs on the zipper of her jacket, and moves towards her.

21

WHEN SHE OPENED HER eyes again, she was not alone. Sarah Tucker sat by the bed. Sarah was wearing her hair shorter than last time Zoë had seen her, with blonde highlights that altered the shape of her face, the way an expensive haircut can. In this light she looked younger, too, which might have been happiness, or might just have been this light. She wore a grey skirt and jacket, so obviously hadn't changed from her trip. Her weight, which she claimed variable, looked the right side of good. Zoë bit something back; she wasn't sure what. That there were people she was glad to see, maybe.

'Tell me,' she said, without moving. 'How did Russell make his money?'

Sarah said, 'I knew there was a reason you'd turned up half dead in a hot-wired car.'

'Please don't tell me it was a lottery win.'

'That's what he likes people to think. No, he wrote a book.'

'. . . That's not so terrible.'

'I haven't said which book yet. Did you ever come across, and I know you did because everybody did, did you ever come across that cartoon book, the male guide to female contraceptive devices?'

She groaned out loud. 'Every loo in the country had that.'

'*What Is This Thing Called, Love?*'

'At least it didn't feature a talking willy.'

'At his lowest moments, that's what keeps him going,' said Sarah. 'That and the stupid amount of money he made. Are you alive then, girl? It's lovely to see you.' She leaned forward, and Zoë barely hesitated before surrendering to her embrace.

For what felt like a long while she surrendered everything else, too; stopped being Zoë, with Zoë-sized problems, and shrank to a warm body, wearing this woman's clothes, wrapped in this woman's arms. It was an uncomplicated place to be.

'Are you running?' Sarah asked at last.

'What, I can't just drop in? I need an ulterior motive?'

Sarah didn't bother to reply, which was fair. Zoë broke away and leaned against the wall. Sarah sat back, and the two women studied each other.

At last Zoë said, 'Your ostrich seems very taken with your man.'

'Gwyneth! Ha!'

'Is that usual?'

'Not uncommon apparently. It's the real thing, too. Poor girl's head over heels.'

'And how about you?'

Sarah said, 'We're happy.'

'That's good. I'm glad.'

'You make it sound like I just had nice weather or some-thing.'

'I'm not knocking it, Sarah. What do I know?'

'You must have thought it would work with Joe, once.'

'Maybe. The reason why escapes me now.'

'He was a good man, Zoë. Don't be hard on his memory.'

'He was a good man in many ways. Not to be married to was one of them.'

'Sounds like you've still got issues, Zee.'

Baleful was the word for the look Zoë gave her. 'Don't call me Zee.'

'Sorry.'

'And don't say "issues." Unless you're talking about magazines.'

'I've been editing a self-help book,' Sarah confessed.

'And I thought I had troubles.' That made Sarah snort. Ever afterwards, whenever Zoë thought about Sarah, it was that snort she'd remember first. 'So here you go again,' she said. 'Young love.'

'I'm thirty-eight, Zoë. It's not like I walked into it wide-eyed and legless. And love's not so young, either.'

'Two years is nothing. You're probably still leaving notes for each other. Still wearing matching underwear.'

'You don't believe in happy ever after, do you?'

'Sweety, I don't even believe in once upon a time.'

'God, woman, I bet you still go in bars on your own, and drink right up at the bar. And get pissed off when men chat you up.'

'It's a free country. I can drink where I like.'

'There's streetwise, then there's stupid. It's right to get angry you can't walk down dark alleys without being attacked. But it's stupid to walk down dark alleys.'

'You're probably right.'

Sarah brushed a lock of hair free of her face. 'But that's what you've been doing, isn't it? Walking down dark alleys. What kind of trouble are you in, Zoë?'

So here they came to it. She thought about saying, *Maybe it's better you don't know*, but had an instant flash of what the response would be. *Fuck off, Zoë. What kind of trouble are you in?* Sarah had changed in the past few years, but Zoë would have been amazed if she hadn't. On their first major encounter, Sarah Tucker had been on a cusp, and the very fact they'd had a second had shown which way she'd fallen. That first time, she'd been full of pills – surrounded by them – and if she wasn't actually on suicide road, she wasn't heading anywhere healthy. The next, she'd been sitting on a bench, staring out to sea. By then, both women had a better idea of what they'd wandered into, and by then, Sarah had made the choices that had formed the person she was today. There had been a missing child, and Sarah had decided to find her. Of the many things that threatened to thwart that intention, none had survived Sarah's rediscovered sense of self.

She said, 'It's kind of a long story.'

'I'm kind of not busy.'

'I'm not avoiding it. Just warning you.' Then Zoë sat up ramrod straight, as if attending a formal interview, and laid everything out, all that had happened since last Thursday morning, in exactly the order she could remember it, which was largely the order it happened. Sarah didn't say a word until it was over; barely took her eyes from Zoë's, in fact. And Zoë, in the telling, found things levelling out in her mind, as if she were just now formulating answers to questions she hadn't finished asking yet.

Some of which must have been audible. When Zoë had finished Sarah sat in silence a while, thinking it through, then voiced Zoë's thoughts. 'These cops. They killed Sturrock.'

'Charles Parsley Sturrock,' said Zoë. 'Yes. I think so.'

'And Wensley saw it happen.'

'It was on his patch. Yes, I expect that's what happened.'

'So they killed him too.'

Zoë opened her mouth, closed it, nodded. She was seeing Kid B, stomping out his nine-year-old venom as she drove Andrew Kite from his world. *Piss the fuck off*, she'd told him, but she hadn't meant him to die. She wondered what they'd said to him, those cops, before they dropped him off that tower block. Definitely meaning him to die.

'He tried to shake them down, didn't he?' Sarah asked.

'He told Andrew he was coming into money. Yes, he tried to shake them down.'

'Bastards.'

'But why they're after me, God knows. I talked to his grandfather. I was late for his inquest. That's about it, really.'

Sarah said, 'We do have our exciting moments, don't we?'

'I shouldn't stay, Sarah. Coming here wasn't brilliant. Anyone with an eye for research could work it out. Anyone online.'

'You're going nowhere till we've worked out what to do next. And we haven't discussed the other one yet. Talmadge.'

'The man who wasn't there.'

'Someone was there. Else those women would be alive.'

'Unless they died by accident.'

'But you don't think that. Do you?'

'I don't know what I think,' Zoë said. 'Mostly, yeah, he's real. I think. But when I got on that bus Monday morning, it was because I'd decided he wasn't.'

'But you thought it was him when that guy followed you on the Tube. You must have believed in him then.'

Zoë thought about it. 'I believed in him when I couldn't see him,' she said at last. 'When I knew I was being followed, but couldn't spot him, I believed in him then. If he exists, that's what he's like. But once I saw this guy, I knew he wasn't Talmadge. Too much of a bruiser.'

Too much of a cop.

'The woman next door to Caroline . . .'

'Alma Chapman.'

'Alma. She saw him.'

'She saw somebody, in Caroline's garden. Okay, that probably was him. But there's nothing solid to connect him to Victoria. It's like the trail between the two was only there because I went looking for it. One of those optical illusions where it's all corner-of-your-eye stuff. Once you concentrate, it's gone.'

'But if it's real, he's a murderer.'

'Yes.'

They thought of murderers they had known. Sarah had found one in her kitchen once, but that was a different kitchen, some years ago.

'There was a guy on the train,' Zoë said.

'Oh yes?'

'Take that look out your voice. He was a guy on the train, that's all. But I bumped into him the following night, in town.'

'In a bar?'

'Yes.'

'And you had a drink together.'

'Don't make it bigger than it is, Sarah. Yes, we had a drink. And yes, he took my number. Or looked it up, anyway.'

'And you saw him again?'

'We had another drink.'

'I'd forgotten the delights of a girly chat. Zoë, this is like pulling teeth. Are you telling me you've found a sweetheart? Or you think he might be a serial killer?'

'If he's Talmadge,' she said, 'that's what he does, right? He picks up women. Lonely women in their forties. With nobody else in their life.'

'This is not you. That's nobody I recognise, Zoë.'

'So? It's what the world sees. This man, Jay, he's a good ten years younger than me. What was he after?'

'You want me to spell it out?'

'I brushed him off and he bounced right back. It's not like I was real nice to him, Sarah. And it's not like he'd have had much trouble, any other bar. Any other night.'

'So, he liked you. It's not that big a stretch, Zoë.'

'Like Talmadge liked Caroline? And Victoria? If it was even the same man?'

'Stop lining yourself up with them. You're nobody's idea of a victim.'

'Reality check, Sarah. I'm not my idea of a victim, or yours. But people at large? I'm a single woman in my forties. Equals lonely, hurting, and desperate. Whether Jay's a killer or not, he saw me as a target.'

'Or he likes you.'

'Or he likes a challenge.'

'Met his match then, hasn't he?'

'Is this helping?'

'Well, your colour's up. That's an improvement.' Sarah leaned forward. Her eyes seemed larger of a sudden; were inescapable in this small room. 'There's something you're not telling me.'

She looked away.

'Zoë?'

'That's the lot, Sarah. You know as much as I do.'

'Uh-uh. Give.'

'Nothing to give.'

'Zoë . . .'

Any other scene, Zoë thought, there'd be a clock ticking. Something to underline the silence; to make sure each second shattered on the floor between them.

'There's a lump,' she said.

'Oh,' said Sarah.

'Doesn't leave much to say, does it?' Except for the statistics and the cheerleader stuff, which she trusted Sarah not to indulge in. 'Left breast. About the size of a quail's egg.' Her voice sounded remarkably steady. 'Well, that's what I've been telling myself. But it's a bit bigger than a quail's egg. I'm scared, Sarah.'

Sarah said, 'I'm glad to hear it.'

'. . . Do you know, that's not the response I was expecting?'

'It surprised me too.' Sarah reached for Zoë's hand. 'Zoë, there've been times this last year, I've wondered whether you were ready to die. I mean, really.'

So there it was: that awful truth your best friends never tell you. You look fat in that dress. The haircut's shocking. I've been wondering whether you're ready to die.

She said, 'That bad?'

'It's been . . . as if your life had stopped mattering. That you were just counting out time, and didn't care where it was leading. So now you're scared? That's good, Zoë. That's good.'

Zoë felt Sarah's fingers link with hers and squeeze softly. For almost a minute they sat like that; Zoë wondering what it would take, these days, to make her weep.

'I think,' she said at last, 'that when you take a life it wounds your soul.'

'Yes,' said Sarah softly.

'He was an evil bastard. He'd have killed us. But taking a life wounds your soul.'

'Yes.'

She freed her hand and reached under the bed for her tasteless cigarettes.

Sarah said, 'Do you think—'

'Don't.' She lit up. 'The week I've had, not smoking would be dangerous and stupid. When I want a lecture, I'll let you know.'

Sarah said, 'Pardon me for being interrupted. But do you think I could have one of those?'

After a while Zoë said, 'I can be a bitch.'

'This is news?'

She passed Sarah the packet. 'I expect you to enjoy that. It's my last.'

They both smoked quietly, using the empty box as an ashtray. Blue tendrils rose to the ceiling, and wafted through the door.

Sarah said, 'Do you think they'll come looking?'

'I would. If I was them.'

'Well, then. Better plan a next move. Something public would be a good idea.' She flattened what was left of her cigarette, stood, and stretched. 'Are you starving?'

'I'm getting there.'

'You look shattered, too. Get some more sleep. When you're awake, come over. Food'll be ready.'

'. . . I haven't asked how things went in London.'

'Yeah, right. We should talk about house prices too.'

'Sarah?'

On her way out the door Sarah stopped, looked back.

Zoë said, 'I didn't come to you because you owe me help. You don't owe me anything. I came to you for help because . . .'

'Yes?'

'. . . You know.'

'Yes. I know.'

Zoë lay back on the bed and closed her eyes.

Passing the ostrich pen, heading for the house, Sarah smiled – it was nice having solid evidence that Zoë was still in her life. A refugee in a shed didn't make for an ideal reunion, but where Zoë was concerned, that was as good as it was going to get.

What had that cost her, anyway? – *I came to you for help because . . . you know.*

Halfway, she met Russell coming to meet her. He was frowning, and before she could ask why, he pointed at something up the lane.

Gwyneth trotted over, and went into lovestruck moron mode behind her fence.

'. . . What's up?'

'I thought I saw somebody. A guy in a black jacket. Among the trees.'

She turned but saw nobody, black-jacketed or otherwise.

As they stood there, a car turned off the road and rolled down the lane towards them.

SIX

THE MOST DANGEROUS ROOM

22

THE OVEN WAS DOUBLE-FRONTED, and had a six-ring range, on one back ring of which sat the largest of Sarah's Le Creusets – which lived here because it was too heavy to move; because she didn't trust its weight to the overhead rod where the other pans hung. On another ring sat the kettle. Sarah was no traditionalist, but the electrics here were nothing you'd trust your life to. The one who seemed the leader – the one who moved gingerly as if, say, he'd lately been sideswiped by a car – nodded in its direction. 'A cup of tea would be welcome.'

He wore a black beltless raincoat over a suit which looked slept in; a tie which he'd knotted in the dark.

'Your ID says Met,' said Sarah.

'That's right.'

'You're a long way from home.'

'That happens sometimes. They call it hot pursuit.'

In the movies they did. She said, 'Remind me of your name?'

He hesitated. Then said, 'Burke. Detective Sergeant Burke.'

'And . . .'

'DC Maddock. And Sergeant Ross.'

Maddock was the one who'd held Zoë's head underwater. He had red hair and washed-out eyes, which might have been something to do with Zoë, and was carrying a little weight. A rugby player heading for seed, was Sarah's impression. For a one-word description, 'policeman' would fit. Ross was older; lately known as Tube Man. His hair was a mess of tight greasy curls starting way back on his forehead, and a prominent vein in his forehead pulsed under Sarah's gaze. But what really claimed the attention was the pirate-black eyepatch giving him the air of an oversized boy dressing up. That aside, he was old for a sergeant. When the others had proffered ID he'd hung back, waggling a pass holder which might have contained his library ticket. Sarah had asked them in for fear of Zoë wandering from the shed while they loitered – that plus the worry they'd have come in anyway. There was no sense provoking an endgame before she'd tried talking her way out of this.

Russell said, 'It must have been quite some pursuit.'

Don't, she thought. Let me handle this. But how many men would have listened? Even sweet gentle Russell.

Ross looked about to answer. Burke got in first: 'And you, sir, would be . . . ?'

'Russell Cartwright. I live here.'

'Of course.'

'And I was wondering about this *hot pursuit*. Two-thirds of you look like you need intensive care. Is the Met that stretched?'

Sarah said, 'Why don't you sit down. I was about to put the kettle on. I'm just back from London myself.'

'Today?'

'Yes. Russell, would you light the fire in the front? It's turned a bit chilly.'

'It's not that—'

'Please?'

They say lovers share unspoken thoughts, and Sarah was positively screaming hers. *Use the bloody phone.* He blinked, and got it.

'Of course.'

Maddock stirred like a tree in a wind. 'A real fire?' Words

spoken carefully, as if abrupt speech might wreck his balance. 'I'm partial to a real fire, myself.'

Trying to squeeze brightness into his voice, like a man forcing his neck into a collar three sizes small.

Don't, thought Sarah: a silent prayer that Russell would refrain from a smart answer.

He did. 'Come through when the tea's done. Five minutes. It'll be roaring.'

'My old man used to make a fire. I've always enjoyed watching it done.'

It was painful, matching dialogue to delivery.

Russell said, 'Of course' again. And this was better; a stranger wouldn't have known he wasn't delighted.

That was love too – finding new surprises in the loved one's graces.

Sarah was left in her kitchen, with two strangers.

So this was what she'd returned to: the Zoë emergency. Sarah was no psychic, and had no time for frauds who were, but this was . . . not unexpected. It wasn't so much that Zoë went looking for trouble, as that she'd not step aside from it if she thought she had right of way. So there was always going to be an emergency, and Sarah was where Zoë would run when she had nowhere else to go. Because however much Zoë fought it, they'd come through too much together to be anything but friends, and being Zoë's friend didn't mean offering her flowers or crockery or pretty pairs of shoes. It meant giving her a wall to put her back to, and standing next to her when she did.

Sarah wished she'd changed, though, once she'd got back. She'd have felt better in jeans. Especially if it came to flight.

Try to take charge, though. 'He's right, you know. You don't look well. None of you.'

Aiming to keep it light. To give no hint that she knew where these wounds came from: which of Maddock's thighs was punctured; why Burke moved as if he'd recently bounced off a moving car.

'We had a bit of a jolt,' said Burke at last. 'Touch of black ice on a corner.'

'No other vehicle involved,' said Ross.

He had the voice she'd have invented for him if so required: a deep raw London rasp. As if he'd shouted himself rusty, practising these lines.

'Late in the year for that,' Sarah said. Then shut up: let them have their story. Fool.

'Treacherous bastard stuff,' he said. 'Black ice.'

She turned away, so he wouldn't notice he bothered her. 'Don't I know it. Some friends rolled their car last winter. Nearly killed themselves.' Listen to her witter. She can do mindless chatter with the best of them. She set out cups; rattled the tin of teabags, as if gauging its contents before daring to open it. All the while maintaining a stream of words: the weather, the neighbours, the trouble on the roads. Outside, the wedge of sky visible from the window screamed grey but calm, as if dangerous weather were a figment cooked up in the kitchen: the most dangerous room. The one where accidents happen.

'Did you drive from London?' Burke asked abruptly.

Sarah reined herself in. What did the innocent do when policemen called? They made tea, and asked questions. 'Yes. And I wasn't expecting company. Would you like to tell me what's going on?' And don't say *hot pursuit*.

'We're looking for a woman, Ms Tucker.' Burke was in charge of polite, evidently. 'She's wanted in connection with various offences. An old friend of yours. A Zoë Boehm.'

A Zoë Boehm, Sarah thought, ridiculously. There's more than one? 'Offences? Zoë? I don't think so.'

'Well, that shows loyalty. But we need to speak to her.'

'I wouldn't mind speaking to her myself. Zoë's not the best at keeping in touch. Tell me about these offences.'

'I can't do that. Ongoing investigation. I'm sure you understand.'

'Well, that shows faith. But I don't. Not remotely.'

'Assault,' said Ross. 'On an officer of the law. In the execution of his duties.'

Sounds like Zoë. But she shook her head: 'There's been a mistake.'

Burke silenced Ross with a look. 'Either way, we need to speak to her. When was the last time you saw her, Ms Tucker?'

'Zoë? About two years ago. Yes, two at least.'

She heard a noise from the other room, but it was probably the normal sounds you got when one man was watching another light a fire.

'That's odd. I was under the impression you were close.'

'I'm not sure why I figure in any of your impressions. But if it's your business, which it's not, yes, we're friends. But long distance. We lead busy lives.'

Burke nodded. And these were the preliminaries, while he worked out his approach. Sarah hoped, whatever it turned out to be, Burke's approach won the day. Ross was on edge, and looked like he favoured muscle. Having Zoë flip a coin in his eye hadn't softened what couldn't have been mild to start with.

. . . What bothered her mostly was, they'd given their real names. They were cops, yes: but. Sarah was no expert, but she read the papers. When a policeman was hurt he was bandaged up and photographed while his mates hit the road mob-handed. Wounded policemen didn't drive cross-country, pursuing an arrest. And the way Burke hesitated when she'd made him repeat his name told her he knew what he'd done. Even his approach wasn't a treat in store; just the best of available scenarios.

Ross said, 'Do you mind if I smoke?'

'I'd rather you didn't.'

'I should have guessed. No ashtrays.'

'Yes, well.' She laughed, or tried. Even to her own ears, it sounded like a seal barking. 'Not much point, really. As neither of us smoke.'

'I see.' He came nearer. There was something of the zoo about Ross; something best caged, and kept in darkness. 'Only you smell like you've been smoking.'

'. . . Do I?'

'It hangs on the clothes, you know? What my ex used to say.'

'I must have been somewhere smoky,' said Sarah.

'I thought you'd just driven back from London. And you not being a smoker, your car's not gunna be smoky. Is it?'

She turned to the stove, where the kettle was reaching the boil. From the corner of her eye she thought she detected movement through the window, though it was hard to be sure: little was visible, above the whitewashed wall. Tussocks of grass hung over its edge. Sometimes, early summer mornings, she'd see rabbits balanced there, stretching for that grass as if food came sweeter with danger attached. The rabbits weren't to know that Sarah presented no danger. She killed the gas. 'Well,' she said. 'You're quite the detective, aren't you, Sergeant Ross? It was Sergeant, right?'

He said, 'Where is she?'

'I'd have thought inspector at least, with that little display. Got me bang to rights, haven't you? Do they still say that? Bang to rights?'

Ross touched a finger to the eyepatch Sarah was sure was plastic. She had a vision of them pulling off a motorway to some desperate joke shop, plying fright wigs and comedy noses to the lost in need of laughter. And she wanted to tell him not to be such a *fucking* idiot, that he needed casualty, that all three needed treatment. But she said nothing, because what she mostly was was frightened – they'd given their names; given their actual names. Without a seriously good plan to get out of this, they were leaving scorched earth in their wake.

'Don't tell Russell,' she stage-whispered. 'I had a fag in the car.'

'Did you now.'

(It wasn't a question.)

She lifted the kettle to fill the teapot. There ought to have been reassurance in this, the domestic heft of it, but it just added to the unreality, as if the kitchen were a stage set, and pouring water her next direction.

'Maybe I'll step outside, then. That be okay? If I had a smoke outside?'

'Help yourself.'

And now he was patting his pockets; one step up from a white-faced fool pretending he couldn't find a door in an invisible wall.

'Would you believe it?!'

She wouldn't. She would.

'Could have sworn I had a pack.'

She looked at Burke, but he was Quiet Cop: hands in pockets, studying April's picture on the calendar.

'But maybe you'd lend me one. In return for keeping quiet in front of your old man.'

Sarah put the lid on the teapot, and practised a sweet smile with her back to them. No. That wasn't going to work. She turned it off, and turned around. 'Well, I would. But that was my last. Sorry.'

'You're sure about that.'

'Very.'

'Where is she?'

'I buy packs of ten. I smoke one or two, and throw the rest away. Because if they're around, I smoke them. You see?'

Burke said, 'Is there a tray? I'll carry that through for you.'

She looked at him blankly. Then caught up: this wasn't a stage set; there was another room. Her Russell was there, with another of this crew; lighting a fire, so they could sit round it drinking tea.

She hoped to God Zoë stayed where she was.

Zoë decided to wander over to the house. She'd just woken – felt sluggish and loggy from broken dozing – and a savage itch told her the handcuff hooped to her wrist was causing a rash. A sunlit circus of dust motes danced in the air. Anything might be happening, anywhere.

Sitting on the edge of the bed, she reached for her shoes. This was such an effort, there must have been a significant alteration in gravity as she'd slept. Zoë felt loaded down by her recent past, as if forced to shoulder it in laundry bags; images of robbed and soaking men had soured her rest. And now she was awake proper her perspective adjusted, and the real threat hove to mind. She was under no illusion that Monday night's escape was conclusive – these weren't men you could hurt and assume they'd forget it. Regardless of their reasons for wanting her in the first place, she'd given them cause to hunt her down.

Her shoes, too, were uncooperative. Their laces confused her fingers.

For a moment she thought about lying down some more, but she was hungry. For the first time in a while, Zoë wanted food, above and beyond the necessity of it, and she wondered if this had to do with seeing Sarah, and being reminded of the simple deep connections that make up life: things like friendship and hunger. Once, she'd found these readily available, but that was before she'd killed a man. *It wounds the soul*, she'd said, and it was as if the words had been growing inside her; an alien growth she needed to expel. Ten minutes with Sarah, and Zoë had said a lot of things. Sometimes it was hard to know who you were supposed to be defending yourself from.

. . . But this achieved nothing. She finished her laces, stood, stretched. The agenda was the same as ever: survive. Protect Sarah and Russell too, which meant removing herself. It had not been wrong to come here – she'd had nowhere else to go – but now she had rested, would soon be fed, and it was time to plan her next move. Talmadge was on that agenda too. Her recent, accumulating history included Caroline and Victoria; Zoë had delved too far into their lives not to carry their load to the finishing line. She'd had a recent taste of how men pursued their interests. Alan Talmadge was next on her list.

She made her way to the open air.

'Who's that?'

They were in the sitting room: Sarah, Russell, three cops. The tea tray sat on the low table in front of the log burner, which was blazing more fiercely than the day demanded; Sarah was wondering about opening the window. By which Maddock stood, looking out towards where the cars were parked on the gravelled expanse bordering the ostrich pen.

'There's somebody out there,' he said.

Five minutes they'd been here, enjoying the tea party from Sarah's personal hell: the one where policemen arrive, and throw their weight around. So far, metaphorically only. Burke sat next to Sarah on the sofa; Russell in the armchair to their left. But Maddock stood by the window and Ross too near the burner, shoulder to the stone fireplace into which it had been fixed. He was sweating, though sweating might be something Ross did as a matter of course. He had that basted look.

It had been Ross who'd said, 'Well, isn't this nice,' while Sarah poured.

'You've come a long way,' she'd said, 'and you look like you need a hot drink. But when you're finished, you can leave. You don't have any business here.'

'You're harbouring a criminal,' Ross said. 'We'll be leaving soon as we've taken charge of her.'

It was as if there were two different scripts: Sarah's aiming for a credible, real-world effect, while Ross's edged towards the ballistic. Burke, nominally in charge, possibly hadn't recovered from Zoë's car-kiss yet. He didn't look comfortable in his bones let alone on the sofa. With every moment that passed he faded like the Cheshire cat, leaving a grimace instead of a grin behind him.

Sarah said to Ross, 'Your dialogue sounds like a second-rate cop show,' and immediately regretted it. She'd been better off acting like Zoë was his fantasy: tolerable, but best disregarded.

'I think it's time we talked about warrants,' said Russell.

Russell was older than Sarah, successful in his own right, and had had student run-ins with the police: drugs and protest, like everybody else. And now, like everybody else, he'd grown out of both, and was generally in favour of the law. So why did Sarah wish he wasn't here? It wasn't just that she wanted him far from danger. It was that she couldn't trust him not to recognise the big gap between everybody else's view of things, and the way they might turn out to be.

This was a gap Sarah knew. She'd fallen into it before.

Burke said, 'It's funny, but as soon as somebody says *warrant*, I start wondering what they have to hide.'

And the lines in the room solidified and set, and Sarah knew this wasn't going to end with polite goodbyes.

He said, 'So you haven't seen Ms Boehm in years?'

It was as if he'd decided Russell wasn't there.

'I've already told you that.'

'Have you spoken to her lately?'

'Once or twice.'

'When, is what I was asking.'

She said, 'I'm really not sure. Do I need a lawyer?'

'Would you be happier with one?'

'I'd be happier with a policeman.'

'We are policemen, Ms Tucker.'

'Why does that not comfort me?'

Maddock said, 'Who's that?'

All turned.

He said, 'There's somebody out there,' and he was looking towards where the cars were parked, on the gravelled expanse bordering the ostrich pen.

Ross was by his side in a second. Burke was stiffer, slower, car-bashed; as he got to his feet Sarah thought *Keep moving*, but he didn't; he halted halfway, and looked back at her and Russell both. The nearest phone was in the kitchen. There was another upstairs. He wasn't about to let her get near either.

She had a mobile of course, but the signal here was atrocious.

'Where?' Ross was asking.

'Over there. Beyond the cars. Far side of that wire fence.'

'Her?'

'It was just a glimpse. She wore a black jacket, didn't she?'

'Until you pulled it off her.'

Sarah said, 'This is ridiculous. You're looking for a woman I've not seen in years. You've no authority here. I'd like you to leave.'

Maddock said, 'Who else lives here?'

'What do you mean, who else? Nobody does. Just the two of us.'

'So who did I just see?'

'You're asking me? You're seeing goblins for all I know.'

'Sarah,' Russell said.

Burke said, 'Let's all calm down. There's no point things getting out of hand,' and said it as if he'd been here, done this, recognised the circumstances: a bunch of rogue coppers, nearly past pretending, and a pair of householders *knowing too much*. Sarah thought *Thanks, Zoë*, and squashed the thought immediately. Last time anything remotely like this happened, it had been her own fault.

Sarah, Zoë had said. *I'm not gunna make a big thing of this. But I can't just walk away. That would make me bad as them.*

'So who did I just see?' Maddock asked again.

'Probably one of the neighbours.' Russell's voice was remarkably steady, and Sarah wondered if he was finding out how brave he was, or if he'd not realised the ground had shifted in the last minute.

'Doing what?'

Russell shrugged. 'We're in and out of each other's places all the time. They keep their tractor here.'

Ross looked at Burke. Burke looked away.

Russell said, 'They've got a key. Never bother with the bell.'

He knew. He knew things had changed.

Maddock said, 'I'll take a look.'

Sarah said, 'This is pointless.'

'She's here,' Ross said. He wasn't talking to Sarah; just announcing his conviction to the room. 'She had no other friends, no contacts. Nowhere else to go.'

'I've changed my mind,' she said. 'You'll never make inspector. That's not deduction, that's plain stupid.'

'Word of advice. I'd keep quiet, now.'

In her own home, he was telling her this. She was still holding her teacup, she realised: on her feet, cup in hand. She pointed at his eye. 'Zoë did that, didn't she? What did you think, she'd go to pieces at the first threat? Jesus, you'd better hope you don't find her again.'

He took a step towards her. Russell moved to her side. Burke put a hand in the air: all he needed was a whistle. 'That's enough.' He looked at Sarah, at Russell. 'You two should sit down.' To Ross he said, 'And you, keep it together.'

'You're not policemen,' she said.

'Oh, but we are.'

But he didn't meet her eyes when he said it.

She said, 'You're not here officially. Are you kidding? You've not said three words that've made sense since you arrived. Best if you just go, wouldn't you say?'

He looked to Ross, and seemed about to say something. What the manuals call a conflicted moment: if it weren't for Ross, this would be close to over; wouldn't have got this far to start with. Sarah could see Ross as the driving force: obliterating Charles Parsley Sturrock; triggering everything that came after. Wensley Deepman had witnessed that killing, and thought he'd found a way inside big money. It had probably taken Ross all of five minutes to find he didn't want to hock his life to a twelve-year-old thug.

Ross: who, as she watched, extended a thick fist and unfolded it for her gaze. In its palm, a silver worm, attached to a metal hoop.

'You still want to say she's not been here?'

Sarah didn't say anything.

And before Burke could speak, Ross went on: 'You told them to sit down. They haven't yet.' He turned back to Sarah. 'This can go clean or get messy. Any more fuss and you're under arrest. You're impeding an investigation.'

'Do you think we're stupid?' she said.

'Don't ask questions you know the answer to. Sit down, both of you.' And to Maddock he said, 'Go and take a look.' He put a finger to his eyepatch. 'And remember. She's got sharp fucking teeth.'

Maddock, limping, didn't need to be told.

But she didn't make it: having pushed the door open, she retreated back inside. There was a new car by the house, a big black one. It could be anybody's – friend or neighbour; salesman or census taker – and if it were any of those, they'd soon be on their way. Zoë was hungry, but not stupidly so. She wasn't about to blunder into company. Pulling the door to, she leaned against the jamb, becoming aware, as she did so, of the heavy smells this confined space contained: of recently opened tins of paint; of something oddly reminiscent of cocoa; of her own last cigarette.

It could be a friend or a salesman, yes. Or it could be a bunch of policemen, mad as stoats, and up for punishment.

. . . She'd punched her own name into search engines the odd time or two; out of vested interest rather than vanity. When your living relied on your reputation, it was useful to know what was said about you. And how many hits had it taken before she'd matched her name with Sarah's? There was only one big story Zoë had ever been involved in, and it was both of theirs. If she'd come looking for herself, how long would it have taken her?

There was something hard and pointy in her back, so she stood up straight, and studied the house through the crack in the door. It gave no clue as to who was inside, except maybe for that curl of smoke working out of the chimney: did you light a fire when heavies dropped round? That was more a friends and neighbours thing. Maybe they'd lit the fire for Zoë. Maybe they thought she'd be cold, without her jacket.

And besides, it could be Sarah's car . . .

So here she was, hiding in the shed from Sarah's car, while Sarah sat warm by the fire, wondering what was keeping her. This was ridiculous. She needed to eat, then be on her way. She ran a hand through her hair, suppressed a wild yawn, then stepped out into cold grey daylight, just as the cop who'd jumped her down by the canal limped round the side of the house.

Sarah stood.

'Where do you think you're going?'

'To the bathroom.'

'Sit down.'

'You are not going to tell me—'

'Sarah—'

'—to sit down—'

'Sit down,' he said again.

'—in my own house.'

'I just did.'

'Ross,' said Burke.

Sarah looked at Burke. 'You're doing this all wrong,' she said. 'You want us to believe you're who you say you are, you shouldn't be playing it this way. Not one bit.'

'Your friend,' he told her, 'is a dangerous woman. You can't blame us if we're on edge.'

'And I'm just back from half a day's drive. You can't blame me if I need the bathroom.'

Ross said, 'Just exercise a little control, all right?'

'I'm having my period. You want me to paint you a picture?'

'Jesus Christ,' he said.

'The problem is,' said Burke, 'we don't want you using a phone right now. In case she has a mobile. You understand?'

'It's not her you don't want me contacting.'

He piled through that. 'So I'll walk up with you. Okay?'

'Does it make any difference if it's not?'

Russell said, 'I'm having difficulty believing this is happening.'

'Oh, it's happening,' she said. 'Don't worry. I won't be long.'

She left him with Ross. The stairs were narrow, 'a feature': it was tempting to shove Burke down them. But it wasn't his neck that needed breaking. Reaching the top, she headed straight for the bedroom.

He caught her by the elbow in the doorway. 'This isn't where you're going.'

'There's things I need.'

'What things?'

There was a look Sarah could do that she hadn't grown up

with: she'd learned it during her marriage. She used it now, and he released her elbow, and stood watching as she took a pair of jeans from the back of a chair, then gathered various items from the top of the chest of drawers.

'You planning a complete makeover?'

'You know what us girls are like.'

As she passed him, heading for the bathroom, he put an arm out to stop her. 'You don't need all that.'

'I'm going to get cleaned up.'

'Put it on the bed.'

She dumped everything on the bed: jeans, talcum powder, tampons, mobile phone, deodorant. The mobile phone, he took, looking like he wanted to say something but couldn't quite find the words. Sarah wondered if it was shame blocking them.

She said, 'You expect me to apologise?'

He picked up jeans and tampons and handed them to her. 'Five minutes,' he said.

As they left the room she closed the door behind her, which had been the object of the exercise.

In the bathroom she used the loo, changed into her jeans, and ran the shower. The plumbing was another feature: like having a steel band on the premises. It took a moment to notice the thumping on the door. 'I told you,' Sarah called, opening the window. 'I've had a long drive. I need to clean up.' He shouted back, but she couldn't tell what. Clearing toothbrush mugs from the window sill, she climbed on to it. Here at the front of the house, she faced a fair fall on to gravel. She'd fallen further, and had the scars to prove it, but it wasn't her best memory. Now, anyway, was not the time to dwell on it. She climbed out.

The ledge was maybe three inches wide. You could walk all day on a three-inch strip, she told herself. All the room in the world. It felt different high up, that was all. She straightened, holding the frame for balance. This was okay. This was really okay. If she kept telling herself so, it would convince. Look neither round nor down. Just edge along, facing the wall; it was yards to the open bedroom window. A three-inch ledge for a couple of yards. There'd been a time she could have managed that on her hands.

But it was only three inches wide for the length of the window.

Things got trickier then. There was no window frame; only a sort of stone dado rail, an inch and a half wide, two feet below her, where the second storey met the first: as if they'd built the second separately, and it didn't quite match. For hand support there was only the stonework, which was rough enough to allow a little purchase. But this wasn't anything she paused to think about; stepping down before her mind changed, she allowed her left foot all the time it needed to find that ledge, then balanced a moment, suddenly sure they were down below, watching her. Waiting for her to fall. But they weren't. With her left hand she found a knobbly edge of stone to clamp on to while she completed the step down. From the bathroom behind her the shower thundered on. It really would be an idea to get that seen to. One thing at a time, though. Stepping down threw her heart in her mouth. Standing flat against a wall was not simple; the height was an added complication. *Don't think about the height.* Her right hand pressed flat against stone; tried to mould a handhold out of unyielding surface, which yielded as she had the thought, or maybe that was an illusion brought on by being scared witless . . . Either way, her fingers found a grip, and she edged an inch further. *This is how you do it, Sarah.* An inch at a time, like the rest of life. It was going to be fine, except her left foot slipped and she fell to the ground: only she didn't. Somehow, she didn't. Her left foot slipped, then found the ledge again; her left hand probed and found another hold. Behind her, the shower thundered; in front of her, the bedroom window yawned open. Bless Russell, who liked a through draught. Another step, and her fingers would reach the window frame. From there, it would be like hauling herself out of a swimming pool: another dumb dangerous moment behind her.

The ledge beneath her right foot crumbled, and fell away into nowhere.

Zoë stepped back into the shed, even as she did so thinking: how stupid was *that*? She'd boxed herself in . . . She wasn't breathing. She made no sound at all. And he didn't, in fact, see her; he was looking towards the treeline, and didn't turn her way before she'd become invisible.

After studying the trees, he looked up at the corner of the house. From here, because of the way the land rose, his head was almost level with the guttering. He stood there a moment before going back the way he'd come: round the house, out of her line of vision.

She let out a long breath and pulled the door to, realising, a moment too late, that she'd made the wrong choice. That she'd just boxed herself in again.

These are the things that run through your mind when you're about to break your neck: that the past few years have been the best of them; that it's not your first love that matters but your last; that the window frames need attention, but remain pretty reliable nevertheless. It was that *nevertheless* saved her; she caught the woodwork before gravity caught her; was gripping it two-handed before that chunk of stone hit the ground. From below, she must have looked like a circus performer. Heaving herself through the bedroom window was the most physical she'd been in recent memory, but she had more to worry about than a few stretched muscles.

And she hoped the shower was still pounding, because she hadn't been too quiet about that last bit.

Which it must have been, because Burke didn't come crashing into the room. Closing the door had helped: damn Russell, who always left it wide open, because he liked a through draught. Falling on the bed, she pulled the phone towards her, lifted the receiver with one hand and punched buttons with the other as soon as the dial tone reached her ear: *nine nine nine*.

Somewhere else a phone rang once, and almost twice, then died.

23

WHEN THE COP CAME back, just long enough later for Zoë to wish she'd made a run for it, he was holding the orange-handled cutters Russell had used to clip the handcuff from her wrist. There was a patch of green on the cop's knee where he'd knelt. The junction box was round that corner. He'd cut the phone line; and the area – Russell had said – was mobile-dead.

She wondered what was happening in the house right now.

There were a couple of certainties: that if this one was here, the others were too; and sooner or later they'd be told where she was. This wasn't a matter of blame or treachery. It reduced to fundamental logic; was almost physics. Laws of action and reaction. You push, and in time you are pushed. Having come all this way, these three wouldn't back off out of squeamishness. They were desperate men, and desperate men resorted to devices. Sarah would shield Zoë to her limit, but still had a limit. Sooner or later, one of them – probably Ross – would discover it.

I just don't want to let anybody down.

Well, Russell would get his chance now.

She did a quick recce of the shed's shelves: the hoes, the spades, the weedkillers that could be converted to semi-lethal use, if there were squirting devices handy. Which there weren't. Through a flaw in the woodwork, she estimated the distance to the treeline, and reckoned it five hundred yards, with little cover; just the tuck and ruffle of uneven ground. And there was no telling when they'd wander outside again, or if they were watching from windows. She wondered if Russell had managed to shift her car. And she wondered why these cops thought she knew anything, when she was simply a frightened woman in a shed.

Sarah, she supposed, would be glad she was frightened. Would take it as further proof that Zoë wanted to remain among the living.

. . . Everything came down to choices. She could stay in the shed, or she could run. She could head towards the house or away. She could make it or she could not. As with everything else, some choices were out of her hands; she simply had to do the best with what was left.

She shuddered. Whatever happened next – whatever choice forced itself upon her – she wished she'd kept hold of her leather jacket. Zoë could have done with that comfort; with something zipped and familiar. She was going to make a run for the treeline now, and had her hand on the door, about to open it, when she heard feet scrunching on the gravelled area, and knew she'd left it too late.

'I got through.'

'She didn't,' said Burke.

'The call was answered. First thing they do, they read your number back—'

'We know the first thing they do,' said Ross.

'She didn't get through,' said Burke.

'They'll be here soon.'

Producing this lie felt like throwing pebbles at a cliff face, while Russell watched her eyes, watched her lips move, and knew the truth.

She'd still been trying to rattle life into the receiver when Burke had removed it; replaced it gently in its cradle, exactly as if she couldn't be blamed for trying. As he'd ushered her downstairs, she'd heard the shower hammering away behind the locked bathroom door. Just as well she'd not opted to run the bath.

Maddock limped in, and deposited one of Russell's tools on the table, probably scratching it.

'Is any of this necessary? We've told you. She's not here.'

But Maddock said, 'Her car's here. Behind the pen where they keep those birds.'

Ross said, 'I don't know about you lot, but I'm fucking sick of this. Let's go,' and pushed Russell, who stumbled over a footstool. He scrambled to his feet before Ross could tread on him. 'Outside.'

'We're going nowhere.'

'You'll go where you're told.'

Russell looked at Sarah then back at Ross, who pushed again, with hard stubby fingers that bit the meat of Russell's shoulder. For a moment, complete bewilderment painted Russell's face, and Sarah wanted to put her arms round him. She doubted deliberate physical harm had been inflicted on Russell in thirty years. Now something had been peeled away, exposing the gristle beneath. And it frightened Russell, but he hid this immediately, and Sarah ached to see it.

They marched through the front door: Russell, Ross, Burke, Sarah, Maddock. Sarah was out of words. Everything was happening too quickly; as if she'd been cast without audition in a part she'd never wanted to play.

On the gravelled area outside the front door, daylight scratched the surface of things. Ross elbowed Russell aside and stalked to the big black car, whose make Sarah wasn't sure of: was it important? Maddock put a hand on her, and she pulled away as angrily as if he'd suggested sex. Ross opened the boot. Burke said words Sarah didn't catch. His moment had gone.

The show was now Ross's, and one-eyed Ross was angry: it wasn't about covering up whatever they'd done any more. It was about getting hold of Zoë. Ross was somebody who paid back hurt he'd suffered: in the big world, this fuelled wars. Here, it wouldn't be pretty either. When he turned he held a twin-barrelled gun in his hands, pointing at Russell. He said, 'Where is she?'

Russell, staring at the gun, couldn't answer.

Ross adjusted his grip. 'Where?'

Sarah shimmered. Maddock's hand was on her elbow again; his hold as tight as if he needed an anchor. And all of this was happening: a fact it would be as well to keep a grip on. The sky was grey, the grass was green; a one-eyed demon had invaded their lives with a life-swallowing shotgun. Sarah opened her mouth: she was going to tell them where Zoë was. Then closed it again: she wasn't. There was no way he was going to kill anybody. Not here, by the green grass, under the grey sky.

Russell said, '. . . I don't know.'

'You know.'

'She was here. But she left.'

'So why's her car over there?'

'She took mine.'

'What make?'

Russell's mouth flapped. Sarah prayed for him. He said, 'Focus. Ford Focus.'

'Colour?'

'Silver.'

'Year?'

'Er . . . Ninety-seven.'

'Plate?'

'. . . What?'

Ross grabbed Russell's shirt; pulled him close so the gun was trapped between them, aiming skyward. 'You're lying. There's no silver fucking Focus. Where is she?'

And it would be easy to pretend it wasn't happening, because now, more than ever like something from a dream, Gwyneth singled Russell out of the pack, and pranced over. Reaching the wire fence she sank to her knees in that at first glance impossible manner, her feet projecting in front of her, and began softly crooning. No idea of what was going on. Love was blind, presumably. Everybody looked for one second, then attention refocused on Ross, on Russell.

'I won't ask again.'

'. . . She left.'

Sarah found her voice. 'Are you mad?' She looked at Burke. 'What happens afterwards? You think all this just goes away?'

Burke said, 'We need to find her,' and his voice was strained and clutching straws.

Gwyneth fluffed her feathers out. It had never before failed to make Sarah laugh: this lovelorn ostrich making a play for her man. Now it had the bad taste effect of a gag at a funeral.

Russell said, 'I've told you. She's gone.'

'I don't,' said Ross, 'believe you.'

'She left,' shouted Sarah. 'Are you out of your fucking minds? She left.'

Ross swung round. 'That's right. I'm forgetting.' He shoved Russell aside. 'Why ask the monkey when the organ grinder's here?'

Burke said, 'Jack, I think we've gone—'

'Shut up.'

Russell lunged at him, and in a manner so casual it hardly seemed to happen until it was over Ross raised the gun so Russell's forehead ran slap into the stock. He stepped back then sat down suddenly.

Sarah screamed.

Russell fell flat on his back. He made no noise during any of this.

Maddock's grip tightened on Sarah's shoulder; less – she thought afterwards – to hold her steady than from simple alarm at the turn events had taken. Burke stepped forward.

Gwyneth flapped: stood, pranced two steps left, then dropped again. Whatever courtship ritual her mind embraced, Russell had just introduced new dimensions to it.

Burke said, 'Is this necessary?'

'You want to die in prison?'

'Jack—'

'Shut up.'

Maddock said, 'He's right.'

'Where is she?'

'Fuck off,' Sarah told him.

Russell groaned. Sarah tried to reach him, but Maddock pulled her back.

Burke said, 'Just tell us where she is. This can all be over right now.'

Ross said: 'You see? Even the voice of sweet reason's come round.'

'Did it take all three of you to kill the little boy?' she asked. 'Or was that just you?'

'Sturrock deserved to die.' His teeth were flecked with spit. 'He was ten years overdue.'

'I don't care about Sturrock. You killed a child.' She spoke to Burke: the weakest link. 'That's why you're here.'

He said, 'He wanted money . . .'

'He recognised you.'

'Are we quite fucking finished?'

She turned back to Ross. 'It was you, wasn't it? Who threw him. Did he scream? Did that turn you on?'

'I wasn't even on the roof, you dumb bitch.'

And now she was looking at Burke again, who opened his mouth then wiped something invisible from his cheek. 'It didn't . . . It wasn't like that. Nobody threw him.'

But he didn't jump, either.

Ross said, 'What is this, true confessions?' He shifted the gun in his hands: letting her know that he unequivocally held it. 'Your turn. Where's the woman?'

Burke went on as if Ross hadn't spoken: 'We meant to scare him, that's all.'

'I'd say you managed that.'

Ross said, 'Yeah, right. So now he's pavement art, and if that don't teach him, nothing will.'

Burke, to Sarah, said, 'None of this was meant to happen. We were righting a wrong, that's all.'

Of course. So now they were here with a shotgun, and her man lay on the ground bleeding. What was wrong with this picture?

In the background, Russell struggled to sit up. Sarah willed him to stay put: just lie there out of the story. But he wouldn't; didn't. He held one hand to his head, and with the other pushed himself to a sitting position.

She strained forward without realising it. Maddock's grip tightened.

'Whatever happened,' she said, 'whatever mess you made, you're making it worse now. Can't you see that?'

'Thanks for the information.' Ross was speaking from beyond anywhere she recognised as rational: a place where he'd helped murder a man for whom, let's face it, she wouldn't be lighting candles. But that wasn't a place you travelled back from easily. And now he was looking for Zoë, who he thought had found him out; and here were Sarah and Russell too – what were the chances he'd be seeing sweet reason himself anytime soon? And judging by Maddock's grip, Ross wasn't alone. They'd all three stumbled over the point of no return.

Gwyneth's crooning became louder; stuttered, stopped. Started again.

Ross waved the gun at Russell, who was holding his head in his hands; trying to rub the pain away.

'You want me to shoot him?'

'You're not going to do that,' she said bravely, unless it was stupidly. How did she know what he was going to do? It wasn't enough to cling to a vision of the way things ought to be: that this couldn't happen, not here in her quiet home.

'You want to bet his life?'

But this wasn't Sophie's choice: Russell or Zoë. She wouldn't get to keep one of them.

She looked at Burke. 'Are you still sane? Or are you as far gone as him?'

'Just tell us where she is,' he said. Answer enough.

'You said it was an accident. You never meant to kill the boy. There was a witness.'

'Christ,' said Maddock behind her.

'Ross,' said Burke. 'Ross was the witness.'

Russell stood, and wobbled like a newborn foal. 'Sarah?' His voice carried a tremble she'd not heard there before: in sleep nor love nor grief. 'Are you okay?'

Gwyneth fluttered at his voice: she was getting beyond a joke.

Ross said, 'Somebody is going to die unless I get an answer in the next five seconds.'

She looked at Russell, who looked right back. There should have been more of an exchange in that glance; they should have been communicating something deeper than just the gap between them. A gap which one or other of them, usually her, had always been able to bridge with one of the simple formulae: I'm sorry/I didn't mean that/I love you. But here and now the few yards between them were too far to travel, because Ross had said *Somebody is going to die* and all of a sudden she believed him.

Russell said, 'Sarah—'

Sarah. Because, she thought, it was always going to be her task: to forgive him, or to betray her friend. It didn't much matter in which order these things happened.

'It's okay,' she said.

He looked at Ross. 'She isn't here. She left,' he said, and that wasn't what Sarah had been expecting.

'Yeah, right, fine,' said Ross. Then he thrust the muzzle of the shotgun through the mesh of the fence and pulled the trigger.

The noise echoed inexpressibly down the rest of Sarah's life. It never stopped. Something screamed briefly, but whether it was herself or Russell or Gwyneth couldn't be told: she saw feathers, blood, meat; something that once lived and recognised humans. Then saw nothing for a second or two. Then saw it all again, and none of it had changed. Ross pulled the gun back through the fence. He looked at Sarah, looked at Russell. 'That didn't have to happen.'

Maddock had let go of her, she realised.

Burke said, 'Oh, fuck . . .'

Russell stared at what used to be Gwyneth, and his lips moved but no sound came out. He licked them. Something gathered at the corners of his eyes, and if it wasn't tears it was blood. He said, 'You cunt.'

'Yeah, right, fine,' said Ross again. There was metal in his voice.

'I'll hurt you for that—'

'Sure. You've got two left. You want to tell me where she is?'

They had two left, but they were gone away into their coop. Would be sticking their heads in the sand if there were sand for them to hide in.

Ross did something to the gun that made a noise. He didn't need to use the words this meant.

Russell cast a look at Sarah. There was nothing in it she recognised as his, though she caught its colours: hurt, loss, anger.

Maybe she nodded her head. She couldn't afterwards remember.

Russell pointed. 'She's in the shed,' he said.

Zoë had left it too late, because they were out of the house now, all of them – she'd pulled the door shut, but even at this distance, she could tell it was all of them, from the different weights and shapes she heard rearranging gravel. Three of them, plus Sarah and Russell.

She squashed into the corner, in the gap where the shelving didn't reach. Fumes from an unsealed tin of paint stung her nose; she had to breathe through her mouth. Various aches and pains woke, stretched and grizzled, but adrenalin responded. There was nothing like immediate danger to put yesterday's frights to sleep. There were words, but she couldn't make out what they were. There were voices, and one was Sarah's. There was a hollow thunk, like somebody walking into a tree. Then Sarah screamed.

And Zoë stayed wrapped tight in her corner. If she walked out now, hands held high, it would be a betrayal of what Sarah and Russell were going through. It was not up to Zoë to take that from their hands. That was what she told herself, wrapped tight in her corner, while minutes crawled by.

Her hand, she noticed, was resting on her breast. She removed it, and stared at it strangely for a moment. Its concerns seemed to belong to another period of her life.

Then a gunshot, and dust rose around her, and danced in the spears of light that lanced through the fissures in the walls.

Her heart stopped. For half a second, that was all she was conscious of; her brief suspension, as if that muscle governed not only her own continuance but the survival of *everything*: this shed, the country surrounding, the world it was part of. Everything stopped when her heart stopped: that was what happened. And that would be death: the conclusion of everything, all of it dependent on the beating of her heart. When she stopped, everything stopped. It was that simple. But this time, she started again.

There came more screaming; one brief fraction of it barely human. Blood pounded in Zoë's ears. She imagined Sarah cut in two; Russell puddled on the ground; the pair of them reduced to their constituent elements. Numbness spread through her, and dissolved immediately in a new wash of adrenalin. She did not know what was happening, but this much was clear: it was time to run. Memories of things left undone jostled in her mind – bills unpaid; letters unburnt – then faded to a fresh white vision of the here and now. Sinking to her knees, she prised the door open. The treeline had grown no nearer. She'd count to three, she decided, while her breathing adjusted: *one two*— And then an instinct from nowhere fell on her, convincing her that this was not the moment, so she pushed the door to again, blanking out the light from the world. Still on her knees, she rested her face in her hands. It was rare that the consequences of a decision were immediate, but these would be. If there was any comfort nearby, that's where it lay: that whatever happened would happen soon. And although they caused her heart to stop once more, she was hardly surprised by the gunshots, when they came.

From the treeline he watches, and can barely believe what he sees: the sudden, brutal murder of an ostrich. There one minute, and the next mince and feathers. Though rationally speaking, it has no right being present in the first place: here on the edge of the Peak District, ostriches aren't what you come looking for.

Zoë is who you come looking for.

The men are the men from the street the other night: who found Zoë, and mostly wished they hadn't. The one who has shot the bird, he's seen before then – he's watched him speak, without believing a word he said. And now this man is turning, pointing the gun at the one who's just struggled to his feet; who must be Sarah's man. Watching from the treeline, Alan Talmadge – a name he still calls himself when he needs an other to flesh out the dialogue he embodies – tucks his hands into their opposite armpits, where the black leather jacket fits tightest. Chiming through his mind is the lyric that dragged him here. Sometimes the songs are more than songs: they're instruction.

Whenever you need me
I'll be there

This is why he's come: to protect. All the other challenges – loneliness, other people's pity – fall away to pointlessness. What he's thought of as the problems he could do something about; the everyday dangers revealed in the eyes of women on buses, in the Tube, in the street. The ones he's grown up beside. They don't amount to much, set beside an angry Cyclops with a weapon. And violence isn't his strength. He's been present at death, has been there when death started to happen, but that was ordained. You can only rescue one person at a time. But this is new, and just for a moment, he wonders whether he's up to the task.

Be my brave boy, now. Be my white knight.

But he has no choice, really: that's the nature of the role. That you do what's required. Though it's difficult to know exactly what's required now, as Sarah's man points to the shed as if giving directions, and the eyepatched man advances on it, gun level in his grip, exactly as if he means to open fire; exactly as if there's a war going on he's forgotten to tell anybody about. So Talmadge simply watches, hugging himself ever tighter, as if some savage transfer is taking place and this black leather becoming part of his skin. Though even watching it happen, it's hard to believe when, five yards from the shed, Eyepatch opens fire; his first blast shattering the landscape, so trees everywhere explode in the same moment, as frightened birds escape into the air and chunks of shed spin free like wooden fireworks. Thick six-inch splinters embed the ground around like flightless darts. He fires again, and part of the roof blows free. And in the sudden shocking silence immediately after

273

— a silence that isn't silence, but rather a clearing away of enormous noise, as it bangs off towards the horizon — it becomes clear to Talmadge that if Eyepatch fires again his task is over because the shed is too small, the gun too big; and if Eyepatch fires again, he'll be tearing a hole through anything breathing inside the wooden shelter. And even as the thought occurs, Eyepatch fires again.

Sarah said, 'No,' but nobody heard her. She said it again. Russell turned — looked right through her, as if the past few minutes had taken him somewhere remote and indistinct, and he just barely carried her picture in his head — then turned back to watch Ross's progress towards the shed. Ross carried the gun level in his hands, as if using it were next on his agenda. On Russell's forehead, a dull red continent of pain was emerging; its shape immediately familiar.

Five yards from the shed, Ross fired the gun.

. . . The noise seemed to whistle past Sarah's head as if it were heading somewhere else entirely, and never had anything to do with her. She imagined it soaring way over distant hills: crashing into someone else's life like a fragment of space debris, unintentional and devastating. Then her consciousness righted itself. She was still here. Ross still held the gun. The shed had acquired a hole, and a lunatic crop of spiky wooden mushrooms had sprouted off to its left. Ross shot again, and part of the shed's roof blew free, throwing up a minor black cloud of tarpaulin woodchips nails glue: all blasted into irrelevance and deposited out of sight. Russell's lips were moving, as if he were trying to find a connection between his words, *she's in the shed*, and this consequence: the shed's destruction, along with everything inside it. Maddock's grip on her arm relaxed. And Burke was swearing under his breath — more litany than straight-forward cursing, as if it had become important to purge himself of all the foul words he'd ever heard: right here, right now.

She looked at Russell, who tensed, as if whatever happened

next would be louder, fiercer, and make more mess. And just before it happened Sarah understood why that was, and dropped to the ground even as he motioned to her to do so.

Ross fired again, and the shed exploded.

SEVEN

FLIGHTLESS THINGS

24

THE FIRST SHOT STOPPED her heart. That was how close it felt: this noise made of metal and splintering wood, that punched everything out of its way, and flailed so wildly in its passage it stopped Zoë's heart even at this safe distance. The second was muffled, as if its target were more inclined to flap than stand firm to be torn apart. Before the third she'd opened the door, dared a look, then stepped into daylight grown old and bruised. The day had walked smack into the utterly unexpected; the utterly never seen here before – this quiet place between hills, with its treeline and moody ostriches. Where a man with an eyepatch blasted away at a shed she'd never been in.

The neighbours keep it here, Russell had said of the small blue tractor behind it. *And its fuel and gear in the shed*.

She tried to picture fuel for tractors, and imagined plastic bins or big tin cans, lined on shelves like ducks at a fair. While a man with an eyepatch blasted away, under the impression she used them for shelter . . .

It was not, all things considered, a huge explosion; hardly Hollywood choreography. Zoë, in motion now, had her back to it, but ever afterwards was able to remember it in acute detail nevertheless. Ross had been quite near the shed when he fired a third time and hit the ducks dead centre, so their hearts burst in unison, scattering liquid fire everywhere.

Whatever Ross had been expecting, it wasn't this. He fell back – flew back, in Zoë's created memory – and hit the ground with a bone-rattling thump, and the gun was airborne suddenly; curving through space like an ill-planned boomerang. Zoë actually *saw* the spirograph pattern it carved on the air, circles inside a circle, before the ground reached up and interrupted its trajectory. And then she was among trees, her vision obscured even in memory. A branch lashed her face. Behind her, smoke stained the darkening sky; a black comma the wind would shred and toss.

If she followed the treeline, she'd reach the road; somewhere on the road would be a car. In the car, a phone. This was how the future broke down, into one plain fact after another, though when you looked back afterwards, it seemed a smooth unfractured process.

It was getting to be second nature: fleeing over uncomfortable ground. Grey light speckled through the trees like rain. The noises that reached her now were suspiciously ordinary: her own breathing, of course, and the pumping of her heart. But beyond that, just the sounds trees made while the wind scraped past them, and the usual distant grumblings of nature. Nothing resembling a car. Zoë reached a sudden ditch, on the far side of which lay the road.

To a more athletic version of herself, the ditch was an obstacle leaped without thinking, but that Zoë was ten years younger. She stepped down carefully, grimacing as mud squelched into her shoe, then scrambled up the far side, smearing her hands in the process . . . Was it just this afternoon she'd bathed? But here was the road: she stood a moment, hands on hips, breathing hard. The road twisted out of sight a hundred yards ahead; behind her, it climbed a hill then dropped into nowhere beyond the lane leading to the farmhouse. Urgency gripped her again. Sarah and Russell were still back there.

Zoë started to jog. There was mud in her shoes and tar on

her lungs, but she had this straightforward task to accomplish: find help; rescue Sarah. And Russell. Round the corner the road kept twisting, and as she ran she became aware of a thudding undercurrent, a soft padding echoing the slap of her feet hitting tarmac, but when she turned there was nobody: only the wind scratching round in the trees. It was just her imagination, running along with her. She was remembering her lost jacket, and how comforting it would be to have it now.

There came the sound of a car, heading towards her.

When the shotgun hit the ground, nothing happened, which was a relief. Watching it lazily plane through the air, Sarah had been expecting a random discharge on impact: something lethal and indiscriminate. *It's not the bullet with my name on it that worries me*, a wise man once said. *It's the one addressed 'To whom it may concern.'* She was on her hands and knees; Ross was down too, his hands covering his head. And Burke looked like a man who'd walked into the wrong room, the wrong entire life, while Maddock had been plain erased: his face a blank white sheet.

. . . As for Russell, he'd collapsed. Her instinct was to head for him, but sometimes you had to go with your brain. Getting to her feet she felt the world tilt, as if that shed had been its fulcrum. And everything was happening just a touch slowly, with the extra care that comes with pretending not to be drunk. The noise in the distance was probably a car. But it sounded drugged and irritable, and lowed like an upset cow.

The gun, though. The gun was what she was supposed to be focusing on.

At a tilt, then, she made for where it had landed. With a curious absence of alarm she realised Burke was coming to life; dragging his attention from the gutted shed, whose occasional pops and whistles were cans and bottles of . . . *stuff* bursting. Paintstripper, turpentine, weedkiller: *stuff*. There would be noxious fumes, and maybe they were affecting her; were maybe

the reason the word 'noxious' floated dopily round her brain
. . . Enough. With a curious absence of alarm she realised Burke
was coming to life, but this was followed swiftly by an entirely
reasonable alarm. He too appeared a beat behind reality, but
he stood nearer the gun. Sarah's dash would have carried her
straight into him, but some self-preserving impulse slammed
her brake on.

Burke didn't point it at her, exactly. But he was holding it
and she wasn't, and that kind of made a point all by itself.

'Just stay there.'

She just stayed there.

Then he lost the script. Looked at the gun as if Props had
fucked up, and it should have been a spade or a banana; something harmless, and more in keeping with the man he'd been
when he'd signed up for law and order. She could almost feel
sorry for him, except, of course, she couldn't.

'She wasn't in the shed, was she?'

'No,' said Sarah. 'She wasn't in the shed.'

He nodded vaguely. 'I'm glad . . . So where is she?'

She shook her head.

He looked at the gun again, as if it suggested a method of
making her tell, and then forgot about it. 'This wasn't . . . this
wasn't the plan, exactly.'

'No kidding.'

It was as if there were just the two of them, and he'd been
saving up for the moment: the moment when he'd seek abso-
lution.

'He deserved to die.'

'He was twelve years old, Burke.'

'Not him. Sturrock. Danny was a friend of mine. Every day
Sturrock was breathing was a kick in the teeth.'

Sarah guessed Danny was the policeman Sturrock had stabbed
to death. 'And Wensley Deepman just got in the way.'

'He saw it happen . . . Recognised me from the station.' A

twisted smile creased his face, as if he were remembering something funny that happened to somebody else, some time ago. 'He was kind of a regular.'

'And he wanted money.'

'Of course he did.'

Sarah waited, feeling as if there ought to be a grille separating them; as if she should be prepared, any minute, to mumble Latin words and set him free.

'I was the one with the eyes. In the car park. I was supposed to make sure there were no witnesses. But he was a sneaky little bugger, that one. Sneaky little bugger.'

His eyes recalled a job undone. Remembered what he'd had to do to make things right.

'I knew he didn't like heights. Can't remember how. You ever get that? Knowing something about somebody without knowing how you know it?'

'Sometimes,' said Sarah.

His grip on the shotgun hadn't faltered yet.

'So I arranged the meet up top of a tower block. For the edge, see? Like we needed an edge. He was twelve years old.'

Burke was weeping, or his eyes were weeping, even if the rest of him refused to acknowledge it.

'We wanted to frighten him.'

Well, they'd managed that.

'Little bastard thought he was indestructible.'

Somewhere behind her, Ross swore. 'Christ. Fucking *Christ* . . .'

To Burke, Sarah said, 'Give me the gun.'

This puzzled him. It seemed perhaps not entirely within the rules of the game. He glanced over her shoulder at the approaching Ross, as if hoping for a clue.

'Burke? Now?'

But there hadn't been enough time; had not been enough talking. If he had finished his story, Sarah knew, he'd have given her the gun.

She heard Ross cough and spit behind her. 'Don't shoot the bitch,' he called. He wasn't far off. 'Give me the gun. I'll do it.'

Sarah reached out and laid her hand on the shotgun's barrel, just as Burke's hold on its stock tightened.

She did not know afterwards why she had done what she'd done: stepped back into the bushes at the roadside and dropped to a crouch before the car appeared. It was best put down to a self-preservation instinct, an awareness – and if Zoë hadn't known this already, the last few days would have taught her – that you never knew where the next blow was coming from. That the light at the end of the tunnel was probably that of an oncoming train. She had the feeling that something was tracking her; something sleeker and more camouflaged than those hard men with their wounds and aggravation. So she dropped, and let a bush fold itself around her uncomfortably. Once the car was upon her, once she'd seen who it was, she'd step out to flag it down.

Though once she'd seen who it was, that ceased to be an option.

Sarah reached out and laid her hand on the shotgun's barrel, just as Burke's hold on its stock tightened, and for a moment she had a clear picture of what happens next: Burke fastens on the trigger, and Sarah ceases, in any meaningful way, to exist. Like Gwyneth, poor ostrich, who died for love. But instead Burke's grip failed him, and she was pulling the gun from his hands like a sword from a stone; was turning, pointing, in a single fluid motion, as if it were something she'd practised in a dream.

Ross came to a halt two yards off.

She said, 'I've done this before.'

'You fucking idiot,' he said, but he wasn't talking to Sarah.

Russell was on his feet. He looked dazed, and the welt on his head had grown no smaller. For a second, she wanted to lash out: give Ross a matching bruise. Watch him collapse like a broken mast. This is how wars start.

'Back off,' she said, then stepped back herself so Burke was in front of her. He might have regrets about relinquishing the weapon. He looked, in fact, like he was having regrets about everything, but was in no state to rectify any of it. She kept the gun trained on Ross while telling Burke, 'Just move over there, would you?' *Please*, she remembered not to add. Polite was a form of weak, to some.

Reading her mind, Ross said, 'You're not going to use that.'

'I was very fond of that ostrich,' she told him, and saw a shadow cross his face, and was glad.

This happened when you wielded a gun. It dragged out demons you didn't know hid inside you.

She said, 'I want the three of you over there. Not moving.' Then called, 'Russell? Are you okay?'

He said something she didn't catch.

'Russell?'

'I think so.' But he didn't sound it. He was patting himself down as if checking he was in working order. Burke, meanwhile, heaved himself next to Ross; Maddock was near enough that she could keep an eye on all three at once. She wondered where Zoë was. Either she'd gone for help, or she'd be showing any moment.

Russell said, 'He wasn't ready for that, I guess,' and gave a cackling sort of laugh.

Ross muttered something under his breath.

A gust of wind lifted her hair. Incredibly, Sarah suppressed a yawn. Her jaw ached. Something that was probably a car hummed in the distance, and it was as if the phone had rung while she was watching TV, and for a moment it was unclear which reality it belonged to. And while she was shuffling between the two, Ross took a step forward, as if he were about to jump – she couldn't have done it on a dare, but she did it:

brought the gun up to shoulder height and levelled it at his head. He stopped dead; or to be precise, dead was what he didn't stop. He stopped a moment before he might have been dead. Even if she'd had her hands free, Sarah couldn't have put either on her heart and sworn she wouldn't have squeezed the trigger.

'I said don't move,' she told him, and even to herself, her voice sounded as if it were relayed through somebody else.

The humming grew louder, and was definitely a car.

Russell approached, unsteadily; a bruise red and wide on his forehead. He was making words, but she still couldn't hear him. Swallowing panic, she said, 'Russell? Come over here now. But be careful of these guys.'

The humming was an engine, all right: attached to wheels rolling down the lane. She didn't look, but her first thought was *Zoë*. Zoë had run to the road; had flagged down a car, which was full of . . . Sarah's imagination let her down for a second. Traffic wardens. No: off-duty firemen, or passing farm labourers. A carload of either would make short work of these stooges.

Russell reached her side, and had sense enough not to touch her. 'I wasn't sure it would do that,' he said, reasonably clearly.

The shed was a wreck: a bright orange heart pumping away, feeding nothing. It looked like a dismantled bonfire. Small clumps of flame littered the area. The blue tractor sat scorched but entire behind it.

'He shot Gwyneth,' he said then, and fell over.

The car came to a halt on the gravel.

'Russell?' she said.

He didn't answer.

Behind her, a car door opened, then shut. '*Russell?*'

Ross said, 'Why don't you put that down? See to the man.'

'Fuck off.' She risked a glance at Russell. 'Sweetheart? You okay?'

'. . . Head hurts . . .'

Somebody was coming. She didn't want them getting closer when she didn't know who they were. 'Just hold it right there,' she called.

Whoever it was kept coming.

'I've got a gun,' she said.

'You're not going to shoot me.'

It wasn't a voice she recognised.

She took a step back, which was wrong: she held the balance of power, but a gun was only useful if you were prepared to use it . . . Russell at her feet, Sarah turned to see who was coming: a tall lean man wearing glasses and a raincoat, still a dozen yards off. She spared him half a beat, and turned back. 'Don't move.'

Ross, almost comically, had put his hands halfway up. 'Oh, we're not going nowhere.'

She turned again, and brought the shotgun muzzle round this time too. The man didn't falter.

'We both know you're not going to shoot me,' he said. 'So it would be best all round if you just gave me the gun.'

He held one hand outstretched; the other was in the pocket of his raincoat. Here was a man who had no doubt that she wasn't going to shoot him. He was right, of course. She could hardly kill him. They hadn't been introduced. Movement behind her: Ross had shuffled forward. You could hold all the cards, but lack the edge needed to win. All she had to do was pull the trigger, but she didn't want to hurt anybody. And firing into ground or air would shout that loud and clear.

The man kept coming. He lacked the physical presence of Ross or Maddock, but there was an authority to him they wouldn't even pretend to. They were knock-down-door types. This one would rap on it loudly; a demand you couldn't ignore.

Russell moaned at her feet. She had maybe a second to decide what to do: to fire the gun or give it up.

In the end, Sarah did neither. Instead, she flung it over the heads of the three cops in front of her, so it swam once again through the smoky air, before dropping, as neatly as if pulled on a string, into the glowing heart of the murdered shed.

25

B ACK AMONG THE TREES, looking down on the ruined shed beyond the ostrich pen, Zoë saw nobody. The grass was pockmarked with burnt patches where scraps of fire flickered, and at the centre of what had once been the shed itself, something throbbed like a toothache.

She'd come back because she'd heard no cars since Tom Connor's, and had no idea how close the nearest house was. Time had become crucial; everything had become different. Tom Connor had brains, and brains were dangerous. This was what she'd thought even before she'd heard the gunshot.

It was dulled by distance – came from Sarah's place – and while it didn't stop her heart this time, her heart sank all the same. Gunshots were never good. These were very bad. Sarah, or Russell, had tricked those thugs into thinking she was in the other shed; now they were stuck with the aftermath. Men like Ross excelled in aftermath, throwing their weight around in exact proportion to whatever displacement they'd suffered. The gun had been lost when the shed exploded; who'd recovered it, Zoë couldn't know. But when she tried to picture Sarah pulling its trigger, imagination failed.

From the farmhouse chimney, smoke still whispered; genteel, compared to the rough beast the shed had produced. They'd gone back inside, Zoë decided; unable to banish a vision of Sarah, Russell, being lugged like coal-filled sacks out of the daylight.

Just inside the pen's fence, Gwyneth's remains lay like a slaughtered mattress. Of the surviving pair, there was no sign.

She thought: I have to draw the men out. That or get inside. Precisely what she did after that would become apparent in due course.

If Zoë stopped to think about it, she would remember this urgency from long ago; the emergency the heart suffered when others, who mattered, were at risk. She'd been ambushed often enough lately: she ought to recognise the symptoms. But she was too busy waiting for dark, without which she could do nothing.

That, and wondering what was happening inside the house.

They were back in the kitchen, as if this were some mad merry-go-round Sarah had returned to, starting to whirl again. Soon she'd be excusing herself to take a shower, and then she'd get to crawl along the outside of her house once more . . . 'Are you okay?' she asked Russell. Because he wasn't; he looked drained and vampire-stricken, and had stumbled twice on the way to the house. This was after the gun, cooking in the shed's embers, had exploded. Sarah had had the sense of something whistling brutally into the air; a stray bullet freed by heat, and pounding blindly anywhere. Maybe it would turn up, if she lived through this evening. Maybe she'd find it years hence, buried in a tree, and know its target had been nominated an instant after detonation. For the moment, though, it felt an open issue.

Russell nodded, numbly. He was leaning heavily on the table, and she wondered if he were about to be sick.

Connor told the others: 'You screwed this up, didn't you?'

'I've been telling them that,' Sarah said.

He looked to her, his lips pursed. He was a different proposition; more a cop who ran investigations than kicked down doors. Who appeared on TV, explaining why things had gone right or wrong. He was tall, lean, with thinning sandy hair. He wore spectacles that were as much fashion statement as functional. And he'd walked straight at her while she held a gun, not believing for a second she was capable of pulling the trigger.

Now he said, 'This is a mess. I'm sorry. You didn't ask for any of it.'

'So how do you undo it? Walk away?'

Ross opened his mouth to say something, but Connor silenced him with a look. 'We need to speak to Ms Boehm. We can still sort this out, we can . . . reach some kind of conclusion. Something we can all live with.'

He was careful not to place special emphasis on this choice of words.

Sarah said, 'She's long gone.'

'I expect she's coming back.'

'Then you don't know Zoë.'

'No. But you do. And you'd not be trying to convince me she was gone if you didn't think otherwise.'

There was no point countering this. He'd made his mind up.

He said to Ross and Burke, 'Go and have a look. One of you check the road.'

Burke said, 'Shall we take the, er . . .'

'Christ,' said Ross.

Connor looked lasers at the pair of them. 'Don't hurt her. Bring her back here.'

Sarah sat next to Russell and put her arms round him. He barely reacted.

Now there were four: themselves, Connor, Maddock. That last non-conversation had been about guns, Sarah knew. This was the most dangerous room, but out there in the landscape, that pair were hunting Zoë with guns.

Connor said, 'Did she tell you what she knows?'

Sarah was beyond lying. The only person she'd be fooling

was herself. 'She didn't *know* anything. Not until those goons attacked her. Then she pieced things together. That the bunch of you executed Charles Parsley Sturrock, and were stupid enough to let a small boy witness it. So you killed him too.'

Russell made a small noise: it wasn't clear that this was voluntary. Maddock, by the door, was chewing something; possibly the inside of his cheek.

Connor said, 'Oh, she knew.'

'The closest she came to Sturrock's case was reading about it in the paper.'

'She was at the inquest.'

'She'd spoken to the boy's grandfather. He asked her to be there.'

'There was more to it. She asked about Sturrock. Said how odd it was, him dying near where the Deepman boy was killed. I told her coincidences happened.'

'And?'

'And she said, "Like dates?" Then said she was thinking about birthdays. That it wasn't important.'

Sarah said, 'Listen. She knew nothing until last night, in Oxford. When these guys jumped her.' It had become important that she convince him of Zoë's retrospective innocence, as if this changed anything. As if they might travel back to the land of the honest mistake, and write this off to experience: shake hands and promise to exchange birthday cards . . . Oh shit. Birthday cards.

She couldn't remember his name. Burke had used it earlier. It didn't matter. Connor knew who she meant. 'It was his birthday. Is that what you're saying?'

'Danny Boyd's.'

'Yes,' she said. Something else was nagging at her now, and her mind pushed it away; refused to let it into the light. 'His birthday,' she said again slowly. 'The day you killed Sturrock.'

'He'd have been thirty-five,' said Connor. He was staring at her, or through her, intently, but the words came out abstracted, as if the same thought she was fending off had just occurred to him. 'Thirty-five years old. Ten years he never got to have. Ten years Sturrock owed him.'

Sarah was watching how the last of the day's light fell into the kitchen; slanting across the room, laying a platform for motes of dust to dance upon. This was always happening: it didn't matter how grown up you got – there always came a moment when you wanted to reel in the last five minutes, and unspeak the words you'd spoken. There was always a moment you saw the light, and it was always five minutes late.

He said, 'She didn't know, did she? She wasn't playing games. It was just words she used I thought meant something else.'

Sarah said nothing.

He looked at Maddock. 'There's no signal here. Is that right?'

'Not a peep.'

'And nobody's used the phone since you got here?'

'Nobody.'

He looked at Sarah, and they shared the same thought again. Everything was still fucked up. But what she'd told him clarified this: Zoë had told nobody about her suspicions – she'd had no suspicions to tell. Nobody knew anything, except those in the immediate area.

Connor mumbled something; Sarah wasn't sure what at first. Then understood.

Containable.

The situation was containable.

Russell shifted dopily, and his grip tightened on her wrist.

Sarah hoped like hell Zoë wasn't coming back.

It was getting dark; was probably after seven. Zoë was watching the back of the house when two men came into view from round the front: Ross and the one she'd swiped with her car Monday night. She shrank back into the shadows, without losing her view of Ross heading to their car; opening the boot. He took something out, some *things* out, and handed one to his companion.

They had more guns.

They did: they had guns. Sideswipe held his as if he'd been gifted a turd, while Ross opened his up, checked it was loaded, closed it again. From this distance, he might have been squeezing a lemon. While he did so one of the ostriches appeared from its hut: the male, Zoë thought. His feathers ruffled in the breeze as he scanned the area with poky jerks of the head. When he saw the men he froze, though they paid no attention; Ross finishing whatever he'd been saying, then heading for the lane that led to the road. Mr O beadily watched him leave. The other man trudged past the house, heading towards the rise where the trees hid Zoë, walking like a man with his strings cut. The gun weighed down the hand he held it in. Something did the same for his head.

She watched as the cop covered maybe half the distance between them, then sat, as suddenly as if he'd not actually intended it, and buried his face, tried to bury his entire self, in his hands. Watching, Zoë's heart beat cold. Not for him, not for him. She had been somewhere similar, and had never completely returned. He was in that desolate arena everywhere turned to when you'd killed; as if a door had opened inside yourself, and locked behind you once you'd fallen through. But it wasn't for him her heart beat cold. It was for Sarah, for Russell; for whichever of them had turned victim.

After a while – she'd lost all sense of time – the cop stood. He remained on the spot a little longer, looking alternately at the gun in his hand and at the surrounding countryside, then shrugged so eloquently Zoë could have sworn she heard him sigh, and put the gun in his pocket. Then he returned to the house, pausing at the ostrich pen. Mr O stared back at him; body interrupted mid-stride – one leg in the air – and resumed his nervous stalking only once the man had gone. He was pacing out what was left of his territory, Zoë thought, now blood had claimed its space.

Looking back along the ridge to where it met the road – a junction obscured by distance and foliage – Zoë saw nothing bar leaf and branch. There was no saying how long it would take Ross to decide she wasn't on the road, and if he headed back via the tree-lined ridge, he'd walk into her. But if her future was heading from that direction, she couldn't see much of it. Then again, if it was, there wouldn't be much of it to see. A sudden blank was all. Diagnosis and fulfilment wrapped in the same envelope; there'd be little time for fretting her long-term prospects. And with that thought came another: that whatever prospects awaited her, whatever *We'll have to fix you up with an appointment* led to, these were at least *her* prospects, and not those imposed by a man with a lump of metal in his hand. She would be there to open the envelope when it came, and then be wherever it directed her to be. Whatever happened after that, happened. Whatever her future, she didn't want to meet it here, now.

. . . Ross appeared from nowhere, cleared the pen and disappeared round the front of the building. Zoë could assume he'd gone inside; that all four of them were in the house. Along with Sarah and Russell, if they still lived.

Burke had been so much of a wreck they'd kept him clear of the inquest; sent Ross as a witness in his place. *He spread his arms like the Angel of the North, and jumped.* From an ex-copper, twenty years behind him, that had worked for the coroner. The fact that Ross had quit half a step ahead of an inquiry was a matter that hadn't arisen.

Burke was no witness now, either. 'Can't see her,' he said.

'How hard did you look?'

'Fuck you, Ross. I looked. You think I'm enjoying this?'

'Different when it's a kid, isn't it? That's more your speed, right?'

Lots of things might have ended then, except Burke had given the gun to Connor when he'd come in. Sarah, listening, decided that killing Sturrock had started as an after-hours fantasy, fuelled by alcohol and vicious misjudgement. *Would you kill him?* somebody had asked. To which there was only one possible answer. Had Sturrock really thought he'd die in bed, his own or anyone else's? *Just think of everything Danny boy never got to be.* Twenty-six, twenty-seven, twenty-eight . . . After a while it became a plan. But Burke, she guessed, had never recognised the turning point, and was probably still hoping he'd wake up.

'Shut up,' Connor told them.

'She's long gone,' Sarah said. 'Can you hear anything yet? There'll be sirens.'

Maddock said, 'They wouldn't use sirens. They'll come quietly.'

Everybody but Connor looked at him.

Connor said, 'No. She's not going to leave you. They didn't see her, but that doesn't mean she's gone. It means she's hiding.'

Sarah forced a laugh. 'Zoë's not exactly countryside material. If you can't see her, she's not there.'

'Well, maybe you're right. And maybe I am. I guess this is one of those occasions time will tell.' He glanced out of the window. 'When's it dark round here?'

'Two a.m.'

'Funny. When does it *get* dark?'

Sarah said, 'Half seven. Round about then.'

He looked at his watch. 'Twenty minutes? Let's let her know how things stand, shall we?' He pulled her from the chair so abruptly, Russell's head, which had been resting on her arm, hit the table, but she barely had time to register this; she was being pushed out of the door, with Connor on her every step of the way. She'd thought Ross was the brutal one, thought

296

Connor represented a higher order of thuggery, but this is what it came down to every time: a man in a corner hit out. It didn't matter who he was hitting. Connor pushed her through her hall. Somewhere on the way he produced the gun Burke had given him. And then Sarah was out in the beautiful twilight, in a part of the world she loved, with a fist clamped round the collar of her blouse, and a gun barrel pressed to her temple. Connor held her for a long moment, his body hot against hers; he turned her slowly through 180 degrees, displaying her to the landscape. And then they were on the move; Sarah stumbling every second step as he forced her round the house, halting at each corner to repeat the display. There were no words. Ross would have shouted his intentions to the hillsides. Connor knew words were unnecessary.

Back in the house, back in the kitchen. Russell sitting up now, barely aware she'd been away. Maddock and Burke were so still, they might have been playing grandmother's footsteps. Greying light splayed the same pattern on it all; the same lazy motes dawdled in its oblongs. Only Ross had broken formation: he'd lit a cigarette. Its smoke grimed the air, like an illustration of the harm he'd brought on the household.

Connor released her, though her arm retained the memory of his grip. What could she do about any of this? She did the only thing she could do; she sat next to Russell, and placed a hand gently on his arm. 'You okay?'

He nodded. 'Fuck 'em, right?'

'Yes.' The tremor in her voice was barely there.

Connor said, 'Geoff, switch the burglar lights on.' He meant Maddock. 'Then go and watch the front. You two, upstairs. Keep it dark. Try not to be obvious.'

Burke said, 'Maybe we should just go.'

Connor said, 'You know what it's like for a cop in prison? You need a picture?'

'I just don't see why she'd hang around.'

'Boehm's hanging around because we've got these two. And she knows what we'll do if she goes for help. I've just shown her that.'

'Are you really going to shoot her?'

Yes, thought Sarah. Answer me that.

Connor said again, 'You know what it's like for a cop in prison?' and this time, he didn't get an answer.

The clock ticked. Upstairs, though it had been going on so long it was almost inaudible, the shower hammered against its empty stall.

Connor said, 'Okay. Enough. Is that door solid?' He was looking at the pantry, whose door had a key in it. Maddock opened it, looked in. Shelves of various foodstuffs; no window.

'Seems okay,' he said.

'Put them in it.'

'Both of them?'

'You're worried about their morals?'

'No, but I'm hungry.'

'We're all hungry. I'll sort something out.'

He said, 'No offence, but can you cook?' Connor didn't reply. 'Make her do it, I would.'

'Have you finished?'

Ross said, 'None of us have eaten all day.'

Watching, Sarah wasn't sure which way Connor would go; which way she wanted him to. Maybe he was conscious of this, because he didn't drag it out too long. 'Okay. Just him.' He nodded at Russell.

Russell looked at Sarah, clearer suddenly. 'They're going to lock me in with the biscuits.'

'I love you.'

'I love you too. Everything's going to be all right.'

'Yes.'

She couldn't say anything more just then.

Russell stood, still shaky on his feet, and walked into the

pantry. Before Maddock locked the door on him, he said, 'What's funny is, I'm the cook.'

Tom Connor said, 'Get where you're going.'

Maddock put the key in his pocket and left the kitchen. Ross went too. Burke followed a moment later. Sarah heard their tread on the stairs.

She said, 'Are you happy with everything so far?'

The gun was back in the left-hand pocket of his raincoat, which he hadn't taken off. It gave him a lopsided appearance; its weight tugging the fabric down, throwing the buttons askew.

He said, 'Sturrock deserved to die. And there are other victims here. Les Burke? He's a good copper. Hell, *I'm* a good copper. You think this has left us undamaged?'

She said, 'I try to be broad-minded. But fuck you, okay?'

'Suit yourself. Now, food. A plate of sandwiches will do. You'll understand if I cut the bread. It's not that I don't trust you.'

'You probably brush up real smart, don't you?' she said. 'You've probably done the PR courses, and all the rest of the human-face crap. But you boil down to the same fucking thug in a uniform in the end.'

'Like I said. Sandwiches will be fine.'

Sarah was getting to her feet. 'It's going to have to be a bit more complicated than that,' she said. 'You've just locked the bread in the pantry.'

26

THE LIGHT HAD LEFT. Zoë's touchstone for this was Gwyneth's corpse, behind the mesh fence. Over the last ten minutes it had grown hazier, and lost whatever it retained of shape and identity. But maybe this always happened with death; that whatever had made a life unique slowly dissolved, until what was left was newly smooth and ridgeless, as if it had been sandblasted in the process.

Some short while ago, Tom Connor had walked Sarah round the house with a gun riveted to her temple. Maybe an ounce of pressure had kept Sarah this side of that smooth and ridgeless existence, and Connor had wanted Zoë to notice that. To think about that ounce, and how easily he could put his hand on it.

. . . He wanted her to think there was a way all this could be resolved, and Sarah and Russell left in peace. But also, of course, to know that this was endgame. Zoë could light out now and bring help, but if she did, there'd be more than ostrich blood spilt.

The chimney had stopped smoking. Whatever was happening inside now, they were no longer playing house.

And the burglar lights would be activated, Zoë supposed. There was a set facing each direction, attached to the roof at the level of the guttering. There was no chance she'd get to the house undetected.

All of this, every strand of it, running through her head simultaneously. While down below, what had been Gwyneth dissolved in the dark.

Sarah took an apron from the back of the kitchen door, and put it on.

'If you had any ideas about boiling oil,' Connor said, 'forget them.'

'Do you want food or not?'

'Sharp knives either,' he said. 'We don't want any accidents.'

She tied the apron. 'If you want a hot meal, that's going to include a certain amount of activity.'

'Just don't get ambitious.'

'Don't worry. Cordon bleu, this isn't.' She opened the freezer compartment of the fridge, and removed a plastic tub that had once held ice cream. 'Bolognese sauce,' she said. Then she lifted a pan down from the overhead metal rod. 'Pan,' she added. She set this on the stove top, on the ring directly in front of the Le Creuset, then opened the plastic tub and held it upside down over the pan. After a moment or two, its contents dropped out in a solid block. 'Mmm,' she said. 'Doesn't that look good?'

'Shouldn't you let it defrost?'

'I'm so glad you brought that up. I plan to apply heat now. Is that going to be a problem?'

He said, 'Just so we both know where we stand. If this results in an attempt to boil, scald or otherwise pain me, I'll hurt him first.' He nodded towards the pantry door.

Since walking her round the house, she thought, his gun pressed to her head, Connor had given up any pretence of being the civilised one. They were here to cover up the crimes they'd committed, and the longer they stayed, the more there was only one way of doing that. Hurting Russell first sounded like a threat, spoken out loud, but Sarah could see beyond the words to the other side. First or last, he'd be hurting Russell eventually, unless something happened to stop him.

What she said was, 'I'm not a fool.'

'Let's hope so. You intend opening any of those drawers, you ask me first. What tools do you need, anyway?'

She nodded at the glass jug by the side of the range, in which a collection of wooden spoons lived. He studied it for a moment, without moving closer. 'Okay.' As she watched, his hand tapped his coat pocket, and it barely mattered whether this was an unconscious or deliberate reminder of what he had in there. It wasn't like she'd forgotten yet. She could still feel the O on her temple where he'd held its barrel against her.

She reached for a spoon and then, with her back to him, turned the dials and pressed the ignition switch that lit the flame. Then began shovelling at the frozen block with the wooden spoon.

After a while he said, 'How long is this going to take?'

'That depends on how frozen you want it to be.'

'It was a simple question.'

'Half an hour. Minimum.'

'And you're just going to stand there poking at it, are you?'

'Unless you want it to burn.'

She was determined not to turn round.

He was moving, and her hand dropped to the dials at the range front, but he wasn't coming near. He had stopped by the mantelpiece, above where the kitchen fire had been before previous occupants removed it. The mantel had survived, though, and it was where the household odds and ends washed up; the out-of-date hayfever remedies, and gifts from the cereal packets they bought when Russell did the shopping. Stray foreign coins, useless now. Stuff that didn't get thrown away without serious effort, and in the new life Sarah had made these past few years, housekeeping didn't rate high priority.

But there was something about this detritus, when she found

it in other people's houses, that always warmed her to them; that gave a glimpse of the messy reality underlying ordinary lives, however tidy they appeared on the surface. There were always fragments of history gathering on untended shelves, to reveal the unsuspected depths friends had. There was a photograph of Russell halfway up a mountain, whose story had revealed an aspect of him she'd never have known about otherwise. And she hoped that Connor was looking at these things, and that she and Russell, in consequence, were becoming that little bit realer to him; that little bit more alive. That little bit harder to kill.

He said, 'This could all still work out.'

'Yes.'

But even with her back to him, she could tell what that exchange meant:

This isn't going to work out.

No.

He lapsed into silence while she stood working with the spoon, reducing the solid frozen block to the thick sauce it had been when she'd made it. A rich smell filled the air, reminding Sarah that she was hungry too; that it had been a long day, with nothing remotely like this in prospect when it had started. And she stirred faster, as if to speed the smell's diffusion; as if domesticity were a barricade she and Russell could shelter behind. Or failing that, as if it might keep Connor from coming too close.

Crawling back to it had been a twenty-minute journey, and in the darkness the shed felt unfamiliar, for all the hours Zoë had spent here lately. It was a moment before she got a handle on where things were. On the wall hung the tools: rakes hoes shears. It was the shears she needed, and she located a pair by touch, putting her fingers to something sharp first – the tine of a fork – but without drawing blood. She lifted them from their hook. At the door she paused, looking to the house, but saw no movement. It occurred to her that if the men came out of the house themselves, the burglar lights would snap on, unless they had the wit to turn them off first. Connor would have thought of that. Ross would come charging like a bull into the brightness.

Zoë stepped outside, and felt the night's breeze on her cheeks.

Something rustled in the near distance. She froze, even though her brain was already telling her what she was hearing. The noise came again, no nearer, no further; something like a scrabble in dry earth. Her heart slowed, though not quickly enough. Her breathing burned her throat. What she was hearing was what she'd expected to hear: the noise of an ostrich prowling its pen. But she couldn't help reminding herself that she only had to be wrong once.

The shears should have made her feel more secure. If anybody jumped her now, all she had to do was hold them out; forward motion would do the rest. A sudden and severe image of precisely this happening sent a shudder down her spine. But there was no time for this. She had to move.

Round the shed again, then; making her way over the slight upward pitch of the ground before it dropped away the far side of the ostrich pen. She walked into, before she saw, the wire mesh of the pen itself and yelped: a thin bat squeak of a noise the air around her swallowed. There was a dull feathery slap to her left, as if a piece of furniture had fallen over. She could see him, in fact – him? Zoë was pretty sure it was the male – standing nine foot high in the darkness, shaped like an ink-blot test, but with twin pinhead gleams above the beak. His gaze followed her as she dropped to a crouch. Was it her imagination, or could she hear a buzzing in the night? Even here, working at the task in hand, she could swear it was right in front of her: the mess that had been Russell's ostrich; flies crawling over it, and the hot stink of spoiled meat making a pharaoh's feast of the air.

The blades forced a way through the thin mesh in front of her, and with all the strength in her lower arms, she brought them together.

It became easier after the first cut, as if there were already a hole, and she was merely tracing its outline with these giant scissors. And though it seemed loud, she was aware that her senses were exaggerating every scuff and scratch she made on the silence, which wasn't silence anyway – there were giant birds here, moving around their pen; there was wind making its way through the trees in the distance. Even here, miles from a city, there was the ambient pulse of life all around: electricity pounding the wires that crosshatched the roads, and animal feet pounding the tarmac below them.

There was her heartbeat, thumping away without cease. If they couldn't hear that, these scratches and scuffs from the shears weren't going to alert them.

She peeled away the section she'd cut, and scrambled through, taking the shears with her. Her night vision was on full now. There was little moon; busy clouds filled the sky. It must have been imagination, but the air inside the pen tasted thicker: rank with birdshit, and avian fear. She was not given to anthropomorphism, but it struck her that this pair had seen their companion destroyed today, and were still burdened with its corpse. Gwyneth, she'd been called. A silly creature which had fancied itself in love. And this brought to mind other silly creatures, or perhaps just overfond ones, who had imagined themselves in similar straits, and met similar ends under trains and in ditches. Love was dangerous, constantly. You needed to watch your back.

When she was sure nothing had changed for at least a minute, she made her way forward.

Movement behind her told her where at least one of the ostriches was, but she didn't turn round. She treated it as she would a dog, and pretended it didn't exist. But information kept slipping past her barricades anyway: that ostriches featured in Roman circuses; that they used their feet as weapons. She had no clear picture of an ostrich's foot, but it was possibly curved and sharp. And they could reach speeds of – what had Russell said? Forty miles an hour? But these were family pets, she reminded herself; kept and fed by humans, for the pleasure their appearance gave. Sarah and Russell must have moved among them time without number. Of course, there'd been three of them then. And they hadn't spent hours sharing their pen with a slaughtered colleague: with her dead stink, and the buzz of feeding insects.

Shears pointing earthwards, she almost walked into the mesh once again.

The house was a dark mass thirty yards distant. A faint glow from downstairs suggested there was light round the back, but the windows facing Zoë were blank. She studied them, waiting for a shift in the shadows' configuration which would tell her which rooms the men were watching from, but the only motion came from clouds' reflections on the dark glass: thick grey mufflers, covering the moon.

Zoë shuddered as something crawled across her grave. Then, praying it was too dark for her to be seen, she followed the mesh round, looking for the gate.

The sauce's aroma had ripened the air, and Sarah's apron was polka-dotted red. Connor stood by the mantel. There'd been a bump from the pantry a few minutes before, but other than that, Russell was quiet. Through the window there was nothing to be seen bar her own reflection: hair a little mad, lips a little red. Eyes giving nothing away.

She kept hearing creaks and aching floorboards overhead. The house, complaining about interlopers.

Connor said, 'Is this nearly done?'

'Hungry?'

'Of course.' This without an edge: it would have been amusing in other circumstances. That he was polite enough to refrain from voicing irritation, but not so much so he'd refrain from killing her when the need arose.

She reached towards a cupboard.

'Don't.'

'What's your problem?'

'Tell me what you're after.'

Exaggerating it – plucking each consonant like a harp string – she said, 'I was reaching. For some. Pasta.'

'Let me get it for you.'

'Where have you been all my life?'

She pointed to where the pasta lived. He came round, opened the cupboard, lifted down a bag of tagliatelli.

'Not that. The spaghetti.'

Connor handed her the packet of spaghetti, then moved back to where he'd been standing.

. . . He's worried, she thought. He thinks the kitchen's a woman's ground.

That was okay. She could work with that.

'I need to boil some water,' she said. 'Is that going to be a problem?'

'Just so long as you don't get clever.'

'I'm cooking pasta,' she said. 'It's not rocket science.'

He didn't respond. She reached down another pan from the overhead rod, this one a stainless steel pot: big, round, twin handles at the lip. Filling it with water made a circus-worth of noises. She closed her eyes, and imagined this was ordinary – another day, another meal with pasta. She'd open a bottle of wine, and share the past few days with Russell. What had she done, these past few days? Being in London was like something she'd once heard about. Toting the pan back to the range, she set it on a ring, and added a splash of oil and a sprinkle of salt.

Outside, in the big world beyond the window, nothing

happened. She was utterly alone. Whatever came next, and whether it made things better or worse, was entirely down to her. Living with the consequences was the best possible outcome.

The Sarah she wasn't glanced back at her from the window. She could have sworn there was a degree of dark knowledge in the look, as if the view from the other side took in all available futures.

Standing directly in front of the range, blocking Connor's view, Sarah turned the gas off. 'I could do with a hand here.'

'Doing what?'

'I need the back ring.' She turned to face him. 'The one with this pan on. It's too heavy for me to lift.'

'There are six rings,' he said.

'And this is the one I need for the pasta. Unless you can wait another half-hour, while I use the slow one. But I expect the troops are getting restless.'

He put something down on the mantelpiece: Sarah wasn't sure what. Something he'd picked up, weighed in his hands, turned over; something of hers or Russell's, or else just something that had wandered among their possessions and settled there, but was soiled now, and always would be. Maybe the whole house was. Nothing remained that wouldn't always remind her of the casual slaughter of an ostrich she'd saved from the abattoir. But she couldn't even tell now what it was he'd handled, because he'd put it down without her seeing, and he was coming towards her.

She stepped aside. 'That one.' The big, cast-iron Le Creuset, which was too heavy to trust to the overhead rod.

'Where do you want me to put it?'

'I just need it out of the way,' she said. 'So I can get at the ring.'

He gave what was almost a smile, as if there were this conspiracy they shared in, one that underlay all male–female dealings, regardless of surface kindness or violence: one that ruled that, when the bottom line was reached, there'd always be a woman asking for help; always be a big strong man to give it. And, still believing this, he gripped the cast-iron pan by its cast-iron handle, and lifted it clear of the range.

It was curious how long this lasted: Connor holding the pan, that slight edge of superiority painted on his face. Sarah thought afterwards that even in the moment of lifting, that edge was melting; giving way to the suspicion that she'd wrong-footed him somehow, the way women always did, when that same bottom line was reached. And the big strong men always fell for it, didn't they? But that was afterwards. While it was happening, what she was mostly aware of was the beating of her heart, and the curious absence of noise. Though the first thing he did, of course, was make noise. It took a moment or two to get through to her, that was all.

In the same moment, lights burst on all around the house.

The two men – Ross and Burke – emerged from the house and split: Ross to Zoë's right; the other to her left, where he disappeared round the corner after a moment's hesitation – there'd been a noise from the house, something like a woman's scream, just as the lights went on. Zoë tensed, but stayed flat on the ground, hands shading her eyes in case reflection gave her away. She was a yard or so inside the gate to the ostrich pen, which she'd fixed open by jamming the shears in the ground like a tent peg. Cutting through the chain hadn't been the hard part; the hard part had been doing it quietly – when the shears' blades met the thin chain between them, the crack sliced the air, and somewhere behind her, the birds – roaming the pen; frightened and curious – ruffled their feathers and spat.

After pinning the door, she sprinted back, flapping her arms to scare the birds through the gate, towards the house. Zoë heard, rather than saw, them leave; they made a noise like something falling down a flight of stairs. A hot stink hung behind them. Then they were gone.

She dropped to the ground an instant before their movement triggered the burglar lights. It was as if God had flipped a switch, and lit everything at once. Seconds later, the two shapes came out: Ross to Zoë's right; the other to her left, and she watched them flat on the ground, on the dark side of the brightness.

The second man disappeared round the corner. Ross, though, came forward to stand on the edge of the darkness: to stare into it somewhere off to her right. That must be where the birds were: they'd disappeared in a mad flap once the lights came on. She hoped Ross wouldn't see them. She doubted she'd get a second shot at drawing him from the house.

Ross had his gun out, aiming at the night. The heavy wooden door to the farmhouse was behind him. It had seemed like a plan at the time: get the bad men out by triggering the lights, then sneak in when they weren't watching. But she'd been banking on more than just two of them emerging: getting inside, even unseen, wouldn't leave her much better off than she was now. But she had to take a chance on moving. Any moment, he'd figure the birds were loose.

She crawled forward; put her hand on something sharp: a stray shard of gravel. Pain was okay, though. Pain would keep her focused. She kept moving.

I'll be there.

It's not just words, that's the important thing. It's not just words and it's not just music: it's a promise. So here he is, keeping his promise.

The man he's watching he saw earlier, crossing the meadow between house and treeline. He hadn't got more than halfway before falling to his knees and trying to bury himself in his hands. This had been moving, but at the same time laughable – like watching a one-man theatre company stage Lear *– and anyway, what he'd mostly been* interested in was the certain knowledge that somewhere among the trees, Zoë was watching too. And he wonders what her feelings were then; whether she felt for the man – his pathetic display to an audience he didn't know he had – or was simply noting him as the weak link. The latter, he thinks. His Zoë, his Zoë: she is tough. She's tough, but she needs him.

And now this weak link stands in the half-world of the light bordering the house; the light that offers security as long as you're wrapped inside it, but makes everywhere else darker. And he feels alone. Talmadge knows this. He feels alone because he's weighed down with the guilt of everything he's done; he's lain awake all night every night since doing it; lay awake last night in whatever God-awful ringroad hotel these men crashed in, nursing their wounds, and working out where Zoë had gone. And all he's waiting for now are words; words he'll recognise because they've been sheltering in his memory for years; words that will speak to him as if they're his alone . . . Words he'll walk towards, because he's nowhere else to go.

Talmadge licks his lips, opens his mouth, and breathes deliberately, feeling cold air channel through his throat.

. . . It's easy, giving comfort. It's a matter of letting people know they're not alone.

He moves through the dark, and knows himself unseen. The policeman stands in the lee of the house, and wouldn't have noticed a battalion approaching. He's supposed to be looking for Zoë, but it's obvious his focus is inward, on the demons gnawing his emotions. This is brutally revealed by the lights hanging from the guttering, and if he gets close enough, Talmadge will be able to describe the man's every last pain. Won't even need the light. Will be able to spread his palm across the man's face and read it in his fingers like Braille; every line an ache, every wrinkle, regret.

Sometimes, it's clear that people need music.

And it isn't just words, that's the important thing. It isn't just words and it isn't just music: it's a promise.

In a perfect world, the last voice you heard would be somebody singing.

People say I'm the life of the party
'Cause I tell a joke or two

Talmadge pauses, and watches the words reach the man, crossing from the darkness to the light; carrying with them everything such words always carry – everyone knows the old songs. Everyone attaches a moment to them. He doesn't just think this: he knows it to be true. He's not been wrong yet. So before his own moment closes, he opens his mouth and sings the lines again.

And standing there on the dark side of the lights, he waits while the other man comes to join him.

All pain involves a stripping away of identity; it pulls the sufferer down a level, nearer to where the unmasked live. This had gone a step further, searing Connor's fingerprints; erasing his individual loops and whorls while filling the air with the stench of scorched meat. The pan handle had been so hot it had taken Connor a moment or two to understand it – he'd had time to lift it clear of the range before pain reached him. Half an hour at least, Sarah had had the gas flamed high, hidden by her body and the pan in front; the acrid smell of warming metal masked by gently cooking sauce. And then he'd screamed and dropped the pan, that expression peeled from his face as if she'd used a blowtorch on it. The pan might have hit his foot. Sarah didn't notice. She grabbed the other pan and hit him on the temple. Bolognese sauce splashed everywhere: if it had been paint, you could have called this decorating. Connor's peculiar, high-pitched scream died instantly. Sarah dropped the pan, dropped to her knees; even before going to Russell, she was going through Connor's pockets. First things first. Outside, the lights had gone on. Here in the kitchen, they went out. A shadow hung in the doorway: Maddock. She scooted to one side; came to rest with her back against the sink unit. The left leg of her jeans was soaked in meat sauce.

Maddock didn't crouch. He stood framed in the light from the hallway. From behind him came a draught: the others had rushed out when the burglar lights went on. Which meant Zoë was nearby; which meant the other pair were hunting her. They'd found her once before, and much good it did them. But this time they had guns.

There was a thing . . .

Sarah said, 'I've got his gun.'

'I don't believe you.'

He leaned to one side, she thought. That would be the wound Zoë had inflicted, down by the canal: sticking him with her penknife, and twisting it till it caught.

'I don't want to shoot you.'

Maddock moved forward. 'I don't want you to shoot me either. But I still don't believe you.'

He was measuring the gap, she knew. The gap between where she sat and where Connor lay; the gap she'd have to close to get hold of Connor's gun, if she didn't already have it. That was what his mind was working on: the maths. Could he get to her before she got to Connor? He had no idea how fast she was. All he knew was their relative sizes, and the fact that the last time he'd jumped on a woman, she'd scraped his bone with a knife.

This time, he'd take no chances. He was a big man; she was an average woman. He'd pound her like meat. That would be his plan.

Of course, he had to get round the kitchen table first.

Whichever way you looked at it, she didn't have time for elaborate schemes. Ross might be back any moment, and then there'd be two. Whatever happened had to happen in the next few seconds; and so thinking, she made her move.

When Zoë looked up, Ross was gone.

It hadn't been more than two seconds, a quick glance away while she navigated rough ground, but when she looked back, he was nowhere. She stayed as motionless as she could. He was too big, too rough, too one-eyed right now to creep quietly up on her, but still . . . One close encounter was the best she could hope to win. If he caught her again, there'd be no leeway. He would finish her.

But there was no future, either, in remaining where she was . . . A breeze ruffled her hair; carried a frightened snickering that might have been the birds again. And there was something else, too, that grew quieter when the wind blew; something like singing. It was out of her mind before she could focus; besides, there were things she had to do. Like move. She waited one beat more, then pushed to her feet and made for the light.

Visualise your goal. Didn't Joe used to say that? Along with *Understand your own strengths* and *Learn to grow, grow to learn.* Whatever he'd picked up from *Reader's Digest*, really. What she needed to do now was visualise herself reaching the door unscathed; see herself stepping through and locking it behind her. That there were more men beyond it was a different problem, and she would visualise how to deal with them next. What mattered now was reaching the door. So that's what she pictured as she sprinted for the house; herself reaching safety, or what would pass for it in the next five minutes. She saw her hand on its wood. She saw herself closing it behind her, and activating its lock.

She saw a shape loom up on her right, and what felt like a shovel, but was only a fist, strike the side of her head.

And then she saw stars; she saw continental drift. She saw everything she'd hoped might happen in the next thirty seconds collapse to the size of a squash ball, with a squash ball's ability to be everywhere at once.

'Bitch.'

She rolled before his foot hit her, but that was sheer instinct; nothing to do with preparation.

He swung again, and this time connected, but she was surfing on adrenalin, and her hip went numb instead of screeching in pain. Knowing what would happen if she stayed on the ground, she scrambled to her feet. If she ran, he'd be on her. If she didn't, the outcome would probably be the same, but once you'd identified yourself as victim, the game was over. Stand, and look like you know what you're doing. It wasn't much of an edge, but beat lying down and taking it.

But she wished she'd picked those shears up.

When he came forward, she moved back. A little dance on the edge of the light, as if this were nothing more than stage business; a distraction from the main event. His lips moved again, but she was concentrating on his feet and shoulders: the giveaways. Though knowing which way he'd lunge wouldn't help much, once he'd lunged.

He spoke again. 'I've been looking forward to this.'

'You're a fucking gorilla.'

'And you're meat.'

Save your breath. She saved her breath. Maybe the lights would die, blanketing everything in darkness again, but that wasn't really going to happen. The lights were triggered by movement. She watched his shoulders, watched his footwork. He was going for her left, so she went right. It wasn't a complicated decision. But he went for her right anyway, and the next thing Zoë did was walk into his reach, and his gun was fixed firmly under her chin.

Sarah made her move, and Maddock was quicker than she'd expected; was round the table before she was on her feet. Connor's prone form lay between them, and instead of reaching for her, Maddock went for Connor. She let him fall to his knees, where he groped for Connor's pocket, then showed him the gun she'd been holding since the moment he'd appeared in the doorway.

'I'd have to be an idiot to miss,' she told him.

He appeared to be about to say something, maybe something along the lines of *I don't believe you* again, or *You wouldn't dare*. And she was ready to ask him, *You want to bet your life?* But in the end he said nothing; he simply subsided, more or less, into a heap next to Connor, who was starting to stir now. Stir, she thought. That almost worked as a joke, given that he was covered in Bolognese sauce. Holding the gun steady, she moved out of Maddock's reach, but close enough that she'd still have to be an idiot to miss. And all the while she was keeping an eye on the door, and wondering who'd come through it next.

She'd had moments lately when she'd almost have welcomed this: being half a squeeze from nowhere. But not here, not now . . . His hand gripped her tightly above the left elbow, and his big face was inches from her own. Zoë could smell his wound, and guessed it was seeping below its patch; a light she'd mostly put out. The grip tightened. 'Happy now?' he said.

It was so nearly the question she'd asked herself, she couldn't have replied if she'd wanted to.

'We've come fucking miles for this,' he said. *We* meant himself and the others, but for a moment he might have meant the two of them, and that this were the terminus of some elaborate journey. He pushed the gun's short barrel against her chin as if he intended to drill through her with his own brute force. 'But I'd have come a lot fucking further. I owe you, bitch.'

It was strange how the mind would not let go of rescue. She supposed this was always so: as the parachute failed to open; as the jumbo screamed into the sea. There must always be that belief there: that this couldn't be happening, not to *me* . . . For some reason, it was Alan Talmadge Zoë was thinking about. The ghost in the machinery of her recent days. He had been following her, she was sure. If these three could manage it, why not him? But as soon as the thought occurred, she forced it away. It was a measure of her desperation that the idea had even visited. It was a glimpse into how much she valued rescue.

She could feel, as if the pressure travelled down the barrel of the gun, his finger tightening on the trigger. She could feel him breaking her life with the movement.

Something crashed behind him.

He moved fast: so fast, she had to piece it together afterwards. He swung the gun, first against her head – and light flared again; supernovas erupted; she hit the dirt – and then round into the darkness, firing twice. He was shouting as he did so, though she never worked out what. And then, it seemed – and this bit wasn't memory; it was her later recreation of events – that the arm holding the gun dropped to his side, and he stood there on the edge of the light, his one good eye staring into his future. Which came out of the darkness to strike him once, making an inhuman noise as it did so, and then vanished the way it had come, leaving him crumpled in a heap next to Zoë, blood leaking from the wound in his stomach: an almost perfect incision, she was told later. Clean and straight; a good inch deep. Not enough to kill him. Shock did that.

When she got to her feet at last, the second thing she did – after collecting the gun he had no further use for – was bend to pluck the feather she found by his feet. Such a fragile thing, it seemed to have nothing to do with what had just happened.

She found Sarah in the kitchen: two men at her feet; a weapon in her hand. Connor was badly damaged; Maddock simply looked deflated, as if the process Zoë had begun when she'd punctured his leg by the canal had reached its obvious conclusion. Zoë looked at them, then at Sarah. But before she could speak, Sarah said, 'That one's got a key in his pocket. Could you ask him for it?'

Zoë said, 'You heard her.'

Maddock gave her the key.

'Could you unlock the pantry?' Sarah said.

'Where's the other one?'

'Burke? Was he not outside?'

'I'll go and find him.'

She released Russell, who came close to hitting her with a tin of kidney beans when the door opened – he stalled at the last moment, and carefully placed it on its shelf before stepping into the room. Before he could reach Sarah, Zoë put a hand on his arm.

'Thank you,' she said.

He touched her cheek. 'You're welcome.'

Zoë was still holding Ross's gun. On her way out, she said, 'I loosed your birds, by the way.'

'They won't go far,' Sarah said. 'They're spooked right now, but they're very territorial.'

'I noticed that,' said Zoë.

Round the far side of the house she found Burke, beyond the reach of the burglar lights. He lay on his back staring at the starless sky with eyes that were open, but reflected nothing. Instead, they were black pools, which had absorbed everything they were ever going to, and were finished now. She had never known him alive – had never known his name until a minute ago – but he had come here planning to harm her. He might have had second thoughts, but that was his business.

There wasn't a mark on him, that she could see.

She knelt and examined him briefly. There were no obvious wounds; no blood at all. But his head seemed unmoored, as if he were an overplayed with doll. The neck was broken. Maybe he had tripped and fallen. But if so, she'd found him in a strange position; as if he'd just lain down, to look at the stars that were not there.

She stood and, realising at last that the gun was still in her hand, put it on the ground. She'd been too close to too much death today. There was nobody left to shoot, anyway.

From somewhere near the treeline, Zoë caught a whisper of sound, a fragment of song, carried on the wind.

Whenever you need me

I'll be there

And then it was gone.

She began to walk towards the trees, as if she might find him if she reached them. But she knew already that Alan Talmadge wasn't going to be found, not by her. Not until he wanted to be. She knew who he was, though. There was only one possibility; she should have known him from the start. Should have recognised him, the way you're supposed to know love when it comes calling. But she hadn't.

Halfway, Zoë stopped, and sank to her knees. He was long gone and she wouldn't know what to do with him now anyway; not out here, miles from anywhere. *I will find you*, she'd promised him, and she would. But not tonight. She was cold and hurt; there'd been too much death. And he had, in his way, helped her.

It was dark, and no one could see her. If she was quiet, no one would hear. Out of reach of any man's hand, Zoë wept as if her heart would mend.

FROM THE FOURTEENTH FLOOR the world looked sensible, or at least a long way off. Zoë leaned against the railing a moment, flirting with vertigo, and when the wind gusted it was like that moment on a station platform when an express whaps past, and hits the heart sideways. It was a reminder of what could happen if you had no roots. She clutched the railing, and did not light a cigarette.

Behind her was Joseph Deepman's flat, though Deepman didn't live there any more. The old man had died the day after Zoë had last seen him, and had lain undisturbed for three days until an angry neighbour crashed his way in to turn the TV off. What Zoë felt about this, if anything, she didn't yet know. She wasn't sure she'd had much more to say to him; was pretty sure she knew the answers to any questions she might have asked. It was another appointment missed, though, of which there had been a number lately.

For instance: she had not found the man whose coat she had stolen, and, while she couldn't yet know this, never would. She had looked for him in the usual places – along the canal, in the public squares – and had found plenty of other invisibles, but no sign of those battered laundry bags. The previous afternoon, though, she'd divided ninety pounds among a group of what she'd heard called junks and drunkies, who had sensibly scattered as soon as she was done. Zoë hadn't thought of this as paying a debt. It was more an acknowledgement that a debt existed that was waiting to be paid.

The wind blew again, and she hugged herself. Her jacket was denim, resurrected from the back of a wardrobe. Her missing leather jacket was another debt, one she intended to collect some day.

Because Alan Talmadge was out in the world: wearing her leather jacket.

She shivered at the thought, or maybe it was the lack of leather that made her shiver. Alan Talmadge had followed her all right; had been there, she supposed, in her hour of need. He had quietly, calmly, broken a man's neck, and had done this for 'love' of Zoë. This was what love meant in some vocabularies. That there was no harm you would not inflict to keep the loved one safe.

(Zoë had asked Sarah, 'Would you have done it? Killed him?' And by *him* she'd meant Connor, or Maddock, or Ross . . . Whoever had been closest.

And Sarah had said, 'To stop them hurting Russell? Yes . . .')

But love took different forms, some more recognisable than others. Zoë, for instance, had not recognised Alan Talmadge when she met him, but then, he had adopted a different character for her – had cut his hair; shifted his manner – as if he'd already known that the shape he'd assumed for Caroline and Victoria wouldn't have done for Zoë. The fact was, no shape would have done that. Apart from anything else, she'd had their examples to look back on. Caroline Daniels and Victoria Ingalls had opened their hearts where they shouldn't, and, when push had met shove, that had cost them everything. Talmadge had ghostwritten his way into their lives and ghosted his way out again, and the ghosts left in his wake were theirs.

But then, maybe they'd always known danger lay ahead, but found the alternative too bleak to countenance: that they were unloved; or worse, unlovable. Maybe this late arrival in their lives felt like a prize they'd won, and the man delivering it the thing itself: their golden ticket out of loneliness.

Zoë could live with being unlovable. There were worse fates.

And meanwhile, unlovable or not, she was everywhere again. Out in the ether, the stories were writing themselves; flying higher the less there was to tie them to the ground. Where she'd spent days answering questions, or trying to; though the list of things she had no answer for spooled endlessly in front of her, while the answers she did have might have been cobbled out of a sick fantasy:

You're saying an ostrich did that . . .?

But they weren't stupid, her questioners. At least part of the story that had threatened to swallow her had travelled the Blue World already: a whisper in the canteens; a rumour in off-duty hours. Everybody knew those cops had known Danny Boyd; had been the mainstay of the anniversary do. That Ross, who'd jumped the force seven years ago, a shade before he'd been pushed, had been the unlikely point of intersection between the upward-looking Connor, the lifer Burke and the workhorse Maddock. And it was known that they'd huddled in corners a time or two; and it was known, of course, that Charles Parsley Sturrock was dead. The shortest distance between two points was occasionally just a line, waiting to be crossed.

You've killed before, haven't you?

She had, and it had scarred her life, but scars heal – the mark remains, but the pain disappears. Zoë was learning that. A few hard hours in police custody weren't going to unlearn it for her.

'You already know I have,' she said, 'so it's not a real question. Now I'll ask you one. Who do *you* think threw that kid off a roof?'

What they thought and what they knew were two different

323

areas. Though it was increasingly apparent that the truth, whatever form it took, wasn't going to look nice on the front pages.

So they had let her go for now, though they'd collect her again before long. It was nice to have some routine to your days. And it was always possible that sooner or later, she'd give them Bob Poland. Unless she decided that his was a debt best paid personally: personally, and over and over again . . .

For the second time in as many minutes, Zoë didn't light a cigarette.

She had another appointment this afternoon; this with Amory Grayling. Who was perhaps wondering if she were still among the living. For some while Zoë had wondered whether he really needed to know how Caroline's life had ended; that long before she had found herself in the path of that oncoming train, Caroline had wandered into the way of somebody at least as directed, at least as dangerous. Grayling might have been happier with his illusions intact, especially if these included – as Zoë suspected – that Caroline's balance had been upset, in the end, by his own perfect unattainability; his own happy marriage. His own being there, every day. So yes, of course he had to know. The fact that a diagnosis might turn out to be unpleasant bestowed no right to hide from it. Even ostriches didn't, in fact, hide their heads in sand; this was one of those myths that came out of nowhere, and gained currency because they were just strange enough to sound true.

And Zoë, too, had been picked out by the headlights that had dazzled Caroline, and poor Victoria. Talmadge had followed her. Had been following her since the night she'd stood outside Caroline Daniels's home, wondering why a car door had opened and closed, and no light had come on. Had followed her all the way to London more than once; even making it look, the first time, as if he'd been there before her . . . She remembered talking to Deepman about him; trying to find out how often

324

he visited, and Deepman had told her *He said he'd come back. And he did.*

Since Friday?

On Friday . . .

She'd thought the old man confused, but it was Zoë who'd muddled the facts. She'd been expecting confirmation that Chris Langley had been a regular visitor. So that's what she'd heard when Deepman told her otherwise: that Chris had been there, left and come back, all in that same morning. He'd arrived after she'd departed on her quest for light bulbs; he'd brought whisky to distract and confuse the old man. And he'd stuck his mobile number on the fridge for Zoë to find, just as he'd attached a tracking device to her car the night he'd followed her home from Caroline's. Which was how he'd traced her to Deepman's in the first place.

He said he'd come back. And he did. He'd said he'd popped next door, but he hadn't. He'd left and waited for her to come back, that was all. And he'd been at the inquest, expecting to see her there, so had heard Ross give evidence; had maybe seen Burke there too, whom he'd later killed. She wondered at which point in all of this Chris Langley – Alan Talmadge – had decided he loved her; wondered, too, if there was any point in wondering about this. Of the heart and its contents, there were no easy answers; instead, there were too many stories. There were too many songs, each with their own definition of love. There were too many endings, and even the happy ones were precisely that: they were endings.

She should have known him – should have picked him out by his shape from a crowd – but Talmadge had been a stranger after all; had shaved his head and become somebody new for her: nervy, diffident, socially concerned. Had he thought that was what would impress her? Or just assumed this was somebody she would never recognise? And what did it say about her that she hadn't? What would it have said if she had?

It was a pity she wasn't smoking today, because now would have been a great moment.

Something happened then in the clouds way above; one of those overarching rearrangements that shift the light a little, allowing shafts of it, in this instance, to break on the City a mile or so to the east. Illumination was always happening elsewhere, it would be easy to decide. Hindsight was the perfect view; it was where the mind said *Take your pictures here*.

. . . She'd seen Jay Harper the previous evening, in Oxford city centre; his arm round a blonde woman Zoë figured for twenty-three, twenty-four. He'd seen her too, and given her that same rueful smile she'd received when he'd occupied what might have been the last seat on the train. As if, under other circumstances, he'd give things up for her; but not, obviously, if it was going to cost him anything. She'd given him the look she'd give a pane of glass, and walked on by. There were songs for every occasion, perhaps, and that was one right there: 'Walk On By'.

Leaving her where?

She let go of the railing suddenly, disgusted by her self-interrogation. Zoë Boehm knew where she stood. She stood fourteen storeys up, gazing down on a city where she didn't belong. She ought to be heading home: there were things to do, there were things to do. And every time one of these things arose, the next step appeared, just waiting to be taken. When that envelope had arrived, for example, with the date of her appointment – two days from today – the next step had proved to be the telephone, and it had been Sarah Tucker she'd rung . . . Because love was unavoidable, really. How long had she spent ignoring that vital truth? Love was unavoidable. It was what the heart did while it was doing everything else. Maybe this, in the end, was what Caroline and Victoria had known. Which did not mean that the price to be paid need always be so great.

There were fourteen floors to climb down, because the lifts were out of order, and Zoë took them briskly, two stairs at a time.

She felt okay – not brilliant, but okay – and she supposed that was a start.